P9-CEC-766

CHILDREN OF EVE

Also by Deirdre Purcell

A Place of Stones
That Childhood Country
Falling For A Dancer
Francey
Sky
Love Like Hate Adore
Entertaining Ambrose
Marble Gardens
Last Summer in Arcadia

CHILDREN OF EVE

Deirdre Purcell

HODDER
HEADLINE
IRELAND

Copyright © 2005 Deirdre Purcell

First published in 2005
by Hodder Headline Ireland

The right of Deirdre Purcell to be identified as the Author of
the Work has been asserted by her in accordance with the
Copyright, Designs and Patents Act 1988.

3 5 7 9 10 8 6 4 2

All rights reserved. No part of this publication may be reproduced,
stored, in a retrieval system. or transmitted, in any form, or by any means,
without prior permission of the publisher, nor be otherwise circulated
in any form of binding or cover other than that in which it is published and
without a similar condition being imposed on the subsequent purchaser.

A CIP catalogue record for this title is available from the British Library

ISBN 0 7553 2621 0

Typeset in Bembo by
Palimpsest Book Production Limited, Polmont, Stirlingshire

Printed and bound in Great Britain by
Mackays of Chatham plc, Chatham, Kent

Hodder Headline Ireland
8 Castlecourt Centre
Castleknock
Dublin 15
Ireland

A division of Hodder Headline
338 Euston Road
London NW1 3BH

For Patricia and Frank Byrne
Old Friends Are Best

ACKNOWLEDGEMENTS

Thanks to Catherine Hogan, who accompanied me as I criss-crossed the states of Arizona and New Mexico while researching for this novel – and who revealed only subsequently that she was permanently terrified while sitting in the passenger seat on the Interstates. Tolerance in friendship is priceless.

Profound thanks to Patricia and Frank Byrne, to whom this book is dedicated; neither has missed a beat, not only in loyalty towards the books but in support for every aspect of my life.

I do give daily thanks for great pals, old and new. We might not see a lot of each other these days because of geographical distance and the general busyness of modern life but I would like them to know they are always in my thoughts and I see the publication of novel number ten as an opportunity to write an honour roll of friendship: Caroline Adderson, Suzannah Allen, Gill Bowler, Pat Brennan, Gay Byrne, Laly Calderon, Glynis Casson, Audrey Conlon, Carol and Roger Cronin, Margaret Cronin, bank manager John Crowley, Rose Doyle, Jacqueline Duffy, Bríd Dukes, Madelyn Erskine, Karen Erwin, Bernard Farrell, Marian Finucane, Frances Fox, June and Gerry Harrington, Eithne Healy, Gemma Hussey, Marie Kennedy, Rudi and Joke Kuper, Pat Laffan, Adrienne McCarthy, Mona McGarry, Deirdre McQuillan, Carmel Milne, Mike Murphy, John and Mary O'Conor, Adavin O'Driscoll, Emer O'Kelly, Jacqueline O'Neill, Tina Roche, Patricia Scanlan, Peter Sheridan, Kieran Ryan, brother Declan, sister-in-law Mary, cousin Barbara Dunne.

Thanks to my terrific agent Clare Alexander, to my rigorous and wise editor Marion Donaldson, to her cheerful assistant Claire Baldwin, to the gang at Headline Ireland, Breda Purdue, Heidi Murphy, Ciara Considine and Ruth Shern, and to Hazel Orme, my copy-editor for all ten novels, who by now can probably predict each peccadillo before it is committed.

Thanks also to former colleagues, Treasa Coady, Felicity Dickson, Jane Wood, Suzanne Baboneau, Martin Pick, Edwin Higel and Joseph Hoban. I haven't forgotten!

Finally, like all the other books, this one was written for the most important people in my life: Kevin, Adrian and Simon.

CHAPTER ONE

I am in the monkey house at Dublin Zoo. The chimpanzees are doing my head in. Screeching like banshees. Demented.

No, dammit, I'm not at the zoo. I'm in bed and that racket is the alarm hammer beating hell out of the tin clock on the other side of the room. I keep it there so I have to get out to turn it off.

'Go away!' I pull the duvet over my head. I'm on breakfasts this Saturday morning, due to clock in at a quarter past six, double dammit, but I don't want to open my eyes. Not yet. I always sleep badly on weekend nights. That's from Thursday to Sunday, these days – I don't know where people get the money for all the carousing lately in Dublin: like, the Celtic Tiger business, all the prosperity and so forth, is supposed to be over, isn't it? Well you could have fooled me. In this house we're persecuted with thugs and gurriers yelling and brawling and smashing bottles in the street outside. After two in the morning it's all the same to us whether they're enjoying themselves or killing each other. Last night was especially bad and I'm particularly affected because my bedsitter is on the ground floor at the front of the building.

The din from the clock is getting on my nerves now, so I extricate myself from the lovely soft warm groove in the mattress to bang it into silence.

I stand there in the middle of the room. Stupid. It's only five o'clock. It isn't the alarm at all.

A telephone call? This early? It can be nothing but bad news.

Rowan. He's in the cells again. Well, this time he can sing for it. How many fecking times have I gone down there to bail him out of the cells in that bloody Gárda station? I snatch up the receiver so violently I nearly brain myself. 'Hello?'

'Am I speaking to Arabella Moraghan?'

1

Ay-rabella Morragayan: certainly nobody I know. The slow deep tone is straight out of *High Noon*. Some bloody customer, probably. Left his wallet in the dining room. Was able some way to find my number and thinks he can ring me any time he likes. 'Yes?' I switch on the bedside light and make myself sound indignant. 'This is Arabella Moraghan. Who's this? It's five o'clock in the morning, you know.'

'I'm sorry to call at such an hour but—'

'Have you lost something?' I cut him off.

'I – ah – I beg your pardon?'

'Have you left something behind you?' Thick with it, I think.

'I – ah – guess we're at cross-purposes here, Arabella. My name is Dale Genscher and you won't have heard of me. I'm calling from the States.'

With that accent? Talk about stating the bleeding obvious – but my skin prickles as though someone has pelted it with a handful of sand. This isn't about Rowan. But whatever it is, the news isn't going to be good. 'Yes?'

'Arabella, I'm sorry to be blunt,' this guy says, 'but are you prepared for a shock?'

I'm clutching the receiver so tightly to my chest that my palm hurts. He doesn't have to say any more. I know why he's rung. My whole life has prepared me for this call. Eve's dead. This man with the cowboy voice is ringing about the arrangements.

Well, screw that for a game of soldiers! Those arrangements are not my concern. My involvement in them has to be *earned*. It hasn't. Not by a mile. Someone else can deal with them. As far as I'm concerned, Eve's remains can rot in a skip.

Against my chest, I can hear my name being repeated: 'Ay-rabella? Are you there?' but I squeeze the receiver tighter and crash back on to the pillows. Damn her. I've loved the idea of her for so long and now she's taken away even that. I've found her in America but too late, when she's already dead. I'll never forgive her for this, ever, *ever* – how dare she?

'Ay-rabella?' Muffled.

'I'm here.' I bring the receiver back to my ear. 'This is about my mother, isn't it? She's dead? Are you a policeman? How did you get my number?'

'Whoa, whoa there. I'm glad to tell you that your mom is not dead. But the rest of the news is not so good. She's had an accident, Arabella, that's why I called. And I'm not a cop—'

'Could she not have rung me herself? Coward too, is she? Getting someone else to do her dirty work?'

Unbelievably, I hear a little chuckle. 'What's so funny, might I ask?' I jump off the bed again. I want to ram the receiver down his throat. Down someone's throat.

'She's far from being a coward,' this character isn't fazed, 'but she was fearful to call you. Now I can see why.'

'All right.' I can't get the words out fast enough. 'So she's had an accident. Big deal! What are we supposed to do about it? How about us? Bit late to be ringing us now when it suits *her* – we could have been having accidents all these years. Rowan could have even been *dead*.' I take a breath, the rant sounding like a piano out of tune as it bounces back against my ears. 'Did that ever occur to her, d'you think, Mr Whatever-your-name-is?'

'Genscher. Dale Genscher.'

The line is so clear I can hear the slow, relaxed breathing. It isn't his fault after all. *Don't shoot the messenger* – that's Greta's favourite line. Greta's my best friend. We've soldiered through various hotel dining rooms together until we landed up a few years ago in the Leicester's. 'I'm sorry, I shouldn't take it out on you, it's not your fault. You have to admit, though, that after the guts of forty years—'

'She felt every week of it.'

'Oh, really?'

The silence at his end is glassy. Crystal glassy. You can almost hear the ting. I force myself to calm down and now I feel something else. Something weird. Fear? Excitement? 'Look, Dale, I don't mean to get at you. I'm sorry. No offence.'

'None taken.'

More breathing. Both sides. Then, it's me: 'What kind of accident? What injuries?'

'Car wreck. She was crossing the highway and she was hit by an SUV—'

'SUV?'

'Sports Utility Vehicle. One of those high four-wheel-drives with the bull bars out front? She hadn't a chance. Her leg is broke some. So's a few ribs – one of 'em punctured her lung. And now she has a chest infection. She's messed up good, Arabella. We've brought her home from the hospital but—'

3

'Is she going to die?'

A chuckle. Then, 'No, I don't think so. Not Eve.'

'Who's this "we"? What's your connection with Eve?'

'I'm a friend. I've known her for many years now and she asked me to call. She wants to see you, and Willow and Rowan. I guess the accident concentrated her mind.'

If that was supposed to be a joke, I ignore it. 'Well, let her come here, then. I gather you have aeroplanes over there – you know, big silvery things with wings?'

'I'm afraid that won't be possible. We did investigate it, but the connections from Arizona to Ireland are too weird, and even with invalid assistance through the airports, it would be too hard right now.'

'Arizona?'

He goes quiet again and the silence pushes and pulls while I try to take it in. She had been thinking about us all these years. That's something, I suppose. But how did she get to Arizona? When? Was it straight away? When I picture Eve, or when Willow and I discuss her, I always feel for some reason that she's in the north of England. Willow's opinion is that our mother is either dead or swanning it in Australia.

I can't adjust. I need a bit of time.

When I'm cornered, or caught in an awkward silence, I gab. And now I fasten on the impossibility of changing my roster at short notice. 'Sorry, I'd like to help but it's not on, I'm afraid. We're very short-staffed, you see. I'm a waitress and it's a fact of life over here in all restaurants, Mr Genscher—'

'Dale.'

'Right, Dale. You see, there's only two Irish waiting staff in our place now – me and my friend Greta. We're old-timers at this stage because the others are kids, Australians, Yanks, Eastern Europeans. We have to teach them, Greta and me. Not only how to wait tables and fill milk jugs but how to say ordinary things like "bacon", "cabbage", "stew", "prawn cocktail". So you see, Dale, I can't just up sticks. My manager would freak.' Gab, gab. On and on until I can't stand the sound of my own voice and slither to a sheepish full stop. What did this man care about the New, or newish, Ireland?

'What's the big rush, anyway, that you should ring me at five o'clock in the morning?' I try to sound brisk. Like my sister, Willow. 'From what you've said, she's not exactly dying, is she? Another little while won't make any difference.'

'She asked me to call. She seems to think it's urgent. She couldn't sleep until I agreed.'

Ice in my eyes. Eve couldn't sleep? Eve nagged him to call us? He's creating a flesh-and-blood person out of this woman who has lived so long like a ghost in my imagination. 'Listen, Dale, I'm not that long awake. Give me your number and I'll ring you later in the day.'

'Sure thing. Don't worry about the time. I guess I owe you one on that.'

'Hold on, I've to get something to write with.'

I fly around trying to find my handbag, and spot it under the latest pile of library books on the floor; I rummage until I come up with an electricity bill and the stub of a Leicester-issue pencil.

When I get back to the phone I can now hear a TV in the background. Speeded-up singing, as though it's one of those clever, cheery cartoons. Jesus, this guy is so laid-back he turned on the TV while I was looking for a pen. But I'm not going to get annoyed again – I'm not, I'm *not*! 'Shoot.'

When he's finished, I check the number by calling it back to him. 'You got it, Arabella.'

'Where is she at the moment? Is she there with you?'

'I apologise that I've given you a shock, but Eve can be persuasive and, anyways, there's no point pussyfootin' around. You should take time to think this through, babe, but not too much time, OK? Let me hear from you real soon.'

Babe? *Babe?*

'You'll hear, I promise. One way or the other.' I bang down the receiver so hard I miss the cradle. I am no longer tired: blood pumps through veins I didn't even know I had, like some in my scalp. How simple! After nearly four decades, my mother has decided she wants to see her family. So she gets a guy to wake me up at five o'clock in the morning after a bad night's sleep to issue the royal summons.

I stare around my personal world, at the forget-me-not wallpaper, so fresh and cheery five years ago. Now it just looks juvenile. As for the black and white lino tiles on what you can see of the floor! And that rickety table, literally on its last legs . . . How can a person of my age live like this? Like a bloody student! Cooking on a two-ring breakfast cooker and in a second-hand microwave. Any mother would hate to see her elder daughter living like a teenager just starting out.

Suddenly it seems very important to tidy the place, make it real clean.

Get a grip, Bel. I stop dead. Even if my mother had deigned to pay me the royal visit, so what? It would have done her good to see how far up the ladder of life I'd climbed – not. It would have done her good to feel guilty.

The alarm is due to go off in less than half an hour. I walk the few steps to the sink, fill the electric kettle, then go across the landing to the gloomy, peeling lavatory I share with three other tenants on the ground floor.

Back in the bed-sit, I open the curtains and gaze out at the street, empty now, under an even, cloudless sky of pearl pink and grey. It's going to be a lovely day. Funny to think that it must still be dark in Arizona.

Arizona. It sounds so exotic. Half the world away. Even if we do want to make this trip, where are we going to get the money? There's no way we can afford it, at least not Rowan and me.

And there's the problem of finding Rowan. God alone knows where he is. If we do decide to go, the Gárdaí, the Vincent de Paul or the Salvation Army will have to help us find him. As it happens, one of my fellow tenants is a member of the Vincent – he helped once before. I didn't ask him a second time, though, because I hated the way he began to make Rowan into a sort of intimacy between us. Plus, I hate being under an obligation to anyone. I'm self-contained. I think that's what people would say about me.

Maybe Jimmy Porter could help. He's a member of the Vincent too: his conference sends him prison visiting. I'm reluctant to ask him, though, because not for the first time I'm at a stage in my relationship with Jimmy Porter where the very last thing I want to do is involve him in anything personal, certainly not something as personal and emotional as this. I can just hear him pontificating. What I should do, what I should say. I try to calculate where I would get the money for such a trip . . .

The row of shuttered shops on the far side of the street seems to lean towards me like a smug jury: *Broke, broke, always broke! Can't pay her own way to America. Why didn't she join the Credit Union when Greta told her to?*

'Shut up, shops!' In more of a stew than ever, I close the curtains.

The kettle clicks off and I cop on. Who made the rule that I have to shout, 'How high?' when, after all this time, Eve orders me to jump? She's the guilty party here. My brother, sister and I are the innocent ones.

The hell with her. We'd waited all this time. She can wait now – she has no right to land in on top of us like this.

But—

Big but.

Suppose she dies? According to this Dale character, the main injury is a broken leg, but he did say something about internal stuff too. Infections. Maybe he was playing it down. Drip-feeding the bad news.

This may be the only chance I will ever have to know my mother. To learn things about myself, dammit.

I sag against the sink. I thought I'd grown out of all that stuff, but here they come again, all the doubts and longings and fears and rages, hissing in my brain like a tangle of snakes.

I make the tea, then climb back into bed. It is twenty past five. If I sip slowly, it will get me as far as twenty-five to six. Only ten minutes to put in after that, then I can start getting ready for work and take my mind off things.

Outside, the sparrows start up on top of the rumbling from the Corpo's street-cleaning machine. Normal, everyday, good sounds of the coming summer.

I've always loved April, maybe because I was born this month, but for whatever reason, since I was old enough to notice, I've looked forward to the immediate stretch in the evenings when the clocks have gone forward. It doesn't matter if it's bucketing or howling from the heavens, I've always fancied that the air on that day is milder against my cheeks and (I know this is going to sound mushy) my imagination fills up with lambs and bluebells, baby birds and clean new leaves on trees.

Not that we see much of Mother Nature down here in central Dublin. It's more the idea of it. You know that a few hundred yards away in the Basin, or in the Phoenix Park, or a short bus ride away in the countryside up beyond Finglas, it's all there. Waiting.

I'll bet you're surprised that someone like me even thinks about Nature. After all, Nature is for people who have the time and money to drive their kids to bird sanctuaries or bogs. People who read posh newspapers and poems. Educated people who have time to save the planet and don't want incinerators. 'NIMBYs', they're called in the newspapers, I think.

Not for waitresses who were brought up in orphanages and who'll never own a car or get Botox.

My tea is almost cold now and I can hear the milk van outside; he delivers to the shops around this time, rickety-clickety-tickety over the potholes as if nothing has happened, as if I hadn't answered that phone. How the hell are we going to get to Arizona?

It will have to be a joint effort. Willow is Eve's daughter just as much as I am: she'll have to take some of the responsibility.

Hey! The solution to the money problem, at least, is obvious. My sister and her husband are dream clients for any bank: two civil servants, index-linked, benchmarked, two good, predictable, pensionable salaries automatically going into their accounts every fortnight. They have a three-bedroomed house, even if it is mortgaged. Feck that. They can't owe all that much now compared to the value of the place; they bought it fifteen years ago, the value of it has to have increased a lot. They can raise money on it – these days, the telly's crammed with ads about 'releasing equity'. For conservatories. For 'That Dream Holiday'.

How about for going to see your long-lost mother?

It won't be as if Rowan and I are looking for charity: I'll pay them back on the never-never, all of my fare and my half of Rowan's, and if Paddy whinges about it, it's Willow's problem not mine.

Too right: I'm now seriously self-righteous. She can do her twitchy I'm-a-mother-and-that's-my-first-priority bit as much as she likes, but I won't bite. It's time Willow and Paddy pulled their weight: I've been left to deal with the Rowan situation by myself for far too long. Like, why am I always the one who has to go to the police station or the squat just because Willow has something on, or her kids have, that can't be changed at short notice? Why am I penalised for being the single sister?

I look at the clock for the umpteenth time. Nearly ten to six. I am now behind schedule. I might even be late, unheard of for me: one of the positive legacies from our bell-regulated orphanage is the virtue of punctuality.

I get out of bed again, this time to face the day. Whether we manage to get to Arizona or not, nothing in my world will ever be the same. Eve is found.

CHAPTER TWO

'I don't believe you!' Greta's blue eyes inflate like tiny beach balls. 'You're kidding, aren't you?' She's having to shout because of the early-morning music programme blasting from the wireless in the corner of the kitchen. We're expecting two large groups of Americans in for breakfast and the pressure is on. Just as well, because if it wasn't I might give in to the sinking, wavy feeling of sickness in the pit of my stomach.

'Nope. You don't think I could make something like this up, do you?' We're filling salt-cellars. (You use a plastic funnel. I've often wondered who invented these helpful things – they must make a fortune and I don't begrudge them a penny of it.) As usual the United Nations, as we call the crowd we have to work with, had only half completed the job of setting the breakfast tables after last night's dinners. We always check first thing for what's missing or out of order: that morning, two of the tables had been laid with only three napkins, one had a knife that was less than clean, there were three suspect coffee cups and more than three quarters of the salts were less than half full. We don't complain any more, even to each other, we just get on with it – hardly noticed, even, when the place changed hands about a year ago and yet another set of renovations started. We could let things slide, Greta and me, but we have our standards, and when there's drilling going on, we just turn the wireless up louder.

Their lack of training or commitment isn't the kids' fault and we have a nice crop right now. Cheap labour, of course, average age about twenty and willing enough. But, as ever, my impression is that none of them plans to make a career out of hotel work or waitressing: they're passing through. If I thought about it too long, I could envy this generation, with their college education and their expectations that every job they do is either just a step on a ladder or a holding operation. Unlike us, whose ambition as youngsters was always just to get a job and earn a living wage. Period.

9

'Have you told Willow yet?' Greta picks up the last unfilled salt-cellar and runs it under a hot tap to loosen the cap. They're a new design and inclined to stick. (They never consult us, you know. What do *we* know, after all?)

I pick up a handful of butters, Floras and Low-Low portions and count them into silver dishes. 'Do you really think I'd ring her at half five in the morning to land a bombshell like this? I'm dreading it, Gret. It's like a fairy story . . . No, not a fairy story. In one way it's like *Nightmare on Elm Street*. I can't take it in, after all these years.' My stomach lurches again. I drop some of the butters on the floor and stoop to pick them up. 'I don't even know whether I even want to go. I'm half terrified to see her, half want to. It's driving me mental.'

Greta rolls the salt-cellar in a dishtowel and twists the cap off. 'It's a shock. But of course you want to go. It's going to be hard, but think of the years to come. You'd never forgive yourself if, God forbid, she died and you'd had the opportunity to see her and didn't. Now, listen to me, Bel . . .' She's glaring at me, head down like a bull calf's.

I know what's coming. 'I'm listening.'

'Don't let Willow get to you this time. Do you hear me?'

'I hear you.'

'I mean it. I'll kill you if you come back to me and tell me that she stomped all over you again.'

'I won't let her.'

'You're too soft altogether.'

'Not this time.'

'Good.' As she resumes pouring salt, I notice how red and puffy her hands are and I'm stabbed with affection for her. Hard work never did anyone any harm. That's what they all say, the nuns, the government. They should spend twenty-five years in a hotel kitchen and dining room! Like Greta, they should raise eight children at the same time.

'How'd this chap find you?' Expertly, click-clack-cluck, she lines up the salt-cellars, a glittering miniature army, on the stainless-steel counter.

'I didn't ask him. I suppose because my number's in the book. I'm the only A. Moraghan – with a *g* – in the Dublin directory.'

As soon as I say it, it strikes me that being so easy to find adds injury to Eve's insult. If it had been that easy for Mr Cowboy, it had been easy all along for anyone. Including her. Since February 1991, anyway, which was when I managed to join the human race and get my own phone.

We know each other so well that I can see Greta is thinking the same thing. 'Maxi plays great stuff in the mornings, doesn't she?' She hums along with the Supremes' 'Baby Love' while flipping switches on the boilers and coffee-makers. She's bossy enough but she can sometimes be very tactful, Greta can.

Under the music, I can hear loud talking and guffawing coming from the dining room. Americans get up early, especially if they're being herded about on a coach tour. 'I'll go out there and start the war, will I?' I pick up my order book. All this might sound as if I'm behaving real normal, but nausea is still a problem.

'Ah, shite!' Greta turns down Maxi. 'We're not supposed to start serving for another ten minutes.'

'The sooner we start the sooner we'll finish. How's the ice?' To us, having Americans in the dining room means we have to have gallons of iced water. Greta bustles to check. 'It'll do,' she surveys our stocks, 'but don't offer. Wait until they ask.'

'Here goes.' I head for the swing door. 'Well, good morning, Dilip,' I say, as one of the Asian kids, still wearing his anorak, rushes in. 'Nice of you to join us.' I aim a pretend box at his ear. 'Get a move on, will you? Most of the tables out there need salt – that's them on the tray there – and . . .' I point to three industrial-sized sliced pans on one of the countertops '. . . that bread needs to be defrosted and separated for toast. The butter dishes are over by the microwaves. I've taken out the rashers and sausages but you'll have to cut up the puddings. Did you see our distinguished breakfast chef on your travels by any chance?' The chef, a Malaysian, should have been with us by now. I had already placed a honeycomb of eggs beside his griddle.

'I saw him pushing his bicycle down the lane, Mrs Bella. I think perhaps he had a flat tyre.' The boy pulls off his jacket and flashes me his Colgate smile, knowing full well that, because of it, every woman within a five-mile radius, including me, will be enchanted and will forgive him everything.

'But you didn't have a flat tyre, did you? What's your excuse? Come on, move your skinny bum!'

Yet I can't help smiling as, glad to be busy, I push through to face the crowd, many of whom are already lined up along the buffet, adding seeds and hi-fibre stuff from personal jars to our Bran Flakes and fruit juices.

Americans care about their bowels. We're used to them now but sometimes, if you're in a hurry, talking them through a menu and what *exactly* each item contains, or is cooked in, can really slow you down. If it isn't dairy or yeast they can't have, it's refined sugar or nitrates or animal fats or sunflower oil or nuts. This morning, thank God, they're quite adventurous. Some of them are even willing to try black pudding as part of their Full Irish.

Two of the girls come in to help with the eight o'clock rush but we're all so busy I don't get a breather to contact Willow until just after half past nine when Greta and I can safely leave the kids to deal with the stragglers.

'I think I'll go to see her instead of phoning. She's at work by now and it's not the kind of thing you land on someone in a busy office, is it?' The two of us are puffing on our post-breakfast fags in the back lane, leaning on the wall beside the rubbish skips and trying to ignore the fragrance of cats and old piss. As usual, I'm trying to give up but doing it the hard way, curving down: twenty a day for the first week, nineteen for the next, and so on. This week, I'm down to twelve but, given the way I'm feeling right now, I have my doubts as to whether I'll be able to stick to that number today.

'Good idea.' Greta stubs out her butt, rolls it in a paper napkin and puts the little parcel into the pocket of her uniform. She is a thrifty person. By some trick of the sun, her hair, blonded so often it's frizzy beyond repair, seems to surround her face like a halo of wire. It's a halo she deserves, does Greta: not only did she bring up her own eight but she and her husband are now rearing two grandchildren, the kids of their eldest daughter, while the daughter and her husband work all the hours God sends to scrape together the deposit on a house.

Greta stares right through me now. 'You're already going easy on her,' she says, 'I can see it, not wanting to bother her and all that crap. Don't worry about her reactions, think about yourself for a change.' She pucks me in the shoulder. 'Be brutal, Bel. She'd be brutal with you.'

'Yeah,' I say unconvincingly.

'And tell Jimmy Porter to get off his arse and do something useful for you for a change. There'll be a lot to do.' Greta's husband is a Jimmy too so we always add the surname to my Jimmy. She feels entitled to give out about him because I met him at one of her parties; like mine, her Jimmy used to work on the buses.

I stub out my own cigarette, number three that day, and put it away. 'I'm not even sure I'll tell him, actually. It might be more trouble than it's worth.' My Jimmy is inclined to see every little thing as a big thing. God knows how he'd respond to something so enormous.

Greta throws her eyes to heaven. 'Suit yourself! Go on,' she gives me another puck, 'fix yourself up. Take as much time as you need – I'll cover for you.'

'Thanks a million. You're a pal.'

'Will you get a move on, ya big mooch? I'll be dying to hear – and, trauma or no trauma, don't you dare cry off tonight.'

'I won't!' I give her a watery smile. 'I'm looking forward to it.' Greta and her Jimmy are twenty-six years married tomorrow. They hadn't been able to afford a party for their twenty-fifth so they'd saved up and are having a big splash tonight, getting the celebration in just before the year is up.

Willow's office is only minutes' walk from the hotel, not that we often take advantage of our nearness – mostly when we want to exchange Christmas presents before she and her family go down the country to Paddy's folks, or there are family birthdays. We usually meet in Clery's rooftop cafeteria: it's reasonably priced and handy, and I have a friend on the staff there who, braving dirty looks from the rest of the customers, reserves a table for us.

Her front office has been gussied up recently. It used to be all dark wood with cigarette burns and splinters out of it, service hatches and grumpiness. Now, with the new openness and transparency in the public service, everything's on view and sincere and mission statements: we're treated to pastels and glass, counters only as high as your waist, and 'Can I help you?' The queues, though, are still long, bored and irritable.

I ask for Willow, give my name, and while I wait, out of habit, take out my ciggies but then see the *No Smoking* sign and put them back into my pocket. It's just as well I'm giving up. Us smokers are being crucified in Ireland. They're talking about bringing in a total ban in all public areas, including pubs, would you believe? *Pubs!*

Willow comes down the stairs behind the public counters and, auto-matically, I straighten up.

She waves to me, but then stops to talk to a colleague. I watch her, trying to be objective, trying to work out for the umpteenth time why

13

my sister intimidates me so much. As a higher executive officer, with security, status and a pension, even the look of her makes me feel inadequate. Spick and span today in her navy suit and starchy white blouse, highlighted hair swinging like a shampoo ad when she moves her head, it's not hard to see why she makes me feel like the poor relation. Which, leaving Rowan out of it, of course I am, with my plastic handbag, Dunnes jacket, worn Doctor Scholls, and my hair scraped back for work in an unflattering French pleat. To say I'm not clothes-conscious is the understatement of the year. For me, Dunnes or Penneys is the height of fashion, otherwise it's Fred's Fashions at the V de P and all the other charity shops. There are millions of them and they're all doing a roaring trade, not only because of people like me but all the immigrants and asylum-seekers. And they've a great turnover. Every week you find new things on the rails.

And it's only when I'm with Willow that I become conscious of the strain on my blouse buttons. By design my sister is lovely and slim; she power walks, works out at a gym, swims, plays tennis in summer, golf in winter.

We were brought up in the same orphanage, had the same foster-parents. We got the same punishments and the same education until we were let loose on the world. To be fair, it isn't her fault that at sixteen I'd had enough of school, wouldn't stay on to do the Leaving, and ended up as a waitress with a sweet tooth and no inclination to do formal exercise.

I shouldn't be in awe of her like I am. After all, I'm the eldest of the three of us, so it should have been the other way round: *she* should be afraid to cross *me*. I'm even an inch taller than her: I'm five eight and she's only five seven.

How tall was – is – Eve? We haven't a clue. It might seem like an insignificant thing but, believe me, it's quite important to know if you're bigger than your mother, or shorter, or what.

Willow glances in my direction and I smile at her too quickly and too brightly, dammit. I close my mouth and narrow it, to show I'm not being craven. 'Craven' is a good word. I looked it up when I came across it in a library book a few years ago and it fits perfectly the way I feel around Willow.

She finishes the conversation with her colleague and comes towards me, eyebrows signalling questions. 'This is a surprise, Bella.'

'Hello, Willow, sorry to appear out of the blue like this, but something's happened—'

'Come through.' Now it's her lips that go thin, but she doesn't have to work at it.

I can see exactly how this meeting will go. Who is this man, Bella? What precisely is his relationship with our mother? When did the accident happen? Where *exactly* does she live? *You mean you didn't even ask?*

She is out of sight for a couple of seconds, then reappears through a doorway a few feet away, beckoning to me. 'What's happened now?' She sighs. 'What's he done this time?'

CHAPTER THREE

This morning was real bad. The wind was coming from the north-east and that's the fucking cruellest. When you've been on the streets as long as I have, you get to know these things – exactly where the wind is coming from, et cetera, et cetera. For instance, did you know that, for us, drizzle is a lot more miserable than heavy rain? Even though the blokes with the Styrofoam cups say that the takings go up during a downpour, we all hate that fucking drizzle. It seems to make you wetter. Certainly more fed up. I'm still trying to work that one out, but it's a fact.

Speaking of Styrofoam cups, the first thing I'll say is I'm not one of that gang. If I ever find myself begging I'll top myself and that's a promise. I've managed to survive without it. All right, some of how I've survived may not be all that legal – but you try living out here on the poxy Social! You try it not for one fucking night as an experiment but one whole fucking month. In November or February. Then come back to me and tell me I'm being mollycoddled by the Social Welfare.

So I look after myself. Right? I do lift the odd time, but even there I have my principles. Only shops. Never individuals.

Except that one time when I did a car. Well, who's really to blame there? I mean, the stiff should have locked his car, shouldn't he? And he shouldn't have left his CDs all over the seats in full view of everyone, should he? (Barry fucking Manilow, would you believe? The Corrs. The Cranberries. The bleedin' Eagles! I got only a tenner for the bleedin' lot. Wanker.)

And, by the way, no violence either. Any time I've been nicked, usually through CCTV – we all *hate* CCTV – I've gone peacefully. The blokes in the inner city clinks aren't that bad, to tell you the truth – if you don't give them lip, that is. They'll even give you a cuppa and, although I hate to admit it, sometimes it isn't too bad to have a mattress up off the floor for the night, even if you don't know who was there before you. Sometimes you're just so tired, you sleep anyway.

No, I don't give nobody lip, not even bouncers or security guards. It's easier all round. They've a job to do. My job is to stay one step ahead of them.

Bet you never thought you'd hear a street person saying the pigs aren't all that bad.

So, to get back to this morning. Early morning is a bad time for me. Maybe I've got to the stage where I'm feeling my age. For whatever reason, I always feel most sorry for myself when I have to get out of that sleeping-bag; I'd give anything to turn over and snuggle in again but, of course, I get no choice.

At least I've got a great pitch at the moment. Haven't had to spend any of the Social on a hostel since I got it.

Some of the hostels aren't too bad but I avoid them unless I'm on my last legs. If I have the flu or something. The noise in them and the smells do my head in. And the wasters that are in there. Dickheads, the lot of them. Although you do hear the odd sob story when you feel sorry for someone. Like an old guy I met who'd lost his entire family in a fire in Croydon or someplace. Had a job and all, he had, but he was away from the house that night. He went off his head afterwards with the gargle, you know. Lost the job, lost the house, lost everything. And would you blame him?

I inherited my pitch from a bloke who decided to move on to Cork. His granny lives there and he was going down to see what's what. He'd had it with Dublin, he said, and even if she blew him off, the competition in Cork isn't as bad as it is in Dublin and he felt he'd make out. We'd become pals, sort of, as much as you can be pals when you're like us. You can make friendships, but they're not very lasting because out here it's every man for himself. This geezer was young, much younger than me, only twenty-two, so he still had a chance of making a go of things. Good luck to him, I say, especially since I'm the beneficiary of his move. I miss him actually, even though you had to be careful around him because he was a header when he was strung out. To be avoided. Anyway, bottom line, if it's a choice between the kid's friendship and his gaff, there's no contest.

The gaff is a doorway, of course, but with a difference: it's grand and deep. Snug. And it has a security gate across the front so you can sleep without worrying all the time if you're going to be fucking stabbed or robbed or whatever. I don't want to say where it is – some other gouger might find out about it and fight me for it. I'm getting too old for fighting, but the reality is that you have to guard your pitch like it's the Holy Grail. There's fellas – and girls – out here that'd take the eye out of your head for a bit of shelter, especially a place as good as this. All I'll say is that it's up near Whitefriar Street church.

Hey – did you know that St Valentine's heart is in that church? It's the heart of the *real* St Valentine. I think they have an arm or a leg or something there too, but it's the heart that tickles me. Much good it'll do me but, still, it's nice to know it's there.

Another great thing about this place is that the gaffer who owns the shop is a good guy. He minds my sleeping-bag for me during the day and even lets me use the toilet in the place. If he's feeling really good about himself, he'll give me a cuppa and a few bob so I can get a breakfast roll. And he saves his cardboard boxes for me so I have a good layer underneath the bag.

That's as far as his charity goes, though – he won't let me hang around during the day. Says I'd put the customers off. I have to be gone by the time the girls come in to open the shop. Like I have the Black Death or something.

Ah, no – I shouldn't slag him: he's a decent bloke. And he doesn't try to convert me, or reform me like my two bloody sisters do all the time.

So, about the two blisters. (I have real blisters too, by the way, the old plates are killing me these days – well, you try walking around Dublin all day with holes in your boots!) They are two pains in the arse. Well, one is more of a pain than the other, I suppose, I have to be fair about it. Bel's all right in her way. Her heart's in the right place. She's the one helps me a bit, gets me out of clink when the pigs ring her up, that kind of thing, slips me a few bob when she has it. But she's still a pain in the arse! Always at me to clean up my act, giving out, doing my fucking head in. One Christmas she even asked me up to her gaff for the dinner. It was nice of her, but no thanks. Her so-called boyfriend was to be there too. Don't know what she sees in him, but, hey, there's no accounting for taste. I've always had it in my mind to tell her she could do better, but she'd hardly listen to me, would she? I'm not exactly Beau Brummel.

Anyway, that year I was invited to the Mansion House for my dinner. It's not bad, turkey, the whole works. It's the Lions Club, or the Knights or something. We don't care who gives it or why – they're probably doing it for the sake of their consciences, to make up for all the dirty looks they give us over the year, but as far as I'm concerned, fair play to them. It's good hot food and no questions asked. Even a few bevvies, although, for obvious reasons, they're stingy enough with the booze.

So that's Bel, she's not too bad, and I know that when I need help she's there.

But the other one? She's a snobby bitch. Thinks I'm scum and shows it. Blood thicker than water? My arse. I'm not scum, right? It's the fucking system, isn't it? Never gave me a chance.

Lookit, be fair. Is it my fault my ma was a whoring bitch? Is it my fault I got the shit kicked out of me in institutions when I was too young to defend myself? Is it my fault now that I can't even get a fucking roof over my head? No. I'm telling you, it's the system.

The blisters think I'm an addict. Sure, I drink a bit. Have a few cans with my mates. And I do a bit of other stuff when I can find the cash, which is getting harder, let me tell you. But I'm not an addict. I can stop any time I want.

To prove my point, I'm clean at the moment. I go to AA on and off (at least the rooms are warm and you get free tea and biscuits) and they say in the meetings that you should take your life one day at a time. But I'm different. I have to have goals. My goal this time is to stay clean until my fortieth birthday. That's in July 2004 and because it's only April 2003 now it's no easy task. It's a milestone birthday, a kind of landmark, so I've decided to do it just to show that I can. It's a quest inside me. A last go at it. Because if I can't do it for even that length of time I'll give up totally. Right? Become a junkie and that'll be the end of it.

I was clean for a whole seven months a couple of years ago. That was the time I had a mot. A good one. She got up the pole and the two of us got clean together for the sake of the sprog, and we even got accepted on the list for a flat.

And then she got sick. Hep. Probably from sharing gear. It was a mockery, wasn't it? Here she was, clean, and then she gets hep from some earlier time. She was so pissed off she went back on stuff, took it wher-ever she could find it, and you know what that means on the streets. You could be sold anything. Rat poison, even. Anyway, one night when she was high, she snuffed it.

So. No mot. No sprog. And, of course, off the list for the flat. It's the system. People like me don't count. We're invisible except when reporters come around to do 'stories' about us. They're all sympathy and quietness and can you read and write, Rowan?

Please! I might be temporarily on my uppers but I'm not a thicko, you know. At one point, the bint interviewing me congratulated me on being so articulate. Give me a break! What did she fucking expect? That just because I'm sleeping rough my brain doesn't connect with my mouth? I decided I'd show her how much I knew about cinema. I turned her questions on her and asked her had she seen the latest French *noir*? 'It's a jewel,' I said. I've struck up a relationship with a guy in one of the arty cinemas – he lets me in for nothing in the afternoons. As a result I've seen everything they show there, French, Hungarian, Polish, the indies from all over. I'm an expert, I am. The problem is I've no one to discuss them with on the streets. Anyway, this bint was so shocked at having the tables turned on her she nearly choked on her *latte*.

I've seen and read some of the reports they do and it beats me why they do it. They're all real angry against the government on our behalf. The system, they say, excludes us. Bit two-faced, wouldn't you think? Like, what do they have against the system? They give out about the system, about politicians and so forth, but aren't they part of it, with their cars and their watches and crèches, their smooth faces and white teeth and nice heavy jackets and windy-round-the-neck scarves? They're making a nice fat living out of being against the system, aren't they? So doesn't that make them part of the system? And if they're that upset about us, why don't they give us some of their big fat money?

Their favourite words about us, the words they use a *lot*, are that people like me are 'the most vulnerable in our society'. But so are the elderly, the handicapped, the first-time buyers, people who live in slums, single mothers. Every time you get to see the news it's somebody else who's the most vulnerable in our society. Like the people who won't pay the bin charges. So who's *not* the most vulnerable in our society?

Actually, sometimes I think they think we're in a zoo. Look, folks! They talk English! They walk on their hind legs!

As a matter of fact I was on a programme recently. At the time, I thought the reporter was very nice. She bought me a cup of coffee and a fry-up in Bewley's. Sat with me for the best part of an hour and a half while I spilled my guts out to her. Told her everything, I did, about my whoring ma and so-called father and what went on in that fucking so-called home, and how I got into H because for a while it was bliss but how it's now the enemy.

She was a great listener, I'll say that for her. I suppose they're trained that way – to get people to confide in them. But she did give me respect . . . at least, I thought she did. Something I haven't experienced much, I can tell you.

And then that night she talked to me again, this time with the camera in tow. She chose the place, an alleyway up near Fatima Mansions. It was filthy, a shit place, but I didn't care where she interviewed me, it was her decision and, to me, the back-streets and alleys of Dublin are all the one. He was nice too, the bloke with the camera. Polite. Not much of that either, round where I live.

'Hey, here he is! Quiet on the set!'

'Action!'

'Ready for your close-up, Rocky?'

That was what I got when I dropped into the Focus coffee shop soon afterwards. The programme had been on the night before and a lot of them had seen it.

All day, I got that and some more all around the streets. Hadn't seen myself, of course. I was in a squat at the time but I suppose if I'd known about it I could have gone into a hostel for the night, but although the bint had told me what night it was on, I'd forgotten.

I pretended to be embarrassed at the slagging, but deep down I was chuffed. Until my mates described the programme. Apparently there were millions of us on that programme. I was on twice. *Twice* only. For less than a minute each time. After the bint talking to me in Bewley's for more than an hour and a half! And then bringing me up that alley and keeping me hanging around for another bleedin' half-hour while the fella with the camera was getting ready, and then making me repeat most of what I told her already in the café. Wasting my time.

Told you. We're zoo people.

CHAPTER FOUR

'How's Maeve and Dermot, these days?' I force myself to sound jolly. Willow's two children, twelve and nine, go to private schools and are paragons of achievement. I am Maeve's godmother but I don't think she likes me: the thank-you letters she writes when I give her presents are obviously written to a formula, probably under strict supervision. I think she's a bit ashamed of having a waitress in the family.

'Great.' Willow walks two paces in front of me along the corridor. Prints of the Dublin docks, fire extinguishers, notices about pub quizzes, union meetings, appeals for Concern, about the whereabouts of lost wallets and pens, ads for house-sharing. We go through the doorway of her office. 'Maeve is doing a project on the decline of the pied wagtail in the city of Dublin.'

'That's marvellous. And Paddy?'

'Paddy's fine too.' She plops into a chair behind her desk. 'They're all fine. Jimmy?'

'He's grand.' I sit on the hard chair in front of her desk, like I'm here for an interview. Willow has never met my boyfriend, if you could call him that, and I suppose when I've talked about him to her, I've been guilty of pumping him up a bit. Or, at least, of not disabusing her of the impression she has that before he went on the disability he was an inspector, and not just a conductor on the buses. 'I'm seeing him tonight, as it happens. We're going to a party in Greta's.'

'No move, though?' Towards the altar is what she means: Willow likes her people packaged in pairs.

'Willow, we've been through this. We're fine the way we are. It's mutual.'

'Well, so long as it *is* mutual and he's not just stringing you along. You're not getting any younger, you know – but I presume you didn't come here just to ask after the health of my family or to chitchat. What's this about, Bella, or need I ask? Rowan, of course?'

Stalling, trying not to take insult at the 'getting younger' bit, I smile at the office's only other occupant, a very young man – boy, really – who is poring over a stack of documents at a desk in the corner of the room. He smiles back. 'Nice office. You had it done up since I was here last?'

'Arabella!' But her phone rings and she has to answer.

I study the nameplate facing me at the edge of her desk: *W. McCarthy*. I don't blame her for using only the initial: one of the many puzzles in our lives has been why Eve gave the three of us such unusual, non-Irish names. And why only two trees? Why was I Arabella and not Chestnut or something? We reckon the names were Eve's choice: our mysterious father rarely figures in any of our family conversations. To me, Peter Moraghan has no body, face or personality; I even see his name flat, like a cartoon, squashed into the road by a passing steamroller.

Willow is saying goodbye on the phone. She hangs up. 'So, what gives, Bella?' Steepling her fingers in front of her chin. Head nun. *Be brutal*, I think. 'It's about Eve. Our mother.'

The steeple collapses. Greta's advice had been spot on. 'What about her? Have you heard something?'

'Yes. Look, I don't have all that much time, I'm only on a break, but do you want to go for a cup of coffee or something?'

'Is she dead?' Suddenly Willow's busy looking for something in a little tray she has beside the phone.

'Not quite.' I know, because Eve's friend told me, that our mother is far from near death, but I also know my sister. To get her to react, I have to be a little creative. It has worked, obviously, because she lowers her head to get her handbag from under her desk. 'I'll be back in a few minutes,' she calls over her shoulder to the boy, then walks ahead of me out of the room.

Although we don't speak again until we get to the corner of Cathedral Street, I can nearly hear the confusion in her brain. This Burger King is all hard surfaces, black, red, a bit of 'wood panelling', but clean and well organised. Inside the door, she attempts to take charge as usual, 'You want tea or coffee, Bella?' but as an act, it's horrible to see. I may have been too brutal.

'I'll get it.' I shuffle the change in my jacket pocket. 'You sit down there. Coffee for you, yeah?'

'Yes, please.' She sits.

As it turns out, neither of us is to take even a sip of the beverages. As I fill her in, as quickly and accurately as I can, colour bleeds out of her face until her lipstick looks like a scab against the skin round her mouth. She's a trier, though: 'So! Our mother clicks her fingers and we're both expected to drop everything and go to Arizona?'

Exactly what I'd been thinking, of course, although I don't say that. Instead I remind her that there are three of us involved here. 'Rowan too.'

'How the hell are we to do that,' she's not listening, 'even if we could afford it? No. We can't afford it.'

'Let's at least talk about it. And Rowan should have a say too—'

'*Rowan?*' The colour is returning to normal. 'It's long past time when that layabout was entitled to a say in anything in this family. How would we find him, anyway?'

'Same way we found him before, I suppose. The Vincent, the Sally Army, Focus, Trust, Simon?'

'You're on your own with that.'

This isn't fair of her, of course, but I can't blame her: while I continue to see good in Rowan – sort of – she can see only the outside. To her, he's a deadbeat, beyond redemption. I don't think she sees him even as a human being any more, only as a sad *thing*.

You'd have to understand this and forgive her. I can remember him as a baby, how sweet and chubby he was (when he wasn't roaring – I've conveniently forgotten the bad bits), but she was too young. And although we had supervised visits to him at the beginning, he never became part of our lives.

Right now, I'm not up to fighting her for ownership of the problem but I still feel she should take some part in finding him. 'His social worker, maybe.'

'I don't even know who that is any more,' she says briskly, 'he's had so many. Well,' she brings her chin up, 'even if we do find him, you needn't think I'm going to be responsible for him – cleaning him up and finding clothes for him so he won't disgrace us.' She's almost back to her usual bossy self so I sit back and let her go full pelt. Did I think she could leave Maeve and Dermot or her job, just like that, at the drop of a hat? Paddy is very busy, she is very busy, there are rules and procedures that have to be followed in these cases. It's outrageous that I should have been rung up like that out of the blue – who do these people think they are? There should have been contact through social workers, the health board. Our permission should have been asked by intermediaries, those laws are in place to protect us, what's the use of having laws—

I make sympathetic noises during all of this – it's good, I think, to let her get it all out. But as she cracks on, I'm amazed that she seems to be turning over the idea in her mind as if it's a possibility.

The penny drops. The enormity of what has happened, what might happen, is rising inside me like a giant mushroom, choking off some of the air to my throat. You know how that is? How when something seems like just a possibility, you can consider it and work it out in your brain, but it's only when it seems really to be on the cards that your heart joins in for real?

Willow winds down and stares into her cup.

I give her a few seconds. Then: 'The bottom line, Willow, is that procedures don't matter now. We have been contacted. We have to make the choice. I have to ring this man back to let him know one way or the other.'

'I don't know how to deal with this, Bella.' She holds her head on her neck as rigidly as if it's a stop sign. 'I'm not sure I want to see her. I was getting along fine – my life is bloody *in order*. I don't want it turned upside down.' But as we look at one another, each reads the picture in the other's mind. Our mother. Eve. A woman we know from one blurry photograph.

'There's no gun at your back.' I'm gentle, and if it hadn't been Willow I would have reached out to touch her. 'You have to make up your own mind, but it depends on you as to whether I go or not.'

'How does it depend on me?' Her face, so much more beautiful than mine, becomes a little less beautiful.

Be brutal.

I stick my chin out. 'I'll need a loan from you and Paddy. I'll pay you back, of course, but it'll have to be on the drip. And if we do find Rowan and he wants to come, I'll pay you back half of his fare too.'

'Half?'

'That's only fair. He's your brother too.'

'Out of the question, Bella.' A red tide rises through the v of her white blouse. 'I'm sorry and all that, but do you have any idea how much it costs to rear children in this city? The fees, the uniforms, the outings?' She's off again. If children are to have any chance, they have to have the same extra-curricular classes as their peers, ballet, soccer, tennis, music . . .

I tune out and find myself thinking about Arizona, about cowboys galloping past cactus plants, those big ones that look like prehistoric hands. About dying of thirst in the desert. About rattlers and coyotes and cruising like Thelma and Louise in a car with the top down. Empty highways unrolling to the red horizon.

I've been reading too much.

I tune back in to Willow, who seems to be coming to the end of the current spiel. '. . . no, Bella, no way. No loans. Whatever about you, no loans for Rowan. It's out of the question.' She's right back on top form now. I'm pleased. That glimpse of a meek, disturbed Willow had been too frightening.

What's more, her aggression helps me make up my mind. I'm going to Arizona with or without her. I'll do my best for Rowan, but if he can't or won't make the effort, so be it. 'No problem.' I stand and zip up my jacket. 'Keep your hair on. Forget I even asked. I'll find the money somewhere. Because you know what? I'm going.'

This feels real good. There has been this great big hole in my life. It won't be filled by saying a quick one-off hello/goodbye to my mother. (Quick because I won't be able to get much time off. One-off because by the time I pay back the loan from wherever I get it, it's unlikely I'll ever have the wherewithal to make the trip again.) But it will fill some of that hole. It will place me somewhere on the scale occupied by normal human beings for whom the past is swarming.

Other women of my age and older, Greta for instance, moan about their mothers, are exasperated by them, give out about how demanding and unreasonable and selfish they are as they get older and more dependent, but the underlying theme is belonging.

From my point of view, even those whose mothers have died enjoy high status. Years after the event, they get sympathy, they have allowances made for them, they're given Mass and thinking-of-you cards. To be motherless by death is far preferable to being motherless by dumping. It's *normal*.

That sounds superficial and selfish, even bizarre, but it's what it feels like to an outsider. These women with heritage know where they fit in the natural order. I was thrown out of it for the best part of four decades. Now I have a mother and I can take my place.

'I'm going to Arizona, Willow,' I repeat quietly. 'You suit yourself.'

CHAPTER FIVE

The rest of that day was chaotic. And, yes, I got the promise of the money from Willow. All of it. For Rowan too. When she saw me marching out of Burger King and realised how determined I was, she caved in. Ran after me. Even apologised. I have stood up to her once or twice before and this has always happened. I guess I'm a bit lazy, confrontation-wise.

Neither of us had success, though, in finding Rowan. All through the rest of my shift at the Leicester, I was sneaking out to the public phone, making calls to all the usual suspects and checking in with Willow, who, in the middle of making bookings for the flight and organising her leave and so on, was making as little headway as I was with the agencies. The last people to see our brother, apparently, had been the staff at the drop-in coffee shop at Focus Point, the homeless place run by Sister Stan down in Eustace Street. But that had been more than a week ago.

I went down to Focus after the lunches. One of the staff there remembered seeing him 'about eight or nine days ago, I think it was', and that he seemed to be in good form. That was a good sign. They're honest down there. She would have told me if he'd been strung out.

'Any word since?'

'No. But that's not surprising. We see people sometimes ten days in a row and then maybe not for a couple of weeks, even months. They move around.'

I decided that, since I'd made the trek all the way from O'Connell Street, I might as well have a cuppa. 'Did you see him on the telly?' the girl, who was the chatty type, asked me while she was making it.

'What telly? Rowan was on the telly?'

'Oh, he's quite the celebrity. We're calling him Rocky, these days. There were two of them on it that we know from here.' She gave me the coffee, and as she filled me in on the programme, I was kicking myself. I'd love to have seen it – why had no one told me? Dammit. As usual, I'd probably had my head stuck in a book. But Jimmy watches a lot of telly – why hadn't he rung to tell me?

'Did you see that programme about the homeless on the television the other night?' It's half a day later, twenty past eight in the evening and we're in the taxi on the way to Greta's party.

'I saw the beginning,' he says back, 'but I switched over. There's enough bloody depressing news in this country without putting even more of it on in the evening when you're trying to digest your tea.'

'Thanks very much. My brother was on that programme.'

'Why didn't you tell me? I'd have watched it. Of course I'd have watched it!' He's wounded now. He takes things personally.

'Forget it. I didn't see it myself. I didn't know it was on.'

'But—'

'I said forget it! Don't go making a meal of it, Jimmy. I only asked you in case you saw it and could tell me your opinion of what he was like. So you didn't see it. No big deal.' It's on the tip of my tongue to ask him now for help in looking for Rowan, but I get contrary and decide to keep my mouth shut. Jimmy has that effect on me. I don't get contrary with anybody else. Is that what relationships are like? Familiarity breeds contempt sort of thing?

I can see he has certainly made an effort for this party. He's wearing a bow-tie and his good suit, the one he reserves for state occasions, and you could choke on the pong of Brylcreem from his slicked-back hair. He's proud of his hair and he has a right to be. It's still thick and full, with only fifty-fifty grey. 'The Porters always had a great head of hair' – if I've heard that once, I've heard it a thousand times, always added on to the bit about when his grandfather died the undertaker had told them he had never in all his born days seen a finer head on a ninety-one-year-old corpse.

When we get to Greta's cul-de-sac it's chock-a-block with parked cars. The house, blazing like Christmas, is festooned with big red balloons and a banner saying HAPPY SILVER WEDDING GRETA AND JIMY – the spelling ruining the effect. 'A bit of a do, eh?' The taxi-driver takes the money from Jimmy. 'Enjoy yizzerselves!'

'We will!' Jimmy's cheerful again. 'Keep the change.'

'Thanks, boss.' The driver grins.

Greta answers the door. 'Come in, come in, the both of you! It's bedlam inside, but that's what parties are for, isn't it? You're just in time for the ceremonies.' She's wearing black velvet trousers and a sleeveless glitter top with a big butterfly picked out in blue sequins over her chest.

'You look lovely, Greta.'

I go to hug her but she pulls back in alarm. 'Mind me hair! It cost a fortune!'

She's had it done upswept, with artificial curls on the top held in place by two big diamanté slides. She looks so happy I'm thrilled for her. 'Congratulations, Greta! Here, this is for the two of you from the two of us!' I give her our present, a set of six wineglasses. They'd been on special in Roches Stores.

'We both chipped in.' Jimmy's anxious to claim credit where it's due.

'Sure what else would I expect, Jimmy?' Greta winks at me. 'I'll just put it here with the rest.' She places the package on the heap of similar parcels beside the coat-stand in a corner of the tiny hall. 'I'm going to have a great time opening all of these. This party's going to go on for days! Jimmy's inside – go on in,' she says to my Jimmy. 'He'll get you a drink. Ask him for anything. He's been practising his crème de menthe frappés!' She waits then until she's sure he's out of earshot. Not that she needs to: The Dubliners are blasting from the sitting-room stereo at a level to damage your eardrums and there are so many kids squealing and running and bumping into everything that I'm already making decisions about not staying too long. Greta's terraced house is two-up two-down. Two bedrooms upstairs, sitting room and kitchen downstairs, weenshy bathroom on the return. You'd wonder how she reared eight of them in it. 'Any developments?' she hisses now.

'Yes and no. Tickets booked for the day after tomorrow, but no sign of Rowan. That's not tonight's conversation, but!' I push her firmly in the direction of the sitting room. 'Tonight's a celebration. Come on, let's join the party.'

And some party it is. There's hardly an inch of free floor space in the sitting room even though they've taken out all the furniture except a ring of chairs of all shapes and sizes around the walls. Greta's older kids, pressed into service as ushers and waiters for the night, are hard put to get anything to anyone but the mood is so raucous and gregarious that it's impossible not to catch the spirit. 'Hello, Granny!' I push through to give Greta's ninety-four-year-old grandmother a kiss on the cheek.

'Bella!' Rod straight on a hard chair, she bends not an inch to accept the kiss. 'Isn't it very noisy?'

Matriarch, sure. But hard to live with, I'd say. 'It sure is. But it's a party, Granny.' I smile at her and go back to Jimmy.

We're among the last to arrive, and within five minutes there's a great tapping of glasses and calls for hush. Greta's brother-in-law, who's a bar manager, has been appointed MC for the serious part of the evening and takes to the task with gusto. However, his speech extolling the blushing couple is mercifully short and when we all toast Greta and her Jimmy the place nearly combusts with warmth and love. I find myself crying, because this is what it is like to be part of a big, real family. Luckily, in the hoo-ha of hugging and thumping and cheering, nobody notices. Then Jimmy Porter gets a rush of blood to the head, calls for more hush, and when he gets it, self-appointed, thanks our hosts on behalf of us guests. 'Another toast, everyone: to the best friends and family in Ireland!'

We all drink again. 'And now,' Jimmy adds triumphantly before we've even swallowed, 'let the proceedings begin. A noble call, anyone?'

This raises a chorus of good-natured groans and moans.

'All right, all right,' he yells. 'I exercise my right and I call on the man of the moment, ladies and gentlemen, the groom himself, to give us a bar. *He-eeeeere's Jimmy!*' He does it like the guy who used to introduce Johnny Carson. We still get that show on satellite TV and Jimmy loves it.

To be fair, this first call raises a genuinely heartfelt cheer. And Greta's Jimmy, although protesting, stands up immediately. His party piece, which I've heard at all of Greta's parties, is '*Abdul El Bulbul Emir*'. We all know it and I get a chance to bury those treacherous tears while joining with the last line of every verse, of which there are an awful lot. Along with everyone else – even Granny's waving one arm back and forth in a little arc – I cheer and whistle for Sheikh Abdul and his harem of harlots, stamp and boo with the best of them at the heinous doings of the villain, Ivan Skavinsky Skavar. All the time I'm worrying because I know what's next.

Jimmy Porter loves performing. It's as if, having lost nearly all joy in real life since he was forced off the buses where, according to himself, he was 'every oul' wan's fantasy bit of stuff', he's channelled every little bit of what's left into standing up in front of an audience. Again according to himself, he was always considered a bit of a card in the Broadstone depot and now takes himself seriously as a comedian. For the past couple of years he has collected jokes and joke books, practised at home in front of a mirror and has recently taken to entering talent contents. He is single-minded about this; the fact that he never wins anything doesn't put him off. He is convinced his day will come. In the meantime, he can't wait for the party pieces to begin. I can see him now across the room, grey-hound in a trap, eyes glittering, as Greta's Jimmy nears the end of Abdul and Ivan's long, convoluted story. He can't wait.

It's too much to hope that he won't get the next noble call, but of course he does, from Greta's Jimmy – and having got it, he's so fast into the tiny clearing in the middle of the room that I can feel the draught.

I brace myself. Despite all the wavering about my relationship with Jimmy Porter, I'm loyal to him and I'd hate him to embarrass himself. When you're part of a couple, you feel sort of responsible, don't you? If they don't laugh, I'll die. I've heard his patter before, though, and some of it is quite good.

But Jimmy has a surprise in store. This time, instead of launching into the well-worn jokes about fat mothers-in-law and thick Kerrymen, he tries out a new act. Seriously vulgar. Women's bits and so forth. I'm mor-tified. I don't think he meant to offend. And it's only now, as he's dying on his feet, I remember he had told me at some stage that Greta's party was going to be the perfect opportunity to try out a new routine with jokes he got off some American website. I suppose he felt that everyone would be so well on that they'd take them in the party spirit.

The opposite happens and in five minutes flat that party goes from jolly to dead. You can hear the ice clinking in the glasses, real quiet clinking as though everyone's fingers are as stiff as pokers. Even the kids are transfixed. To give him his due, he gets the message and after two awful stories involving licking (I can't bear to tell you) he tries to retrieve the situation and goes back to a standard gag out of his blondes repertoire: 'This little blonde girl, you see, comes home to her mammy and says: "Mammy, we learned to count today. Everyone else only counted to five but I counted to ten. Isn't that very good? Isn't that because I'm blonde, Mammy?"

'"Yes, dear," says the mammy, "that's because you're blonde."

'The same thing happens the next day with the alphabet. "Mammy, Mammy," says the little blonde girl, "all the other girls only got as far as D, but I got as far as K. Isn't that very good, Mammy? Isn't that because I'm blonde?"

'"Yes, darling," says the mammy. "That's definitely because you're blonde."

'The third day she runs in to tell the mother that at school today, they all went swimming. "And all the other girls had no breasts, Mammy, but look at me! I'm thirty-six D. Isn't that good, Mammy? Isn't that because I'm blonde?"

'"No, darling," says the mother. "That's because you're twenty-five!"'

At least that one gets a few titters, but it's too late. Greta's parlour has a carpet on the floor and, crowded though it is, I can hear every step of Jimmy's feet as he returns to his place. She glances towards me and I mouth at her that I'm sorry, but I can see she's bucking. I don't dare look at her granny.

It's not over yet. There's worse to come. Jimmy's not thick and he knows he's bombed. He doesn't even make his noble call and Greta has to call it. In desperation probably, she calls on one of her aunties, a woman who sings in her local church choir and whose rendition of 'Panis Angelicus' kills the party even deader than Jimmy's jokes did.

Everyone's in bad humour now and drinking too much and not knowing where to look, even though poor Greta tries to get a singsong going with another of her aunties, a big, happy woman whose speciality is 'The Dublin Saunter' à la Sonny Knowles.

Then, disaster upon disaster, one of Greta's sons takes a half-hearted swipe at his da for giving out to him about drinking and refusing him another lager. Jimmy Porter, obviously anxious to make amends, is up like a light to intervene, smooth things over. He trips on someone's handbag and cracks his skull against the mantelpiece.

Blood. Lots of it. End of 'The Dublin Saunter'.

At least it gets us away, me apologising and grovelling and Greta telling me insincerely that there's no problem.

Jimmy's a basket case but he feels so bad I reckon it'd not be on to say what I feel so I keep it zipped.

Thank God it's a quiet night in A and E: sometimes you'd be there for a whole night and half the next day, but we're waiting for only four and a half hours. When he's eventually called in he gets fourteen stitches.

In the taxi on the way home, I tell him about America and Rowan. He's gob-smacked, of course, but picks a fight – probably because he has to have a go at someone. 'Where's the fire? You've waited this long, you can wait another week, can't you?'

If I'd been determined with Willow, I'm rock now. 'How about if I just want to go? How about that?'

'So you're just going to dump the plans we have for next week, are you?' These involve a trip to some cousin of his who has a holiday home in the North of Ireland near the Giant's Causeway. I'd been lukewarm about it in any event. The cousin drinks too much. 'We can go another time, Jimmy.' I notice the taxi-driver earwigging and I keep my voice down.

'So it's all right, is it?' Jimmy has no such qualms. 'That's it? I can just ring him and tell him he can stuff his invitation? That you've found something better to do?'

'Jimmy, shut up!' I lose patience. 'You go. Tell your cousin what you like about me. I'm going to Arizona. And it's not just something better to do – it's me and Willow finding our mother. Cop on!'

He slumps back into the seat and closes his eyes. We part not the best of friends.

You're probably asking yourself – and not for the first time – why I stick with Jimmy Porter if he's such a whinge. Well, he wasn't always a whinge: when we met first he was gas – and from time to time we still manage to knock a bit of fun out of each other when I can persuade him to take me to a dance: he's light on his feet. And, being practical about it, you can see that with my shift patterns it's handy to have someone who's nearly always available. Swings and roundabouts. You have to put up with each other's quirks, don't you? And I do feel sorry for him.

So OK, I do have to think about me and Jimmy. But not right now. I've bigger things to consider now. Like my trip the day after tomorrow. Jimmy isn't perfect, that's true, but – I ask you – am I such a great catch?

CHAPTER SIX

I can't find a smoking area anywhere in the arrivals hall so I'm trying to distract myself by gawking around. Given the reason for our visit here, it might seem trivial to be doing the tourist, but you've got to remember what an unadventurous traveller I've been up to now: think Manchester, the Canaries and Belfast, and that's about it. So leaving the Eve situation aside, this trip for me is the equivalent of Greta's granny zipping the Zimmer to a dog sled and upping it to the North Pole.

So far I can see nothing exotic in Phoenix airport (although it's imaginatively called 'Sky Harbor'); in my limited experience, everything looks to be much of a muchness in every airport. As far as the architecture and décor go, there's probably a little guy somewhere, a Wizard of Oz type behind a curtain, who's going a bomb and sees no reason to change his winning formula: *let's put huge cactus plants in this one and palm trees in that one, and pictures of Irish dancers and round towers in the Irish one with lots of green and Aran jumpers and things. There you go and Bob's your uncle. No one will ever notice that everything else, mall, Tannoy system, even type of floor, is the same.*

But having connected this time through Dublin and Heathrow airports, jittery places where I felt I was on the verge of losing something vital, what strikes me about Phoenix isn't the proper air-conditioning or the lack of litter but the absence of hustle. Everything feels quiet and slow: people are strolling, rather than rushing, smiling even, so that everyone, the elderly included, looks healthy, tanned and relaxed.

And then there are the outfits. I've always thought, for instance, that the Yanks at the Leicester who dress like cowboys are doing it for show, in the way we'd wear green for St Patrick's Day if we were on our holidays in Tenerife. But it seems I was doing them a disservice. A huge proportion of them, men and women, are wearing Stetsons, string ties and tooled leather boots – curly toes, stacked heels and all; as for the others, they're mostly in denim, although I can see a sprinkling of boob tubes and polyester pants suits. By comparison, the travel-weary linen and cotton we're wearing look dowdy and cheap.

One thing is the same all over: the long, long wait for the luggage. We've been here about ten minutes now and the empty conveyor belt keeps bringing round one frayed blue strap and a half-burst plastic bag, packed beyond its capacity with baby clothes.

'This is ridiculous.' Willow looks even more exhausted than I feel. Maybe it's because she's thin. Fewer reserves.

'Yeah.'

'This is supposed to be the most technically developed country in the world and they can't even get a few suitcases off an aeroplane.'

'Chill, Willow. Giving out about it won't bring them any quicker.' I've pushed the reason for this trip to the back of my mind. I'm gasping for a puff.

'So what are you going to do about Jimmy Porter?'

Willow has to have someone to bitch at.

'What do you mean?'

'What do you mean?' She imitates me. 'You know what I mean. You can't put up with the kind of thing that he went on with at that party, surely – it's demeaning. It reflects on you.'

'Hey, there's nothing I can do about it now from this distance, is there?' I want to tell her to butt out, but having confided in her during the long flight – must have been the altitude and the in-flight gin – I can hardly do that now. 'We've more important things on our minds, eh?'

Mercifully she doesn't pursue the subject.

'At last.' She shuffles closer to the belt as the first set of suitcases plops on from the chute.

'Thank God. Nearly there now, eh?'

'If this man turns up like he said he would.'

'Of course he will.' But she's put doubts into my head. During my last telephone conversation with Dale Genscher, he'd said he'd collect us. But when I asked how we'd know him, the answer hadn't been all that reassuring: 'Oh, shoot, I'll know you, Arabella.'

I hadn't pressed it, which, of course, irritated the hell out of Willow: 'I can't *believe* you didn't insist on having a description. Phoenix is a big city, the airport will be busy, and now because of you we could spend hours walking around like a pair of idiots.'

'Sorry. I'm sure it'll work out. We can page him, can't we?'

Despite the bravado, I find myself getting nervous while we try to spot our luggage. Willow had a point. Suppose he didn't show? All we have is one telephone number: suppose we ring it and there's no answer? We have no address for him, Eve or anyone else. No hotel, no car hired. I've been too trusting.

As for the Event, to say I have mixed feelings doesn't cover it. In fact, now that I see my suitcase approaching from the far side of the carousel, I want to grab it, run to the departures area and get on the next plane home.

What am I going to say to my mother? What's Willow going to say to her? I'm wondering if she's feeling the same thing and steal a sideways look: her jaw is tight, a little muscle ticking just above the bone. She's dreading it too.

Dear God, that bloody suitcase is trundling round the corner of the belt . . .

For the past day or so, in the rush to get here, the vision of meeting my mother has been kind of misty, a *potential* meeting, but the sight of that scuzzy bag swimming like Jaws towards me is bringing it into focus. This might really happen.

Another feeling. Anger towards Eve. A splurge, fuelled by lack of nicotine. Who's she doing this for? Hardly for us! Contacting us from her sickbed could be seen as the supremely selfish act of a most selfish woman. That woman not only abandoned us, she is responsible for wrecking our lives.

The case arrives and I pull it off the goddamned belt, crash it on to the floor. 'I don't feel like going to see her straight away, I need some sleep first.' I don't even look at Willow.

Her case, a wheelie-bag, is not far behind mine and she pulls it off. 'Fine. We'll tell this Dale that we need some space to get acclimatised. Anyway, it's probably too late tonight to bother her.'

'Yeah.' I can taste the relief. 'It'd be cruelty to land in on top of her tonight. We'll tell him we want to leave it until the morning. He'll understand. We've been travelling for the best part of a whole day and night – it's four o'clock in the morning back home.'

We straggle through to the outside.

'Good evening, ladies!'

Dale has spotted us straight away. Just as well because in the crowd he's the last person I would have picked to be our guide. He has a long tail of hair, as thick and grey as a badger's, bunched into a floral scrunchie (a *scrunchie!*) under a black cowboy hat. 'Good evening, Dale.' I force myself to sound normal and stick my hand out. It's caught in a grip so strong it nearly breaks my fingers. 'That was quick, how did you know it was us?' It's impossible to guess what age he is. Forty? Fifty? Sixty, even? His face, to be kind, is 'weathered', so lined around the eyes it's hard to see what colour they are.

Then he smiles and takes years off himself. 'How could I not know Eve's daughters?'

'Thank you for collecting us.' Willow is as prim as only she can be.

'You're welcome.'

We all stand there. I can't think of what next to say and Willow's busy folding her passport into a little compartment in her handbag.

Dale seems in no hurry to fill the conversational gap. People amble past, embrace each other, backslap. You know when you have a mental snapshot of someone? From the sound of his voice, I had imagined this man to be beefy and bandy, a John Wayne type. He's tall all right, but there the similarity ends, and instead of being massive all over like the film star's, Dale Genscher's body is as thin as a knotted rope. Think Lyle Lovett, stretched.

At least I had pictured the clothes right. He has the hat, of course, the check shirt and the jeans, almost white from wear along the thighs and knees; he has the stacked boots. But what I would never have foreseen are the tattoos: heavy blue-black ribbons of blossoms and ivy curling up his neck from under the collar of his shirt. Then there's the fistful of jewellery: huge silver rings on three fingers, a turquoise earring and, to complete the set, a heavy silver buckle on his belt.

Clear as glass, I can see what Willow's thinking as she looks this character up and down: *We're entrusting ourselves to this?* Compared to me, she's had a sheltered life. At least we get all sorts at the Leicester.

'Well, I think we should get goin', if you ladies are ready?' Our new friend seems to think we have all given ourselves enough time for the preliminaries. 'Do you want to come right out tonight? It's only 'bout a hundred miles or so, take 'bout a hour'n a half. Or would you prefer to wash up, have a night's sleep first?'

'A hundred miles?' This was Willow. A hundred miles in Ireland is a long day's outing. 'Yes. Definitely we'd like the night's sleep. We're both exhausted. Is there a decent guesthouse or B-and-B around here? We don't want anything too expensive, you understand.'

'I know the place. Let me make a coupla calls. Got my cell here.' He taps the mobile phone in his breast pocket, then picks up both bags as easily as if they are candy-floss. 'I have the car outside. Let me get it. I'll show you ladies where to wait.'

We follow him across the airport concourse. Outside, like dark fireworks, the crowns of palm trees are cut into the starry sky and the smells are foreign, unknown perfumes and aftershaves, warm concrete. Dale shows us where to stand, then strides away. 'So, what do you think?' I dive into my handbag, extract my cigarettes and light up; the smoke, like an old friend, hits my throat and slides down.

'What do I think about what?'

My sister is staring at a middle-aged woman dressed entirely in shiny fake leopardskin: tight leopardskin trousers, leopardskin blouse strained across a large bust, leopardskin hairband on dyed black hair. Through lips as big and crimson as cushions in a brothel, she's giving out socks to a much younger man with a hangdog expression. Son? Toy-boy? Willow's thoughts are clear from her expression: *what have I let myself in for?* 'Willow, pay attention. What do you think of Dale?'

'How do I know what I think? For heaven's sake, Arabella, I just met the man. He could be a murderer or a loan shark or Mother Teresa reincarnated, for all I know.'

'How old do you think he is?'

'Fifty? A hundred? What does it matter?'

I concentrate on the blessed smoke.

Five minutes later, a small pick-up truck draws up alongside us. Our guide hops out and comes round the front. 'Let me help you up, ladies. We got ourselves a deal on a room – watch the seat there, it's a little cosy.'

We pull into the stream of buses, taxis and stretch limos, then exit the airport on to a motorway through a series of terrifying multi-lane roads. I assume I'm having my first bout of jet-lag as a wave of fatigue threatens to swamp me. So far Eve has not been mentioned.

'How was Eve today?' I'm in the middle of the pickup's bench seat between Willow and Dale, and against my thigh, I feel Willow's body clench.

'I had business in the city,' he changes gear to switch lanes, 'so I haven't seen her since early morning. But in general she's doin' real well. She's frettin', though. She's not used to bein' trussed up, says she feels like a hog.' He smiles fondly. 'You'll see. She's a feisty lady, a real Irish gal. How long do you two plan on stayin'?'

'We haven't decided yet. Our tickets are open. We paid an arm and a leg for them.' Willow is having to semi-shout to compete with the noisy engine but her tone is designed to discourage familiarity from a tattooed stranger.

But the lady-of-the-manor stuff cuts no ice with Dale: 'Yeah, those airlines!' He changes lane again, accelerating through a gap in the traffic whizzing alongside us.

I don't drive and am a nervous passenger at the best of times. This is not the best of times; by my calculations, the gap isn't big enough for us, and if we're going to miss the bonnet of a house-sized lorry, it will be by approximately two inches. I close my eyes but open them again smartish when the lorry driver makes his displeasure known with a long, deafening blast on his klaxon. 'Hog!' Dale grins across me towards Willow. 'Don't worry, ladies, they do that all the time – just lettin' off steam.'

He settles us behind one of those motorhomes, one with a small two-seater car latched on to its rear by its two front wheels. 'What happened with Rowan, if that's not too personal?'

'He couldn't make it.' With a glare, Willow warns me to keep my mouth shut. I care little who knows about our unfortunate brother's circumstances, but for some reason Willow feels that Rowan's lifestyle reflects on her. She turns her attention again to Dale. 'He might come on later if – if his work will allow. Speaking of work, Dale, what do you do for a living?'

'Oh, this and that.' For the first time, our host sounds cagey. 'Not much of anything right now because of the crisis.'

'Iraq? Have you someone over there?'

'Oh, no!' Dale seems amazed that she would think such a thing. 'I meant the crisis we have with Eve.'

Well, there's no answer to that, is there? So I look through the window at America. We've just come off a motorway and, so far, America is so, well, *American*, full of all those makey-uppey names you see on TV and in the movies: Tire City, Suds'r'Us, Dunkin' Donuts, First Bank of various places, Deli4U, a little supermarket called Basket O'Plenty. The houses in the residential areas between the strips of shops are mostly one-storey; people in sleeveless tops and shorts are sitting outside on garden furniture and camp chairs; kids on bikes and rollerskates, beer and outdoor lanterns — and, here and there, clouds of smoke from barbecues.

Dale turns into a wide boulevard planted with three rows of trees, one on each side, one down the middle. No people sitting outside here: this suburb is posh — some of the houses are as big as hotels. They're floodlit. They have security huts at the gates with guards watching TV inside. They have turrets and sprinklers whooshing water all over the gardens. It's Hollywood, but more discreet — I've never seen anything like it, even in the richest suburbs of Dublin. My eyes are out on stalks. I'm like a kid at Funderland. I've almost forgotten why I'm here so I give myself a mental dig, tell myself to be serious. To be as on the ball as Willow.

Maybe she's right to be suspicious. Like, have we any real proof that this Dale Genscher is even on nodding acquaintance with our mother, let alone that he's her friend? He could be a serial killer. Serial killers are charming and plausible: that's how they get their victims.

Dale Genscher could have murdered Eve. Then he had discovered my name among her effects and, because he wants to cover up his crime, he is driving me and Willow to the Hoover Dam to throw us over and drown us.

He has his mobile with him but he didn't offer it to us to ring her, did he? Not that I would have been ready to talk to her. Right, I think, it's showtime. 'Hey, Dale, does Eve live in a house or a flat? You never said — and what age is she now? I can't seem to work it out. How did you two meet?'

He shoots me a lazy glance. 'Let's see now, one thing at a time. I never ask a lady her age, but I reckon maybe Eve's in her late fifties. And I'll let her tell you how we met. It's a nice story. So what else?'

'Where does she live?'

'Oh, yeah. Trailer. It's a nice park. You'll like it. And she has a kitty, nice old guy. We don't see much of him during the day — either of you ladies allergic?'

'In a trailer park?' Willow's disbelieving tone could cut through steel: the air around her screeches its echo. *Trailer trash? Sleeveless vests? Jerry Springer?*

'You'll change your mind when you see it.' Her tone still hasn't bothered Dale. 'I know what you're thinkin', but this ain't like one of those white-trash movie-set places. The part we live, it's fix up real good. Guess you'd like to call her. You're welcome to use my cell.' He reaches for the phone in his shirt pocket.

'Ah, no.' My stomach flips. 'I wouldn't like to disturb her. Time enough tomorrow. Unless you want to talk to her, Willow?'

'Tomorrow's fine.'

Well, I tell myself, Dale passed that one. He hasn't killed her anyway.

I've always flattered myself that I'm a good judge of character – most professional waitresses are – and no matter what alarums my imagination had come up with earlier, instinctively I'm inclined to trust this guy, tat-toos, ponytail and all.

CHAPTER SEVEN

'Get your arse out of here, sunshine, you've got visitors.' The voice is like blunt razor blades across the back of my head. For a few seconds I don't recognise where I am and I think it's the gaffer come to open the shop.

Then I remember. The canal. The flagon. The mill. The paddy-wagon. Shit. I'd done it again. 'What visitor? Who is it?' I struggle into a semi-upright position on the side of the cot but the screw is already outside, talking to someone.

Need I have asked? Who else would it be except the blisters? I groan and it isn't all to do with the state of my head: it's primarily to do with getting thumped around by Mental. I swear on Phil Lynott's grave (when you haven't a ma you have to swear on borrowed graves) I didn't touch a drop from his poxy stash. I don't know who it was robbed half of it but it wasn't me. I'd meant it when I said I'd stay clean until my fortieth birthday but – give a dog a bad name – there was no convincing Mental. When Mental gets something into his head there's no shifting it. I'd nicked his hash and that was that, but for once I was lucky. A patrol car happened to be passing on the bridge above where we were milling or I might have been seriously hurt. When he's mad, especially when he's in his cups, a mill with Mental is a serious matter.

How did they find out I was here? I hadn't rung them. There isn't any bail involved this time: the pigs know Mental as well as I do and putting me in here last night could be classed as protective custody.

Needless to remark, they don't provide you with mirrors when you're a guest of the Minister for Justice so I just drag my fingers through my hair and hope for the best. 'Shite!' I mutter to myself. As if spending a night in the clink – and possibly losing my lovely gaff to someone else

– wasn't bad enough, now I was in for another fucking lecture about getting my act together.

'Where are they?' In the corridor outside, I interrupt the screw's fascinating conversation about house prices. 'At the desk?'

He nods. 'And shut the door on your way out,' he yells, then continues what he's saying about Clonsilla not being so bad and you can get houses there for half the price you can buy them in the city and if you leave early enough in the morning it'll only take an hour and a half, 'max two hours', to get in to work. He knows he doesn't need to show me the way to the front desk.

When I get outside I'm in for a surprise. Standing there, cool as a breeze, is not Bel, or even Willow, but Willow's husband, Paddy. Except he's not cool as a breeze. He's Paddy. The last time Paddy was cool had to be around the time of the Eucharistic Congress. He's holding out a big brown envelope. 'Here,' he says, 'take this – and for God's sake clean yourself up. You can thank your lucky stars you have two sisters who seem to feel there's hope for you yet.'

I refuse to react to the insults. I get them whenever my path crosses with this geezer's, which is rare, thank Christ. We got off on the wrong foot at Willow's wedding because I was hammered. Well, what else are you supposed to do at a wedding? I wasn't the only one. 'What's in it?' I take the envelope.

'Tickets, money and a passport application. You can get them to sign it here for you, and there's a photo machine over in Busáras across the road. You know where the passport office is? They're expecting you.'

'Wha'?' This is doing my head in.

He shoves his face so close to mine I can see his pores. 'You have to go to America to see your mother. She's sick and she's sent for you all. The girls left yesterday. That ticket in there is for tomorrow morning. There's a telephone number you're to ring when you land if you don't see them there to meet you, and if they ask you at Immigration, that's the phone number you use as a contact for your visit. The guy's name is Dale Genscher. D-A-L-E G-E-N-S-C-H-E-R.' He spells it out like I'm a defective. 'Got that? It's all in there in that envelope. The money is so you can get yourself a suit and a clean shirt – they'll turn you back at the airport if you go up to the immigration desk looking like that.'

He stands back, waving his hand in front of his face. 'And have a shower or a bath. Well, I've done my bit, I'm out of here.'

He turns to go but I grab his sleeve. I'm not quite taking this in. *You have to go to America to see your mother?* 'How did you know I was here?'

He looks at his sleeve. 'Take your hand off me, please. You can thank Jimmy Porter for finding you. He knew where to look, all right. The man you're to see in the passport office is called McConnellogue. Do you want me to spell it for you?'

'No.' I was still trying to understand what was happening.

'He'll be available from ten o'clock this morning. Got that? Do you want me to write it down for you?'

'McConnellogue. Got it.' I'm still stuck and I've already forgotten the name of the spelled-out guy with the phone number. Just as well it's written down for me. But I'm nodding my head up and down and that seems to satisfy Paddy. So he leaves.

I stare after him. I can see him outside getting into his car, a Starlet. I can even see his fucking nodding dog in the back window. And the reg: 87 WX. The thing is fifteen years old. Paddy went all the way to Wexford for a bargain, surprise, surprise. Before I got hammered at that wedding I remember him shitting himself because the waiters were giving out too much wine with the meal. 'McConnellogue,' I say out loud, earning myself a funny look from the pig writing in a notebook propped against a box of tea bags.

I come to my senses. I need more information here. 'Paddy! Paddy! Wait!' I race out after him but his car is just pulling away. I run after it but it speeds off up Talbot Place and I'm left standing, like a paralysed duck, looking after it.

What about my gaff? Someone'll surely take it if I leave the country.

You have to go to America to see your mother?

What the fuck is that all about?

CHAPTER EIGHT

The highway teems with trucks, towers of chrome thundering past us, sucking at the air inside our cabin and dazzling us with our own reflected headlights. I don't want to think about it. 'Did you meet Eve here in Arizona, Dale?'

'Nope. New York.'

'How long ago?'

'Oh, maybe fifteen years or so. No more'n that, I don't think. You gals up for some music?' Without waiting for an answer he turns on the radio and we bowl along for the next few miles to the twanging of a country-music station. Soon we wheel on to a slip-road at a spaghetti junction, then turn immediately into the forecourt of a motel. 'Just a minute.' Our host jumps out and lopes inside.

'Great!' Willow looks with distaste at the two fake palm trees in front of the glass entrance doors. 'Tat City!' She's hissing, although Dale is well out of earshot and, anyway, the trucks rumbling by on the overhead highway less than a hundred feet away would drown out a brass band. 'And did you hear that? Our mother lives in a trailer park!'

'Don't jump to conclusions, Willow. He also said it was nice. That we'd like it.'

Before she can answer, Dale is back and opening the passenger door. 'This place ain't bad, ladies. Clean. Owner's a friend of mine. He's not here but you'll be well taken care of. And you can't argue with the price of the room. Thirty-four dollars.'

'Quite right! You can't argue with that, Willow!' I say loudly and cheerily, as we climb out and trail after him through the millpond of hot air into a small lobby. More palm trees, faded pink walls, leatherette arm-chairs, a Coca-Cola machine and a huge picture of a sunset over a beach, although by my reckoning we're hundreds, if not thousands, of miles from the nearest ocean. Willow shows her credit card to the bored clerk, signs something and that seems to be all that's required.

Dale pushes his hat to the back of his head. 'So what's the agenda for tomorrow, ladies? Are you early risers?'

'We're really sorry to be putting you to all this trouble. Have – have we to go far from here?' I'm shaky now. Eve's presence suddenly looms close.

'Not far at all. Seventy-some miles – I'll be here about nine. That suit you, gals?'

I'm getting used to Dale's lingo but I can see from her face that Willow isn't. Quickly, I put out my hand to shake his. 'That suits us fine, Dale, and thank you very much for everything. We really appreciate it, don't we, Willow?

'Thank you.' Stiffly she, too, shakes his hand. When he has left, she turns to me, her eyes furious. 'Gals? What's with this man? At home I'd have him up before an equality commissioner for that.'

'Shut up, Willow, we're in a different country now. And he's been really good to us. Come on, I want to get into bed. I'm knackered.' I stride ahead of her towards a staircase I can see behind a glass door at the end of the lobby. I'm fed up with her whingeing. And I need another smoke.

'We won't get a wink of sleep.' As if it's a naughty child, she punishes her wheelie-bag by bouncing it heavily on each step as we climb the concrete stairs. 'Wouldn't you think they'd have a lift? And do you hear those trucks outside? This is a great place to put a hotel, isn't it? Under a motorway flyover.'

I've reached the top of the stairs and stop so quickly she nearly collides with me. 'If you don't stop bitching, Willow, I'm going to spend the money and get another room. Why didn't you speak up when you had the chance? If this place isn't good enough for you, check out and take a taxi to the Ritz.'

I'm instantly sorry because I can see she's shocked. 'Lookit,' I lean against the wall, 'be reasonable. We're both exhausted. It's only for one night and we're not here for the good of our health, are we?'

Surprisingly, she doesn't rear up. 'Sorry. I'm tired, that's all.'

I should yell more often. And it's coming easier . . .

As it happens, our room turns out to be at the back of the building, and although we can still hear the traffic, it isn't too bad, just a soft, continuous roar. It certainly isn't going to bother me. I'm used to far worse.

The first thing I do notice, of course – yippee! – is that there's an ashtray on the table. 'Do you mind, Willow?' I pull the fags out of my jacket pocket.

'I do, actually.' She's back to being sniffy. Then, hastily, on seeing me gather breath: 'But why don't you go out on to the balcony? Or into the bathroom? There's probably a ventilator because there's no window. I checked.'

I decide not to argue and go meekly out on to the balcony where there's a strong odour of bleach. Then I see the glint of water below. The smell is chlorine – a swimming-pool? All for seventeen dollars each? Unreal. I do sums in my head. It would be cheaper for me to live in this room full-time than pay rent on my bed-sit at home. Now I understand why Americans can travel around their own country so much. And why they complain so bitterly about the prices in the Leicester Hotel.

I light up and suck the warm, gorgeous smoke across my tongue and into my chest. This is only the tenth ciggie of the day. Or I think it's only the tenth – I've lost track. To reward myself for doing so great, I smoke it right down to the filter.

When I get back into the room, Willow is already in bed and on the phone to her answering-machine at home. We've arrived safely and all that. She'll ring again the next day.

After she hangs up, she says goodnight to me, turns her back and, within minutes, is snoring. Genteelly, of course.

Unlike me. As soon as I lie down, my brain sets up shop and opens for business. If anyone had told me forty-eight hours ago that today I would be in Phoenix, Arizona, about to meet my mother—

What does she look like now? Will she be anything like that early photograph?

What will I say to her? But more to the point, dammit, what will *she* have to say to *me*?

And what about this Dale, then?

Yak-yakkity-yak goes the brain, tootling like a trumpet. I came in such a hurry, I don't even have my library book. Or anything else to read, dammit.

I concentrate on surveying the room. Framed prints of pink roses over each of the beds, big dressing-table with cup-ring stain, built-in wardrobe, TV on a stand, one knob missing. Clean, though, as Dale had promised, and although they aren't the softest I've ever slept in, the two beds are extra-large doubles. Yes, a serious bargain. In Tenerife, Greta and I always stay 'self-catering' in an apartment, so this is the first time in my life, believe it or not, that I've stayed in a hotel room.

I'm dying to switch on the telly to see what the American channels are like but I don't want to wake Willow and get another ear-bashing. As if she hears my thoughts, she whimpers in her sleep, then turns on her back.

It feels odd to be in the same room as her, stretched out and obviously dreaming, mouth and eyelids quivering. I can barely remember the last time we shared a room. By arrangement with the state agencies, she stayed with our foster-family until she had done her Leaving Cert and then got into the civil service. By the time she came out, I was well established as a kitchen worker in a small hotel, with a bed in a good hostel and my own friends, especially Greta.

From the day I arrived in the first kitchen in a little dive on Parnell Square, Greta took me under her wing – I don't know why, because I was seriously shy, awkward and clumsy. And when I broke one too many dishes in that first place and was shown the door, she downed tools and walked out with me. It was she who had got us every job since, including, finally, the one at the Leicester. 'We come as a pair,' she said to me then, and still says. I owe Greta, I do.

So, with her to mind me and Willow all fired up to improve herself, by herself, it was no wonder that my sister and I grew apart, especially since she was so clever and educated and went immediately into such a good, steady, well-paid job.

I study her sleeping face. Her beauty shows when her face relaxes. It's heart-shaped, with smooth skin, a wide, full mouth and long thick eyelashes that don't need mascara. They're fluttering now and she makes a sound, a high-pitched 'eeh' like a newborn kitten.

One of Willow's more surprising talents is that she has a lovely singing voice, not that I've heard it much. She's a member of an amateur musical society but she insists on staying in the chorus and won't take any principal parts, even though I know she could because she used to be pulled out of our choir to sing solos at Benediction at St Camilla's. She says she's too busy to learn parts and attend principals' rehearsals, but I think that's all my eye, part of her buttoned-up personality.

I hope this dream she's having isn't frightening. It's rare for me to feel tender or protective towards my sister – she's so quick and prickly she doesn't invite it or act as if she needs it – but right this minute I want to build a spiny hedge of roses all around her to repel all danger. She'd go bananas, of course, if I tried. These days, Willow acts bitter about everyone in her small family – me, Rowan, her ma, of course. If we found our da – if he was still alive – she'd be bitter about him too. At least, I think she would. Hard to know, of course. She reminds me of a tortoise, or a cockle; something with a hard shell, anyway.

I think it all comes from being put in an orphanage. Every aspect of it. Being there in the first place, the food, the nuns, the coldness of the water, the punishments, the lady-bountifulness of the women who donated stained dresses and blouses, frayed jumpers, serge gym slips that were shiny around the bottom region. (Even knickers with waist elastics stretched beyond use.)

This iffy patronage never bothered me: my attitude was that it was better to have stuff than not to have stuff, so, whatever else I might have a problem with, I'm not sour about the orphanage. These days, Ireland is awash with tribunals and investigations into the abuse that went on in religious institutions and orphanages around that time, but I have to say that we were among the lucky ones. Our nuns were fair enough, in their own way. For sure they didn't let us away with much and, yes, we were slapped, spanked, strapped, thumped, boxed, deprived of food, put into freezing cold baths, all that stuff, but we weren't actually tortured. That was what they call now *the regime of that time*. Children were punished like that in nearly every house and school in Ireland. I won't go so far as to say it didn't do me any harm, because who knows what's underneath, in my subconscious, like, or how I would have turned out if I hadn't been in an orphanage? But I'm still here, amn't I?

What I can see now is that, with limited resources, those nuns tried to equip us for the outside world so that by the time we left we could read, write, spell, add, subtract, mend, sew, darn and cook simple food; we also knew how to keep ourselves and our surroundings clean. They even set up a commercial course, I believe, but neither Willow nor I benefited: by the time it was introduced, we had been taken out by foster-parents.

To get back to the dodgy donations: when they came in what I grabbed were not the clothes or the toys but the books. Torn, filthy, pages missing, I didn't care. I fought other girls for possession, or at least first read. The pleasure I get from books has been lifelong and now I'm on such familiar terms with the librarians in the ILAC Centre, they show me pictures of their kids' First Communions and Confirmations. All I've ever wanted from any book is a good story, and by the time I've reached The End to have learned at least one thing I didn't know before.

That's one terrific benefit I got from St Camilla's. It was there I discovered that a book could be a magic carpet or time machine that took me off to the Australian outback, a ballet theatre in Russia, the American Wild West, an English boarding-school, places far, far away from the echoing, clanking place Willow and I found ourselves in so unexpectedly one Christmas when we were little more than babies.

It was a hard transition. One minute, it seemed, the three of us kids were in our tenement room with Eve, lumping in together around our 'table', two orange boxes covered with a bedspread, squabbling over the last bit of bread. The next minute, us two girls were sitting, terrified, at a long refectory table, wearing paper hats but – even though it was Christmas – forced to eat everything on the plate, lumpy potatoes, mushy sprouts, fatty ham and all.

This frightening new world was run by what I saw at the beginning only as huge black beings with no legs who clacked along corridors. These corridors were lined with flinty-faced statues busily subduing serpents, or pointing with manicured hands to their dripping blood.

From then on, instead of rainy afternoons and cold nights with Rowan, my mother and sister and me all nestled together in our cosy bed, us two girls had to sleep in hard tight bunks alongside rows of snivelling, lonely stranger-children. Both Mammy and Rowan had vanished, Mammy to God knows where, Rowan, we were told, to 'a boys' place'. Up to then, our baby brother had been a squally nuisance in my life, but I missed him dreadfully.

As for the man who had been our father, he didn't figure because he had never figured much, except as an occasional smelly, threatening presence who evicted us from our mother's arms and bed.

Everything had changed completely. By day, instead of playing jacks and swinging out of lamp-posts in the tenement yard, we had to sit upright and pay attention at desks in a draughty kindergarten room with bars on the windows and a door that locked with a big key that made a noise like a drum. At playtime, instead of the pretty china doll with three changes of clothes Mammy had found for me in the Daisy Market, I had to make do with a bald teddy bear whose head wobbled.

At the beginning, in fact all through my life in St Camilla's, I couldn't shake off the feeling that our banishment had come about because of me. I had been too bold. Back answering and not doing what Mammy told me to do. Not minding the two younger ones properly when Mammy had to go out for a while. Wetting our mattress when we were thrown out of Mammy's bed to make room for the noisy but secret things that went on between her and the man who was our father.

You might think that this is a lot to remain in the memory of a child who was not even four years old at the time but, believe me, it's all there – soft and hard, but mostly hard.

CHAPTER NINE

There's a thousand dollars in that fucking envelope. A fucking grand. And three hundred euro. What I could do with those kind of readies – what I couldn't do . . .

And there's more. That airline ticket isn't refundable, they made sure of that (I've already brought it into a travel agent), but what I found out is that it's changeable for an extra few bob. I could sell it, I could. There must be a hundred geezers I could find in this city in half an hour who want to go to the States and who'd pay good money for that ticket. With everything, I could probably get the total up to eighteen hundred.

Jesus, it's Christmas!

Yeah, yeah, there's a note signed by the two of them. A very *stern* note telling me that I'll probably be asked at Immigration how much money I'm carrying and I'm to show them the grand, and giving me a phone number and I'm to say that I'm coming on a two-week holiday to relatives. So I'm to carry the dollars but the euros are to pay for the passport, the taxi, a new suit and new shoes.

And then at the end of this note, in big fucking capital letters and exclamation marks, 'ALL THIS IS A LOAN!!!!'

Yeah, right. Loan.

But, holy hell, *one thousand dollars*. Three hundred euro. Even without the fucking ticket, that's almost twelve hundred total. I checked with that foreign-exchange place in O'Connell Street.

Do you know how long it'd take me to scam that kind of dough? And how much stuff it would buy me? H is seriously cheap on the streets right now. There's a glut.

I could even set myself up. I've plenty of contacts, *loads*.

I'd buy a grand's worth, sell it on for two grand in individual twenties. That's the way you start. Then buy fifteen hundred's worth and sell that for three, and so on. I've heard fellas talking about it often enough. I'd be set up for life. Get my own place. I'd buy it here but I'd go to Cork or Limerick to sell it—

No. Not Limerick. Limerick's too dangerous if you don't know who you're talking to. Galway, maybe. Or Waterford. And it's not as if I'd be a drug-dealer or anything, I'd just be small-time, nobody'd be interested. I'd just be getting myself a start. I'd quit when I had a set-up of my own. Maybe get a decent mot for myself. A clean one. Start a family.

God, it's lovely to be thinking about a future.

You know, I'd nearly do it to spite them all. I'd love to see their faces, theirs and Paddy's . . . Give a dog a bad name. I have the bad name, might as well live up to it, yeah?

I've lived this long without the tender touch of my so-called ma, who's a whore and a bitch anyway. I could live without it a bit longer – couldn't I?

Think, man, *think* . . .

CHAPTER TEN

Willow sighs and I think she's waking up, but she's not. I've often wondered if other real-life sisters have such complicated relationships. When you read novels or magazine articles, sisters all seem to be 'there' for each other. There's a lot of mutual weeping, and putting arms around each other, and where there are fights or fallings-out, there is quick forgiveness and great huggy scenes of them getting back together and vowing never to let anything come between them again.

Willow and I have missed out on all of that.

Here's what I think: I think that the two years of separation, when she stayed in the foster-home and I went out into the big world, proved critical in stunting the relationship between Willow and me. We had been close throughout all the years in the orphanage and the foster-home but we were never confidantes after our early teens. For instance, I didn't find out she and Paddy were going to get married until quite close to the wedding date. And I wasn't her bridesmaid. Instead, she asked one of the girls she was working with. Stick insect.

All right, Arabella, stop running yourself down.

I'm not *fat* but sometimes, God knows, I look at myself in the mirror and wish I could be more like my sister. It's to do with grooming, I suppose. I don't have to look like a model for work so I don't. Maybe I've got lazy.

Mind you, if she'd asked my advice about getting married to Paddy, I'd have told her to run a mile. Maybe she twigged this subconsciously and that was why she didn't ask.

Whether or not I'd have been right in my advice, I don't know. In my opinion, no couple escapes the ups and downs of this world, but if you listen to her, everything is always great or grand in Willow's life. Everyone in her family is perpetually in top form and forging through the world, achieving as they go. It's as if they're marked out for special blessing. I find it difficult to believe, though, that alone of all families in the universe, hers is the only one that has no problems whatsoever; and because Paddy seems to me like a pontificating skinflint, her cover-up irritates the hell out of me.

I'm ashamed of this: it's nothing to do with me, after all, and I could be wrong. (I read once that one of my former heroes, Bing Crosby – lovely relaxed Bing – was as mean with money as Jack Benny pretended to be!) You don't ask my sister searching questions ('Are you happy, Willow?') about herself. You just don't.

But on one of the rare occasions when we were relaxed in each other's company, I risked asking her what she saw in him. We were side by side on a bus, I remember, with her children and six of Maeve's friends on the way to McDonald's for the child's birthday treat. Instead of biting my nose off, as she would have done normally, Willow looked me straight in the eye. 'Security – if it's any of your business.' Before I had time to back off, as I thought she wanted me to, she turned away and gazed through her window, sort of working it out as she spoke: 'I know that, to the out-side world, Paddy's not Mr Charm, but I also know he's not going to go off with a young one. I know he's not going to lose his job. I know I'll always have a roof over my head and food on the table. He's not a drinker. He doesn't gamble. He's not violent. He's not nasty to the children. He doesn't lose his head in a crisis.' She turned back, challenging: 'He's *in my corner*! Anything else you need to know, Arabella?'

'No.' Although I did think privately that a list consisting mostly of what a husband *didn't* do was a peculiar basis for a good marriage. But that wasn't fair of me: I'm not married so what do I know? Anyhow, she had trusted me with the information and I had no right to diss it. 'Your turn now.' She was still gazing at me. 'What gives with you and Jimmy Porter?'

'What do you mean?'

'You know what I mean. If you two aren't going to get married, what the hell are you at? You could do better, Bella.'

The bus lurched round a corner, throwing us all into each other's laps and giving me the opportunity for a quick think. 'Well,' I said then, 'you might be right, but have you met any available men lately? Jimmy and me – we're happy enough with what we've got. We like dancing, for instance. I've told you he's very light on his feet?'

She looked sceptical. 'But that's not—'

'Look, Willow,' I rushed on, 'from my point of view, Jimmy's the devil you know, right? He's handy for being available at the last minute, for going to the pictures, drinks on a Thursday night, having someone to go to parties with – you know my shift patterns. Someone who can work round them is not to be sneezed at . . .' I trailed off. She looked away again. The back of her head was *very* articulate.

She stirs again in the motel bed and I look across at her; she has kicked off the coverlet, exposing long, lovely legs.

I suppose mine are long too, and not bad, if I ever stopped to think about them – but out of uniform and clunky waitress's shoes, I prefer trouser suits and long skirts because you don't have to wear tights. I *hate* tights with a *passion*. It's the claustrophobic, confining, synthetic feel of them. Although that could be more laziness, couldn't it? All that pulling and being careful not to put your finger through them . . . Willow said to me once that you have to suffer a little to look good.

Nope. Don't feel like suffering to look good, thank you. Better and nicer things to do with my time.

To get back to Jimmy Porter, maybe she was right that time on the bus. Maybe I could have done better. So why do I hang in there with him? He means well, I know that, but sometimes he'd put years on you, especially since he went on the disability.

He was stabbed on the top deck of a number thirteen when he asked a gang of little gurriers to put out their cigarettes (the stabber was only eleven). After a lot of to-ing and fro-ing, medics, psychiatrists and so on, the company – and the state – accepted that although he had recovered physically Jimmy's continuing panic attacks were for real and that the psychological damage meant he could no longer work on the buses. Since he was not found suitable for any other employment, he was given compensation and half-pay until his pension kicks in at sixty-five, fourteen years from now.

That incident changed Jimmy, there's no doubt about it. He used to be great gas when we met first, but since that stabbing he's sort of gone into himself, and with no work to go to, he has too much time to think of all the different ways that Dublin's gone to the dogs. What really riles him – he broods constantly about this – is that the little gurrier who injured him got away with it. He still has nightmares about it, not that

I'd know much about them: sex between us has dwindled away to nothing since the Incident, as he calls it. I don't know whether he misses it. *I* don't, not really. I suppose I could say I miss sex in general, not that I'm all that experienced – ha! Chance would be a fine thing. But I don't miss it with him.

I suppose the bottom line for me is that I never got back the pre-stabbing Jimmy but I couldn't be cruel to him. Dropping him because of something that wasn't his fault? What would that make me?

So day to day we jog along and, anyway, what's the alternative? Dublin is a city for the young. It's also a city where single women hugely out-number single men and where any man free of baggage is hard to come by, let alone one who might be interested in a woman in her early for-ties. But, anyway, by what law is everyone supposed to be one of a pair?

And I do have to examine my conscience about my attitude to Willow's Paddy and her marriage, because my exasperation at the way she talks about her cosy-dotey life could be pure jealousy. Like, who am I to be high-minded? Who's the one with the house and the good job and the family? And who's the one with the rented bed-sit and the job with no prospects? Arabella Moraghan has the nerve to look down her nose on Willow's Paddy and then defend her own relationship?

Arabella has no right to look down her nose at anything to do with her sister. Here's something I did to Willow during our early childhood, something I'm still so guilty about that I can't think about it without going cold all over. It happened the first Lent we were in our orphanage.

In that place, Lent was the most depressing time, with everyone tip-toeing around, statues and pictures wrapped in purple sheets and the clapper on every handbell muffled with a cloth bandage. Just coming up to our first Easter, though, us little kids in the Low Babies' classroom heard a commotion outside the door. The apple-cheeked nun in charge of us went to investigate and when she came back she was in great form, even grinning. She was carrying a shoebox, punched with holes: 'See what I have, children! Gather round!'

Great excitement. Her family down the country had sent us six day-old chicks to mind.

Immediately everyone scrabbled and scrapped to hold the birds. 'Don't shove, children,' Sister ordered, but kindly. 'Stand back. Everyone will have a turn – they're not going anywhere.'

By then I had been long enough in the place to know it was every girl for herself, so I elbowed in and joined the ruck. 'Me, Sister! Me! Me!' I managed to grab one of the chicks. I held it to my face. I could feel the little heart going, like a ticking clock. So delicate. So fragile. Such little bones. I felt like crying.

Sister's rare soft mood lasted for most of the day and we took full advantage of it, loving and grooming and playing with our new pets. She gave us each a handful of seed to sprinkle on the floor, then brought in a scrubbing brush and a clanking bucket so we could each take a turn in washing the smeary droppings off the tiles. We felt useful and busy and went to bed happy.

But next morning after breakfast when we ran in to say hello to our charges, we heard no cheeping. No sound at all. The box had been moved. It had been pushed right under the cast-iron radiator. Sister pulled it out.

Someone screamed.

Six little heaps of yellow thread. Twelve dead button-eyes.

The post-mortem was immediate. We were put sitting at our desks. One by one we had to stand up to answer Sister.

'Did you come down here last night, or early this morning, Mary One [or Mary Two or Mary Three or Jinny, or Kathleen, or whoever] and move that box?'

'No, Sister!'

'No, Sister!'

'No, Sister!'

'It wasn't me, Sister!'

'Right.' When we'd all denied it, Sister opened her desk. 'All of you. Line up.'

We knew what was coming. Some of us started to cry in anticipation. But even the application of the ruler across each of our bare backsides produced no result. You got the wooden ruler when you were little and graduated to the strap only after First Communion.

I wavered when I saw Willow getting it because she wasn't even three, but because I hadn't owned up immediately I'd be in double trouble. I was the guilty party. After we had gone to bed the previous night, I had sneaked back to the classroom and, having kissed the little beaks one by one, had shoved the shoebox tight under the radiator to keep the chicks nice and warm. Instead, of course, I roasted them, suffocated them, probably,

59

because I had pushed them in so far they couldn't get enough oxygen. I was never rumbled. Getting away with it wasn't worth it, though, because it haunts me to this day. I am a traitor. I am a chicken murderer.

I've been able to come to terms with the punishment the others took: none of them ever took the rap for me, shit happens, nothing is fair in this world, all the rest of it. But I've never got over what happened to Willow. Even though it's so long ago and I'm forty-one, nearly forty-two and Willow is forty, going on forty-one, I've never told her. I'm too ashamed. Big sisters are supposed to look after little sisters.

Quietly, careful not to make the bedsprings creak, I reach down to the shoulder-bag beside me on the floor and extract the tin box. I always take it with me, even on holidays to Tenerife.

This tin, oblong, with a corroded picture of a bouquet on the hinged lid, is my most precious possession. When you open it, you get a musty scent, whose origin I've never been able to figure out: tea, maybe, or cake – an Oxford Lunch or a Swiss roll. I was found clutching it after our mother deserted the three of us in the Palm House of the Botanic Gardens. On the issue of this tin box, I pull rank and won't share the contents with Willow or Rowan. I'll let them look and handle, but I'm its guardian and they're not allowed to take anything away with them. I tell them it's essential to keep the stuff together, that that's what Eve would have wanted, that she entrusted it to me, as the eldest.

I have blanked out a lot of what happened that day.

Apparently she left us just before closing time so the keepers would be sure to find us – she did that much at least.

I don't remember us being found. I don't remember her giving me the tin box, or anyone taking it away from me, and it was a huge surprise to me when the nuns in the orphanage produced it for me on the day I was 'graduating' from care.

After the initial surprise, I was furious with them for not having given it to me as soon as I was old enough to understand its significance, but time has mellowed my anger. What's the point in holding a grudge? Attitudes to children and children's rights were different those days. If you hold on to bitterness what do you achieve? You damage no one except yourself.

There's a swank new Palm House in the Botanics now. The old one's been restored and is one of the wonders of Ireland, but I'm half sorry they didn't leave it alone. For obvious reasons, I went to the Bots a lot over the years, particularly that Palm House. I liked the sweetish smell that came off the rusty, peeling ironwork supporting all that glass. It was a kind of connection to Eve, because when she left us there she must have noticed the same smell: you couldn't miss it. And, just as I did on each visit before they refurbished the place, she must have seen the mould, very bright green, on certain bits of the glass near the joins with the iron.

Carefully, I open the box and lay the contents on the bedspread. I always look at them in the same order.

1. A photograph of Eve – obviously one half of a wedding photograph. She's wearing a flower (it could be a sweet-pea) in the lapel of her coat; one of her arms is linked under the coat arm of someone else. You can see a shoulder a little lower than hers – she was taller than the man she married. The angle of her pillbox hat is a terrible contrast with the sad expression on her face. She was very young, sixteen. She is also visibly pregnant. That would be with me so I'm in the picture too. The second person, the owner of the shoulder, the husband, has been carefully cut out. On the back is written: *To my Dear Children, this was My Wedding Day, 19 Jan. 1961.*

2. A Victorian silver crown, wrapped in a remnant of white silk. This had to be from the wedding ceremony. Worldly goods. 'Silver and gold I give you.' No gold in the box, unfortunately.

3. My parents' marriage certificate.

4. Three baptismal certificates, one for each of us three children, each in the name Mary Moraghan: *Mary Arabella, Mary Willow, Mary Rowan. Father: Peter Moraghan, soldier. Mother: Eve Moraghan, née Rennick, house-wife.*

5. A cheap china ornament: a black and white mother cat with three kittens tied to her on three tiny chains. They sit in a one-and-a-half-inch green china basket with *A Present From Rush* printed on it in faded gold. *Made in Hong Kong* is written on the bottom.

6. A photograph of the three of us, obviously taken in a studio. Rowan is just a baby, wearing his christening shawl. That's the one that I study most. Rowan looks so gorgeous. He's beaming, looking a little bit away from the camera as if someone is making him laugh. Maybe our mother. He looks as if he has a whole brilliant life ahead of him.

7. The christening shawl, made of Carrickmacross lace, so delicate and

fine that it is folded into a four-inch square. It's gone yellow on me, even though Greta and I got advice from the best cleaners in Dublin and wrapped it in black tissue paper. For some reason this object always makes me cry. It's so innocent − or hopeful or something.

8. A note, scrawled on a torn piece of exercise copy, the kind with blue guide lines and a red margin line down the left-hand side:

Dearest Arabella, Willow and Rowan, this is for the best. I had to go for resons I'll tell you about. Don't hate me, because I WILL come back for you and I will have mony and we will by our own little house and be happy. Do not forget me because I will not forget you. Until we meet again, God and Our Lady Bless you, Your Loving Mother.

The word 'WILL' had been written in letters much larger than all the rest and underlined three times. Although they're touching in a way, I find the misspellings irritating. I'm a natural speller myself.

On a practical note, those baptismal certs had been very useful. They were accepted as proof of our existence and we were able to get duplicates birth certs from them. I like to think she kept the originals. The way you'd keep your baby's first shoes.

By the way, don't think I haven't tried to find my father. I have − but half-heartedly, and mostly because, down through the years, a lot of kind people said I should and offered to help me. Soldiers, even former ones, leave trails, and if I'd made a career of it I probably could have tracked him down. The truth is, though, that I don't really care about Peter Moraghan. Maybe that's hard to believe but it's a fact. Willow *says* she doesn't care either, but I know her better than she thinks I do and I'd be willing to bet she does.

What Rowan feels, neither of us knows. Only that he is very angry and messed up about everything in his life. I wonder sometimes if, for his sake, us two girls shouldn't have tried harder to find our dad. If we had, and had been successful, maybe he could have been straightened out. Maybe a soldier would have caught the danger early enough and licked him into shape. But we didn't, and he didn't, and that's a fact too, and there's no point in me beating us up over it.

I feel now that since this is the last night when to us Eve is not a real person but transparent, like a ghost, I should mark it in some way. Say goodbye to something. But I can't think of anything to do with the contents of the box that wouldn't be melodramatic. Like kiss them. So I do nothing, just replace everything, drop the box back into the shoulder-bag, click off the bedside lamp and settle down to sleep.

Or try to: I kick off the top bedcover, a dead weight on my legs. Our Americans in the Leicester are always complaining about the cold in the dining room. Now I know why. One drawback of this room that I haven't mentioned is that the heat is chronic. Like a sauna. It isn't a cold night, or all that cold by our standards, but the central heating is on full blast. The control is stuck and we hadn't been able to lower it.

I might have chanced leaving the door to our balcony open, but Willow had been horrified at the suggestion: 'This is the Wild West, for God's sake. You'd never know who'd be out there. Every night on CNN you hear about crazy gunmen and drive-by shootings and murderers high on crack cocaine.' She and Paddy have Sky Digital and pride themselves on their knowledge of current affairs.

'Hardly coming up two flights of stairs from the swimming-pool, Willow,' I pointed out.

'What's more, there are bears and coyotes in this part of the world. And what about rattlesnakes? They can climb, can't they?'

I didn't know whether rattlesnakes could climb or not so I left things be.

At least in her litany of horror she'd had the grace not to include men with ponytails and tattoos.

CHAPTER ELEVEN

It's morning, not soon enough, too soon, and the sun, despite the air-conditioning, scorches through the windscreen of Dale's pickup. I've had my eyes closed for a lot of the journey: although I can see that Dale is a good driver, the speed of those killer trucks unnerves me. Willow, a fruit basket jammed between her feet, is asleep, her head bouncing gently against her window.

We turn off the motorway in a big loop and the butterflies in my stomach wake up to have a party. Despite them, I have enough fuel in my curiosity tank to notice we're on a two-lane blacktop (I love that phrase, so literal, so American) and that instead of mile after mile of dusty brown flatness we've entered a lopsided landscape, flat to our right, but erupting to our left with peaks of red rock, Technicolor red, as red as fresh blood. Surreal.

With the change of pace and tone of the pickup's engine, Willow wakes. 'How far do we have to go now?' Her voice is tight.

'Not far.' Dale glances at both of us. 'Maybe another ten, fifteen minutes?'

Sure enough, ten minutes later we turn off the highway to cross a bridge over a stony, dry riverbed and bounce along a rutted track between high, messy hedges. Too soon, we're approaching a large wooden sign, blue paint hand-lettered on white board: 'WELCOME TO ROBINIA MEADOWS COMMUNITY! SET A WHILE!' The notice is tipsy and seems to be held upright by a jungle of nettles and weeds.

Willow picks up the fruit basket and, sitting as straight as a telegraph pole, holds it on her lap as if protecting her chest with a shield. We had left it to the man in the shop to provide whatever he thought suitable. My gift to our long-lost mother is an armful of pink roses. 'I hope she likes pink.' I attempt to sound jaunty. 'Do you know if she likes pink, Dale?'

'Pink's her favourite colour.' He smiles.

We turn through a pair of rusty iron gates, past a second notice: 'WEL-COME, SENIORS!' and drive slowly through loose rows of caravans and mobile homes, pickups, motorhomes, shacks with corrugated roofs, old cars, rusted engines, junked bedsprings and heaps of anonymous iron-mongery, all drowsing under a canopy of television aerials, satellite dishes, jokey windmills and US flags. The residents and their apathetic dogs give us no more than a quick glance. I'm gob-smacked. I'm also not sure it has been 'fixed up good'. I daren't look at my sister. 'It's huge, Dale.'

'Yeah, maybe a thousand homes here.' He hauls the pickup round a narrow corner between two vans connected together untidily by sagging overhead electricity or telephone wires. 'But don't judge us by these first streets.' It's as if he has picked up my thoughts. I was judging. And not favourably. 'These are transients. No one up this end stays long and they're always buyin', sellin' and tradin' the homes and other stuff. We're civil with 'em, of course, but these people are gonna move on. Us settled folk are further down back.'

When I'd heard Eve lived in a trailer park, I'd imagined it as a few cara-vans in a muddy field on the outskirts of some deadbeat nowhere, the kind of place you'd find on the fringes of a seaside resort. This settlement, however, is as big as a small Irish town. 'We're nearly self-sufficient.' Dale picks up on this thought too. 'We got our own drugstore-cum-groceries, an ATM machine, even a little liquor store down the back there. And the medical centre's staffed four days a week. Routine stuff only, but it's nice to know it's there.'

'Medical centre?' My notion of trailer-park living crumples. I glance at Willow. Hers hasn't.

'Yeah, a few of us got together and set one up.' Dale warms to his theme. 'This is a mixed community, but we got a high proportion of seniors. Gotta look after 'em. They built this country for the rest of us.'

'We? Is this where you live too?' This is Willow.

'Yup. Been here nearly ten years now.'

The dirt roads give way to gravel, the rows become more regular, the sites bigger, and the homes, with a few unkempt exceptions, more cared-for, even pretty. Some sport pocket lawns or flowerbeds behind miniature picket fences. 'That's my place, the one with the magnolia.' Dale points through the windscreen in the direction of what seems to be a brand

65

new mobile home, pale blue, surrounded by a garden. 'Got myself two plots. I like to grow my own vegetables.' Sure enough, sprouting from the clay surrounding it, I can see neat green rows, bamboo stakes and climbing frames. So he doesn't actually live with Eve, I think, not knowing whether I'm relieved or disappointed.

The pickup jerks to a halt. 'Well, here we are.'

The Cellophane on my bouquet starts to rattle, and before I can register any details about Eve's place, Dale has cut the engine and is looking kindly at both of us. 'Good luck.' He opens the cab door, jumps out and helps each of us down.

'Aren't you coming in with us?' Willow's voice is quivery, like a child's or an old lady's.

'I'd think three's a crowd.' But he senses our fear. 'Don't worry, I won't be far away. I'll be just across the street in my van, OK? Any problems, all you need do is holler and I'll come right over. Mario's with her right now. He'll leave, naturally.'

'Who's Mario?'

'A good guy. You'll like him.' Dale looks at his wristwatch. 'He's expecting you right about now.' He stoops to stroke a marmalade cat stretched across the bottom step of what must be Eve's caravan. 'Hey there, Ginger – everything cool, dude? Making me out a liar – I told these ladies you's a night owl.' The cat ignores him, arches its back and stalks off, tail held upright and stiff as a poker. Dale smiles at us. 'That don't mean he don't love you.'

'Is he Eve's cat?'

'That's the one. Well, I'll be seeing you . . .'

He hops back into the pickup and drives away, leaving the two of us stranded on the roadway in the heat and dust and glare, hello gifts crackling in our arms. I don't think I have ever been as nervous in my life and yet, pressing against my chest is a growing bubble of excitement.

Eve's van is white. It has two doors, the first leading to a railed wooden deck – a sort of balcony – the other at the top of a set of scrubbed wooden steps. Both are open and hung with beaded curtains, not the stringy plastic variety you see at the back of Indian takeaways: Eve's beads flash in the sunshine because they're made of crystal. Her lawn, small as it is, is perfectly clipped and of an emerald green you'd see only in *The Wizard of Oz*. Someone really cares for this garden – someone with a sense of humour: a green leprechaun, barely six inches high, grins up at visitors from behind a plaster boulder at the foot of the steps to the deck. It's so unexpected, so merry and cheeky that I feel tears rushing upwards through my throat. I put a stopper on them. That's be the last thing any of us needs right now.

'Are you OK?' I touch Willow's arm. She doesn't look OK. In the intense white light, the skin around her eyes is tracked like a shunting yard and I can see she needs her roots done. She reads what I'm thinking and turns away. 'I'm fine,' she says. 'Let's get this over with. Do we ring this or what?' 'This' is a ship's bell suspended from a curved iron bracket on the balustrade of the deck.

'I suppose so.'

But as I reach for the clapper, there's a tinkling sound and a man pushes through the crystals at the top of the steps. 'Well, hi there!'

'Hello!' I shade my eyes to look up at him. 'You must be Mario. Dale told us you're expecting us. I'm Arabella and this is my sister, Willow.'

He bounds down the steps and shakes our hands. 'Yes, I'm Mario. Pleased to meet you — it's so great you're here. You like my leprechaun? Isn't he precious?' He points proudly to the ornament. 'I got it for her last Paddy's Day in Vegas. She loves him. But come on up — she can't wait.'

Physically and in manner, Eve's second friend is poles apart from her first, and as we follow him up the steps I find myself making comparisons. Despite the long hair and the tattoos, the skin like an old road map, Dale, who smells like the outdoors, is casual but buttoned up and the best word to describe his physique is 'stringy'. Mario smells like good soap, wears no jewellery except a small gold sleeper in one ear, is barefoot, tanned and toned all over, and bulges like a weightlifter out of a body-hugging vest and *very* tight shorts. His cropped hair is severely bleached. They say opposites attract. Are they partners?

The thought is only a blip: my concerns are far more pressing than the sexual orientation of two American strangers.

'How's she doing?' Willow whispers. We've clumped to the top of the steps and are clustered on the deck.

'Wonderful,' Mario whispers back, 'thank the Lord. We're doing real good this morning. We're real excited as a matter of fact — we've had our hair done.' Then, in a normal voice: 'You want I should take those from you?' He reaches for the flowers and fruit. 'They're *gorgeous*! Okey-dokey,' he winks, 'shall we enter the temple? Mustn't keep a lady waiting.' He holds the crystals open and trills: 'They're here, sweetie! And wait'll you see what they have for you!' He stands back to let us enter, winking again as we pass, so heavily this time I can feel my hair blowing in the gale from his curly black lashes.

After the brightness outside it takes my eyes a few seconds to adjust to the interior of the trailer. We've entered a kitchen/dining area, dominated by a fridge-freezer.

I've never before been inside even a caravan, let alone anything like this trailer, which on first impression, is ultra-luxurious and makes my bed-sit in Dublin look like a slum. The décor is pastel, mostly pale blue and cream. There's a small dining-table with four chairs, a proper cooker, a microwave oven and a double sink. Even a dishwasher.

At the far end is a couch and, at right angles to it, a wing chair on which is a heap of pale pink. A blanket, maybe. A fan on a stand revolves in front of it.

Four years ago, Greta inherited a huge old camera from an uncle; it's not automatic so you have to fiddle with a bunch of dials and buttons. It might have been up to my eye now, because as I try to figure out the detail down there at the far end, everything stays sharp for a split second, then slips back into a background haze. Bit by bit, though – this all seems to take a very long time but it can't be more than half a second – I can make out a canister of oxygen on the floor, a side-locker holding a couple of pill bottles, a carafe of water, a glass, a couple of framed photographs, and what seems to be an old-fashioned exercise book.

Now into the picture comes a halo of blonde hair, blowing slightly in the breeze from the fan, a blue cardigan over a cotton dress in a glad shade of yellow. A footstool supporting a cast under the pink blanket. Two piercingly bright eyes.

On the plane from London to Phoenix, with Willow asleep, I'd fallen into conversation with the woman on my other side. She gave me her card; her story was that an agent in Santa Fe had contacted her via her website and she was on her way to meet him. So of course, tit-for-tat, I'd told her why we were on board. She was fascinated, and, maybe because she was an artist with a good imagination, asked me to describe what I thought Eve looked like now.

Now, my brain knows that a fifty-eight- or nine-year-old woman isn't exactly on the scrap heap, but to this artist, I found myself saying that my image of my mother was that she was a humpbacked, frail old lady with thin, frizzy white hair and a sad face. A shrunken, wrinkled version of the girl in the wedding photograph.

The woman I'm looking at now, despite the oxygen and the pink blanket and so on, is far from this.

While we look at one another, me doing a Lot's wife, Willow passes me. 'Hello,' she says in the formal tone I've heard her use with tradesmen. 'I'm Willow, the middle one – but of course you know that. This is Arabella. I'm sorry, but Rowan couldn't come.' She moves aside a couple of cushions and a little beanbag on the couch (for Ginger?), sits down and folds her arms across her chest. 'So. How are you, Mother?'

CHAPTER TWELVE

O h, God! Don't turn Your back on me now.
    They're so beautiful, both of them. Rowan must be beautiful too.
I wonder, is he an artist? Or maybe he works in a bank. He was always
a placid little thing, always smiling, at least for the time I knew him. So
intelligent. He was sitting by himself at just after five months! He's
approaching forty *years* now. I can't believe that sometimes. I see them all
as babies still. I suppose that's natural.

Stop looking at them like you're a guppy or a goldfish. Say something
clever. Say the *right* thing . . .

I can't think of anything to say.

Help me, God – quick, quick! I know I haven't been faithful to You,
but isn't there more rejoicing in Heaven at the return of a sinner, or
something like that? Well, listen, God, I'm a sinner and I'm returning. I
promise. From now on, I'll be the biggest and best craw-thumper in this
state and then some.

You must not cry. Don't blow it, Eve. You'll turn them off.

They're very different.

This is Willow here beside me? She's gorgeous, like a fashion plate.
Very calm. Although, I wonder, has she a hard life? She looks kind of
closed-in, in spite of the glamour – oh, Christ! I can see Petey in her!
Today of all days! That guy still haunts me.

Goddamn him to hell, with his goddamn fists and his stinking, boozy
breath and his wandering eye. I hope he's dead. I hope he died roaring.
I hope his brain rotted and his teeth fell out and his stomach went black.
I hope—

Stop with the cursing, Eve Rennick! Your *daughters* are here. You haven't
exactly been Mary Poppins have you?

Arabella – I wish she'd move away from the door: from this distance

70

she's more like me, I think, or the way I was at her age. She's tall. Well built. Good shoulders on her and look at that lovely hair—

I'm not going to cry.

I've imagined and imagined what they look like. All three of them. I knew they had grown up – I knew that, no matter what my circumstances were, I tracked every year, every birthday, but I never imagined them this good. Oh, God!

Please, dear God, remember? It's me! I'm back! Down here!

Let me get through at least the first bit of this without making a mess of it, and don't let me cry. I don't like to think of myself as the crying kind. In anyway, I should be cried out by now. Where's it all coming from?

I'm terrified they won't like me. Maybe the only reason they're here is they're so pissed with me they want to get on my case for what I've done to their lives.

You might have to crawl. Big wup! You should *have* to crawl.

You *crawl* to them two girls, Eve Rennick, and you crawl *good*! This story is going to have a happy ending. I'm determined . . .

CHAPTER THIRTEEN

'Let me put these in water and then I'll leave you three alone to chat – you want I should cut you some fruit, Eve?'

'No, thank you.' The voice is surprisingly strong. And composed. Why do I say 'surprisingly'? I've got to adjust to reality here.

'Later, then, sweetie!' *Rattle-rattle.* Mario tears into the Cellophane. 'Ooh! What fabulous grapes – and kiwi. You like kiwi, don't you, Eve? Have a tiny piece of kiwi.'

'No, thank you. Not now.'

I hardly notice the ripping, the tap running at full blast, the clinking of ware, cupboards opening and closing as I go up to join Willow on the couch. I'm mesmerised. Those piercing eyes are Rowan's; given our brother's chosen way of life, it is often difficult to see their true colour, but they're very distinctive. Willow and I both have hazel eyes but Rowan's, exactly like Eve's, are a striking shade of pale grey with a navy blue rim. This is our mother, all right.

One of the side effects of picturing her was my fear that she would be so delicate I wouldn't have the heart to say some of the things I needed to say. That I wouldn't have the guts to kick Bambi.

Now I can see I needn't have worried. This woman looks far from breakable. She is robust, with large bones, feet sized seven or eight, and work-roughened sturdy hands. Hands like my own. Used to manual labour. So far no sign of the feistiness described by Dale, if I read the meaning of that word right. Early days, though, early days . . .

She hasn't answered Willow's question as to how she is. Instead, she continues to look at us with an expression so passionate it's difficult to watch – like she's eating us with a spoon. Inside my skin I can feel all the muscles quiver. 'This is something, isn't it?' I attempt a laugh. It sounds ghastly, like drain cleaner gurgling down a plughole. 'After all these years,'

I add helpfully. Jesus – talk about lame! Get a grip! And stop watching for every twitch and flicker. You're making everyone, including yourself, nervous.

Still she doesn't answer. And, of course – I think I've already told you how I react to awkward silences – I run true to form. 'Yeah,' I say, 'that phone call from Dale was the last thing we expected. I got quite a shock when the phone rang. And Dale told us all about your accident and the complications – is that why you have the oxygen? Because with the broken ribs you're finding it difficult to breathe?'

She stops me dead by shooting out a hand and grabbing mine, so unexpectedly that Willow and I jump as if we'd been stung; her face crumples like old newspaper while huge tears pour from her eyes. 'Dammit,' she blurts, grabbing handfuls of tissues, 'I promised myself this wouldn't happen—'

Consternation all round, certainly from my side: I'm like a sponge, the worst kind of softie – all I have to see is two people embracing at a railway station and I'm off. Here I am now, out of control and in full flow. My own tears are as big as Eve's: in sympathy with her, certainly, but also with myself, with us all, with mothers and abandoned children and orphans everywhere, and war and September 11 and *Free Willy* and Iraq, with the whole sorry world. I'm giving full whack here. A circus of tears.

To get control of myself, I try concentrating on physical sensations: the effect of the fan's breeze on my burning cheeks, Eve's bony hand digging into mine. Yet all the time I'm fastened to those eyes of hers.

'Oh dear!' Mario is beside himself, pulling more and more tissues out of the box and waving them around like bunting. 'Please, no tears, no crying – people, *people*! Eve! Eve, sweetie,' he mops her face, 'you know how sensitive I am. I can't *bear* this.'

She lets him mop, doesn't react or move. Neither do I.

'This is awful, awful.' His voice rises higher. 'Will I go get Dale? He's better at handling drama than I am. Or Robert?'

'What did you expect?' Willow's voice cuts through the hullabaloo. 'No need to fetch anyone. Thank you, Mario. We'll be fine. You can leave us now. We'll manage.'

'Sure. Thanks. No worries.' He dumps the tissue box on Eve's side-table, then, from a carafe, pours water into a glass so quickly that it slops on to the floor. 'Don't forget your noon medication, sweetie.' He swabs the spill with his bare hands, succeeding only in spreading it. 'Remind her, will you?' He addresses this to Willow, clearly having identified the Alpha female of the group. 'She knows what to take but she's inclined to let the time slide. 'Bye now, see you later, people. Lovely to meet you.' He flees, the crystal beads in the doorway singing behind him.

Willow stands up and walks towards the sink. 'I'm going to make us all a cup of tea. Do you take sugar and milk, Mother?'

The absurdity of the question, given what's going on, puts a stop to Eve's and my tears. 'I take milk and sugar, yes, two spoonfuls, in tea,' our mother gulps, but, thank God, lets my hand go. 'But could I have coffee, please?' *Caw-fee*. Although her accent still bears deep traces of Dublin, there's a lot of the States in it too. 'There's some already perked. On the counter beside the sink. I take it black and strong.' She blows her nose. 'I'm sorry to blub like this. It was certainly not what I had planned for you. I had it all worked out—'

'Don't fret yourself, Eve – may I?' I grab a handful of the tissues and bundle them against my nose. It's too soon and we're all too emotional – at least, Eve and I are – to get down to business. Unlike my sister, there's no way at this early stage that I can call this woman 'Mother'. 'We've plenty of time,' I go on, my voice muffled by the tissues. 'All day if you like. And tomorrow. Excuse me.' I blow.

'Coffee all right for you, Arabella?' Willow, the hostess with the mostest, turns enquiringly to us from her place by the sink.

'Coffee'll be fine, thank you, Willow.' My voice is coming from the bottom of the sea. I steal a glance at Eve. The tears have stopped, but her knobby hand is squeezing the ball of tissues so tightly that the knuckles are white.

Expertly, because she has an electric coffee-maker at home, Willow opens lids and peers inside. 'It's already perked, as you said, Mother. I'll just heat it up a little, shall I? No sugar and and just a little milk for you, Bella, isn't that right?'

'That's right. That would be grand.' We're not meeting our long-lost mother, we're attending a coffee morning. I can't get over how Willow is handling this. As far as I can see, her hands are quite steady but I know that underneath all the managing and coping and being-in-charge stuff, she must be as confused and all over the place as I am. And of course I'm behaving as weirdly as she is.

The compactness of trailer-living is becoming clear to me. Because of the free-standing couch, side-table, large fan and Eve's chair, there is hardly any vacant floor space, while every inch of wall is covered with seating, or storage presses, or display cabinets – and it strikes me then how bizarre it is for such a huge event to be happening in such a small space. With the width and depth of emotion involved, you'd think you'd need the Abbey Theatre to contain it.

Willow presses a switch. A red light glows. We all concentrate on the percolator as if expecting it to blast off any second from Cape Canaveral.

'Would you like the air-conditioning on?' Eve jerks her head towards the machine stuck into one of the windows behind her. 'I do feel the cold but I know how warm you girls must find Arizona after the temperatures and damp of the old country.'

'Not at all. We're grand, thank you. It's lovely and cool in here.' *Like hell it is.*

'Here we are.' Willow has found mugs. She puts Eve's coffee on her side-table, having moved the dog-eared exercise book to make space for it. It's only now that I see the framed photographs are of us as babies. Me and Willow and Rowan.

'Here you are, Arabella.' Willow presents me with my coffee. 'Be careful, it's rather full.' Then she fetches her own and sits down with us. We all sip.

CHAPTER FOURTEEN

Congratulations, Eve Rennick. You're a putz, so give yourself the putz prize.

So much for planning, preparation and thinking forward, you have made a dog's dinner of it. What are you? Some kind of teenager? You promised yourself you wouldn't cry. Why couldn't you just do the right thing for once? The elegant thing?

I'm all out of ideas. I've frightened them.

Think! Be quick about it! Don't let them see how upset you are — you'll drive them away.

Drink your coffee. Be calm. They're calm. Certainly Willow's calm. Be like Willow.

I can't get over how lovely they are. Even with Petey's nose and chin, Willow looks fabulous, as groomed and well turned out as a bandbox. Arabella has the potential to be even more stunning — she has someone else's nose. I don't know whose — how could I? I can see she's sort of careless with her looks: she could do with going to the beauty shop to get that gorgeous hair, so thick and shining, shaped a bit. I should make an appointment for her.

How could Petey and me have produced these girls? I don't deserve daughters like them . . .

When things were bad, I tried to keep in my mind the snuggly bits of them first three years: me and my three little kids all in the bed together on a rainy Dublin afternoon; the baby smells of them after the bath in front of the fire; one of them smiling at me for no reason. It was them kinds of things kept me going through my life in America and you'll notice Petey doesn't figure. Bastard.

Do they despise me for living in a trailer park? I know it would be death for some people. I can see them looking round the van. Do they like it? I can't read Willow's expression but Arabella's an open book: she's admiring things – at least I think she is.

Willow seems to be married. No engagement ring, though, just the one gold band. Does she have a house or an apartment? Kids?

There's so much I don't know. Arabella's not wearing a wedding ring. How come she's not married? Maybe she's divorced.

She's looking again at the kitchen. I think she likes the refrigerator. We have similar tastes. I love that refrigerator too. It's so stately. I'd miss it if I had to move. I love other things too, like the smoothness of the Formica on my table. I love its cool feel.

These are the first worldly goods I've ever owned, you know, the first decent ones in anyway because I don't count the make-do crap Petey and me had in that room in Dublin for them few years, and since I came to the States, until now I always rented or shared. Yeah, 'shared', that's a laugh. Bunked in with other losers in places all over Queens and the Bronx. Roaches under the sink, Murphy beds, stink in the hallways.

No more, thank the Lord. I can be proud of my stuff now. My social security don't spread very wide, but Dale has this knack of finding things for half-nothing in Goodwill or the Salvation Army shops, decent things. He'll just roll in here with something in back of that little pickup and he'll make me guess what he paid for it. 'How much do you think, Eve?' I'll say a sum and he'll laugh out loud. 'When's the last time you went shopping? This here loveseat [or air-conditioner or garden chair] is from Goodwill, not Bloomingdale's!' So he'll tell me maybe five or ten bucks and I pay him, next cheque I get.

To tell you the truth, I never thought I'd be happy living in a caravan like a tinker. (I can't remember the right name for tinkers, even though I do see about them in the Irish newspaper Dale gets me sometimes when he goes into the city. 'Itinerations' or 'travellers' or something?) It's a peaceful life here and much cheaper than in an apartment: you can live on your social security and nobody in the place is letting on they're any better than anyone else. The lads and Gina are great friends to me. I struck it lucky when Dale came along. I don't know what I'd do without that guy.

What do they think of him?

Hey, are you wondering why I don't have a job? Sponging on the US taxpayer, like?

Well, I tried for jobs after I settled down here at the Meadows, I really did, but I had no references worth talking about – there isn't much demand for priests' housekeepers in Arizona – and although I answered a few ads for cleaners and kitchen staff, I was always outflanked by younger, more eager Filipinos and Latinos, fair play to them, who'd do the job for half the wages I thought I was worth. And it wasn't only them I was in competition with: it was the Hispanics too. The economy of Arizona was pretty depressed at the time I was looking but it was even worse in New Mexico, and a lot of Mexican illegals were coming across here to do the dross jobs for half nothing, cash in hand. I got discouraged.

In anyway, did I really want to spend the rest of whatever life I've left scrubbing floors and cleaning toilets for rich people in Phoenix? Would you? In my opinion, I've given a fair degree of labour to the world, between one thing and another, so to tell the truth of it, I think of myself as honourably retired.

I can smell perfume. It's probably Willow's. Arabella is more the down-to-earth type. She's the one that's most likely to be soft, but I can already tell she's nobody's fool. I should be careful.

This is torture, this silence. Break the ice, dammit. *Talk!*

First thing, they're going to want to know why you did it. Well, that's covered in anyway. That's the diary. If you can't think of the right words to say, read the goddamned diary out loud to them. I have to trust the diary now. So, putz, you're going for the sympathy vote, big deal, but what else do you have?

Oh, Lord, I'm so tired suddenly. It's like a wave, high up, coming down fast . . . It's all that medication and the result of the anaesthetic when they were setting my leg. For God's sake, Eve, push it away, push it away . . .

If you can't read the diary to them, give it to them. Please let them at least read the blasted thing.

The diary will take care of the early times. What about since then? Are you going to tell them about New York and Atlantic City and every dump and dive? The booze? The boyfriends?

Are you going to cut to the chase, Eve Rennick?

Finish the goddamned coffee. Stop using it as if it's a holy sacrament and you mustn't talk while you're receiving it. Say something.

'I'm sorry' might be a good start?

CHAPTER FIFTEEN

All three of us continue to sip at the dregs of our coffee, making a meal of it, Willow and I hooked solid on our mother's stare as silence, thick as bristles on a brush, sweeps the trailer. As if to emphasise it, here comes scrunching on the gravel outside followed by cheerful ribbing: 'Hot enough for ya, Hank?'

'You're such a wuss, Robert.' Laughter and more scrunching, until silence falls again. I let it run on. And on. And on. I'm determined not to be the blabbermouth this time.

'Do you need a hand there, Mother?' My sister who, on the surface, doesn't seem as uncomfortable as I am puts down her mug and half rises as Eve, hampered by her cast and coverings, reaches again for her tissue box.

'No, thank you.' Eve shakes her head, manages to reach the box, blows her nose but doesn't let up on the staring. It's very unsettling.

My mouth is glued to the lip of my empty mug. I'm sucking its marrow. What am I doing here? It was a mistake to come. I was fine. I should have let well enough alone. What you don't know doesn't hurt you. La, la-la, la, la . . .

'This climate must be very good if you have—'

'I want to say something—'

Eve and Willow had spoken together.

'You first,' says Eve, drilling hard into the two of us with those eyes of hers.

'I was just remarking,' Willow picks up her mug again, 'how good this climate must be for people with rheumatism.'

'Oh, stop this!' I put my own mug on the floor with such force the handle comes off in my hand. Dumbfounded, I look at it, with the yellow bauble of glue that didn't do its job properly. 'I'm terribly sorry. I'll replace it.'

79

'Don't be silly, Arabella. It's only a piece of junk.'

'I insist – I'm really sorry, Eve, it's china too. I'll give you the money before we leave.'

'Arabella, she says it's all right. Don't go on about it.' This is Willow.

Suddenly I want to yell, like I did yesterday. The noise is already in my chest – I can hear it, distant thunder. 'We have a lot of very important things to say to each other,' I go, voice all trembly with the effort to hold in the din, 'all three of us. Willow and I have come a long way to say these things, Eve. We should get on with it and stop this farting around.'

Willow's eyes are wide with shock. She's still not used to this new me but now that I've started I'll finish. 'Excuse the language. I apologise for that, but not for what I said.' I take a breath and start again. 'Lookit, Eve, and you too, Willow, we're not here to drink coffee or arrange flowers or make conversation about the climate. This isn't a social call to a stranger or some nice auntie we don't see very often. We have real things to discuss. A lot of real-life, serious things.'

Eve seems to grow taller in her chair. 'You're right. How right you are.'

'Thank you.'

Then she wrongfoots me. 'So. Tell me about Rowan. Did you bring a snapshot of him?'

'Could we leave Rowan out of it for the moment—'

'There wasn't time to organise that kind of thing, Mother.' Willow has regrouped and cuts in, warning me to get back in my box. She laughs with a sound like a blunt saw on a log: she has to be holding in the yelling just like me. 'In any case,' she says, 'snapshots of Rowan are few and far between.'

'Fine, no photographs, not a problem.' The gimlet eyes are darting from one to the other of us. 'Dale said he couldn't get away. What does he do?'

'He has your eyes, Eve.' I send Willow frantic signals with my own because, despite my fine words earlier, I think it's still a bit early for our mother to get the full whack, Willow's view of our brother. 'And he's quite tall,' I add, 'maybe six feet one or two, a bit thin, mind—'

'He's delinquent, Mother.' The diversion hasn't worked; Willow's yell is in danger of breaking through.

'Willow – don't . . .'

I might as well have appealed to the pink blanket: my sister doesn't even glance at me. She leans towards Eve so their faces are almost touching. 'Your son is a dropout, Mother. A bum, I suppose you'd call him. He can barely write his name unless it's to collect his dole.' She spits the word.

'Easy.' I put out a hand to slow her down, but she swats it aside. 'Shut *up*, will you?' Then, so close now to Eve that I can't imagine how either of them can see the other in focus: 'Our brother has been in and out of gaol since he was fourteen, and despite everything everyone's done for him, social workers, myself and Arabella, care agencies, even some of the judges, who were kind enough to give him several last chances, he blew it all back in our faces. No one can control him, he's into drugs and drink, and to say he has worked six weeks in any one year of the last ten is probably an exaggeration. We don't know how he lives, where he gets the money to feed his habit – it has to be by stealing, so he's a thief as well as everything else. Nor do we ever know where he's sleeping, what filthy squat or hovel or shooting gallery. He's a burden on the state and on us. I'm sick of it. I'm sick of him. Bella can do what she likes,' she glares at me, 'but I've done with him. To tell you the truth, I'm delighted he isn't with us over here. If we'd found him I might not have come. He's a leech, a blood-sucking bottom-crawler. Well, I've washed my hands of him and of the whole sickening Rowan situation. No more, and that's that.' Panting, she throws herself against the backrest of the couch.

Like a virulent firework, the outburst hovers over the three of us, splinters into yet another silence, but leaves a bright, complicated sparkler. *This is your fault. You brought him – and us – into the world and then ran off as if we were three dandelions in your lawn. You didn't give a shit what happened to us, who rooted us up, what dump we landed in. If Rowan's a fuck-up, you're to blame. We're all fuck-ups thanks to you.*

In novels when a character has been wronged, or is in distress of some kind, they are sometimes said to display a 'ravaged countenance'. The first time I came across this I looked up both words and found that 'countenance' is a fancy way of saying 'face'. 'To ravage', though, is to lay waste, plunder, make havoc or destroy. So much for nice neat print on a nice neat page. Here before me on Eve is what that phrase actually means.

I have been cursed all my life with empathy. I feel whatever sadness

81

anyone else is feeling and want to bloody *fix* it. But I can't fix this so I am paralysed by Eve's pain: I am confused about the boundary where my pain ends and hers begins. I can't think of anything to say or do to take ownership of this crisis.

As for Willow, I could kill her.

On the other hand, I'd never before heard her so passionate about anything. That cool façade is obviously just that. Nevertheless, it's a blessed relief all round when she gets up and walks back to the coffee-maker and when my mother, having looked after her for a second or two, covers her face with her hands so I don't have to look at either of them for a while. I can get back inside myself. Stop feeling everything for everyone. Remind myself that, however uncomfortable our mother is, Honesty Is the Best Policy.

If that woman is distressed so be it; she is not the wronged party here. Willow has a perfect right to say what she feels. So do I, for that matter. I just don't have the guts. Not yet.

Now I can hear humming outside. A woman's humming. I can even identify the tune: it's the English national anthem, of all things, 'God Save the Queen' . . . I have to use all my self-control not to bloody laugh.

'Sorry, Mother.' Quiet now, Willow is standing at the kitchen counter with her back to us. She doesn't sound sorry. 'I didn't plan on it all coming out in a rush like that but it's the truth.'

Eve lets her hands fall slowly from her eyes and rests them in her lap. 'I'm the one that's sorry. I'm so sorry.' Here she goes again with the big fat tears. Where's 'feisty' when you need him? Me – I'm not going to get caught again, no, sirree, Bob. I read the label on the pink blanket: 100 per cent acrylic. Tumble dry. Warm. 'Will you girls forgive me? Will you let me explain?'

No, no, no, I'm not going to get caught. 'Would you like a drink of water of something, Eve?' I'm chirping. I'm a daytime TV presenter.

'I know I don't deserve the time of day from you,' Eve goes, as though I haven't opened my mouth, 'from either of you or Rowan. I know there is no excuse whatsoever for what I did. And I wouldn't blame you if you walked out of here right now.' She takes a big breath. A big, shuddering breath.

La la la-la la – not going to get caught here . . .

'You were right to have a go at me, Willow. I deserve it.'

No bleach. Made in Thailand.

'I don't expect forgiveness. I want it, of course, but that would be too much to ask, at this early stage in anyway. But I can't tell you how grateful I am that you have given me a chance. Maybe in time you'll be able to forgive me.'

This is excruciating. Of course I want her to apologise. I want her to feel awful. But I'm faced with her feeling awful and I hate it. I'm beginning to dislike this woman. Pink blanket, my big toe. It should be white with black spots. Evil black spots. I want her to be Cruella de Vil: that would be a lot simpler. 'Eve – don't—'

Was that my voice there?

'Ssh!' She smiles weakly at me, then turns to Willow again. 'For what it's worth, I've been sorry since the day I left you.'

Oh, yeah? You're sorry since the day you left us? What about the Big Chill? Nearly forty years of it? I look at the floor of the trailer. Pretend tiles. Vinyl. She's pushing me into unknown territory and the space is too wide, too high. If I can forgive her so easily, what does that say about four decades of confusion, anger, betrayal and indifference? Am I to take it now that those feelings weren't real?

I'm not buying. It's an act: I have to convince myself it's an act. She's crawling to us now to get into our good books. The woman deserves an Oscar.

Say something! Where's the yelling waitress when I need her?

'Arabella!' Willow comes back to us and, although there isn't a tear on my face as far as I know, she hands me a tissue from Eve's box. 'This is ridiculous. Unless we all calm down, I'm leaving right now. In fact, that's the best idea I've had all day.' She wheels and makes for the door of the trailer. Click-clack-click, heels like an old-fashioned typewriter.

I rush after her. I don't want my sister to go. I don't want to be alone with Eve. I grab the sleeve of her blouse but she tries to dislodge me. 'Let me go.'

'We've come all this way!' I tighten my grip and it's touch and go for a few seconds, but then she looks me straight in the face.

'If there's any more of this – this –' she struggles for the word '– *excessiveness*, I'm definitely out of here.'

'No more. I promise.' I let her go.

When we turn to take our seats again, the pink blanket is heaving. Eve is trying to cough. She seems to be choking. She's flapping one of her hands, trying to tell us something. She's upstaging us again. But we rush across to her and it's Willow who twigs: 'The oxygen. She needs the oxygen.'

She's not trying to upstage us.

As I'm nearest to it, I pick up the heavy cylinder. 'How do I turn it on?'

'Here, let me – you put the mask on. Put those elastic bits behind her ears.'

Between us, by trial and error and with the help of the instructions on the cylinder, we manage to get the mask on her nose and the oxygen flowing. Our mother's face is as grey as old snow. But the jury is still out – I keep it out for my own sake.

We stand over her as, gradually, her breathing becomes regular. She doesn't open her eyes. She seems to have fallen asleep. Talk about an anticlimax.

We sit. 'Should I go and get Dale or someone?' I look at Willow. 'I'm out of my depth. We both are.'

'Let's wait a few minutes.' Willow looks at her watch. 'It's eleven forty-five. She's due her tablets, whatever they are, at twelve. We'll have to wake her up for that.'

Eve is not asleep. Eyes still closed, she raises both hands to the mask and pulls it sideways so that, like a big green carbuncle, it rests against her neck. 'Please. I've got to say this.' She takes another long breath (no shudders, thank God), then opens her eyes and locks on to us again. 'If this doesn't sound too creepy or melodramatic, let me tell you what happened.'

Willow looks at me and I look at Willow, then we both look at our mother.

From somewhere I find the courage. 'I don't know, Eve. Not yet. I don't think I'm ready yet. I want to know, of course, but I need to settle down a bit first. OK?'

She nods, a tiny movement. Then she reaches for the exercise book I had noticed before. 'At least read this, will you? It might help you understand.' She hands it to me. Muggins. In my hand, the thing is floppy and feels like cloth. It's stained with God knows what.

'What is it?'

'It's my diary.' She takes the mask, puts it back over her nose and closes her eyes again. What we're left with in the trailer is the slow swish of the fan and the hiss of the oxygen.

CHAPTER SIXTEEN

'That was a bit harsh, wasn't it? Right off like that. Couldn't you have waited a bit? You really upset her.' This is me, whispering, while in another part of the forest I'm kicking myself because I'm arguing against my own case. Like, a minute ago wasn't it yours truly that was all on for awarding Eve an Oscar? What the hell am I at?

'Tough.' Willow picks up her mug and, making no effort to be quiet, walks towards the sink.

I glance at Eve, partly to see if she's still asleep, partly to check she hasn't heard, then follow my sister. 'She's not doing this for fun or on a whim,' I'm still whispering. 'Whatever she's done in the past, she's our mother, Willow.'

No response.

'At least admit you went too far. It's too much all in one go – she's sorry. It's terrible that a woman of her age feels she has to humiliate herself in front of us like that. I mean she's only short of asking us for mercy. Is that what you want?'

'Do you want more coffee? I'm having some.' She picks up the percolator.

'No thanks. Lookit, Willow—'

But she turns on me. 'Shut up, Arabella. Just shut *up*, will you? Keep your Pollyanna notions to yourself.'

'Ssh!' I look back over my shoulder again. 'At least don't let her hear us arguing about her.'

'I don't care whether she hears us or not.' But Willow lowers her voice. 'Listen, Arabella, the world doesn't work your way just because you want it to. You forgive her. You have mercy on her. Do whatever you like. I have no feelings for that woman one way or the other. *None.*'

'I don't believe that.'

'Suit yourself.' She pours the coffee, a brown stream, thin as venom, into her mug. 'But just know this: I'm giving this a maximum of a week. I've more to do with my life—'

'Willow, come on! Give yourself a break – give us all a break. You can't catch up on a lifetime in one week!'

'Maybe not even that long.' Her lips have done that narrowing thing again. 'You stay as long as you like – I'm going outside to drink this. The atmosphere in here stinks.' She dives through the curtain and sits on the steps outside.

I stare at her back for a few seconds, at the sun-struck brightness of her hair flashing through the crystals. She couldn't have meant all that. She isn't that cold. She intimidates me, sure, but I do remember little things about her that she's probably forgotten: the period when she was afraid of the dark and, braving Armageddon at the hands of the nun in charge of the dormitory, used to creep into my bed for a cuddle; or the time she sat the civil-service exam and was convinced she hadn't done well enough to be called. That night, she came running to the hostel I was in at the time, nearly breaking down the door in her haste to get to me and, when she did, crying her eyes out in my arms until she fell asleep. I smuggled her into my bedroom and kept her there until morning, when the veneer, since perfected, was back in place and she couldn't get out of the place fast enough. She didn't contact me again for weeks. It's true what they say: you are never forgiven if you do someone a favour.

Slowly, I go back to sit beside Eve and catch sight of her exercise-book diary, perched like a siren on the arm of the couch where I'd left it. It is so quiet that, from outside, I can hear the little 'ding' as the rim of Willow's cup accidentally hits her teeth. She's not coming back inside any time soon. Now is my chance to read the thing . . .

I open it quickly. Like her note to us in my tin box (the paper might even have been torn out of here), these pages have horizontal blue lines and the red margin. The top page is covered with black, blotted hand-writing and, flicking on a little, I can see that some of the others have been written on in red or blue, sometimes both. It's like homework done by a child in a hurry.

I can't face it. I have to calm down, get my thoughts in order. I put the thing in my handbag, which, luckily, is big enough to hold twenty exercise books.

The air blown into my face by the fan is hot, because the temperature in the trailer has risen to an almost unbearable level. Or maybe I'm noticing it properly only now and my dress, bought as a crisp white broderie-anglaise shirtwaister from Penneys, now feels as cool as clingfilm. I hold the neck-line out from me as far as it will stretch and lean towards the fan, trying to cool myself by channelling the breeze at my breasts.

'Having a nice visit, Arabella? Uh-oh – she asleep?' The crystals swing and clink in the draught as Dale walks towards me down the aisle of the trailer. He has removed his shirt and is wearing a sleeveless black T-shirt; revealing tattoos not only on the sides of his neck but creeping, vine-like, across his shoulders and half-way down his upper arms.

Mortified, I jump back from the fan. 'It's stifling in here,' I say loudly, shooting to my feet to inspect the switches on the air-conditioner behind Eve. 'Will we turn this on? It seems straightforward.' I'm blushing.

'Sure,' he says comfortably. 'It's a hot one, all right.'

'But first I have to close the door, don't I?' In the rush, I knock over a little magazine stand. I pick it up, stuff the magazines back inside, straighten up, close the door and catch one of the goddamned crystal strands in it.

'Well,' says Dale, as if nothing has happened, 'I just came over to make sure everything was OK. Seems so. Eve! Wake up! Have some manners.'

I'm back with my switches. Although the air-conditioner is whooshing and whirring into life, I'm monitoring it as if I'm in a space capsule blasting off for the moon. Oh, why the hell doesn't the man leave?

'It's probably her medication that's making her so sleepy.' I chuck again at a dial that's already pointing to 'Full'. At last the machine cranks up. 'There she blows!' From behind my back, I hear him chuckle.

'That machine don't owe us a dollar – fifteen years old if she's a day.'

I have no choice but to turn and face him but he's not looking at me, thank God. He's gazing down at my mother. 'Come on, doll.' Gently, he nudges Eve's good foot with the toe of his boot. 'Open those baby blues.'

When there is still no stir, he smiles wryly. 'When the going gets tough, the tough go to sleep. And, make no mistake about it, she's tough, our Eve.'

'Are you saying she's not really asleep? You think she can hear us?' I remember the conversation between Willow and myself and blush harder, if that's possible. I am a pillar of fire. I have not been so scarlet since I went to my first dance and was asked to dance by a guy with a bad case of acne and a blob of Brylcreem on his lapel.

'Who knows?' Dale shrugs. 'Don't forget to give her the medication. It's coming up to twelve. Give her a good shake, that'll get her – and if she still don't play ball, come and get one of us. You know where to find me?'

I nod. It's all I can do. 'Thanks, Dale.'

Instead of leaving, he looks down at me with a quizzical expression. 'Your sister OK?'

'She's fine.'

'Don't look fine, out there on the stoop.'

'She's fine. Believe me. What's that you said about Eve being tough? Willow's Eve's daughter. I am too, by the way,' I add hastily.

'I beg your pardon?'

'I'm tough too.'

'Yeah.' For a second he hesitates, then, 'OK. I'll close the door after me. No use coolin' the whole park.' He walks away through those bloody crystals and closes the door.

I glance over my shoulder at my sleeping mother. I've got to get out of here for some fresh air. And to pollute it with a cigarette.

Willow is sitting on the step, staring into space. I sit beside her. 'Sorry for the outburst.' Her manner is offhand. 'We're two different people, Bella, that's all.'

'We sure are.' I light up and inhale.

'So don't let's go on about it.'

Although it is on the tip of my tongue to do exactly that, I agree. One of Greta's wise old sayings, parroted from her granny, is: *When you have an advantage, the best advice is, don't use it!* Willow had said sorry in her own way.

'Give us a cigarette, will you?' She holds out her hand.

'But you don't smoke.' I'm flabbergasted.

'So?' Her eyes are challenging. 'Are you going to make a Supreme Court case out of this? May I or may I not have a cigarette?'

In a daze, I take out the pack again and offer it to her. I light her cigarette and she puffs, blowing out the smoke immediately the way non-smokers do. 'I must phone home.' She looks at her watch. 'I wonder what they're doing? I hope Paddy's giving them a proper meal. When I went away to the conference that time, Maeve told me – smugly, I might add – that she loved it when I went away because they had great food. That they always had takeaways for their dinner at night and that their dad always gave them the leftovers for their breakfast next morning. Lamb balti at half past seven in the morning! Chicken nuggets?'

'I suppose I should phone home too.'

She looks at me, astonished. 'Who have you got to talk to?'

'Greta.' But she had caught me on the back foot. She was dead right. Greta would be delighted to hear from me, I knew that, but she was hardly family. 'Jimmy Porter,' I said. 'Maybe I should ring him and tell him we've arrived safely.'

'After he made an eejit of himself and you too?'

'None of your business.' I'm more annoyed than ever now that I've told her about that party. 'Listen, Willow,' the words burst out, 'I'm sorry about the chickens that time.' You know how that happens sometimes? When you say something out of the blue and you hadn't planned it?

'Chickens? What chickens? What are you on about now?' She frowns. 'Honestly, Bella, sometimes I wonder about you.'

'Don't you remember? We were in St Camilla's only a few months. Those day-old chicks that got killed? We were all punished. Including you.' I look directly into her eyes. 'It was me who did it. And I didn't have the guts to own up.'

'For God's sake—'

'It's haunted me all my life.'

'Christ almighty, Arabella, I haven't a clue what you're talking about.' Slowly, she shakes her head from side to side, as if faced with someone really, really dim. 'Haven't you nothing better to be worried about than events that happened aeons ago?'

'Are you sure you don't remember?' I can't seem to stop. I need her to remember. 'You got smacked with the ruler – we all did. But I could have saved everyone. I should have saved you. I've felt like Judas ever since. At least say you forgive me.'

'Forgive? Not you too!' She groans as if she's in a play. 'It must be something in the water. What the hell's infecting everyone in this place?' She pulls irritably at the Alice band holding the hair off her forehead. Then she sees I mean it. 'All right, I forgive you. For whatever it was. For one of the hundreds, if not thousands of punishments I got in that place. Does that make you happy? Now, can we talk about something more pertinent than chickens? Please?'

'Are you sure you don't remember? Day-old chicks? In a shoebox? Dead the next morning?'

'*Arabella!*'

'All right, all right, sorry. I'll shut up about it now.'

'For this, much thanks.'

We sit there, smoking, side by side, although she's making not much of a fist of it. The heat has bleached the sky to the colour of bone and I fancy I can see the air simmering over the street in front of us. Although the shade from the awning over the deck is welcome, I'm suffering.

'Remember Dirty Doreen?' she says, out of the blue.

I'm astonished. 'What brought her into your mind?'

'I dunno, really.' She blows a cloud of smoke, real wide, like amateurs do. 'I suppose it was you bringing up those chickens. Which,' she turns to glare at me, 'I do not remember and do not want to discuss further.'

'So what about Dirty Doreen?'

'I just felt sorry for her, that's all. When I saw what happened to her day after day, I think it made me pretty careful never to step out of line. I think I decided then that I was not going to let anyone get under my skin. That I wouldn't give anyone any reason to.'

This is more than astonishing. This is beyond belief. My sister confiding a weakness? And is this a sort of roundabout way to explain her behaviour towards our mother? Best not to ask directly. 'You were pretty young, Willow.'

'Did you not make any decisions about your future in that place?'

'Can't say I did – I was more a get-through-one-day-at-a-time sort of person.'

'Yes, well, I wasn't.' Said in such a way that it cuts off any follow-up and we lapse into silence again.

Poor Doreen, an inmate of our orphanage, was a sickly, pale child who was constantly wetting herself or her bed; she was frequently smacked for it, forced to parade her smelly sheets in front of us, then wash them, and herself in cruelly cold water in the bath.

Our nastiness to her – the sniggering, the showy wrinkling of our noses when she walked into class – must have been even worse for her than any physical punishment, and I'm ashamed to say I was as bad as the rest. It was mob rule in that place, the strong versus the weak, and if you didn't belong to a gang you were dead. Our gang – all the gangs – cast Doreen out and felt mighty.

Early on, Doreen vanished from our lives. At the time, none of us knew where she went or why. The waters closed over her smell, and the gangs, always regrouping in any case, quickly found other targets. Then one day a grave-faced Sister bustled into our room and made us kneel to pray for the repose of her soul. 'She's with the angels, children.'

I remember being struck with belated remorse so heavy it was like being buried under a pile of rocks.

Willow and I are joined by Eve's cat, purring and waving his tail. He inspects us from the bottom of the steps. Then, gracefully, he covers the distance between us in one, rippling leap, landing on Willow's lap. 'Get off me! Get off me!' She jumps up in terror. Willow hates cats.

Rejected, Ginger lands softly on four paws beside me and looks from one to the other of us with an injured expression on his triangular face. Then he turns his back to us, sits, sticks out one of his back legs and begins furiously to lick it.

I feel like a cretin. All that time I'd been beating myself up about those chickens and for nothing. She doesn't even remember. There's a lesson in there somewhere but will I ever learn? And it's going to take me a while to digest the revelation about why she behaves as she does, as if she's an armadillo or a crocodile or something. Armour-plated in any case.

'There's more,' says this sister of mine.

'More? More what?'

'I rang every Moraghan in Ireland, England, Scotland and Wales. Luckily there aren't too many spelt that way.'

'You were searching for him?'

'Around the same time I was searching for Rennicks. Do you never wonder where he is, Arabella? What he's doing now? What he's like?'

'Not a lot. Not lately anyhow.' But I'm seriously intrigued with this new insight into my sister. 'Did you try the army? How long ago did you do all this ringing around?'

She looks at me and I can see that the deviation from normal business is over. 'Of course I tried the army. I tried there first. I'm not stupid, Arabella, but they said he no longer collects his pension – or whatever it is. And it was quite a while ago. Let's go back inside now.' She gets to her feet. 'We have to wake that woman up.'

CHAPTER SEVENTEEN

They think I'm not with them, that I can't hear them. I can. Not all the time, I'm in and out of it, like I'm in a train carriage travelling through a series of tunnels.

Sometimes I'm in their conversation but then my own stuff comes back and blots them out. Stuff from now, stuff from my past, things I'm thinking, or have thought last night or yesterday or ten years ago. It's that kind of frustrating, dozy sleep that you can't seem to escape. You'd think it would be frightening, all a jumble, but it's not: it's nice, actually, even enjoyable. Peaceful. It's most likely the oxygen.

The only bad thing is that Petey's in there. The bastard.

Death is the ghost at the feast, as Dale would say. Well, that's for sure and death is pretty personal for me since the wreck. Not the one lately that has me here like this, but the one years ago, the bad one. That was when I met Dale. I was told later in the hospital that he saved my life. He was hanging out on the sidewalk, right by the junction where the crash happened, and he pulled me out through the window of that car just before it caught fire. (It would have to be a gas truck that hit us, wouldn't it?) The funny thing is that although I can still see the face of the guy who was driving, the terror on it just before we hit that truck, I've never been able to remember his name. I was too busy fighting for my own life to go to the funeral or even to send a card. He was just some guy. We'd picked each other up in a bar in Queens and we'd pitched up outside this garage at this junction on our way to his place. We were both drunk. It's probably what saved me. Dale says it was no problem to pull me out through that window: I was just like a rag doll.

Apparently I was unconscious for four and a half days and I had one of them near-death experiences. Well, I don't know how near it was for real, but I was pretty far gone, that's for sure and medically proven. So I have news for you. From what I saw, death is white, like soft cotton wool. No God or welcoming Jesus or tunnels, but 'yes' to the bright light you hear about. Not dazzling, just lovely and bright and friendly, like a sunny day, giving you this comfortable feeling like you're drifting along in your own company and have all the time in the world. Which, of course, you have if you're going to be dead.

You do hear people talking about you, and dings and dongs and bleeps, but none of it bothers you. And you don't care about anything you're leaving behind, not even people. In my case not even my kids that I hadn't seen.

Oh, God, they're arguing about me now down there in the kitchen area. This is horrible. *A maximum of a week,* Willow says. *As long as it takes,* Arabella says.

It makes it worse, in a sort of a way, that they're whispering. Sometimes whispering sounds really vicious.

Arabella's the one I should concentrate on. She's my best hope. Although I'd bet my bottom dollar that this cool, composed puss of Willow's is a sham. Put on to hide that she's deep-down terrified of the world. I can see it, you know – it's behind the eyes. I could help fix it if she'd let me but I don't think there's much I can do about it just yet in anyway. That attitude seems to me pretty well practised. Poor little thing . . .

What I've done to those girls . . .

Don't go there, Eve . . . Stay cool.

Did I tell you already about the other things in my tin box? Besides the diary, I mean – stuff like the three locks of hair, one from each of them. The couple of photographs, rosary beads and so on. If I'm repeating myself, forgive me.

Or did I tell you about the tin box at all? I'm getting confused. Maybe it's this second accident, but I find some details hard to get out of this soupy half-sleep I'm in. In anyway, this tin box is all I have left of the old country, a few souvenirs. The most important thing in it is the diary. I've added to it over the years, as I thought about things, so it's a little out of sequence. It's not a proper diary either, because I wrote all of it after the events.

You see, unless they tried to find me, which I doubt (but wouldn't that be awesome?), they know nothing about me, except for the few pitiful things I left with Arabella (in a tin box too and that wasn't an accident or a coincidence: it was deliberate).

So this diary is for them. Did I give it to Arabella already? I think I did . . .

Down the years I was always real careful to make sure that whatever deadbeat I was with understood properly that, if I passed while I was with him, I had one dying wish: that the tin box with the diary in it should be preserved, and that he should do his damnedest to get it to my kids even if he had to do it through the CIA.

You know, after that first accident, when I was nearly creamed for good and Dale and me became friends and fellow-travellers, in a manner of speaking, as soon as I began to trust him, I spilled my guts out to him about the three of them. 'Why don't you try to get in touch now?' was his attitude.

For a while I put it off – I could just imagine how much they'd hate me – but then, with his help, I wrote off to the Irish Department of Health; we'd figured that they'd know the names of kids who went through all the orphanages. There might be a chance that if we could find those places someone might have kept in contact.

Although it took about a year, I guess, and we had to write two more times, they did come back with the names of two 'institutions', as they called them; the girls had apparently been placed together, Rowan was put in a different one; but the letter said that neither was in existence any more and that the department kept no records of the children in subsequent years after they were discharged at the age of sixteen.

Dead end.

I didn't want to give up, though, so we got on to the Irish embassy and they gave me the address of the place that registers births, marriages and deaths. But that place misunderstood my letter and sent me back a note saying if I wanted copies of the three birth certificates, I'd have to enclose an international money order and all that kind of garbage . . .

Dale and me were on the move by then but when we had settled in the Meadows, I figured now was the time to try again. So we tried the Irish Information for the phones, and even though I could give them no addresses, I have to say the operators were very helpful. None of my kids was listed, however, so we figured they might not be still in Ireland. Or if they were, and the girls were married, they'd be under different names.

I planned and planned to contact them. I really did, God help me (hey, God? Down here? Sinners? Back? More rejoicing?). I planned to go to

Ireland and search for them in person but, as you know, I never did. I kept putting it off. I'm sure what I did made the papers at the time, and even though it was a long time ago, reporters have long memories and I kept imagining somehow that the minute I set foot in the country I'd have to go through rows and rows of people who were all waiting to give out to me and shake their fists and tell me what a *bad* person I am. Stupid, I know. No basis for that whatsoever. No logic at all. And a sign of awful cowardice. No need for anyone to point that out to me, or to tell me about my badness either. I've told myself enough times about *that*.

I guess this time I didn't care who thought badly of me except the kids themselves – and I was willing to go through any hell they'd design for me just so I could start putting things right.

Before the kids read that diary, though, I want to get my spake in to you about what's in it, but in case you think that, by telling you, I'm trying to make excuses for myself, I swear I'm not. There are no excuses I could make. I'm just putting it out there for you. First of all, I won't bore you at this point with stories about what they call nowadays my 'disadvantaged childhood' and whatever. Tons of people have disadvantaged childhoods but turn out OK and don't abandon their children: look at Oprah. She's some woman and she doesn't whinge.

Here she is, back again to sit beside me – Arabella, I mean. She's a good person. I can tell. I wish I could push aside this fog and talk to her one-to-one; my hands feel like logs. Maybe I'll get the strength in a minute . . .

In anyway, my time in the orphanage was pretty standard for that time and we all just got through it. I was set loose at fourteen and went into service. That was the way it was done in them days. You got to be fourteen and you were out on your ear and into some rich person's basement or attic.

The way it worked was that the bigwigs would come by appointment, or sometimes they'd just turn up at the front door. They'd ask for 'a strong country girl', and it so happened that when the Portmans of Iona Road, Glasnevin, Dublin city, knocked on the front door, I was the one on offer and they had to make do with me. I was strong in them days in anyway, and of a cheerful enough disposition, so in my opinion them Portmans didn't get a bad bargain.

I'll never forget the actual day. I knew it was going to happen, of course, but when I was told to dress in my best bib and then put into the nuns' parlour, I was shaking so hard I was sure those people would hear my bones rattling.

The parlour was a place of high shine and smells of wax polish, dark green pot plants and snowy white antimacassars that I'd been allowed enter only as a scrubber and polisher before. 'And mind you don't touch anything,' warned the nun in charge of exit interviews.

It was hard to obey. Even though I was so nervous, I was also very hungry because I hadn't been able to keep anything down since the previous night – and here was a tea tray on the piano, set with china cups and seedy cake and a piping hot teapot under a cosy that was embroidered with a picture of the Good Shepherd. Plus sherry and whiskey in cut-glass decanters and delicious little fairy finger biscuits. They'd know if I touched them, so I didn't, but when I was sure I was on my own, I deliberately spat a big gob into my hand and smeared it up and down the side of the piano. Kind of leaving my mark. I knew they couldn't do anything to me once I was gone. It was stupid and childish – and that was a real nice piano. Plus I was just making work for some poor misfortunate who'd have to clean it off later. It sure made me feel good, though.

The door opened. I'd been taught to bob in a little curtsy and I did this now. 'Good girl,' said this woman, Mrs Portman, all feathers in her hat and a lovely coat with big pearl buttons, and high-heeled court shoes. 'And is she honest?' she asked Sister. 'You can vouch for that?'

'We certainly can,' says the nun, all smiles and twinkly eyes and putting her hand on my head as if I was her favourite pet dog. The same nun that'd beat hell out of you quick as looking at you.

We had tea, and Mrs Portman had a small glass of sherry too. I minded my manners, because if I didn't God knew what the next woman would be like. At least this one didn't have horns. 'She'll do,' she said briskly, standing up and brushing a few crumbs on to the floor. You could tell she was used to someone else picking up after her.

So that was it. I'd do!

I *did*, all right. The house was one of them big old red-brick ones with bay windows, stained glass in the front door and miles of tiled floors and marble hearths and brasses to be polished. Winter or summer, I had to be up first in the morning to get the fires set and the range going. The house didn't have a basement so I was put sleeping in the scullery, but that was all right. It was grand actually: the kitchen was always warm and I had a nice feather mattress, good sheets and a warm Foxford blanket. Mrs Portman was a hard mistress and wasn't above giving me a clout, but I was up to her and never showed her I was afraid of her. I wasn't either, to be honest. As I told you before, I was tall and strong in them days. The food in the orphanage had been plain, mostly spuds and coarse bread, but the nuns got good milk, eggs and butter from local farmers and, except for the ones who got consumption, we all left there as healthy as trouts.

What did piss me, though, was that I had to call the two little Portman brats – and brats they were – 'Master' and 'Miss' and let them order me around, and them only a couple of years younger than myself. I had to go along with it, though, if I wanted to keep my job.

Dale's been and gone. How dare he? Hinting to Arabella I'm faking it. I'm not faking it. I can't open my eyes. Here. I'll try.

See? I can't. The eyelids weigh a ton but, yes, I accept I've got to wake up. There's precious time bleeding away. Especially with Willow being so antsy and all. I wonder what they think of Dale.

I'll wake up in a minute. I'll make another big, big effort. It's so nice down here, though, so floaty – and I'm so comfortable with my own thoughts and my own peace.

I never found out what Mr Portman did. He went off every morning early. He was always immaculate though – thanks to me and Sunlight soap and a lot of elbow grease with the flatirons – so I suppose he worked in some kind of an office. Maybe a bank or an insurance company.

In them days in the old country, not like now, you got time off at the pleasure of your employer, and mine's pleasure was that I got an hour for Mass on Sundays and holy days and a half-day to myself every Wednesday because Mr Portman had a half-day that day and he and Mrs Portman went out themselves, to the pictures, or to play golf, if it was fine, or to the Theatre Royal or the Queens or a tea party. So it suited them.

Well, in anyway, the first few Wednesdays, maybe even every Wednesday for the first few months, I didn't know what to do with myself on my half-day. The first time, I'm ashamed to admit it, for the whole six hours I skulked around the laneway at the back of the Portmans' house, the one with the gates for the cars and that. I didn't know where else to go. I made myself a little grotto in a gap I found in the weeds and bushes on the verge and pulled them back tight over me so no one who happened to be passing by would see me. It was lovely and dark and cool, I remember, and I fell asleep there for a while so it was night time nearly when I got back round to the front. 'Did you have a good time, Eve?' says Mrs Portman, when she opened the front door to me.

'Yes, ma'am,' says I, bold as brass.

'Where did you go?'

'Town.'

'And what did you do there?'

I was ready for this, in case she asked me what picture I'd seen or what café I'd been in or what. 'Oh, I just walked around, ma'am.'

'Good. You're just in time to do the vessels after the children's supper.'

So that was the holy all of my first outing after I went into service.

It took me four, maybe six goes, or seven, I don't remember exactly, a lot of Wednesdays in anyway, to get myself on to an omnibus and really into town. The conductor was kind: he thought I was a country girl (there was no mistaking that I was a maid, of course) and he counted out my farthings and ha'pennies for the right fare. 'You want to get off at Clery's, now, love,' he says. 'Sit there with your back to the engine and I'll look after you.'

It's hard to believe, I suppose, but in all the years at the home I'd never been into town. Not once. My life was the nuns and our dining room, our work and our chapel. It was a hard life but it was safe. You knew your place in the world. There was some of us that had fathers in gaol, or whose mothers had died of consumption and for them it was *really* hard because they knew what they were missing. I never knew what it was to be cuddled so I only imagined I missed it. There was a lot like me too, who didn't know where they were got. No one has ever had a clue where I came from. I think the police made enquiries and so forth after I was found, but nothing ever came of them. I've given up wondering. It would be nice to know something before I die, especially now that I've found my children and you'd never know, maybe grandchildren too. But that's a sort of hazy thing. Not real. And I don't feel a hole in my life or anything. Not any more.

One Wednesday, in July, a year and seven months into my employment, I was in the Broadway Café in O'Connell Street, treating myself to a cup of tea and a milk bun. I knew my way around the city by then and was quite relaxed.

Then, I remember it like it was an hour ago, I realised that here was this soldier casting his eye on me. Petey had a gamey eye, I'll give him that, and he used it to good effect with yours truly. Promised a lot of fun, that look did, and of course I fell for it. Great thick hair he had, and although he was a wee thing, smaller than me, he was well made. Here's what he does. He slides into the chair opposite me and gives me a wink. 'What's a nice country girl like you doing in the big city?'

Now, Dublin at that time was full of sailors and soldiers in uniform and it wasn't the first approach I'd had. 'I'm not from the country,' I say, bold as you like. 'I'm a Dublin woman. And I'll thank you to leave me in peace.'

He didn't. He got round me, oh, that guy! He could charm the birds off the bushes when he wanted to, and at the beginning Petey Moraghan threw everything he had into charming me. You win some, you lose some.

Oh, no! Willow's shouting, 'Arabella!' outside as if she can't stand it any more. Day-old chicks? That couldn't be about me, could it? I can't make out what they're saying now: that damned air-conditioner. It sounds like a locomotive with asthma.

Whether you believe it or not, America was always supposed to be temporary. I was going to make a few bob, first to pay back the loan to Maura, then to have a nest egg, come home, claim back my kids and be able to set us all up in a house somewhere, minus Petey Moraghan. I had this stupid vision of us all in a little cottage, with a whistling kettle. When I think back, I know now it came from a poem I learned by heart when I was very young. I can still say it:

> *Oh to have a little house,*
> *To own the hearth and stool and all*
> *The heaped-up sods upon the fire,*
> *The pile of turf against the wall.*
> *To have a clock with weights and chains*
> *And pendulum swinging up and down,*
> *A dresser filled with shining delph,*
> *Speckled and white and blue and brown.*

The poem is called 'The Old Woman of the Roads'; she's homeless, you see, and there's more in it, about being busy all the day sweeping and polishing and shining her speckled store of delph, but you get the picture. Yeah, I know it's sentimental, but it sounded so cosy and independent and free of hassle.

Did I ever think I'd fetch up in Robinia Meadows Trailer Park, Sedona, Arizona? Did I squat! However, that's life and all that garbage.

Voices raised again from outside. Willow's shouting again ... *Get off me!* Christ, they're having a boxing match now. Get up immediately, Eve Rennick. Pull yourself together ...

CHAPTER EIGHTEEN

'You wake her.'

'No, you. I don't want to touch her.' Willow picks up the pills and examines them, or pretends to. We're silent, listening for the slightest sound, watching for the smallest move. But although her eyelids are twitching big-time, Eve is stubbornly still, breathing easily, the green mask a little fogged.

The door opens. Then, clink-clink, yet another man, balding, early sixties, plain, short-sleeved white shirt tucked neatly into his chinos, is pushing through the beaded curtain. 'Hello there! I'm Robert, Mario's partner. Poor Mario is very agitated. He thinks you guys are a little upset. He's the sensitive type,' he smiles affectionately, 'so I guess you'll have to make do with me.'

I sense Willow's 'aha!' For some reason, I experience a little jump in my chest. As a 'partner', he isn't Dale's. Not that it matters a jot, of course.

'You're Arabella – so you must be Willow.' Having chosen correctly, this Robert shakes hands with us in turn. Dale, or Mario, must have filled him in as to which was the good-looking, glamorous one. Then he bends low over Eve and shakes her a little. 'C'mon, Eve! Wakey-wakey. It's party time, sweetie!'

Eve's eyes open. Milky. Looking from one to the other of us.

Now he hunkers in front of her. 'It's Robert, sweetie – you know, your little circle of friends? Robert and Mario? Dale, Mario, Robert, Gina? And you know Arabella, don't you? And Willow? They've come all the way from the Emerald Isle to see you.'

'It's white,' she says indistinctly.

'You having a dream, Eve?' He gets to his feet again and gently removes the oxygen mask. 'She's not been sleeping nights,' he says to us, 'and the painkillers are strong. Give her a little time.' Then, to Eve, while he's popping the lids off two pill bottles, 'So you've been having a nice visit, Eve? Such excitement, eh? Let's see here . . .' He takes a pair of glasses from the breast pocket of his shirt, checks labels. 'Here we are . . . Two of these, one of these – mmm . . . Wish I could take one of these myself. And don't you look like a baby when you're asleep, Eve.'

She's not paying attention to him but gazing at us.

Robert pours water from the carafe into a glass. 'Now, be a good girl.' He puts an arm round her shoulders and, cradling her head in the crook of his arm, feeds her the three tablets one by one. I feel like an intruder: these men and Gina, whoever she is, are Eve's family, not us. I'm over-whelmed by the need for a cigarette. But right now I can't get it together to make my excuses and go outside.

As soon as he has dispensed the tablets and a few more pleasantries, Robert says he and Mario have to go to town, wherever 'town' is. The emotions whizzing along the wires between Eve, Willow and me are too raw and unstable for the three of us to be left again without the pres-ence of a friendly outsider. 'Would it be OK if I asked Dale to come and join us?' It's out before I know it.

'Sure thing,' he says calmly. 'I'll tell him. No problem.'

We cover the gap left by Robert's departure with fussing over whether our mother is too warm, or too cold, or too much in between. More air-conditioning? Less? Does she want more coffee?

'Or perhaps tea, Mother?' Willow offers. 'I brought some Lyons tea. I thought you'd like to taste it again. I suspect it's been a long time since you had a cup of Lyons tea. I have it in my handbag. Shall I get it?'

'I'm fine,' Eve says finally. 'No tea, no coffee, no more blankets. I'm fine. But thank you.' The milkiness in the eyes has already given way to that paralysing stare.

Dale arrives, thank God, and with his quiet interventions we stumble through the next half-hour or so by not talking about anything that could be thought private. The sensitive subject of Rowan isn't mentioned except carefully in passing – nothing controversial, to give Willow her due. But it's early days so I'm watching everyone. Especially Dale. If he shows any sign of restlessness or of leaving us, I'm prepared even to rugby-tackle him to force him to stay.

So we catch up only with the basics as they currently stand in Ireland or, as Eve calls it, 'the old country' – a phrase I thought existed only in novels or films written by Irish-Americans. We range across Willow's perfect kids, Paddy, Willow's great job, mine (less great) at the hotel, my friendship with Greta, Willow's nice house, my less nice flat, what Dublin is like now, the skyline full of cranes, how Eve would hardly recognise any of it, with all the construction and urban renewal and so on.

'Sounds like a fascinating place.' Dale stands up and stretches lazily. 'Don't know about you all, but I hate air-conditioning. Why don't we go out on the deck?' He's not looking at either Willow or me, but at Eve. Somehow, though, I have the feeling that he's rescuing me. I don't want to be rescued, dammit. I'm perfectly capable of rescuing myself.

There's a palaver getting Eve out, opening doors for her, with her protesting, 'I *hate* this! This is dreadful! I'm not always this feeble, you know,' and that covers things a bit.

The light outside is still dazzling, and after the coolness in the trailer the air, hotter than before if that's possible, feels like we've entered a pizza oven. While Willow and I sit in a pair of canvas director's chairs, Dale settles Eve into a hammock-like seat, slung between two steel poles, then hands her a straw hat and a pair of large sunglasses, framed in tortoiseshell and decorated at the corners of the eyepieces with pink sequins. Think Dame Edna Everage.

With no sunglasses or a hat, I have to squint. It hurts. And after only two minutes out here, I can feel my scalp burning where the hair parts.

Dale to the rescue again. Before he sits down, he plucks a remote control from a side pocket in Eve's seat, presses a button and, from over our heads, an awning drones outwards from the side of the trailer, giving shade to the entire area. The guy is beginning to irritate me. Is there no end to his fecking goodness?

'Hello there, Dale, Evie. Lovely day?' A woman who has to weigh the best part of twenty stone under her electric blue muu-muu waddles up to us in that leaning-back, wide-legged way of pregnant and fat people. 'I'm going to the store. Want anything? It's lunchtime.'

'Thanks, we got it covered.' Dale crosses his legs.

The woman hesitates a bit, fiddling with her long, lank hair, and I know she wants to be introduced but he says nothing more and she barrels off. 'That wasn't Gina, was it?' Curiosity overcomes my being mad at Dale and I lean out to look after her. 'Robert mentioned that Eve had another friend called Gina.'

'No. That's not Gina.' He laughs to himself. 'That's Mary. We call her Mary Wu because she's our local Western Union. A flea don't jump on a dog but Mary wants to know why. You'll like Gina. She's a good one, lives a few streets away.'

'Will she be around today?'

'Should be. Gina don't like to rise early.'

'Is it always this hot here?' Willow kicks off her sandals.

'Shoot, it's only April. You all come back here in August!' Dale, too, bares his feet, slipping them out of his flip-flops. 'We're having a bit of an early heatwave right now, but it's not too unusual this time of spring. Tell 'em how you felt about the weather when you first came to Phoenix, Eve. That was August?'

Eve laughs. The outlandish sunglasses have slipped a little and she pushes them back up on to the bridge of her nose. 'I thought it was punishment for my sins – a preparation for the hobs of hell – especially coming from Chicago at the time, where the winters would freeze your toes off. I said that at the time, didn't I, Dale? I asked you. I said, "Why are you bringing me to this place that's hotter than the hobs of hell?"'

'Yep, that's what you said.' He smiles at us. 'She complained about the winters in the east, summers and winters in the midwest, nothing suited her. "Jesus, Mary and Joseph," she'd say to me, "where we goin' to next?" Our girl was religious back then – or acted as if she was. I think she pretended just to be ornery. She liked to quote your Irish hellfire missioners at me. We had many a doctrinal disagreement over the years, your mother and me!'

'"Back then"? Have you lost your religion, Mother?' Willow sits up. She and Paddy are quite holy: as far as I know, they all kneel down together as a family to say the Rosary before the kids go to bed. It has to be mainly Paddy because I remember Willow when she didn't believe in God. (I know I'm not being fair about Paddy, but I can't help it.)

'Lost my religion?' Eve is in no way put out at the implied disapproval. 'I'm not sure, actually. Sometimes yes, sometimes no. Will I tell you what I think death is? And heaven? And hell?'

'Hey, c'mon, Eve.' Dale stretches his long legs. 'It's sunny, it's a nice day, and these daughters of yours have just arrived. Give 'em a break.'

'No, that's all right, Dale.' Willow, on safe ground, speaks strongly. 'I'd like to have this discussion. I'd be interested in hearing our mother's views.'

Eve glances shrewdly at her. There is no longer much trace of the earlier disorientation. Far from it. 'Well, death first,' she says thoughtfully. 'I think death is quiet and glidey, with the pain shrinking down to nothing, and all of a sudden you're not responsible for anything any more, for nothing and no one, not even for the trouble you've caused. It's just you now. And everyone will think better of you. At least, they'll talk better about you, say nice things. That's what I think death is. Relief, really.

'As for purgatory and hell . . .' She pauses, eyes flickering from Willow to me and back again. 'That's all garbage dreamed up by powerful people to make us suffer in case we'd get a bit uppity and think we should be happy and that. Look at what happened to Limbo.' She leans forward, suddenly and scarily passionate. 'Gone with a stroke of a pen after all them centuries of heartbreak for people like Maura, who was crucified every day of her life because she thought her little unbaptised baby would never see heaven for all eternity, would never see her, or she'd never see him. "I don't want to go to heaven, Eve," Maura said to me, over and over again. "How could I go to heaven and him not with me?" That's the kind of thing that them high-up clergy used to be trying to get us to believe. Sure how could you be happy in heaven if you knew that you could never see your little baby ever again?'

Abruptly, the passion dies and she sits back, pained. 'There was no talking to her about it, though,' she says quietly. 'Maura was religious and she believed in everything they said, Limbo and all. She thought I was a heathen. I was, I suppose. Still am. I used to pray about you girls and Rowan, shouting at God and pleading with Him to do something, to help me make things right. But not in a good way, not accepting His Will and all that kind of thing. That's not religion, is it? It's more like habit or superstition or bribery. Well, that's what I think in anyway. You did ask.' She clams up. Looking at something inside her head.

'Who's Maura?' I ask faintly. Well, someone has to say something. Dale just looks amused. Willow is speechless.

But not for long. 'Excuse me,' she gets to her feet, 'if you don't mind, I need to ring home. They'll be all there and eating by now. My mobile doesn't work here. Is there a public telephone anywhere?'

'You can use my cell.' Dale reaches for his breast pocket.

'No, thank you.' Willow is already backing away. 'I'd really prefer to use a public booth.'

'There's a few . . .' Eve gives directions and Willow stalks off.

'Anyone feel like lunch?' Dale unfolds himself from his chair. 'It's all in the icebox. Mario does a mean shrimp salad. I'll bring it out. Ice water OK for everyone?' He doesn't wait for an answer, but goes inside.

Eve calls after him: 'And bring out the Kisses too, will you?' She turns to me. 'Have you tasted Hershey's Kisses, Arabella?'

'No, I can't say I have.'

Like a little girl's, Eve's face screws up with glee. 'They're swirls of pure chocolate. You'll love them. I had Dale get them especially for you and we've kept them in the refrigerator so they'll be nice and fresh and hard. They're scrumptious.'

I can't help smiling. Such a lovely old-fashioned word, 'scrumptious'. I hadn't heard it for years. 'Eat your stewed apple, girls, it's scrumptious.' Sister Marcellus. Or Martirio. Or one of the others. 'Great.' I smile at Eve.

What I'm thinking, though, is how, during the last forty-eight hours, the past, which for years sat at the back of my brain like a big, grinning onion, layer upon layer of it, has become as live as the present and feels as real. Dale's phone call had peeled away those layers, exposing them all and scattering them about, so when I pick something out of it, there's no dividing line between what *feels* like history and what's going on right under my nose.

He returns with a stack of plates, cutlery and the Kisses. 'For dessert, Eve,' he warns, and to me, confidentially 'Sweet tooth. Oh, my!'

'I'll set the table.' I take the ware from him and he goes back inside. Now I feel cheated. While Willow and I had been left with virtually nothing, this Dale seems to have a storehouse full of Eve's life.

She's watching me again. 'Tell me the story, Arabella,' she goes. 'What happened with Rowan? Why is Willow so horrible about him? Surely she should be trying to help him. You don't hate him like she does, do you?'

Carefully, too carefully, I lay the first place setting on the low garden table around which our chairs are arranged. 'She doesn't hate him, Eve. I don't either – it's just that . . . It's just that recently—' I stop. How am I going to explain to this woman that after our childhood, and even before Rowan's descent, her two daughters and son rarely spoke to each other, let alone met? No doubt she has fondly believed that after our incarceration in the orphanages, the three of us, who up to now had no other family, at least had each other to cling to for support. 'Willow doesn't seem to like much of anything at the moment,' I say lamely. 'She's OK, though. It's probably just a phase. And you should see them two of hers, Maeve and Dermot,' I say jollily – if there's such a word, 'they're dotes, they truly are. Maybe you'll get to meet them some day.'

'Maybe I will.' I haven't fooled her: she looks down at the deck.

I finish the place settings, taking my time about it.

'I'm glad we're by ourselves for the moment,' she says slowly.

There's something coming and I don't want it. I don't want a one-to-one. Not yet. So I straighten those knives and forks as if we're going silver service for the King of Siam.

'There's something I need to give you.'

She just won't stop, will she? No, she won't, is the answer. 'Will you go inside, Arabella, please, and ask Dale to get my tin box, and will you bring it out to me?'

'You have a tin box?' I'm so flabbergasted at the coincidence that I drop a spoon.

'You've answered my next question.' She watches me pick up the spoon. 'I was hoping you still had it. They're not quite identical, but mine is as near to yours as I could find. I searched high up and low down in yard sales and junk shops. I know it sounds stupid but I was trying for some kind of connection. I left mine to you in my will. Big deal, I hear you say.'

I can't stand looking at her – at all that intensity. 'I'll get it.'

Inside, Dale is spooning salad from a food container into a ceramic bowl. 'Not long, dressing's ready. Maybe you'd take the ice water out?' He points to the tray set with glasses and jug.

'Eve asked me to fetch her tin box.'

'She did, did she?' He wipes his hands on a tea-towel, then goes through a door, to the bedroom, presumably.

Eve's tin box is even more decrepit than mine. Like mine, it's oblong with a hinged lid, but instead of flowers, the corroded picture on it is of a lake and mountains. It might be Killarney. Greta and I went there once on a day trip by train: five hours each way with four and a half hours there. It was lashing rain and the wind was howling. 'A change is as good as a rest,' Greta said, so we bought a pack of cards in a souvenir shop and played gin in the lobby of the Great Southern Hotel until it was time to go home. They relayed music through the train's loudspeakers and people did party pieces and we ended up having a great time.

'Are you going to take it out to her, or will I?' Dale brings me back to reality.

Eve watches every step as I arrive back outside. 'Open it.'

On top is a document tied with a piece of frayed bias-binding. I take this out, exposing a layer of flimsy fabric, yellow and spotted with age. 'What's this?' I don't touch it, afraid it might fall apart in my hands. 'It's the baby dress I was found in,' she says. 'Christmas Eve 1944.'

This will take some time to sink in. I untie the bias-binding and unroll the documents. Eve's birth certificate. *Child's name: Eve. Sex: F. 24 December 1944. Mother: unknown. Father: unknown.*

I think this is the moment when Eve becomes real to me. There's something moving and permanent about a birth certificate. It's a formal record – and recognition – that you exist. Have existed. And now I hear it again, clear as diamonds, the sound of a voice. It's faint, faraway, high and musical: *'Arabella Moon! Come out, come out, wherever you are!'*

We must have been playing hide and seek, Eve and me, I can't remember where, it certainly wasn't in our room. The only visual clue I have is a hazy one, of being inside a big piece of brown furniture – a cupboard or a wardrobe. And the smell: cloth, maybe. Or precious wood, mahogany or cedar. Even more than the sound of her voice, the pleasure comes from what it represents. Eve might have had a pet name for the others but if she had they don't remember because they were too young when she left. She had one for me, though, and I remember. I am Arabella Moon. It's so personal and special it makes me shiver to think of it.

She's still watching me. 'I was found in a shoebox. A few hours old.'

'So small? Must have been a big shoebox?' The image was unbearable.

'I believe I was premature,' she says quietly.

'Why are you showing this to me? What about Willow?' Shakily, I put the certificate back in the tin. I don't dare look at her: I don't want to think about what she has just said. The world feels fragile around me and I feel I'm in danger of destroying something. Maybe her. Maybe even my idea of myself. I know it sounds ridiculous, but that's how it feels.

'All in good time. You're the eldest, Arabella. Aren't you going to look at the rest of it? Are you going to read the diary?'

'I haven't had a chance yet, Eve. I have it in my handbag.'

'It's sort of my life story.' She seems to be pleading.

I hate this. I don't know what to say.

'It ain't pretty but it's what happened,' she goes on. 'I added to it over the years. I always prayed I'd meet you, Arabella, and I'd be able to tell you in person so you wouldn't have to get this through some big-shot attorney or something – oh!' Her tone changes, 'Here's Willow back again! I hope there's nothing wrong at home.'

I look up. There has to be something wrong – my sister is half running. She never runs, except officially, for exercise.

'Paddy was as mad as hell that I didn't ring earlier,' she gasps, as she rushes up the steps on to the deck. 'He didn't realise that my mobile doesn't work over here. They found Rowan yesterday just after we left. He's on his way here – his flight is due to land in just over an hour and a half.'

CHAPTER NINETEEN

Fucking A! If I don't get a smoke soon I'll kill someone. I mean it. I'll strangle someone with my bare hands or kick someone's head in or do something desperate. I don't care if I'm arrested. I'll give myself up. I'll walk up to someone in a uniform, blow smoke in his face and invite him to arrest me. It'd be worth it for just one drag – my mouth is like a sandpit, my teeth are on fire. See that fucking cactus plant over there? It's dead meat. I'm going to shred it, I am. *I have to have a smoke . . .*

I've never been on a plane before. At my age. Can you believe that?

It looks all great on the box, smily bints bending down on their ankles and giving you glasses of champagne with little serviettes. Jeez. How wrong can the telly be? Your knees up to your chin and a pain in your arse from sitting for what feels like three whole days and people snoring and your nose all stuffed up. Kids throwing stuff around and knives that break if you try to cut anything. Not that there's anything to cut. Mush. Crap mush.

And they make these announcements about not hesitating to call them if they can be of any help but if you push the little red bell thing over your head they come down and snap it off, 'Yes?' and glare at you as if you've farted into their handbags.

Christ. It's the last time I'm getting on a plane, I can assure you of that. And once you get on the fucking thing you can't get off. They don't give out parachutes. Only lifejackets, for fuck's sake, like you're on the fucking *Titanic.*

I'm an arsehole. I should've done what I wanted to do in the first place. Set myself up with that money.

What got into me?

I'll tell you what got into me. Softness in the head – that's what got into me. Me mammy! The little boy wanted to see his mammy.

111

Well, I've news for everyone. I'm not a total pushover. All right, I got the fucking suit and the shoes and all, but I got them in Fred's Fashions for twenty-two notes all in. Including a suitcase. So that's me up nearly two eighty of their clean-yourself-up-Rowan money. Well, two. I bought a few cartons of smokes to bring with me.

It was Mental who told me Fred's had a new delivery. Yeah, after the mill and all, you're probably surprised that we're on speaking terms, but where that's concerned Mental makes the rules. And he's not the type to hold grudges.

I ran into him when I was coming out of the passport office. He was trying to do a car on the opposite side of the street but when he saw me he left it and came over. I think he was feeling guilty about the mill. Didn't apologise, of course, just said he probably overreacted. 'I just lost it. You know how it is, Rosie?' He calls me 'Rosie' but I value my health and I don't argue. Then he offers me a smoke. They were only roll-ups but any port in a storm and we light up. 'This is a bit off your patch, Rosie?' he says then. 'What the fuck are you doing in there?'

He's looking a bit aggrieved, like I'm muscling in or something, so I tell him I had to come in to the passport office because I have to go to America. He relaxes. 'That'll be nice, Rosie,' he says. 'That'll do you good. This place is fucked anyway.' He takes a drag. 'The U-nited States of A-merica,' he says then, drawing it out and letting the smoke curl through his nose, 'land of the Pil-grim Fa-thers.' Then he looks me up and down. 'You going in them threads?'

'No. I have to find something.'

So that's when he tells me about the new delivery in Fred's. And leaves me with a handy little profit. What they don't know won't hurt them.

For fuck's sake. Another fucking queue here for the luggage. I wouldn't mind but all I brought was a few socks and cacks. And the sleeping-bag. They're not worth waiting for.

I'm telling you, I'm going to light up. One more minute is what I'm giving it and I don't care if they send me to that place in the middle of the sea. The one with the Birdman. I don't care if they put me on Death Row. I don't care if they fucking shoot me.

CHAPTER TWENTY

Phoenix Airport is still relaxed. There are a few more kids around than when we arrived and it's hotter in spite of the air-conditioning. Willow frets, looking at her watch for the umpteenth time. 'That flight landed hours ago.'

'Twenty minutes,' I point out.

'If you ladies will excuse me, I'm going to the john.' Not surprisingly, Dale leaves us. Being with us right now has to be like keeping company with the Twitchy Sisters.

When we heard Rowan was coming, the lunch was abandoned. Dale went off to get his pickup, while Willow and I made sure Eve had everything she needed during the time we – and Robert and Mario – would be absent. 'He's coming? He's really coming?' Eyes shining, our mother submitted happily to our fussing. Everything we'd revealed to her, or that Willow had revealed to her about our brother, seemed to have had little effect. Even the gossip lady, Mary Wu, evidently sensing drama, stopped by, adding to the confusion by asking questions, offering to help and generally getting in the way.

Controlled chaos, I think they call it.

For me, shattered anyway, the prospect of Rowan's imminent arrival, which I saw as a sort of black whirlwind, was nerve-racking. Still is. I don't have to tell you why, I hope, but if he comes off that plane either stoned or drunk, as I fear he will, how are we going to handle it? It's always a worry. You'd never know what state he'll be in. In Dublin it hardly matters, except emotionally, but in front of Dale? And if things aren't right when he's meeting Eve for the first time?

Shit – I'm doing that empathy thing again, feeling his pain, her pain, feeling responsible for inconveniencing Dale. All the way to the airport I turned myself inside out apologising for taking him all the way back to the airport so soon, but he batted me away until I copped myself on and got back into my shell. Willow, stiff and uncommunicative, also played to type, tapping her fingers on her shoulder-bag like it was an accordion, seriously getting on my nerves. Sometimes I wonder how we came out of the same womb, her and me; maybe one of us was put into the wrong cot in the maternity hospital.

'This is ridiculous.' She has carried the tapping with her into the arrivals hall so, naturally, I take on *her* fears now and my need to make everything right kicks in.

'I never thanked you for organising the fares, Willow,' I go, in my most sugary voice. 'Thanks a million. I'll pay you back every penny, don't worry, and half of Rowan's, of course.'

'It wasn't easy, you know.'

'I know. Don't rub it in.' So much for sweetness. I had been about to ask where she got the money but I had no desire to prolong the humiliation. On the other hand, things are going to be tough enough for poor old Rowan when he lands in; the last thing he needs is to come out to the two of us snapping at each other. 'Hey, Willow, I meant to tell you –' I have to hand it to myself. I'm a trier '– but I didn't get the chance. Eve has a tin box like ours. She gave it to me to look at. I haven't been through it properly yet, though.'

Silence from Willow.

'I haven't got it, actually, I left it behind when we were in such a rush to come here, but somehow I don't think she had it easy.'

'Did we?' Straight ahead.

'By the way, one thing I did see. Her birth certificate is in it.'

This brings her round sharpish. 'When did she show you all this?'

'When you were off ringing Paddy.'

'Why didn't you tell me before?'

'This was the first opportunity I got. I didn't want to blab it out in front of Dale. Be reasonable.'

'Reasonable? You're the one who insisted on leaving messages for Rowan – now look what you've got us into. Well, you can look after him.'

'We've been over and over this. The bottom line is he's her son. He deserves to see her every bit as much as we do.'

'If you say so.' She goes back to staring rigidly ahead. Then, pretend-casual, 'What's on this birth certificate anyway?'

'Nothing we don't know. Just her first name. Eve. Female. Mother and father unknown.'

'So!' She pulls a face. 'No apple-cheeked grannies for us, surprise, surprise!' Then, quietly, looking at her shoes, 'If her mother and father are unknown, where did she get the surname Rennick that she put on our birth certificates as our mother? I never told you but a few years ago I rang every Rennick in the Irish phone books. I spent a fortune on Directory Enquiries here and in the UK, getting lists of Rennicks in England, even in Wales.'

'Did you ring all them too?'

'Yes.'

'Thinking we might have relatives?'

'Yes.' Her expression warns me not to get too close. 'So where'd she get the Rennick?'

'Who knows?' I shrug. But of course I'm gob-smacked: after her telling me about trawling for our father, this second revelation from a woman who has moved on, put everything behind her, is simply not interested in our dysfunctional family? 'At the first opportunity, we'll ask her.'

'Did she show you anything else?'

'I didn't see much more but there is other stuff in that box. The dress she was found in, apparently. She was only a few hours old, Willow. And guess what? It's a coincidence, I suppose, but she was found on Christmas Eve just like we were.'

Willow gets it immediately, as I had. She stares at me in horror. 'You mean she deliberately chose the same date for us?'

'It was her birthday. And she was only twenty.'

'That's sick, Arabella,' Willow wasn't buying, '*sick*.' Then something catches her eye and, in a different tone, she says, 'He's not wearing any socks, dammit.'

'Where is he?' I look where she's looking and see Rowan scanning for us as he makes his way slowly through the crowds. Last time I'd seen my brother, some months previously, he had been clean-shaven, sort of, with a rash of dark stubble, and a buzz-cut, less than a quarter-inch away from bald. Now the hair is collar-length or even longer and he's fully bearded. (One-third grey. Now, there's a jolt!) The new suit hangs well on him although the trousers are a bit short; when you see Rowan hunched up and filthy in his jeans and holey jumpers, he looks much smaller than he

115

really is. He isn't staggering or wandering. He's upright. He's clean. The lights above his head create a shine on his hair. 'He seems fine, Willow.' I'm dizzy with relief. 'Steady. Maybe things are going to turn out great. Doesn't that beard suit him?'

Willow is far from smitten. 'Yes, of course our drug-addict brother is going to behave like St Francis of Assisi while he's here.'

'Well, the suit's not right but he has the beard and the Jesus hair.'

She shoots me another of her looks.

'Come on, Willow, where's your sense of humour?' I wave to catch Rowan's attention. 'Give the guy a chance.'

He spots me and speeds up a little. As he comes closer, I notice that the suitcase is bouncing in his hand with each step: he hasn't much in it. And Willow's right about no socks: he's showing six inches of skinny ankle under the too-short trousers. By and large, though, I'm delighted to see he has made such an effort. Or that someone, probably Paddy to give him his due, has made the effort on his behalf.

Rowan and Dale reach us at the same time. Just as well, too, because our brother is not the chattiest person in the world; simply by being there, the American acts as a sort of bridge between us all.

Guess who takes up the slack here, introducing the two men and so on (a waste of time because Rowan, rooting in a pocket for his cigarettes and lighter, doesn't have the courtesy to extend his hand) and making small-talk about how I hope the flight was OK. But, having continued to ignore Dale as though he is a taxi-driver, Rowan is now ignoring me too and cuts across my welcome speech: 'Is there anywhere in this kip to have a fucking smoke?'

I give him a dig in the ribs, a hard one. Keeping him between me and Dale, and my voice low so our host won't hear, I say, 'Language! This isn't Dublin. Try and respect what's going on here. We're with nice people. People who don't use curse words like that, so just watch it, right?' Then, brightly, 'Sure, Rowan. You can have a cigarette outside. Then I suggest we all get a move on and go back to the trailer park straight away. Eve can't wait to see you.'

'I'm starving, but!' he objects.

Willow and I, acting together for once, take an arm each, with Dale ambling behind us. 'If you're hungry, Rowan, we can get a hamburger or something on the way.'

While we wait for Dale to come with the pickup, I join Rowan with a cigarette of my own. 'So, everything worked out?'

'Yeah, yeah.' He drags deeply. Willow, meanwhile, is standing four feet away. *Who are these people? Certainly no acquaintances of mine . . .*

'So do you want me to tell you about Eve, or should I not say anything in advance, let you make up your own mind?'

'Fuck off, Arabella. Leave me alone. It was a mistake coming here.' Then, furtively, 'Sorry. I'll try. OK?'

'The one thing you need to know is that she's had a car accident, nothing too serious, but she has broken ribs and a cast on one of her legs. There's an oxygen bottle, but don't get a fright, eh? It's cool.'

'So when I meet her, the message is, I'm not to say, first-off, "Howya, Hopalong!" Right?'

It's feeble, of course, but it's a long time since I heard Rowan crack a joke. This is historic. Nevertheless I don't push my luck, just smile and nod and pretend to watch out for Dale, while I'm thinking that maybe it was a mistake to press for Rowan to come. So far so good, but this could go either way. I steal a sideways look at him. He's allowing the smoke from his cigarette to curl upwards, watching it make shapes. With a start I realise that, cleaned up and without the scowl he wears like a uniform, he is very handsome: great cheekbones and Eve's marvellous eyes. Looks a bit like Daniel Day-Lewis, actually. He senses me looking at him: 'What?'

'I'm glad to see you looking so well, Rowan. It's a treat.'

'Don't start, Bel . . .' but I can see he's pleased.

With the best will in the world, the pickup's cab can't accommodate four people so Rowan has to ride in the open bed at the back. 'No problem, mate.' He smiles at Dale. Unlike those of his contemporaries on the street, Rowan's teeth have survived pretty well. 'I'm knackered so I'll just bunk into this and everything's game ball.' He opens his suitcase and pulls out an ancient, stained sleeping-bag. I'm mortified but I cop myself on. *Remember he's making an effort. Give him credit. And he's not your son, or a teenager, he's a separate person. He's your brother and an adult . . .*

We set off and each time I check through the little window behind my neck, our brother is asleep, or seems to be; the sleeping-bag is a violent green and, having wrapped himself around the suitcase, using it like an anchor, he looks like a big caterpillar.

'Time's gettin' on, ladies.' Dale's voice makes me jump.

We're half-way back to Robinia Meadows and all three of us in the cab have passed the first part of the trip locked into our own worlds. I had been lost in a fantasy involving Eve and myself in a *Little House on the Prairie* scenario where I would pluckily nurse her back to health, or at least be her companion and lead her to a Happy Death. Prayers for a Happy Death had been big in St Camilla's.

'We should make plans as to where you're going to bed down tonight,' he continues. 'You want I should book you another motel? They're pricey in town, but maybe I can do a deal. I don't think you'd all be comfortable in Eve's trailer, since you're not accustomed to trailer livin'.'

'Yes.' I glance at Willow. 'I suppose we should think about that.'

'You want to leave it to me? You happy with that?'

'Of course we are.' I signal Willow to take some part in this but she keeps her eyes trained solidly on the road ahead. 'Thank you, Dale. I don't know what we'd have done without you.'

'Wouldn't be here, would you?' He laughs, a surprisingly hearty guffaw. Then: 'It's my pleasure. Eve has changed all our lives.'

'Oh? And how's that? How did she do that?' As alert as a hare now, Willow sits forward in her seat and leans out to look across me at him.

'Ohh,' Dale says in his deliberate, slow way, 'she's a very special person, your mom. She gave us all somethin' to live for. Before Eve came into our lives, we were pretty much swingin' in the wind. Separately, of course. Eve and I weren't acquainted with Robert and Mario and Gina and the others before. But we got here and it all made sense. I had no one. Gina had no one. Robert and Mario had each other but they fight so much over nothin' – or they used to in those days, that sometimes it was like they had no one either.'

'Where did they come into the picture?'

'When Eve and me were passin' through this little place in Alabama. I don't know if you know this, ladies, but at that point Alabama wasn't exactly puttin' out the welcome mat for queers.'

'I can imagine.' At home I'd never dream of calling a homosexual 'queer'. 'Go on, Dale.'

'Let's put it this way: if Eve hadn't intervened, they might have been tarred and feathered.'

'You don't mean literally?' I'm shocked.

118

'Naw. Of course not. But she has this way with her, you know? So next thing everyone's bein' real polite and the two of 'em are taggin' along with us. It's not like we're a convoy or anything, it's just that our paths kept crossin' and then we all ended up here. So now we all have Eve, all of us together, because in a way she was the one who brought us all to the Meadows.' He grins at us. 'Makes no sense to you at all, does it?'

'Of course it does, Dale.' Nice and all as he is, I'm getting a little bit irritated with the ducking and diving. 'So you met her in New York?'

'Yep.'

'Please, let us in on it. What's the big secret? What are you both hiding?'

'No secret. It's your mom's story, though, ain't it? She'll want to tell you.'

'I'm sure she wouldn't mind. We have four lifetimes to catch up on, hers and three of ours. And we haven't got all that much time.'

The story proves to be a short one. Dale had been out 'socialisin'' with a few buddies one evening in Queens, New York, when 'I'm on my way home and, Lordamighty, right in front of my eyes this Chevy climbs up the back of a gas truck at a red stop light. The gas starts leakin' and with both the engines still runnin' it's only a matter of time before she blows, so I run over to the passenger side, because that's the side that's seems farthest from the truck — although it's a toss-up. And what do I find?' He chuckles reminiscently. 'The door's buckled and stuck shut but here's this lady, one leg out through the open passenger window and one still inside, and she's tryin' to drag this big heavy guy out through the window with her. Herself, she's like a broken doll, I can see that already. One arm's danglin' by her side, there's blood all over her hair and face where she hit against the windshield and her chest is all bloody too, but here she is, half-way in and half-way out, her good arm around this guy's neck, pullin' and haulin' and heavin' at him. It's a waste of time, you know, because he's already a goner. His neck's broke but she don't see that. I try to grab her but she fights me and tells me she's not goin' anywheres until she gets this guy out, but I grab her anyway and run with her to get out of the way — and bam! We make it just in time. She don't hear the explosion, though, because she's already passed out in my arms. That lady was your mom and that's how we became friends. And it's the mercy of God that they were drivin' that night with the windows open.'

119

It was a long speech but Willow doesn't give him time to recover. 'Who was the driver?'

Dale shrugs. 'Dunno. I stayed with your mom, brought her to the hospital and so forth, but I was right. The guy had died instantly, it said in the newspaper next day. Weren't news to me, his head was hangin' sideways. The driver of the truck survived, though, and it was probably him that told the newspaper your mom was a heroine. She got headlines.'

'Did she ever tell you the man's name?' Willow remains unimpressed by our mother's heroism. 'Or how she knew him? Or what she was doing with him that night?' She is so tense now she's shaking, head to toe. Dale either doesn't notice, or is too polite to indicate that he has. 'Nope,' he says. 'And I didn't ask, none of my business. She was unconscious for days. We nearly lost her.'

'Can you remember anything at all about this man? Colour of hair? Was he a small man?'

'He was middlin'.' He glances curiously at her. 'Don't remember about his hair, though. Why? Do you think you might know who he was?'

'Not at all, I was merely trying to fix the image in my mind.' My sister sits back in her seat.

I want to give her a hug but that might prove catastrophic. She certainly wouldn't welcome it. You see she thinks – thought – that this man might have been our father. That wouldn't have occurred to me.

CHAPTER TWENTY-ONE

I can't wait to tell you this. It's night again; Willow and I are in a B-and-B type hotel in this amazing town, Sedona. It's really worth describing and I'll tell you about it some other time but, right now, I just have to tell you about the most extraordinary thing that happened this afternoon when we got back from the airport with Rowan. If I were a religious person I'd say it was a first-class miracle.

I've got to tell you *exactly* the way it went. So bear with me because I'm going to explain it step by step, as it happened, including everything that led up to it. It's just too exciting to blurt it out straight; it's the kind of thing I want to get story value out of.

Right. Here goes.

First off, Rowan sleeps the whole way back to Robinia Meadows. When we get back, there's Eve, still in the chair where we left her. As soon as she sees us, she gets up under her own steam (she has the crutch all ready) and comes to the top of the steps, so she's standing there, waiting. We get out. Willow goes straight up into the trailer to use the bathroom. I wake Rowan. He gets up, hair mussed, suit creased. His two feet haven't even hit the ground when Eve starts crying.

Rowan stands at the bottom of the steps like a big lunk, ankles showing, not knowing what to do or say. She holds out her arms. He does this sort of shuffle thing with his feet, like he's deciding whether or not to do a runner, but at the last minute he goes up the steps and lets her hug him. He doesn't put his arms round her, mind, he's as stiff as a wooden ladder, but from where I'm standing, I can see his eyes are closed. Hers are too but tears are pouring out from under the lids.

I feel my own waterworks springing up and decide this will not do anyone any good so I look behind me, searching for Dale, but Dale's walking away towards his own place.

I can hardly get back into the pickup or hide under a bush.

I can go inside to join Willow, I think, so I work my way round Eve and Rowan, muttering, 'Excuse me,' as I go.

It's lovely and cool inside and I breathe hard, nearly panting. I hadn't realised I'd been holding my breath. No sign of Willow, but I can hear water running behind the bathroom door. I'm trying not to eavesdrop on what's happening on the deck – it'd be difficult to make out anyway because of the air-conditioner going full blast. I can just about hear a low murmur: don't know which of them is talking, though, male or female. My guess is it's Eve.

I sit on the couch. Beside me, Eve's tin box seems to raise itself up on its hind legs and crook a finger at me: *open, Sesame* . . . I'm trapped here, I think, so I might as well – and before I know it, I'm rifling through it, breathing in the musty, sweetish smell, like burned paper, that comes from it.

I'm careful with the fragile baby dress, putting it gently on the couch. Underneath is a worn manila envelope; inside it are letters, several, on different types of stationery, all with American stamps. They're addressed to 'Maura Rennick, c/o Bernie Rennick' at an address in the Irish midlands, but every envelope is covered with additional handwriting: 'addressee unknown' or 'not known at this address'. There's also official 'Return to Sender' franking from both the Irish and US postal services. All have been torn open and numbered from one to seven, big figures in red biro, obviously printed by Eve herself. I hesitate for a second, then extract the letter from number one. The pages have been folded and refolded many times. The handwriting is childish. Page one seems to be missing so it begins at page two:

hard work Maura them fires is a killer. They use a lot of wood in them over here its a fine kind of ash that woud chok you but one grate thing they have dum waiters (electrisity) so you dont have to cary the food up all the stars and cary the vesels down again to the kitchen. You get a haf day off every week and a whole day once a month as well so I will have lots of time to write to you. I am lerning to drink coffee its not too bad when you get used to it. My imployer is a real lady. She is a Jewess her name is Mrs Finkelstein and I can tell you my eyes are opend because she coud teech catolics a thing or two about how to treet peeple. She dusnt ask nosy questions all she wants to know is if your honest and not afrad of hard work. We have another maid from the Filipeens but I don't have much to do with her becase shes mostly takeing care of the children and the cook is from Mexico. Them two don't speek English very well but they are nice. Its a nice atmosfeer in the house the children (2) are well behavd. We all have our own rooms mine is nice and cosy with good warm blankets and a big wardrob. We dont anser the door. Mrs Finkelstein ansers it herself in case its the law looking for ileegals. Im not worried. Mrs Finkelstein says she knows a lot of highup peeple and if anything hapens they'll look after me.

As you know I am a lot of times in aggony when I think about what I did with the children. But Maura I had to think of whats best for them. This way they will get an education beter than what I got I am sure with the beter times thats coming soon in Ireland. I hope that they will forgiv me somtime but even if they dont what kind of a mother was I to them not able to feed them proper even with all the skivying I did in the big houses in Ranelagh and b and bs in Drumcondra at five oclock in the morning and up all ours washing other peeples sheets. If I left them with Petey Id be afrad hed harm them when hes drinking theres no talking to him. One of them probably Arabella shed be dead you know what hes like when he has drink and she would anoy him mabe by aksing to many questions. No they are defnittly better off. And since he didn't come home lately I'm sure as sure he didn't look for them. I wonder dos he know yet? I get very lonly sometimes when I think about the 3 of them. But I try to keep bisy and not to mope. I do hope dear Maura that you will think kindly of me when you go to Mass. I am never going to Mass again as long as I live. Where were them clergy when me and my kids were hungry? And how dare that old bee in the confeshon box tell me to go home and make peice with my husband that time when I complaned him.

I tell you what I am not sorry about as well. I am not sorry I hoked my wedding ring and my silver broch that Petey gave me that time when he won at the dogs and was sorry sorrying all over the place. No suveneers, a clean brake good ridance!!!!! I am still anoyed that I only got 28 pounds from the pawn for the ring and the broch and all my few bits of sticks from the room. And that mattres was a good one too Maura. But it is all water under the brige now.

My God if I hadint you dear Maura I woud of never had the money for my passage. Thank you thank you. May God be good to you and I will be sending it all back to you as quick as I can. Not all together Im afrad but as much as I can evry month like this month Im sending you 43 dollars I hope it arives safly and is not robd by robers in the post. Im on a good wage here so after I pay you off Ill be able to save and that way Ill see you and the children again real soon. When you get this leter don't forget to write me back and give me your new adres and by the way please thank your cosin Bernie for takeing this leter for you. I hope your hapy in your new home wherever it is and that its what you have wanted all your life.

So goodbye for now dear Maura. The next leter Ill be sending you with some more money Ill tell you all about New York. Its just like Id imagind only nearly beter. Its very hot now because its the sumer but they have great parks and air condishon in the houses and all the shops. Ill tell you all about the shops next time. You can by anything you want. And Im geting to like Jewish food. Woud you beleiv that! Its called deli over here.

Your loving friend,
Eve

PS Some of the men over here are nice as well nicer than youd meet at home in anyway defnittly nicer than the mickydazlers I met in my time! Some of them back there youd think they were from the zoo no names no pak drill Maura!

I can hear footsteps coming across the deck towards the door into the kitchen and I shove the pages back into their envelope any old how.

And now Willow is coming out of the bathroom. 'What's that?' She stares at the letter, then sees the baby dress and the other envelopes scattered around the open tin box. 'Is that what you were telling me about at the airport?'

'Yeah – ssh! There's someone coming, I'll fill you in later.' I hold the letter behind my back.

Rowan comes through the crystal curtain. Above the beard, his cheeks are pink, but of course, I tell myself quickly, it's a hot day. He stops just inside the door. 'She says why don't you come outside?'

'Sure.' I'm flustered. 'Willow and I are just getting a few lunch things ready. I know you're starving. And I'm sure Eve must be too. Tell her we'll be out in two shakes of a lamb's tail.' I hesitate. 'Are you OK, Rowan?'

He doesn't reply to this, but pushes back through the door. 'What's in that?' Willow reaches to take the letter out of my hand as I go to return it to its manila envelope with the others. But I hold it out of her reach. 'Later, Willow, please. We have to get out there. Anyway, it needs a bit of discussion. There's a bunch of them here.'

'From whom?' Willow always becomes grammatically correct when she's tense.

'It's actually from her to this friend of hers she mentioned. Maura. There's more of them, all the same, I think. Look, Willow, we'll talk about it later. I promise I'll show you. But now's not the time, not with Rowan's just landed in and all.'

'I'm her daughter too, you know!'

'I know. I promise.'

There's a small stand-off. But I'm not giving in. I know that for all my accusations about Willow's unreasonableness I'm the one guilty here, but I want to go through these myself first. Something (again) about being the eldest? I'm Arabella Moon. Eve entrusted that stuff to me. 'When? When will you deign to show it to me?' My sister's face is turning red.

'When all three of us get the opportunity to be together. Tonight when we're in a motel or something. OK? I promise.'

Another stand-off but then she turns away, and while I tidy away all the stuff on the sofa, she opens the door of the fridge. 'There's too much food here, even with Rowan being an extra. How much will we take out?'

I spot a serving tray on a wire shelf above the sink and pull it down. 'Let's put out as much as this tray will hold, OK?' She doesn't answer and so, wrapped in her thick, offended silence, we sort out the food: Mario's salad, some cheese and cold cuts, potato salad and a little dish of olives. Leaving her to figure out how to extract ice from the icemaker on the fridge door so we can have ice water, I pick up the laden tray and go out.

Rowan's sleeping-bag and suitcase are in a corner of the deck, but of him there's no sign. 'Where is he?' I ask Eve, who's back in her perch, eyes covered with the Dame Edna sunglasses.

'He said he'd be back in a moment.' She sounds uncertain.

I set about unloading the tray. 'How did it go?'

She hesitates, fiddling with the buttons on her cardigan. 'Arabella, can I ask you something?'

'Shoot!'

'Was Willow exaggerating about Rowan? He seems very quiet. It's hard to believe all that stuff about him being a junkie and a bum.'

I'm standing in front of her, wondering how to handle this, when a voice sounds right beside me: 'Have a nice trip?'

I jump. 'Sorry?'

It's a woman. She's wearing those moccasin things so she can walk without making a sound. Even on gravel, apparently. 'Did you have a nice trip?' she repeats, not looking at me but giving the side of Eve's hammock a friendly little thump. 'How you doin' today, lady?'

'Great. Gina, this is Arabella, my elder daughter.' Eve remains subdued but smiles from one to the other of us. 'Arabella – Gina.'

The woman (girl?) finally turns to me and shakes my hand. Another who likes to break bones. I try not to wince. 'Very nice to meet you, Gina.' In my imagination, Ginas are Italian film stars, with sultry eyes, pouty mouths and hourglass figures. This one is small and scrawny, with sun-leathered skin, a lazy eye and hair dyed to the colour of nasturtiums. She's wearing ripped jeans in a size far too large for her so they're hanging precariously on her skinny hips, and a sleeveless vest that was once white. It's impossible to tell what age she is, anything from thirty to fifty. 'This sure looks good.' She surveys the table. 'Mario make that salad?'

'He did, yes.'

'Great! That guy sure makes an awesome salad.' Without being invited, she moves to the table and I notice she has a limp. She sits in one of the chairs, back to the wall of the trailer.

'Help yourself,' I say, too late, as she has already plunged the servers into the bowl and is transferring piles of lettucy things to a plate.

'I'll get another place setting.' I'm mentally calculating how to fit it on to a table full enough with four. 'Two, actually, Arabella.' This is Eve. 'Don't forget Dale will be along too, I'm sure.'

Now I don't think I'm behind the door when it comes to imagination, but never in my wildest fancies would I have conjured up the crowd of oddballs surrounding Eve. One thing we were taught in our convent, however, was to know our place. Eve's friends are her own business. So I squash down the impolite enquiries or comments that are bubbling up.

What happened to your leg? Where do you fit in with Robert and Mario? Are you a lesbian? And if you're not, have you a relationship with Dale? Is that how you got involved in this ménage?

Unaware of my scrutiny, the new arrival is chewing heartily. 'So where's the other one, Willow?'

'She'll be out in a minute. Speaking of Rowan, you didn't happen to see him, did you, Gina? Tall, longish hair? Beard?'

'Good-looking guy wearing a suit?'

'Yes.'

'Aha!' she says. 'Thought so! A guy in a suit in the Meadows? Yeah, right – I saw him for a second. He was walking down that road between Dale's place and Mary Wu's – he's hot! Except for the suit, of course.' Now she sees something over my shoulder. 'This him?'

Sure enough, our brother is walking slowly towards the trailer. I wait until he gets within earshot. 'We were getting worried. Where'd you go?'

'For f—' Rowan pushes forward his chin, then remembers where he is and mumbles, 'I had to have a slash.'

I make a mental note to inform him that mobile homes have bathrooms these days. 'Come and eat.'

He climbs up to us and I introduce him to Gina.

Now here comes this amazing thing, this first-class miracle I've been leading up to all this time. She stands and sort of bellies up to him, cocking her head to one side. 'Hi there, Rowan! Welcome to the Meadows. I'm Gina.'

'I'm Rowan.' He smiles down at her and something happens.

I swear to God, as true as I'm lying here in this bed, as true as Willow's cheeping again in her sleep, I actually saw and felt something weird happen between Rowan and this woman. I have never experienced anything like it before. The only way I can describe it is to tell you that a kind of shiver jumped across the air from one to the other of them and back again. If I were to draw it (I can't draw, of course) it would be like that bright blue lightning zigzag you see in cartoons or commercials on the TV.

On my sacred word of honour, I swear to God I didn't imagine it, and I'm not now retrospectively Mills and Booning it. The sensation lasted probably a millionth of a second, but it was as real as the heat from the sun, as real as the beam from the lamp shining on Eve's tin box on this bedside table.

Can you believe it?

127

CHAPTER TWENTY-TWO

It's very quiet here tonight after all the excitement. I'm exhausted but I can't sleep – you know how that is? Too excited, my brain like a whip against a spinning top: Arabella-Willow-Rowan-Arabella-Willow-Rowan, their eyes, faces, hair, voices, hands and fingers, clothes, Arabella-Willow-Rowan. I can't decide which one to concentrate on.

The girls have gone to a hotel in town. Arabella's the easiest, I think; Willow's holding back. She's the one who has the real problem with me, determined not to give me an inch.

Rowan is the mystery. I can't get a handle on him at all. The guy I saw, the son I hugged, who ate, smiled and nodded – a guy who wouldn't say boo to a goose, it seems – is not the person Willow described with such fury. She couldn't have been making all that up so there has to be something there; I just haven't seen it yet.

He's staying in Dale's trailer. I know I'm repeating myself, but Dale is such a good person. He's a Christian in the proper, loving, charitable meaning of the word.

So if you asked me how it went today, I couldn't really say. I don't know whether I made things better or worse. It was quiet one minute, frantic the next, to-ing and fro-ing to Phoenix airport and food and Dale and Gina – and Rowan arriving unexpectedly and all the questions, asked and unasked, all the half-answers from all of us. Too many emotions that we were all trying to manage. Too much carefulness. If you put a gun to my head I might say, being real cautious, that something did open up rather than close down.

I can say one thing for sure: now that I've seen them, if I find tomorrow that they've all flown away like birds in the night, my life will never settle again.

I wonder what time it is. I guess it might be three o'clock in the morning but I'm comfortable here in my little bedroom and it's too much trouble to turn over and look at the clock. I can't wait until I get this clumsy cast off and the lighter one put on.

Trailers creak at night, you know, just like old houses, something to do with cooling down. It's not only the trailer either; it took me a while to get used to the night noises from outside – lizards skittering across the roof, cicadas, raccoons turning over the garbage can. You always have to tie up your garbage real well against those critters.

Some nights you hear the yip-yip of foxes or the scream of a captured rabbit; and thank God you hear coyotes only in the distance because it's a lonely sound they make, like they're putting out messages with no hope of reply. Although they get plenty from Robinia Meadows. Every mongrel in the place sets up a racket that'd hurt your ears.

Even with all that and being alone at night here, I've always felt safe, much safer than I did in any of the flophouses or apartment hotels, or even in the Finkelsteins' lovely house that I worked in as a domestic soon after I got to the States. Five storeys, no elevators, the legs worn off me, but they were real nice people. Gentry. So it wasn't them. What made me worried all the time at the Finkelsteins' was the thought of being caught as a working illegal and being sent home in disgrace, with no money and no husband – except Petey Moraghan, wherever he is, useless lump of garbage – so no means of support and no way to get my kids back.

In the end, I had to leave the Finkelsteins' in a hurry. She got a heads-up late one night from some well-connected friend of hers that the following morning early the law was going to come to all the big brownstones in our district looking for illegals, so that was the end of that. Weeping and gnashing of teeth from Carmencita and Maria – they were the two other hired help – but I didn't shed a tear because what was the point? I never saw either of them girls again. I guess they went back to their own people.

As for me, I got work wherever I could find it as an illegal, moving, moving always to keep a step ahead of the law, cleaning in Irish pubs or working in Chinese laundries or sewing labels on jackets in sweatshops down in the garment district. Going from low to low, you might say.

After about a year of this, I got a break, got hooked up with one of the Catholic missions, housekeeper to a Father Moriarty. He was from County Mayo. He found me sitting by myself in a park at around nine o'clock in the evening. I was well on and he knew it; I didn't try to hide it, I didn't care.

I had started drinking. I can see now it was out of self-pity, although alcoholics don't need an excuse. You learn that pretty quick when you join AA . . . But at that time I was all over the place. I had finally realised that, with the low wages I was getting and the rent I was having to pay, even for one-room coldwater walk-ups, I'd never get home to pay off my debts so I'd never see my kids again. That's just an explanation, not an excuse. No excuses.

And you're probably asking yourself where I got the money to drink.

In them days, you'd be amazed how little you had to pay for low-grade liquor in the States if you knew where to look, and I knew. When you don't eat much you can get smashed on very little.

Anyhow, Father Moriarty sat down beside me and offered me a cigarette, which I refused because I never smoked. He recognised my Irish accent and, after a bit, persuaded me to come home with him to the rectory to clean up. It wasn't a hard sell: I was too far gone to put up much of a fight, although I did try, out of politeness.

The next morning we were in his kitchen. Clean enough, but you'd know immediately you were in the house of a bachelor. Very dilapidated and old fashioned, worn-out oilcloth on the table and an ancient stove, one of them grey and black ones on curved legs that were manufactured in the twenties or thirties. The decoration was just one spindly busy lizzie in a baked-beans tin on the windowsill and a parish calendar pinned to the wall. I learned later that Father Moriarty's last housekeeper had run off with the sacristan more than a year previously and he'd gotten such a shock he hadn't had the heart to get a new one. I was trying to get down a slice of toast and he was watching me.

He'd already dragged some of my history out of me. 'I've a proposition to put to you,' he goes suddenly. 'I could do with a housekeeper to keep me straight. The pay isn't marvellous, but it's better than you're getting now, which I gather is zero, and you'd have your room and board. There's one condition: you have to stay off the booze, Eve. Do you think you can do that?'

I couldn't believe this. I nearly choked on my toast. I was delighted. Well, as delighted as a person can be with a goddamned great big hangover at nine o'clock on a freezing January morning. I didn't want to blow it, though, by sounding too eager in case he changed his mind. 'Stop drinking? Of course I can, Father,' I answered respectfully, trying to show him what an honest, intelligent and calm person I really am. Priests, I imagined, needed their housekeepers not to be flighty.

'Are you sure about that?' He smiled at me. 'It's not going to be easy, you know. If I'd a dime for every poor unfortunate who promised to go on the wagon I'd be a rich man. And you mightn't like the job.'

'I'll like it,' I said firmly. 'I've been as good as a housekeeper all my life. I can do anything in a house. You'll get good value for your money. And I won't squander the housekeeping money either. I'm used to bargaining.'

'And the booze?'

'I'm not drinking all that long, Father, and not all the time either. It's only since I hit hard times here. I never drank in the old country.'

You see, at the time I felt deep down I wasn't a *real* wino, that it wasn't an addiction or anything like that.

After I settled in, we rubbed along well, the priest and I. I was no longer afraid of the law because I knew I had protection now. He had good connections – the clergy always had good connections in New York at that time – so there wasn't any fear of me while I was working for him. I sent money to Maura (but it came back like all the rest, unfortunately, I'll tell you about that some other time). I even managed to save a little out of my pay. I scrubbed and polished and cleaned until that house shone. I whitewashed the kitchen walls and made him give me a few bucks to buy a new stove and material for new drapes and cushion covers for the parlour. I planted wallflowers in the yard. It was the nearest I ever got to my 'little house, hearth and stool and all'. I was almost happy.

For the time I was in the parochial house, staying sober was no problem at all. I ate well and got my energy back.

One of the best things was the way Father Moriarty acted at all times like a gentleman to me, even though I would have nothing to do with religion. We'd argue about it but he never got mad and in the end he would just laugh – his whole body shook and wobbled because of all the doughnuts and chocolate milk shakes he indulged in – and then he'd say that, whether I liked it or not, I was still one of God's children. I wouldn't say we became bosom buddies exactly because of the difference in our stations, and I was always careful to keep that in mind, but we were easy with each other.

The parishioners respected me too – well, most of them. There were some, of course, who didn't take to the idea of a pagan as a priest's house-keeper and got up a petition, but that's human nature, isn't it? Father Moriarty blew them off, politely, of course.

After a little while, I confided in him about the Palm House in the Botanic Gardens and deserting the children – this is the conversation I still have to have with the three of them and I'm dreading it – but he didn't condemn me. When I had finished the whole sorry saga, all he said to me was that it was so sad. He didn't try to offer me absolution or any-thing. I was waiting for that, but he didn't. (I had a laugh about it pri-vately: where religion was concerned, Father Moriarty knew when he was bet.)

When I was nearly a year with him, he helped me sort out my docu-mentation so I got my green card. 'You have to live here without leaving the States for an unbroken year, Eve,' he said, when he gave me the good news that I was approved, 'but after that, if you feel ready, you can go home to find your children. You'll be able to come back and forth. If it works out, you'll even be able to get them in here with you. I'll help.'

Then, only a month after I got that green card, Father Moriarty didn't come down for breakfast one morning; I went upstairs and found him dead in the bed. The new man brought in his own housekeeper, so that was the end of that job and, once again, I was out on my ear.

Green card or no green card, jobs were hard to get for priests' house-keepers but at least they knew I was trustworthy and hardworking, at the beginning in anyway, so I became a waitress for a while in Atlantic City. I waitressed in all kinds of dives, burger joints, fast-food places all over New York and New Jersey, even in one or two posh restaurants, but I'm afraid I hit the sauce again. It just crept up on me, you know? On my days off, then after I quit work, then, sometimes, to cure the hangovers. I wasn't able to keep jobs for long: I was turfed out any time the boss smelt drink on my breath. You'd be surprised how word travels, even in a big place like America, and after a while my name got to be mud so on one would hire me. This is how I stepped down the ladder and became a cleaner, of restaurants first, then sleazy apartment hotels, then hotel kitchens. The stories I could tell you about cockroaches . . .

Isn't it weird Arabella is a waitress too? I'm sure that's not out of necessity, though. A bright, kind person like her? She could be anything she liked.

Speaking of waitressing, I think I noticed something developing this afternoon between our Gina and my Rowan. It could be my imagination, but would that be a gas or what? She's a good person, straight A. She wasn't always a waitress, she was a social worker, you see, while she was married to a no-good country singer, but now she works nights in cocktail bars, freelance, because she doesn't like to be tied down.

As I said, that ex of hers is a real no-good – she's still having to chase him for her alimony, and this is three and a half years after the divorce was supposed to be finalised. He makes a good living too: he and his band play in bars and at country fairs and rodeos all over the south and southwest, but he told her when he bought her the trailer that that was it and no more. Her attorney says this is garbage, that she'll get it, back payments and all, with interest – but the question is, when? His work keeps him moving across state lines and that sure suits him because Gina and her attorney keep having to pursue him and start new proceedings. Jerk. But that Gina sure packs a punch in that little body. Great guts.

At least she got the trailer out of him and she was lucky in that there were no kids to worry about – God, when I think of the creep I married and the place I lived . . . That room! Cooking on the fire with my bits and pieces all rickety on shelves made with bricks and bits of wood I'd find in skips. The only piece of furniture that was for real was the bed; the rest was all orange and apple boxes, padded with newspapers and covered with ancient sheets I'd buy for a few pence in the Daisy Market.

We nearly had a rag rug to cover some of the floorboards but unfortunately I never got it quite finished. It was part of the bundle I gave in to the pawn when I was raising money to come here. I wonder where it is now. Probably in some dump. Nobody nowadays would appreciate all the work that goes into making a rag rug.

What time is it? I have to go to the bathroom so I must move my ass. Jeez, it's only twenty of four. This sure is a long night . . .

CHAPTER TWENTY-THREE

It's four o'clock in the morning. Actually it's 4.02 a.m. I bought myself a digital watch at the airport on the way out here. It's great. I love it. You can see the time even in the pitch dark if you press a little button at the side. I haven't had a watch since I fucking can't remember when.

Gina's trailer is a cracker – not like my ma's, which is all old-lady and pink blankets and stuff: this one is pure rock. Seventies, I think, although I'm not up on that interior-decorator shit. Furry, I think, would be the best way to describe it. The bed has a furry cover and so does the couch; the carpet is long-haired, kind of a mustardy colour; her crockery is yellow too, with those round smily faces on it, and she has this huge birdcage in a corner of the living area with big, spiky plants growing out of it.

It's so long since I kipped in a real bed I can't fucking sleep. The mattress is too soft or warm or something, but Gina'd probably freak if I got up and she found me flaked out on the floor, wouldn't she? She'd be insulted. Bints are like that: they want to know how you're feeling all the time and she'd probably interpret it that I didn't want to sleep beside her after the deed was done, that all I wanted was her body. I don't want to piss her off. We were good together in the sack. I don't mean to boast but she said I was one of the best she'd ever had.

I know, I know, it's the oldest fucking line in the book, but she said it as if she meant it.

I have to be careful, though, because I don't want to go off the deep end with this. Like, I haven't had a girlfriend – in fact I haven't got laid – for a long time. I had this mot, as I told you, and we were going to get a life together with the sprog and the flat and all that and when she upped and snuffed it on me, I kind of closed up shop so it's a bit weird that I have all these tumbled-around feelings hitting me now. Like, just a few minutes ago I found myself thinking of my dead kid and getting real emotional, that he'd be about three now and what he would be like. If it had been a girl, she would be just at the stage where she'd be getting all girly about clothes and dollies and stuff. I haven't thought about that shit for ages. I wouldn't let myself think about it. You can't let yourself get soft when you live on the streets because that way madness lies. What you do is you just get on with it. You move on. You survive.

Her name was Caroline. The mot, I mean.

I'm telling myself it's happening now because of not being with anyone for so long, or because I'm in a bed, or it's four'clock in the morning, or I'm over-tired from the flight. Where Gina is concerned, I'm trying to keep a bit of perspective and not get caught up in something I haven't been prepared for, although there's no question of her trapping me or anything like that. Gina lays it all out, she does. Told me straight up when we were both real excited but before we even took our clothes off that this wasn't a one-night stand for her, that she wasn't a one-night-stand kind of person, that I'd better know this before we did anything. I went ahead anyway even though that's kind of scary, because with Gina I instinctively knew there was going to be more to it than just getting laid.

There's something about her. I can't describe it properly but something happened to me the minute I saw her. She has this smile. It seems to spread right from her chin up to her nose, which wrinkles up, and makes a dimple in one of her cheeks. You feel good when you see her smile at you like that, you know? And you can't help smiling back. And you forget about her funny eye. At least, I did. She has a grand little body too, a bit thin, but strong. Wiry. She feels like one of those whippet pups that Mental likes to take around with him until they grow up and have to be given to the pound.

It was obvious right from the off that she was coming on to me. The smiling, the cocking of the head, the handing me food and taking too long about it, that kind of thing.

It's been so long since any bint smiled at me like that, or came on to me so strong, that at first I thought it was my imagination. Must be the suit she's looking at that way, I said to myself, but then, when I looked at *her* gear, I changed my mind. This is not a woman who takes much notice of clothes. Right away I could feel myself behaving differently. Behaving like a guy in a suit, with a watch. Being polite. Watching the language. I could see it made sense, what Arabella said, about these being decent people. Actually, I was so afraid I'd curse, I hardly said anything at all. My ma probably thought I was a bleedin' dummy.

You see, on the streets you don't even notice these words. Take Mental. When he's trying to get through to someone that he wants a favour (or else!) he'll look that person straight in the eye and, with a pleasant smile, say something like 'Do you underfuckingstand, my friend?' and you can be sure the person gets the message and certainly does underfuckingstand! It's for emphasis, like.

By the way, Gina coming on to me, and me being polite and not saying anything, happened in front of my ma, the blisters and that geezer Dale, whatever his name is. He's weird. He's so laid-back he's fucking horizontal. All those tattoos! He'd give Mental a run for his money there – and that pony-tail? For fuck's sake, it's as grey as . . . as . . . it's fucking light *grey*! I'm glad I didn't have to take up *his* invitation to stay! Anyway, I could see my ma and Bella were watching what was going on between Gina and me—

Fuckit, I don't want even to *think* about my ma. Not yet. My head's done in about that subject.

All right, I'm not a fucking eejit. I knew beforehand she'd cry and tell me she loved me and all that stuff – and she did and all, and I was ready for it, or I thought I was, but I didn't think it'd upset me as much as it did. I had to leg it away from her so she wouldn't see. I pretended I had to have a slash.

Maybe 'upset' is the wrong word.

Shag it, I don't know what the right word is and I'm too wired to spend time on it. I don't have my fucking dictionary with me, these days . . .

I'm gagging for a smoke. Will I chance it?

Ah, I'll wait. I don't want to wake her up. It's so dark I can't see her properly, but she's lying on her back and I think she's sucking her thumb. I must be going off my head, I must, because for some reason that makes me emotional too. Poor kid. She has this limp from when she was a kid and her dirtbag of a stepfather caught her leg in a door accidentally on purpose . . . I can't tell you how bad it made me feel when she told me that. I wanted to find the guy and knock his block off. She's only a little thing.

For fuck's sake. I have to pull myself together. This is too dangerous.

But it's nice—

Ah, I don't know anything any more.

CHAPTER TWENTY-FOUR

Willow's gone. She left this morning after a row with Eve. Well, no, you couldn't call it a row, exactly, it was more Willow expressing her feelings. Or, as far as I could see, not expressing them. Correction again: more like not being able to express them. She's so furiously angry it's choking her. But she won't admit it.

It's seven o'clock in the evening now and the sun has just set. Eve has taken an early night; she was tired, she said, but in my opinion she's stressed because of what happened. I don't know where Rowan is – I really can't figure out what's going on with him. Something has happened between him and Gina, though, that's for sure. That miracle that I talked about.

As for me, I'm sitting in the bar attached to a western-themed restaurant in Sedona: horse tackle, spurs and saddles and so on, rough log walls, guns in glass cases, country music through the speakers, spittoons, and although all the tables seem to be full, the conversation is subdued. I've found that here people don't shout at each other when they socialise. But what's really striking is the quality of the air: not a trace of cigarette smoke. I've just had my own fix outside and now I'm temporarily alone while Dale is off talking to someone on his mobile phone: he apologised when it rang, said he had to take the call and that it might be a long one. He and I are going to eat here. His pony-tail has been freshly done.

So, there you go: our whole family comes together for the first time in yonks and splits up again at the earliest opportunity.

I know I'm not telling this very well. I'm suffering from delayed shock, I think, and things are moving very fast. It seems to me I can't blink but when my eyes open again something else has happened. (I'll never again complain about having a boring life.)

Maybe if I describe in some sort of sequence what happened . . .

Willow and I got up early this morning – our time clocks were baw-ways and we were both awake from six o'clock on. We weren't due to be picked up by Dale until nine. Poor Dale, I thought, in the shower. We sure were stretching his patience and hospitality to the limits and, to put the tin hat on it, he had had Rowan to contend with during the night.

'I hope Rowan behaved himself with Dale,' I said to Willow, who was still in bed when I got back into the room. 'Let's hope he wasn't too outrageous in the language department.' I glanced through the window: the sky was cloudless, that endless deep blue just before the sun comes up. 'It's a beautiful day – will we go for a walk before breakfast? They don't start serving until seven.'

Willow jumped out of bed. 'You go. I want to have a bath and then I have to ring Paddy. I'll wait for you to go down to the dining room.' She closed the bathroom door. I left her to it and went outside.

Our B-and-B for last night was a sort of country house, set plonk in the middle of the extraordinary landscape I mentioned. There was a difference, though: the plains around this house were not as I had seen before: beige-brown, studded with dusty cactus and weak, floppy grass. These were lush green swards, with trees just coming into leaf, but always leading the eye up towards the ridges and cliffs of jagged, naked red, brightening by the second in the increasing light. The house had a stables attached and I stood at the railings of a paddock to watch a lad and two girls, all wearing Stetsons, psyching out the horses in order to put bridles on them. Horses might be beautiful but I think they're also quite stupid: they all saw what was happening to their colleagues, but each was caught in the same way.

First, the girl would walk slowly towards the target horse; he would let her get quite close then kick up his heels to gallop away, snickering in triumph. From a safe distance, he would turn to gloat, but she would be walking away. Ears pricked as he monitored her departure, the victor didn't notice the two lads sneaking up on him from behind in a pincer movement to throw a rope round his neck in one quick movement. It was lovely to watch: the high spirits and grace of the animals, the relaxed demeanour of the handlers. It was also laugh-out-loud fun.

The first rays of the sun were creeping across the paddock by the time the horses, fourteen of them, were all safely roped and being led towards a wooden enclosure dotted with mounting blocks. As I watched them, three plodding chain-gangs, I basked in the morning: the growing warmth on the back of my neck, the air filled with the nattering of birds and the drone of insects, the smell of earth and dung, hay and budding trees. For a few glorious moments, liberated from Eve, from Willow, and Rowan and Jimmy Porter – from my whole bloody nerve-racking existence – I entertained the mad thought of applying for a job in this place. Catching horses didn't involve genius-level intelligence. I could catch horses. I could clean out their stables. I'd be willing to do (literally) shit work while learning the horse business.

But such a big move – I'd miss home, surely?

What *exactly* would I miss?

The honest answer – that I'd miss nothing and no one except Greta, maybe Tayto crisps and *Fair City* on the telly – shocked me. This constituted my attachment to Ireland? To Dublin?

What about Willow and Rowan?

The answer to that one was even more appalling. *They'd be nice to visit occasionally.*

Sneakily, I explored further. What about my boyfriend? He seemed very far away. I hesitated to use the word 'irrelevant', but it might be accurate.

And what was holding me to the Leicester Hotel? Certainly not the wages. Definitely not the appreciation of my manager. So, what?

A big fat nothing.

I let this train of thought run away with me – mind you, I have to admit I'm inclined to do this every time I escape from Ireland. In Tenerife, for instance, I found myself asking a friendly barman one night if any waitressing jobs were going in his bar/restaurant. Shades of Shirley Valentine.

Nevertheless I became seriously excited. I needn't be confined to the stables, I thought, because wasn't I well qualified to work in the house itself? In return for room, board and enough money to keep myself in clothes and the odd trip to the pictures, I could clean and change beds, I could do laundry, I could certainly waitress in the guests' dining room. If push came to shove, I could even do some plain cooking . . . Great fantasy. In it, even the green card – maybe the Morrison visa – was easily got.

The fantasy went on hold when I looked at my watch, saw it was after seven o'clock and visualised Willow's impatiently tapping foot. I filed it away, though. I had options. I was a free agent. Why had I not seen that before?

When I got back to the room I found my sister, fully dressed and frozen-faced, sitting on the bed. Her suitcase was open beside her and she was folding her nightdress to put it in. 'What are you doing?' I was surprised. 'We don't know yet if we're moving out of here today. Remember? We said last night we'd decide before Dale came for us. That's still two hours away. I like it here, Willow, even if it is a bit more expensive than we planned.'

'Paddy wasn't at work,' she interrupted. 'He had to stay at home because Dermot has a chest infection. The poor child is on antibiotics. I have to get back as quickly as I can. Today.'

'A chest infection? Surely that's not serious enough to send you flying home?'

'I think I'm better placed to judge the seriousness or otherwise of my child's illness, Arabella.'

'But we've been here only two days or whatever it is, Willow. We haven't even begun to know Eve.' Dismayed, I sat on the side of my bed.

'It can't be helped.' She picked up her travel alarm and folded it into its leather case. 'You stay, of course. But I have to get back.' Her tone left no room for argument.

'What'll we tell Eve?'

'Tell her whatever you like, Bella. Tell her the truth, that one of my children is sick. I've ordered a taxi for eight thirty. No need to trouble Dale this time.' She stood up and turned her back, closing the lid of the suitcase and snapping the locks shut. *Speck. Spack.*

'You're not even going to say goodbye?'

'You can say it for me.' She wouldn't look at me. Instead she continued to fiddle with the locks.

'The airport is a hundred miles away. What's that taxi going to cost you?'

'I have the cash. Look, Bella,' she stopped fiddling and whirled to face me, 'please stop interrogating me. Please!'

I stared at her. One of her eyelids was twitching. 'Just remember one thing,' I tried to sound neutral and reasonable, 'now that you've met her, nothing will ever be the same. She's a person to us now. When she dies, we'll have real memories of a real person. You should make sure that your memories aren't all of what might have been.'

'Well, thank you for that, Arabella,' she snapped. 'Thanks for the ama-teur psychology. I'll deal with my own memories in my own way, thank you.'

'What's this about, Willow? Does Dermot really have a chest infec-tion?'

'How dare you?' It was clear I'd hit a bullseye. 'Are you calling me a liar?'

'No. I'm just asking what's going on. If Dermot is on antibiotics, as you say, he'll be nearly better by the time you get home to Dublin. Antibiotics are very effective.'

'So now *you're* telling *me* how to be a mother?'

There was no answer to that. There were layers of insult in that.

Our room was on the ground floor. I got up, went to the window and stood looking out at a gravelled area where a cat was keeping an eye on two kittens batting a raggedy ball of grass to and fro. Behind me, I heard the creak of Willow's bed as she, too, stood up. 'You'll never forgive your-self if you go without saying goodbye to her,' I said quietly. I turned to look her straight in the eye. 'I'll never forgive you. I mean that. I can't – I *won't* do the dirty work for you. If you're afraid, you're afraid. But I'm not explaining anything to Eve. I'll just tell her that when I got back after my walk this morning you had already left.'

'That's terribly unfair.' Her eyes were brimming. 'Why won't you help? I have to get to that airport as soon as possible. God knows what con-nections I'll be able to get.'

'Fair or not – although personally I don't think fairness comes into this – that's what I'm going to say.' I shrugged.

We watched each other. Then, slowly, she sat on the side of her bed again. 'What's got into you, Arabella?' She seemed genuinely perplexed.

I shrugged again. 'Nothing's got into me. I'm simply telling you what I'm going to say to Eve.'

'But it won't be the truth.'

'Won't it?'

'You'll know why I left. Dermot.'

She looked so forlorn I almost felt sorry for her. 'Yeah. Dermot. Chest infection. You told me.'

As she continued to look up at me, the sound of the kittens scrabbling in the gravel came through the open window. Nice. Normal.

Nothing normal in my life.

I relented a little. 'Come on, Willow. All right, I accept you're going home – for *whatever* reason,' I wasn't going to let her get away with pretending, 'but a couple of hours is not going to make that much of a difference. At least give the woman the courtesy of saying goodbye. She's all geared up. It would be cruelty—'

'Cruelty?' she flashed, fists clenched. 'What about what she did to us?'

'She's apologised. I can see she means it even if you can't.' I had pushed aside my own anger: time enough for that, no point in feeding Willow's.

'Words are cheap, anyway, it's all become too emotional.' She was fiddling with her wedding ring.

'Emotions are good. This is an emotional situation, Willow. You'd want to be a stone—'

'Good for you. Not good for me.' She stood up. The discussion was over.

To my astonishment, she then asked if she could take Eve's tin box with her. 'Obviously, now I won't get to see what's in it unless I do. But, as I said, I'm her daughter too. I have just as much right—'

'Fine!' I agreed. 'Not the diary, though. I'm keeping it here – and keep everything safe, won't you?'

'I'm hardly going to dump it in the Liffey.'

The upshot was that when Dale came to collect us, she was waiting with me in the driveway of the B-and-B and we both had our luggage with us. The compromise we'd hammered out was that the taxi would collect her at Robinia Meadows at half past ten. She had taken literally my remark about the couple of hours.

CHAPTER TWENTY-FIVE

The two hours before Dale arrived to drive us to the trailer park passed somehow, although right at this minute I couldn't tell you much about them. We ate breakfast. We checked the room to see if we had left anything behind. We sat in the lobby of the B-and-B. We hardly spoke. I was so grateful when I saw that dusty pickup barrelling up the driveway that I nearly fell on Dale's neck.

'You made your flight reservations yet, Willow?' He swung the cases into the back of the pickup. His reaction to the new arrangement was as cool as ever, although I noticed that he didn't offer to take Willow to the airport. His hair was loose. Sitting Bull. Or Sitting Bull's brother, the one who'd been on the Atkins Diet.

'No, not yet,' Willow mumbled, 'but I'll be there early enough to get whatever's going.'

We passed the journey in yet more silence, except for the chatter of a news station broadcasting mostly advertisements with the occasional weather and traffic report.

The transients area of Robinia Meadows snoozed in the morning sunshine. Some doors were open and through the air-conditioning vents of the pickup I could smell bacon frying; as we passed, a child, nappy dragging on the deck of his trailer, looked up from his plastic cereal bowl and two mongrels decided to chase us but only half-heartedly: after a few seconds they flopped back into the dust. In 'our' part, further back, the parking bays were mostly empty: the commuters had left for work. I thought it was time to say something. 'Is Rowan up and about?'

'Rowan? I dunno.' Dale shrugged his shoulders. 'Maybe.'

There was no sign of our brother when we pulled up in front of Eve's trailer but our mother, dressed in a flowered skirt and loose pink T-shirt, was supporting herself on her crutch at the rail. The garish sunglasses were perched like a hairband on her head. 'Isn't it a glorious day?' She clunked across to greet us at the top of the steps. 'Shoo, you!' she waved the crutch at Ginger who, having been snoozing on the top step, moved approximately three inches and curled up again.

The smell and sizzle of frying batter floated from inside: pancakes! And I could hear the clatter of ware. *Rowan making pancakes?* 'It sure is a beautiful day. Not too hot yet either.' Probably because I knew what Willow had in store, I kissed Eve's cheek. 'Good morning.'

She threw her free arm round my neck and almost overbalanced. 'Sorry. Got a bit carried away!' Her smile of joy caused my stomach to flip. At that moment I wanted to punch Willow in the jaw. 'Who's inside? Is it Rowan?'

'No.' Eve waved her arm. 'It's Mario.' Puzzled, she called to Dale, who had put our luggage on the gravel and was walking away, leaving the pickup parked where it was. 'Did Rowan not go with you to the guest-house?'

'No, ma'am,' he called back.

'Come and have breakfast with us. And tell that boy to get over here.'

'You got it! But I'll take a raincheck on the breakfast, Eve – I have to go into town. I'll be back for the car. See you later.' By this time he was level with his own place but, strangely, kept going.

Eve wasn't noticing where Dale was going. She was noticing Willow hanging back. 'Come on up here, don't be shy.' She blazes again into that joyful smile. 'We have a treat this morning. Mario's cooking up a bunch of apple pancakes. You like pancakes with maple syrup, honey?'

'Not particularly, and we've already had breakfast, Mother.' But Willow, seeing Eve's crestfallen expression, gave in. 'I suppose I could manage one.'

'Great. Come on, let's all sit down. Let's be waited on hand and foot by the best pancake-maker in Sedona – in the whole of Arizona. Mario should set up his own pancake house.' The latest change in Eve was remarkable: it was as though she had decided overnight that whatever serpents lay in the grass she would not call them up.

As we settled ourselves around the table, I kept an eye on Willow, who was looking at her shoes, but if Eve had noticed anything wrong – anything *extra* that might be wrong – she was ignoring it. 'So tell me more about the old country. About Dublin.' She addressed herself to me.

Since I had already covered the cranes and the construction work, I cast about for something new to say about the city. 'Well, as I think I told you before, Eve, you'd hardly recognise the place.' I was matching her cheeriness, chirp by chirp. I was so cheery I made myself sick. 'But I don't think I told you about the Luas – that's the new tram system they're building. Or the Spire. Did I tell you about the Spire?'

'No, I don't think so . . .' Eve, barely paying attention, was watching Willow, who continued to find worlds of wonder in her own two feet.

'This Spire,' I carolled, 'is in the middle of O'Connell Street – we Dubs call it the Spike, or the Stiletto in the Ghetto.' Heigh-ho, I was away, eulogising Dublin's newest landmark. Actually, it was no hardship to wax enthusiastic about the Spire because, as it happens, I love it: I love the way it's not supposed to represent anything except itself, glowing silver in the winter sunshine. From the front door of the Leicester, we were able to watch it from the beginning: first, the erection of what we heard was the biggest crane in Europe, then the lorries bringing in the massive cylindrical sections in ones and twos, tantalisingly wrapped in what looked like brown paper. And I was among the crowd, clapping and cheering on the final day when the last tapering cone, like a fairy wand, was carefully slotted on top.

It's not the kind of thing people like me are supposed to love, of course, because we're not supposed to have the vocabulary to convey why we love it. So when people like Willow are giving out about it, and moaning about the money it cost 'when you consider how many hospital beds are closed off and the scandal of homelessness and everything, and anyway what's it supposed to *be*?' I keep my mouth shut.

Having described the thing as best I could to Eve without any help from Willow, I babbled to a conclusion: 'And it's the tallest sculpture in the world, more than seven times the height of the GPO, Eve. It's where Nelson's Pillar used to be. Did you know Nelson's Pillar?'

'I was up it! Three times! The third time it was a clear day and we could see all the way to Wicklow on one side and the Mountains of Mourne on the other. It was great!' She turned deliberately to Willow. 'So, what about you, Willow? Do you like the Spire?'

'No, I don't.'

'What's the matter, honey? Cat got your tongue?' Playfully, Eve slapped Willow's arm. 'Get out of the wrong side of bed this morning?'

Now, I know that the last thing someone should do when trying to butter up my sister is tease her. Eve, of course, does not know that. Or did not know it then.

Willow gave her a frigid stare. 'I'm sorry, Mother, but I cannot discuss something as trivial as this. I have a sick child at home and I have to go back to Dublin as soon as possible. Today.'

Eve's smile kidnapped itself. 'Today, but—'

'I have a taxi arriving here,' Willow consulted her watch, 'in fifty minutes' time.'

'That's awful, honey. Which one is it? Maeve or Dermot? And what's wrong?'

'It's Dermot. He has a severe chest infection.'

'Oh, the poor little thing. How awful. Is he in the hospital?'

'No.' Willow had the grace to hesitate, but only for a fraction of a second. 'Actually he's in the house. Paddy – my husband – is looking after him. I have to go home.'

'But if your husband . . .' Eve trailed away into a terrible silence.

I could hear the hands of my digital watch jerk along the seconds – or, at least, I imagined I could.

'I have to go home,' Willow repeated flatly. She was no longer looking at her shoes but sideways, at something she found interesting in the fabric of the trailer. Eve turned to me. A different woman now. A woman with no solid ground under her feet.

But this was between Willow and her. 'I'll go and see what's keeping Rowan,' I said quietly, getting up. 'He should be awake by now.'

'Don't go!' they said together. Now they were both gazing at me, and if it weren't so serious, I'd have laughed. Like, when did I become Brown Owl? 'All right.' I sat down again.

Jerk. Jerk. My watch was getting louder. A car sputtered into life somewhere on the site. Inside, Mario dropped something and we could hear him: 'Shit-shit-shit-shit-*shit!*'

Eventually, I took two – no, three breaths. 'Tell her about the tin box, Willow.'

'I'm taking it with me – if that's all right? I'll return it to you, of course.'

Eve darted a look at me. 'Sure, honey. That's fine.'

'Are you sure I shouldn't go and look for Rowan?' Again I stood up.

146

'Since Willow is going so soon, I think it might be useful to leave the two of you alone for a few minutes.'

Neither of them answered. I sat down again. 'What's going on here is not my business,' I tried again. 'So?' I gazed directly at Willow.

'So what?'

'So say what you have to say.'

'I don't know what you're talking about.'

'Really?'

Eve watched these exchanges as if she was at a tennis match. Then, softly and sadly: 'You're very angry, Willow?'

'No, I'm not. What's the point of being angry? The past can't be undone. Oh, this is useless.' Willow stood up so quickly she stumbled. 'It's too late, Mother,' she said, when she had righted herself. 'I shouldn't have let Arabella talk me into this. I just want to get on with my life as best I can now. I *was* getting on—' She swallowed hard. 'Look,' she picked up her handbag and held it in front of her stomach with both hands, 'I don't think there's much pleasure in this for any of us, or much benefit either. Thank you very much for your hospitality – and those pancakes do smell delicious, but I think I'll wait for my taxi down at the entrance, if you don't mind.'

For a moment or two, I thought Eve was going to crumple like she had the day before. But she didn't. She simply sat. Staring with those eyes of hers. 'Whatever makes you happy, Willow. I'm truly sorry.'

'I'm sorry too, but as I said, it's too late,' Willow muttered. 'I'll write, OK? I'll drop you a line after I get home – and I'll keep your tin box safe. I'll get it back to you.' She backed off, then plunged down the steps, grabbed the handle of her wheeled suitcase and walked with it away from the trailer as quickly as the gravel would allow.

'Oh dear – I hope there's not another drama.' Mario, a loaded platter in each hand, appeared at the doorway and noticed immediately that something was wrong.

'No drama, Mario.' I rose to take the platters from him. 'Willow had to go home early, that's all. One of her children is ill.'

'How dreadful! But where's Dale – shall I fetch him? He's driving her? She's walking in the wrong direction.'

'Her taxi's coming to the entrance.'

I have to break off with this story soon because I can see Dale is nodding and smiling as if he's finishing up his phone call . . .

147

I'll give you the rest of this mad day real quick. Eve did crumple after Willow left and she also showed herself to be seriously perceptive. 'What's your sister so afraid of? Do you know? She's terrified of any kind of emotion, it seems to me.'

'Willow has always been—' I was caught between honesty and loyalty to Willow.

'Buttoned-up?' Eve supplied, gazing intently at me.

'Not exactly.' I was remembering earlier days in the orphanage. 'I think she might even be the most emotional of the three of us, actually, but she's determined to keep looking ahead all the time. I think she made that decision long ago.'

'You can't run away from your past.' Eve is barely listening. 'Believe me, I know. It's all waiting for her. Somewhere, some day.' Although I did think this was a little rich, coming from the person who had caused Willow's 'past', mine too, and Rowan's, I let it go. 'I'll run after her. Make sure she's all right.'

'No. I should go.'

'I'll come with you.'

'No.' Said with such firmness that I couldn't argue.

'What about my pancakes?' Mario, who'd been hovering, was seriously disgruntled now.

'Keep them warm.' Eve was already hopping awkwardly down the steps. He made a face, then rushed back inside.

'I'll go get Rowan, shall I?' I called after her, as she moved, surprisingly quickly, along the gravel street.

'Yeah. Do that,' she called back, without looking round.

And of course then, to continue with this day's theme of surprises, when I went to find Rowan, didn't I discover that he hadn't spent the night with Dale at all but with Gina? They were having breakfast in her place.

So when Eve came back, she, Mario and I ate the pancakes (big as plates, moist, full of real chopped apples, delicious) but it was a weird occasion: no Rowan, no Dale, no Willow, Robert or Gina, just the three of us, Eve silent, brooding, me and Mario rabbiting on about feck all. 'How'd it go with Willow?' I asked Eve, when Mario was inside, fetching coffee.

'Fine.' She wouldn't look at me. By the sound of it, however, I'd say it had been anything but fine.

Later, when I went for a walk by myself, I got a chance to skim a bit of Eve's diary and it blew my mind (she was a drinker!) but I'll tell you about that later because I see Dale has finished his call and here he is coming now. Smiling at me.

As I said. Mad. I don't even know where I'm staying tonight but right now I'm here in a place called the Saddle Horn, ears pounding from too much Willie Nelson, sipping a frozen margarita and about to have dinner alone with a man I barely know . . .

CHAPTER TWENTY-SIX

I have just opened our mother's battered tin box. I haven't delved through it yet, although I can see the tied-up birth certificate Arabella mentioned; under it there seems to be some sort of garment, so old it's as thin and transparent as tissue. The baby dress? The diary Arabella has kept was probably the most significant element of this collection and I suspect that everything else will be of the 'souvenir' variety, significant to its owner, of course, but, mere tat to everyone else.

I had to cool my heels in Phoenix airport for almost five hours but we took off at last about an hour and a half ago, bound for London. Luckily for me, the aircraft is not full. I managed to secure a seat by the window in a row of just two with an empty one beside me so I should be able to sleep. We're flying east, of course, so it's already dark.

I have to admit that as we climbed into the sunset, then made a wide turn, leaving it behind us, the sky was dramatic: yellows and pinks, even a sort of deep purple on the horizon. In different circumstances, I might have liked Arizona. The landscape is certainly unlike anything I've seen before. Paddy and I holiday in the West of Ireland. The weather there is unpredictable, of course, but we both want Dermot and Maeve to have some appreciation of their own country.

I'm sure you're surprised to hear from me at this stage. I don't really want to be part of this story, as you will have noticed by now, but it's probably past time for me to set out my side of it; I shudder to think what the other three are saying about me back there on that campsite.

By the way, I'm not a snob. It's quite a nice campsite, as they go, and although it wouldn't be my choice of a place to live, don't think I look down on the type of people who are forced to make their homes there. Our mother seems quite happy, as does her collection of strange friends.

I could not have stayed there another minute. The visit had become encased in such a feverish, even romantic emotionalism – *vide* our mother and my sister both agog about some kind of silly love affair they think has developed between Rowan and that odd-looking person with the carrot-coloured hair! Even this business with tin boxes shows how overblown the whole situation has become: our tin box, her tin box – and here am I with one of them on my lap. I know I asked to take it so I'm proving the case. The fever is catching. However, as I have brought it up, I must put down a marker here about Arabella's custodianship of 'our' version. I have always thought it high-handed of her never to let it out of her possession. Whatever about Rowan, what did she think I was going to do with it? Pawn it?

To get back to the point, I like an orderly, calm life, right down to the smallest detail: I like to know that situations in which I am involved are under control. For instance, this is why, if at all possible, I choose to travel with British Airways: I get the impression that its personnel is on top of things. Take this plane: the stewards and stewardesses are polite and civilised but keep a proper, professional distance and don't feel they have to ask you where you got your tan or if you have enjoyed your holidays.

And here's another thing: every time I was in her presence, I could see our mother watching me and analysing me, trying to figure out how to get under my skin so I became as obviously affected by our so-called reunion as my sister. *That* had to be nipped in the bud. If I need psychoanalysis, and I will be the judge of that, I will go to someone qualified.

I've had enough drama and intrusion into my private life – what the Americans so appositely call 'space'. I avoid both at all costs and if this indicates my character is flawed or deficient, as I would guess *some* people think it does, so be it.

She came after me, you know. I wanted no histrionics or tearful goodbye scenes. We had had enough tears and I simply wanted to make a peaceable, dignified exit, but would she let me? No, she would not, but came hobbling along on that cast of hers, trying to persuade me to change my mind. I heard her before I saw her, hopping and dragging in the gravel. 'Willow, Willow – wait a moment,' she called. I had no choice but to obey.

There then followed the most absurd conversation, given the locale and circumstances. Remember, we were standing in the middle of what was little more than a dirt track, with the hot sun beating down on our bare heads and curious residents straining to hear what was going on. I do not exaggerate: they literally lined their decks. 'Keep your voice down, Mother, please!' I was embarrassed and angry, justifiably so, in my opinion.

'Please, Willow,' she would not be diverted, 'can't I persuade you to stay a little longer? Please?'

For some reason, perhaps due to a build-up of stress, embarrassment and resentment at the present predicament, or simply general fatigue, I lost command of my tongue – although at the beginning, I managed to keep the volume down. 'What about him, Mother?'

'Who?' She was taken aback. 'What about who?'

'*Him!* My father. Our father. What about him? You haven't uttered a word about him.'

'But—'

'You walk out on him,' I could not stop myself, 'you take us up to the Botanic Gardens and leave us there to our fate. It's Christmas Eve, Mother. How do you think he felt when he got home on Christmas Eve and found us gone?'

'You don't understand.' She went very quiet. 'You don't have the full picture.'

'I don't need to see the full picture,' I stormed, aware that my voice was rising but, for once, shamefully uncaring about how I sounded or who heard. 'The picture I see is that you kidnapped us from our father, abandoned us to strangers, then swanned off to the bright lights. That's the picture I see.'

'Willow, listen—'

'No. *You* listen.' I moved closer to her and the handle of my wheelie-bag slipped out of my hand so it dropped into the dirt. I did not pause to pick it up. 'I think your behaviour has been contemptible, *Mother*. You don't deserve that name since you deprived us not only of our childhood but of *both* of our parents. And if I am no daughter to you it's because you made me that way. I won't even apologise to you for shouting like this – you don't deserve it. And, yes, I'm going home simply to *go home*. My son is perfectly healthy, thank God. I made up that story about his illness in a misguided effort to spare your feelings. I certainly wouldn't do it a second time. As far as I'm concerned, you don't exist.'

I was shaking so hard my teeth were chattering but, thinking back on it, her reaction was strange. The tirade I had unleashed on her seemed to have relaxed rather than intimidated her, and instead of slinking away, or yelling back, or even defending herself, she waited until I had finished, then smiled and touched my shoulder. 'Poor Willow,' was all she said.

She has my brother's extraordinary eyes, I'm sure you know that already – although I hope Arabella has been accurate in describing the customary unhealthy state of his; the expression in them was disconcertingly unafraid and open. I became impaled on that stare. Its gentleness winded me. It was as if she was a hypnotist. 'You poor thing,' she said again.

'Please don't patronise me.' I managed to break away from her but the heat had gone out of the battle and, with as much decorum as I could muster, I picked up the wheelie-bag and walked away from her.

One minute previously, I had wanted someone to vaporise me, remove me instantly from this place and this chaos and this woman. Instead, as I walked away, I felt odd. It is hard to describe – 'empty' is not the correct word. Neither is 'deflated' nor 'light-headed' because I did not feel any of those things precisely. Perhaps a combination of them all. And while I hated what had just happened for its vulgarity and unseemly lapse of restraint, I felt that something significant had taken place between her and me. *Which I did not want.*

For whatever reason, I was shaken. Isn't that ridiculous? In the meantime, I had to keep going through the massed ranks of gapers (that's an exaggeration, but there were a couple of dozen or more) with her looking after me wearing that Bambi expression, knowing full well whose side of the brouhaha was being taken by the residents of Robinia Meadows.

However, one magician's trick, if that's what it was, does not alter the basic truth. And while that last encounter did have an effect on me, I still want nothing more to do with my mother.

Arabella seems to be taking all of this in her stride. And she also seems to have some memory of her early life with our mother and father. I do not. I don't invite conversations about our past, not any longer, although I have some warm memories of her comforting me when I was distressed about something in that institution. For instance, when I was very young I was afraid of the dark and would sneak into her bed in our dormitory. She never complained, but would cuddle me and whisper to me, trying to get me to remember games we played in the house where we lived. When we were older, she painted a picture of the last time we saw our

153

mother. She claims to remember watching our mother leave us: 'Think, Willow! Try to remember. Do you not remember the heat? And the big huge plants? And the smell? You were wearing a little coat with a velvet collar.'

I have no memory of this incident – and do not want any. And I sometimes wonder if she does remember, or if, on subsequent visits to that Palm House, she has simply *constructed* this memory. I know she has been there. I have not.

Now you are asking, if Willow is so resistant, why did she travel to Arizona in the first place, since she clearly came with her mind made up *not* to give any leeway?

Why indeed? Don't you think I have been asking myself that?

Curiosity? Definitely.

Need? Perhaps . . .

You'll remember I used the word 'misguided' to her. Well, I suppose I came out here (or allowed myself, against my better judgement, to be persuaded) in the misguided notion that maybe, just *maybe*, I might find a parent. I am human. I have been lonely. I have been envious of colleagues who take their mothers on holiday, even of those who become irritated when their mothers telephone them at work. I have wondered what it would be like to have a mother.

But I certainly did not find one in Eve Rennick. I accept that she is remorseful; I accept that I did not let down the barriers; I accept that if I were a good Christian, I would forgive her, and that Arabella is in the process of doing so.

Evidently I am not a good Christian because I cannot even begin. On the contrary, each sighting of her during these past few days brought back images and feelings I had thought I had contained so they could no longer distress me: the orphanage, the beatings, the humiliations, the crucifying loneliness. The useless fantasy that my father, whose face I cannot recall, would come and rescue me.

The dawning realisation, somewhere between the ages of six and seven, or perhaps eight, that nobody was coming for me, that no one ever would. Nodding and smiling like the good little orphan everyone wanted me to be, I fixated on the fact that my mother had prevented him from coming. I became furious with her. I still am, and no self-serving pleas will ever change that.

I *hate* these emotions. I *hate* being brought back to childhood again, feeling as if I have no say, no control, having to jump this way and that at someone else's command or even whim. I *hate* the feeling of having no one in my corner – although Arabella did try to look out for me but how could she? She had the same troubles as I had.

Most of all, meeting my mother brought back in vivid detail the cast-iron decision that no one would ever, *ever* be in a position to abandon me again. By the time I left St Camilla's and the carousel of foster-parents, social workers, Health Board systems, I had decided that, no matter what, I must never be weak: therefore I must never allow emotion or fantasy to rule my will.

Although we never discussed it in fine detail, my husband seems intuitively to understand this and asks few questions; neither does he make demands I cannot meet. It is one of the reasons I married him, I think. In fact, looking back, I never cease to be amazed that any man could have been interested in me because I was 'a hard nut to crack'. I suppose that we worked together in the same department in the civil service meant that Paddy had the opportunity to observe me when I was concentrating on things other than keeping my guard up.

In any event I never dissembled with him, or pretended that I was other than I am. 'What you see is what you get,' I told him, on the night he asked me to marry him. We were strolling down O'Connell Street having been to see *The King and I* for the third or fourth time; it's our favourite musical. We both like musicals and met while we were singing in the chorus of *The Mikado* for an amateur society. We had stopped outside the Happy Ring House to look in the window – casually, I had thought, but then Paddy grabbed my arm and pointed upwards. 'What is it?' I couldn't see anything out of the ordinary beyond the flashing neon 'engagement ring' sign above the shop door. 'Was it a bat?'

'For God's sake, Willow, I'm trying to ask you to marry me.'

I was taken aback. 'Are you sure?' I asked him.

'Of course I'm sure. I've a deposit on a ring in there.'

I got excited then. Who wouldn't? But ten minutes later I felt I had to make things clear by telling him I was not for changing and he would be disappointed if he tried. 'You're someone I admire and look up to, Willow,' was his answer. 'I'd be honoured if you'd become my wife.'

'Then the answer is yes,' I said. He kissed me right then and there and

I let him, even though I was a little embarrassed in the middle of O'Connell Street.

That night, safe in my bed, it felt good to know that my future was safe. Someone would *have* to be in my corner now because marriage was a legal contract, but even then I knew that he was a level-headed person who would honour his word. And we would have a real home. I knew that too, because as we walked away from the Happy Ring House towards my bus stop, he told me he had enough saved for a deposit on a house. He had it all planned out.

I know what some others, Arabella, for instance, think of Paddy – that he's mean, for instance. It might appear so from the outside, because even when we were courting Paddy watched the pennies. It might seem miserly to others but, given my background, I have always thought it a good, sensible thing to do. After all, one never knows when poverty will strike. He is not mean, but careful, and has been a good provider and husband to me, a good father to Maeve and Dermot. He can be a little controlling but so can I, and we have come to a sort of accommodation with this. In any case, controlling people can be relied upon in a crisis. Who was it, for instance, found our brother and got him to Arizona?

We love each other in our way and I would be bereft if he died before me. But I would not go to pieces. I will never go to pieces.

'A cold fish' do I hear you say?

Not in my opinion. Although I am generally engaged with work and family and have made no close friendships, I can and do empathise with others' misfortunes, not with ready tears or gushing sympathy but in a practical way. I bring food to wakes and funeral parties; I babysit for one of my colleagues who was widowed so that she can try to rebuild her life. I run several standing orders at my bank in favour of charities, I listen to my workmates' woes and give advice if I am asked.

I am rearing my own children to be self-sufficient too. As a mother, I believe I am doing the right thing in preparing them for the cruelty of the world at large, teaching them that, at rock bottom, they can rely only on themselves.

Although I work outside the home, I have chosen flexitime hours so they don't always have to come home from school to someone else's house; I am there when they get into trouble, never 'fixing' but encouraging them to find their own solutions; I give them the best education, provide the best extra-curricular activities; I read to them, I cuddle them, I discipline them with love – because I do love them – but I'm afraid I do not understand the phrase 'unconditional love' and there is a part of me that *no one* will have. Not even them.

If all of that to you spells 'cold fish' – again, so be it.

Although I am going home shattered, thanks to Eve Rennick and my sister, who talked me into coming out here, I'm glad I came. All doubt is removed and now I *know* who I am. I am Willow who stands alone, who never breaks in any storm.

For those at home and at work who will ask about it, the visit went smoothly. I will tell them that of course there were no miracles but I wasn't expecting any, and now we must all step back and wait to see what develops next.

Here comes the stewardess again with the drinks trolley. I have had a martini already so I don't think I should have another although I feel somewhat reckless – unusual for me. But alcohol and flying do *not* mix well. I let her pass.

So, what will develop next?

Having said all that I've said and meant every word, I will admit the following only once, and only to you. Probably because that first martini was powerful!

I do get tired being strong.

I did allow myself to hope that a miracle might occur in Arizona.

And, finally, the tiny flame of hope (see? One martini and I become quite lyrical!) still flickers that something can be worked out between my mother and me. For instance, Maeve and Dermot deserve to know they have a second grandmother. And quite an exotic one too!

One strange effect my mother has had: I cannot remove the imprint of her eyes from in front of mine. They are still staring into me, even through me, as they seemed to do during that final confrontation just a few hours ago. Very unsettling.

I have changed my mind. I think I will have another martini, after all. In the meantime, I suppose I had better go through this damned tin box of hers and get it over with.

Yes, this is the birth certificate Bella told me about and this fragile fabric is a baby dress. There seems to be the remains of smocking at the neckline. I won't unfold it.

157

I think the easiest thing to do would be to upend the tin gently on the seat beside me; that way I won't destroy anything.

So . . .

A Miraculous Medal. Tin, the kind churned out by the thousand in Lourdes. Rosary beads made from imitation pearls with a mother-of-pearl crucifix; the links are black with age; and here's the large envelope containing the letters Arabella would not allow me read. I'll put them aside for later.

Three twists of old grey tissue paper. On opening the first, I find a lock of baby hair. Damn! Maybe I shouldn't put myself through this . . .

But if I don't go through these things now, I won't be able to dislodge them from my mind. They'll be waiting for me, like something nasty concealed in the undergrowth . . .

At least I don't have to open the other two twists. I know what *they* contain.

Here's another envelope, containing photographs, three obviously taken by proper photographers. Well, I've already seen the first two: this one is 'the wedding photograph' I know from 'our' tin box. Our father has been removed from this one too. And this woman wants our sympathy and forgiveness? The phrase 'do unto others' springs to mind.

The second one is a copy of the one we also have – of the three of us as very young children – but here is a First Communion photo: three rows of little girls, maybe thirty or forty, lined up on tiered benches. They are all steepling their hands in prayer, wearing identical veils and white socks but a variety of communion dresses, some fitting, some not. A few of these children are smiling, showing they are missing milk teeth; many aren't, probably because the sun is in their eyes and they are squinting. In the back row, the head of one of the larger children has been circled. Eve's? Impossible to tell as the veil is lopsided and covers half of the face.

This next one, amateur, is definitely of Eve. With arms round one another's shoulders, she and another girl are standing on a beach in front of a towering but wonky sandcastle. On the back of the snapshot is written, in careful, childish handwriting, 'Philomena and me. Rush. Julye 1953. Best Freinds For Ever.'

And here is a tiny snap of a group standing in front of a flowerbed: a smiling woman who is stooping in an effort to turn an obviously uncooperative little boy towards the camera; Eve, also smiling, is leaning sideways to balance the baby in her arms on her large pregnancy bump. There is lettering, not greatly improved on that in the previous snap, on the back of this one too: 'Maura and me with Arabella. Peeples Gardens. Pheonix Park. Sumer 1962.' I was soon to be born.

I must not get sentimental over this. I must not, I *must not*.

I touch the call bell for the second time in another attempt to order my martini. So much for BA efficiency . . .

As I wait for a response, I carefully repack everything, keeping aside the envelope of letters to read when I feel a little calmer.

Now I see, jammed between the back and the armrest of the empty seat, a folded sheet of old-fashioned, lined notepaper. I extract it carefully. The writing on it, in thick black ink, greenish now with age, is large and firm (male?) but slanted backwards so heavily I suspect the writer was disguising the hand. It is in capitals:

WE CANNOT KEEP THIS INFANT. PSE TAKE CARE
OF HER. GOD BLESS YOU. GOD FORGIVE US ALL.

We?

The shock is intense.

I had concentrated always on my sense of deprivation in relation to having no father or mother. It had occurred only vaguely to me that there had to have been a whole previous generation.

Even if my grandparents are dead – and everyone at some stage has two sets – I may have living aunts.

Cousins? However far removed?

For the first time in my life I understand the meaning of the phrase 'the hairs rose on the back of her neck'. It prickles.

CHAPTER TWENTY-SEVEN

'Do you never drink, Dale?' For the first time since ten years ago in Tenerife – a night *not* to remember – I was out to dinner with a man (except for Jimmy Porter, who likes Abrakebabra and Burger King: 'It's food, Bella. What's the point in spending hard-earned cash on fancy sauces?'). It took me a while to realise my dinner companion was drinking only juice.

'No, I don't drink alcohol any more.' He smiled. 'Not for more'n twenty-two years. Twenty-two years, four months and eleven days. Exactly.'

'Oh!' Hazily, I twigged. 'You're . . .' I didn't like to say it. Anyway, it had too many syllables. Because of delayed jet-lag I'd been having difficulty with my tongue this evening.

'Yes.' He helped me out. 'I'm a recovering alcoholic.'

Well, there was no answer to that, was there?

We had finished the main course – he'd had snapper, I'd had steak (I'd asked for French fries with it but instead had been offered 'freedom fries'. The waiter seemed a little shifty about this and Dale had intervened: 'Don't ask, Arabella. It's to do with Saddam Hussein and Iraq'). I had declined his offer of wine with the meal, because I had discovered margaritas.

It turned out they specialised in margaritas in the Saddle Horn: they use freshly squeezed lime juice and it goes down easy, like homemade lemonade on a summer's day. I'd had four or five. By the way, did you know there are more than fifty brands of tequila? Maybe a hundred? I didn't. You learn something new every day, don't you? Especially in the Saddle Horn . . . Lovely place. Lovely.

I remembered something. Eve's diary had seemed to imply that when she first came to America, she'd had a drink problem too. 'Hey, Dale, is that how you met Eve? Through the drink?'

'I met her through a car wreck, actually.'

'Oh, I know that bit,' I waved this away, 'but people meet people in acc— in car crashes all the time. But they don't necess—' I couldn't say 'necessarily' so I abandoned it. 'They don't keep in touch for years afterwards like you two have. They don't end up living side by side in his-and-hers trailers. Is it the drink that you have in common or what?'

'This is always confidential, but since you seem to have guessed anyway, I was Eve's sponsor in AA. It's not one way, though, Arabella. She's been good to me too. We've been good for each other.'

Bingo! *I have you now, Mr St Francis of Assisi* . . . I know all about AA and sponsors because of Rowan. I pounced. 'I thought you weren't suppose to sponsor anyone of the opposite sex?' That came out grand and clear. No stuttering or anything.

He didn't bite. 'It's not encouraged. But it happens.' He was patient. He was maddening.

'Here's another thing,' I enunciated carefully, 'I've – I have been wondering why you're being so good to us. So generous. You don't know us from Adam. I mean, me and Willow and Rowan. You don't know us at all. And you are being so . . .' I searched '. . . so *good*. Why are you being so *good*, Dale? Are you a saint or what? What's the story, Dale?'

He sat back in his chair. Tonight he was wearing a sort of fringy thing – you couldn't call it a shirt – in pale cream suede. The fringes moved when he moved. It was fascinating, the way they moved. In between the tracks of the music, you could hear them making a little sound. *Frip. Frip.* 'When you say "good",' he said slowly, 'Eve is a good person. You probably don't know her well enough yet, Arabella, but you'll see. She has overcome a lot.'

'We've *all* overcome a lot. She *deserted* us, Dale. Do you know what that means? To be deserted?' I leaned forward and looked at him with belligerent, piercing eyes. 'Were you ever deserted, Dale?'

He shook his head and it was my turn to sit back. To consider the injustice of three little kids being deserted by their heartless mammy. *Abandonatas. Abandonistas?* Whatever . . . No point in going on about it to Dale any more. *When you have the advantage, don't use it*, yeah? Greta always says that, or her granny does. I forgot which.

So I decided not to beat Dale over the head with Eve's heartlessness. Nevertheless, as I reached again for my margarita (lovely glass, by the way,

161

heavy, good weight in the hand) the well-worn picture in the Palm House assembled itself again behind my eyes.

The three of us.

Three pathetic mites dwarfed by giant lily-pads.

So little. So alone.

No one to speak up for them.

It was tragic. *Tragic.*

I sipped. But my glass was empty. 'Uh-oh!' Puzzled, I looked down into it.

'Would you like another drink, Arabella?'

'Maybe.' I faced up to Dale. 'That's if . . .' I got cunning. Planned what I was going to say. 'That's if it doesn't compromise your non-drinking principles.'

I was delighted with myself. That had been a great sentence. I stared hard at him. I wanted this teetotaller, this friend of my alcoholic, immoral, abandoning mother, to object to my having another margarita. Let him just try.

Instead, he raised a hand and caught the attention of a waiter. 'Another margarita, please, Sam, and I'll have coffee.'

'Would you like to see the dessert menu, Mr Genscher?' The waiter had got sort of huge suddenly. Maybe eight feet tall.

Dale looked enquiringly at me.

'No.' I waved the giant waiter away.

Dale smiled at him. I saw him signal something to the man with his eyebrows. I took this as an insult. 'What are you apologising for?'

'I didn't.'

'It seems to me you did. At the – at the very least you were patron-patronising. If there's one thing I do know,' ponderously, I put down my glass and wagged a finger at him, 'if there is *one* thing I *know* about, it's waiting tables. I didn't insult that waiter.'

'You didn't.'

'Stop agreeing with me. What's the story, Dale?'

'I don't know what you mean.'

'What's the *story*, Dale? Why won't you answer me? What's the fucking story?'

That's where the memory stops. It's now just after seven o'clock the following morning. I'm on a bed in someone's trailer. I'm supposed to be back in my lovely country-house B-and-B, but I'm certainly not there. I know this is a trailer because of the lowness of the ceiling and how small the metal window is. It is open and uncurtained, the sky is bright and I can hear scuffling in the gravel outside. A bird, maybe, or Ginger. I'm fully dressed except for my shoes, not between the sheets but on top, with a light blanket over me. I can't move. I'm afraid to move. I'm pinned to the spot like a horrified butterfly.

My first sensation on waking a couple of minutes ago was disbelief. *Where am I?*

The second was physical: as if I was drowning in hot sand.

The third, the worst, was a detailed recollection of the exhibition I'd made of myself in that restaurant with Dale. Every drunken word is written in clear capital letters on every surface in the bedroom, and no matter how much I go over it, not one changes.

The poor waiter is the final actor in the scene. I have a foggy memory of him bringing the last margarita – then nothing. Did I fall asleep? Did I pass out? What? The rest of the evening is a blank.

In case you ever feel like having a few margaritas with your dinner, let me share with you how I feel now. I can't lift my head from this pillow because the room tilts and spins if I try; my tongue seems to have swollen; light from the gap between the curtains hurts my eyes; not much pain elsewhere yet but there is severe nausea and fatigue. My legs and arms are without muscles. Mentally and emotionally, each thought, word and image from the previous night arrives packed in shame, regret, horror. As soon as I can, I'll get a roll of toilet paper and write *I'm sorry, I'm sorry, I'm sorry, I'm sorry* on its entire length from this bed to the entrance to Robinia Meadows . . .

Oh, God. I've just heard Dale cough. There's a coffee smell. He's making coffee in the kitchen. This is Dale's trailer. The embarrassment. The mortification. Did he put me to bed? Did he have to carry me?

And who else saw me in that condition? Did Eve? The rest of her gang? Dear God, please not Rowan – after all the lectures I gave him. Not Rowan, please . . .

I want to vanish from the face of the earth. I'll abandon this whole exercise. I could be back in Ireland in twenty-four hours; no one at home would ever know what a show I made of myself. I'll make it up to Jimmy Porter for every bad word and unkind thought I've ever said or had

163

about him. I'll settle quietly and happily into spinsterhood. I'll baby-sit Greta's grandchildren and I'll be everyone's favourite aunt. I'll love the Leicester and Dublin and all the yobbos and little gurriers I've been so mean about . . .

Yes, that's a good plan. I'll escape as soon as I can manage to get out of this bed. I'll leave a note. Say I was called back urgently to work . . . Yeah, to serve an urgent sausage.

Shit, there's no way out, even if I could manage to move. I'm trapped.

It serves me right, what happened – oh, God, here's another memory: me challenging Dale in the pickup. *Whaddya mean when you said Eve played games . . . ?*

I think it was the pickup – we were moving and my head kept banging off something. *You said she always pretended to be asleep when the going got tough. Did you or did you not say that, Dale? That's an insult to my mother, Dale . . .*

Flip to yet another picture. Pin-sharp. Dale is pulling the blanket over me, looking down at me: 'You'll need water, Arabella. There's ice water in that jug on the bureau.'

Christ! He seems to be coming towards this door. I'll close my eyes. Pretend I'm still asleep. Maybe he'll go away. He might have to go to town. That'll be my chance.

He's knocking. He's knocking again. 'Hello, Arabella? You awake?'

Keep eyes closed. Breathe slowly and evenly.

'Arabella?'

Go away – go away, please go away.

'I'll leave these here for you. Washroom's the inside of that white door.' I hear something being put on the dressing-table. Feel something landing gently across my feet. Footsteps. Door closing.

When I'm sure he's gone, carefully, inch by inch, I struggle to a sitting position and when the whirligig of stars and stripes in front of my eyes slows down to bearable speed, I find that Dale has given me a set of towels and one of those bathrobes you get in hotels. Plus a disposable toothbrush complete with miniature tube of toothpaste and bottle of mouthwash, all neatly packed in an unopened plastic bag. On the dressing-table is my handbag. It wasn't there when I opened my eyes. He'd had to rescue that too. Dale Genscher, the Bionic Samaritan. I can't stand it.

I lie back. There's no escape. I have to face it. Him. I have to face *him*.

Head low, I make it next door to the shower, sluice water from the hand basin on to my face, dash some into my mouth, undress. The effort causes me to throw up, but at least I make it as far as the toilet bowl. After a minute or so in the shower, I have to rush out to throw up again.

I have a second shower. A long one, hot, then cool, then hot, cool, hot and cool again, letting the water flow across my head and face until I feel marginally better. I wrap myself in the robe, break open the plastic bag, brush my teeth and use the whole bottle of mouthwash to rinse the taste of vomit out of my mouth. Then I pray.

In the kitchen area of his mobile home, my host, whose hair is loose and darkly wet, is dressed in jeans and snowy T-shirt, squeezing oranges in an electric juicer. 'Good morning! It's going to be a lovely day.' While my stomach heaves again, I search for condemnation, jeering, judgement. 'Would you like some breakfast?' he asks.

Sarcasm?

'No, thank you,' a dismal whisper. I clear my throat. 'Look, Dale . . .'

'Food would be good, Arabella.' He juices the next orange as though he hadn't heard me. 'You need starch. And lots of water.' He pours some from a clinking jug and hands it to me. 'At least have waffles. French toast?' He pops open a cupboard. 'And here – take two of these.' He hands me a pack of analgesics. Excedrin, it says on the pack. Never heard of it. It'll do.

'I don't suppose you have tea?'

'Let's see what we got.' He opens a second cupboard, exposing ranks of packets and pots, lined up according to size and bulk as if arranged by a stylist from a glitzy interiors magazine. He surveys his stocks. 'Earl Grey? Or good old Lipton's? Hey! Look here – how about some Irish Breakfast?'

Sick and all as I am, I'm awed and all I can do is nod.

'Cream or lemon?'

'Milk?'

'You go on out to the deck. Sun's up but we don't get it out there until later in the morning. I'll bring your tea when it's ready.'

'But I'm not dressed.'

'Hoo-oooh, boy!' He chuckles. 'It's cool! We're in Robinia Meadows, Arabella, not some country club.'

It doesn't seem to occur to him that I might worry about what people think. A woman in her dressing-gown coming out of a man's trailer at half seven in the morning? But I'm too sick to care. Let them think what they like – after I leave, I'll never see any of these people again. Self-consciously, I pull the belt of the robe tighter round my waist and step past him out on to the deck.

In his trailer, pottering about his calm, uncluttered living area (at first sight the impression is of lots of cream, white, no gew-gaws or even family photographs, lots of stainless steel in the kitchen area), Dale seems different somehow, less laid-back. I suppose people act differently in their own place.

I sit in one of his chairs and swallow the tablets he gave me, then raise my hot, scratchy-skinned face to the sky, close my eyes and will the hangover to be merciful, Dale's memory of last night to be erased, some miracle to happen.

No miracle, but Ginger comes across the deck and, with no warning, leaps, purring, on to my lap and settles down.

Willow, I think, should be nearly home, if she's not already. I'm too tired and sick to work out the timings.

It's very still, the purr of the cat emphasising the quiet. From various trailers around me, I hear relaxed domesticity, the clink of dishes, the flush of a toilet, the scraping of a chair across a deck. Right now I could do with a good book to distract me and wish I hadn't forgotten to bring my library book. Anyhow, I'm so sleepy I wouldn't be able to concentrate. I'll just close my eyes for a minute . . .

'Good morning, Arabella!' I'm jerked awake. A car has stopped in front of Dale's deck. It's Robert, shiny and shaved in a flawlessly white shirt, calling to me through his open window. I sit upright. 'Good morning.' The cat, offended, jumps off my lap.

'Enjoying our good old Arizona weather?' He smiles.

'It's lovely. I should make the most of it. It's probably raining at home.' Irish weather is always good for conversation. 'Are you going to work?'

'What else? Another day, another dealer, another dollar.'

'What do you work at?'

'Me and Mario got a art gallery in town, some good stuff, some not so good, but it's the not-so-good that pays the rent – or, in my case, the alimony. It's a gas, really, my ex-wife's one of our top sellers. As it happens she's in town and doing a few shifts at the gallery, probably checking out if I'm doing her out of somethin'.' He laughs, but without bitterness.

'Suits me. Gives me more free time. You must come in some day. Sedona's tops for artists, you know. Millions of 'em, and gallery owners, flies around the honeypots. Ask Dale to fill you in.

'But, hey, Arabella, Mario and I would like to invite everyone to a barbecue this evening. It'll be a squeeze, our deck isn't that large, but we've managed before. Mario will cook. I'll do the drinks. How about it? And don't worry, I won't be asking my ex-wife. We're not *that* friendly!'

At the thought of barbecued meat, my stomach lurches, but I manage to control it. 'That'd be great. I'd love that.'

'Great. Seven, seven fifteen. Spread the word. Pity your sister had to go home so quickly.'

'Yeah.'

''Bye!' He drives off just as Dale comes out with a little tray. 'Was that Robert?' He draws up a little table and puts the tray on it.

'He's invited us all to a barbecue tonight. I assume he means Eve, Rowan and Gina as well – listen, Dale . . .'

'Drink your tea, babe. I know what you're sayin', I know how you're feelin'. Been there. Think nothin' of it.' He sat down in another chair. 'That was yesterday. Today is another day, thank the Lord.'

I stare at him. 'Are you very religious, Dale? Evangelical?'

'Lord no.' He laughs quietly, then becomes serious. 'At least, not lately. Used to be. I was a JW.'

JW? 'I beg your pardon?'

'A Jehovah's Witness. No longer, I'm afraid.' For the first time since I encountered Dale Genscher I see a look of pain on his face. Maybe I'm super-sensitive because of the hangover.

'Did you just get fed up?' I had in mind the pairs of Jehovah's Witnesses I'd encountered in Dublin, trained, no doubt, in how to maintain a safe distance from slamming doors. I'd often felt sorry for them – they were so sleek and nice and eager, but welcome nowhere. Once I'd even asked them in for a cup of tea, then regretted it because it was hard to get rid of them without being insulting.

'No, not really,' Dale says. 'Actually, I was disfellowshipped.'

CHAPTER TWENTY-EIGHT

I think I hear Robert's car going by, which means it has to be some time after seven-thirty because it's his early shift in the gallery today. I'm going to have to get a clock put where I can see it when I'm lying on this side.

Today I'm going to break through to Rowan. It's not going to be easy, but I'm determined. I tried yesterday, I really tried, but he's a tight one. Gently does it, I think. I hope we'll have enough time. If I can break Gina away from him for a while.

Him and Gina, now there's something no one expected. I think Arabella approves.

He's a sweet boy, you know. So sweet it's still hard for me to accept what the girls told me about him . . .

I suppose it's time I got up. I'm so comfortable, though. So tired – and so sad. I didn't think the world could hold so much sadness. Isn't that typical? Just when you get excited, the world kicks you in the stomach. It's awful that Willow rushed off like that. I was right not to believe that it was about the kid. It was sticking out a mile that the problem was me.

Oh, for God's sake, Eve Rennick. Get a life. Stop feeling so sorry for yourself. You have two of them still here. That's two more than you ever thought you'd see. You're alive and you're healthy – at least, you'll be healthy when you get this goddamn cast removed – and the pain is less every day. You're not dead yet, are you?

Who's to say you won't go to Ireland after all? You have grandchildren to see. She won't keep you from your grandchildren. You can get to know her then. For now, just keep your mind on Arabella and Rowan. It's a privilege to have them here – make the most of them.

Feels like it's going to be another scorcher . . .

Yeah, that's definitely Robert's car. It's the only one around here that makes that sort of chug-chug sound. I think it's because it's a diesel. Robert's a decent man. I don't really know his wife, although I have met her from time to time, but it must be awful to wake up one day and find out that your husband, whom you thought you'd be living with for the rest of your life, wants to leave you for a man. At least he told her straight up and honourable and didn't let her find out for herself, like some people I've read about.

You know, having thought about it until I'm blue in the face, I'm not all that sure I should tell Arabella and Rowan the full story about why I left them. I know that's the rock bottom of what they'll really want to know, but maybe I should fudge it a bit. Willow certainly thinks that their daddy is the hard-done-by one in this story – she left me under no illusion about that. Mightn't it be better to leave it so? Let them have one fantasy parent? If so, I'm going to have to get that diary back from Arabella lickety-split.

Am I getting noble in my old age? What about the Eve Rennick who ducked and dived her way through some pretty hairy situations? Wasn't she the one who, smashed as she was when she was brought in D and D to the precinct station, was still cunning enough to pretend she was pregnant so the young cop would feel sorry for her and not throw her in the tank? Wasn't it her who piggy-backed on Dale Genscher's generosity for years? Who, until she ran out of heartrending stories, preyed on his sympathy so she could keep drinking?

Was this the same Eve Rennick who's thinking noble about Petey Moraghan?

No, schmuck! This is the Eve Rennick who's thinking noble for her kids' sake. So she should. If they're ever going to have a relationship with her . . .

In anyway, Petey Moraghan, Prince of Parents? That's a laugh.

Him and me started walking out quite soon after we met in that café in O'Connell Street and one thing led to another. I found myself in trouble just before Christmas that same year. There was no point beating around the bush. I'm a straight person. When I told Petey, though, he vamoosed. Immediately. Took the mailboat.

In the house in Iona Road it was Mr Portman who found out. He heard me crying in the scullery one night when he came downstairs for a glass of water, and before I knew it I'd chucked up the whole story.

There was murder, of course. I was their third maid to get into trouble in four years and they were mad as hell. I couldn't stay with them, naturally, they said, because of the scandal. Mrs Portman was for throwing me out straight away, but Mr Portman felt sorry for me and said he'd find Petey and make him face up to his responsibilities if it was the last thing he did.

He did too. Traced Petey through the army. I'm not sure how, it's all gone a bit fuzzy, but I think it was because Petey was stupid enough to apply for discharge papers or a pension and gave the army his address in England.

So he was hauled back and we got married on 19 January 1961, three weeks after my sixteenth birthday. Arabella was born the following April but I'm not going to go into the whole rigmarole of the next three years. It's all in the diary anyway. All I will say here is that I had three kids one after the other in a single room in a tenement house; that my husband turned out to be a drinker and a wife-beater (although when he didn't take me by surprise, I gave as good as I got – I was bigger than him); that he was so bone idle I had to take in washing and skivvy any place I could find work so as to put bread and milk into my children's mouths.

The last straw came on 16 December 1964 when I was lumping the two older kids home after trying in vain to get a few clothes for them for Christmas from Ozanam House, the St Vincent de Paul depot on Gardiner Street. I'd arrived too late: the place was closed for the evening. So, bone weary, half dragging Arabella and carrying Willow, I set off for home.

I hadn't gone fifty yards and was passing the Hill 16 pub on the opposite side of the street, when who should I see coming out through the door but my darling husband who was supposed to be at home minding the baby. He had his arm round a young one and the two of them were giggling and kissing with not a care in the world. Remember, I was still only nineteen.

It's funny the things you notice and remember at times like these. She had on fishnet tights, red shoes and a waspie belt round her waist over her jacket, which was a dark-coloured thing with brass buttons. I remember there was a hackney car going by at the time and a messenger boy on a bike. I remember there was half a chewed apple in the gutter beside where I was standing. I don't remember her face. I don't think I even looked at it.

A coldness came over me. I stopped hustling Arabella, who was whingeing and asking to be picked up. Instead I dawdled and let the two lovebirds get well ahead of us.

I hadn't known about Petey and women – I had thought his late nights and early mornings were just drinking – but that sight of him outside Hill 16 was sort of a relief. I had to do something about him now. Those few minutes, while he and his tart canoodled their way down to Summerhill, made up my mind for me about my husband and his fists, his drink and his keeping us in rags. Never again would I lie under the beery breath – and my kids would get the foundation they deserved.

I kept the coldness going. It wasn't hard, because when I got to the room I found the baby in a terrible state, crying and freezing in his own filth. I cleaned him up, and when I was sure he was OK again I went downstairs to Maura's room.

Maura was my friend in the house. She was what they used to call in them days a Deserted Wife and we'd clicked straight off, right from the day I'd moved in. We told each other everything. She had recently found herself on the pig's back because, out of the blue, her auntie in America had died and left her money, quite a lot by our standards in them days. As a result, she was looking around for a better place for herself and her kid, even thinking of buying a little house.

I didn't even sit down for a cup of tea, although Maura, God bless her, had a real mahogany table that she got somewhere out of a skip. (People were throwing out dark heavy things then; I knew from cleaning their houses that the nobs were changing to blond wood and Maura had gotten herself a lovely big mahogany wardrobe too.) I stood in that room, which was bigger than ours, and, cold as stone, I asked Maura for a lend of money, straight out. I told her I couldn't stay in that house for one month more. I told her about Petey and the tart, and that I had to get away. 'And I'll pay you back every penny, Maura, you know I will.'

I didn't tell her everything. I didn't tell her I was going to leave the kids, in case she tried to stop me. I told nobody that. I let her believe I was taking them with me and that it was England we were going to, but even before I got home I'd decided I'd be going on my own. How could I bring three babies with me when I had to be available for any work that was going, day or night? Probably day *and* night.

Maura was always talking about America, how well her auntie had done there, how easy it was to get work and 'the one thing about America, Eve, is that I believe they're willing to give you a chance. They don't care what your background is.' So that's what made me choose America over England.

Plus I wanted to get far away from Petey Moraghan as possible.

My lovely friend gave me that lend with a heart and a half and no questions asked. 'There's no hurry paying it off, Evie,' she said, giving me a hug. 'Get yourself fixed up first. Sure there's enough here to do us all, and what's it for only to be used? I'll go to the bank first thing tomorrow morning and you can come with me. Oh, Lord, Eve, did I ever think we'd be going to a *bank*?'

That's how I was able to book my passage to America.

Petey turned up home at about four o'clock in the morning that 16 December – the seventeenth, as it was by then – drunk as a skunk. I heard him come in. I felt him getting into the bed. He stank, but I didn't move in case he touched me. The kids and I left for the day before he got up next morning. He'd left a manky bunch of chrysanthemums on the table for me, going brown and mushy at the stems. Robbed out of somebody else's vase. Hers?

After I booked my passage, I showed the passport office the ticket and told them I had to go quickly because I had a sister who'd been in a bad car accident. I cried at the counter when I was telling them. It wasn't hard, them tears were genuine, stinging all the time in the skin below my eyes when I thought about what I was doing. But I was determined. Me and my kids were going to be survivors.

They felt sorry for me in the passport office: they hurried up the procedures and helped with getting me the visa from the American embassy. It was almost too easy – it must have been the Christmas spirit in the place: there were tinsel decorations and a little tree and I suppose they were all in a good mood and feeling charitable. Times since, I've thought that if I'd hit opposition at any stage I mightn't have gone through with it.

Mostly I managed to avoid Petey for the next while. He didn't come home some of the nights and I never opened my mouth to complain. I didn't even have a row with him about his tart, just gave him his dinner and his tea, if he wanted to eat, which he didn't a lot of the time. Once I caught him looking at me, sort of puzzled, and twice he tried to provoke a row but as soon as he started, I always left the room and went down to Maura. I knew he wouldn't come after me to her place; whited sepulchre that he was, he never wanted anyone *else* to think badly of him. I'd wait until I heard him clomping down the stairs and then I'd go back up to the kids.

There were no goodbyes to Petey. I did leave him a note, but I don't know if he got it. He hadn't come home for a couple of nights before Christmas Eve. I don't know if he came home for Christmas Day, even, that year. Maura would have told me, but since I wasn't able to contact her I never knew. Saying goodbye to her was hard. No point in going into it here. You can imagine . . . Especially as I was lying to her. My best friend.

Well, not exactly lying. I just let her continue thinking what she thought. She gave me extra money to buy them sweets. 'But they'll be calling it "candy" over there, Evie! They'll become little Yanks, they will.'

'No, they won't!'

That was when I nearly lost it. I started to cry but she hugged me real quick and shoved me out the door. 'Go on. Ye'll be late.' Maura's original family was from the country and she said things like 'ye'. She closed her door while I was still standing there.

The ticket was through London, a return ticket, and when I got to New York the immigration people let me through without any bother. Maybe they were infected with the Christmas spirit too. The guy who examined my visa was black. I'd never spoken to a black man before but he was very nice. Maura, God be good to her, had lent me a costume too, and I was wearing the little pillbox hat, like Jackie Kennedy's, that I'd worn for my wedding so he may have thought I was gentry. He even said, 'Welcome to America.'

I made myself welcome, all right. Too welcome.

After about five months, I posted a bit of money to Maura – that was as soon as I could manage. I sent it with a letter telling her all about my adventures in America and I promised to send the rest as soon as I could. Because she didn't know where she'd be living, she had given me the address of one of her cousins down the country, but the letter came back 'addressee unknown'. I was horrified. I wrote again, this time without the money, but that letter came back too. I wrote and wrote but every one of them letters came back. I have them still in the tin box. I wonder, has Arabella read them yet?

Poor mite, holding her own tin box with the white little face on her in the gloom of that Palm House. I'll never forget the smell. Sort of sweet. Like rot.

After I left them there I don't know where I ran to first, although I had planned to turn right from outside the gates and head towards town. When push came to shove, though, my blood was driving me hard, like an accelerator, until it felt like it would burst out through my face. So I must have turned left, up and over the bridge, because the next thing I knew I was sitting on a seat beside the Tolka, on that special walk down below the Wooden Church, and a man was sitting beside me and asking me if I was all right.

I wasn't all right, but I told him I was.

He wouldn't leave me alone. He was doing my head in, keeping on asking and asking why I was crying. I think he thought I was going to throw myself in.

He had a point. It had been raining heavily for most of the week and the Tolka was very high, nearly up to the banks, and running fast. Although it wasn't something I'd thought of, if I'd stayed there looking at, it might have dawned on me to drown myself that day. It would have been quick. A few minutes and no more pain. Ever.

Upset and all as I was, I wasn't going to throw away the plan, though, because, honest to God, I was going to come back for them. So, to get rid of the do-gooder, I pretended I'd had a row with my boyfriend but that I was sure it was just one of those barneys that most people have and that it'd probably all blow over. 'Are you sure?' he goes. 'Are you sure you're not lying to me now?'

'Why would I lie about a thing like that?' I made myself sound indignant. All the time I was seeing my three little children. What was happening to them right this minute? Were they being taken away by the police now? Would the people that got them to take care of be nice to them? Suppose they were given to cruel people?

I nearly jumped up and ran back to the Botanics but it was too late. There was no going back now. If they were to have any chance at all of a half-decent life, I was doing the best for them. Although it doesn't take away the guilt, I still think that and no one will tell me different.

The Good Samaritan gave up, but not before handing me a Miraculous Medal that you'd hang round your neck on a loop of blue wool. 'It's from

Lourdes. I put it into the Grotto, and when I was in Rome, I had it blessed by the Holy Father during an audience in St Peter's Square. Say a prayer to Our Lady and the Little Flower, Martina.' I'd told him my name was Martina, I've always liked that name. 'If this boyfriend of yours is a good lad, he'll see that whatever it is, it isn't that important in the larger scheme of things.'

'I will,' says I. 'Thank you, sir.'

I waited until he had gone and then, just in case he was still watching me, walked as slowly as I could manage down the River Walk towards Mobhi Road. It was the longest walk of my life.

It sure is going to be a hot one today. I can feel the heat already. I wonder, is Arabella up yet? Did she like the Saddle Horn? Dale likes it. He eats like a horse and the portions are huge there. I don't know how that man stays so thin, like a twig. Maybe I should have gone with them – he did invite me, but I was sick sore and sorry after Willow running off like that. I wasn't in the mood.

We didn't arrange any definite time for Arabella to come back today. I hate that: I like to have something to aim for. I should take it as another lesson in patience, I suppose, and humility. I was never big on humility. For sure I was downtrodden – you only have to hear my life story to know that. For sure I had no parents or family and it's too late to find any now. For sure I wasn't educated except in the basic three Rs (although someone reading my diary might wonder even about that!). I wasn't, amn't, one of those heroines who fights against her station and triumphs to become a happy millionaire – you can see that for yourself.

All that stuff is on the surface, however, and there's a big difference between being downtrodden and feeling downtrodden. Deep inside, no matter what happened to me through the years, I never accepted that anyone in the world, even the Queen of England or the Tsar of Russia, was better than me. That's something I probably inherited from my parents, whoever they were. Dale has this great line on that. Nature versus nurture, he calls it, and in my case nature, wherever it came from, won out. What kept me going, even through the booze and the worst times, was that I could always look a person straight in the eye.

I don't feel like looking at anyone today. Willow's gone, the itching is murder inside this goddamned cast and I need to go to the bathroom, but I know that as soon as I move from this position in the bed, my goddamn ribs are going to act up. My arms are killing me, too, from using those goddamn crutches.

Oooh! Poor Eve. Moan, moan, moan.

Why don't you think up something else to moan about? Here's an idea. Go back and live totally in the past. Tell everyone again how hard-done-by you were. Lie here. Don't move. Wallow. Let your kids see what you're made of. Wallow for the whole day. That'll get you two pints and a daisy.

CHAPTER TWENTY-NINE

My experience of hangovers is limited, but one thing I have noticed is that, despite the pain and the shame and the guilt, you feel relaxed. It's as though the body is saying to you: I've had enough. Stop bothering me with emotional stuff because I need to take a bit of time out. Chill!

So as Dale and I sit on his deck, him with his orange juice, me sipping tea, I'm not that bothered about anything. For once it's soothing to be an observer, noting the slow coming-to-life of the site: doors being flung open, decks swept, cars slowly driving by, neighbours surveying the cloudless sky and saying, 'Good morning,' to each other on their way to or from the site shop – they call it a 'store' – to collect newspapers, milk or breakfast food. The deck feels silky and cool under the soles of my bare feet. I catch a strong waft of coffee. There is unfinished business, however. 'Please will you let me say something, Dale?'

'I know what you want to say – you feel like a fool, right?'

'Right.'

'If you gotta say it, say it, but you're not a fool, Arabella. You got high once in your life. No big deal.'

'But you had to look after me.'

'Yes, ma'am – would you have had me leave you in the Saddle Horn?'

'But you had to carry my handbag.'

His expression makes me laugh. 'All right, all right. I give up. Just take it that I'm suffering now for my sins.'

'Drink your tea.'

'Thanks.'

Instead I tuck the mug under my chin and, luxuriating in the warmth of the china and the steam, I watch the sun's yellow-gold frontier creeping steadily towards us from the far side of the gravelled 'street'. Probably because of my shattered physical condition, not least the fatigue, I'm mesmerised, almost hypnotised by its slow progress. I can anticipate its glow – I can almost feel it.

Whuff! A large handsome bird I know to be a blue jay – because I had been startled by one the day before on Eve's deck – lands on the rail six feet away from where we sit. It regards us with a bright, brazen eye. Eve said that these are a species of magpie. One for sorrow. I'm not going to be superstitious today. I stare back and the bird, deciding there's no profit to be had here, takes off, flashing its colours in dismissal. The spell has been broken.

'Are those people away?' The trailer opposite, two down from Eve's, seems to be empty. The window blinds are pulled down, the plastic chairs stacked in a corner of the padlocked deck.

'We don't know much about 'em. They keep themselves to themselves. Seem to be OK people, though.' He lapses again into silence.

'And who owns the one on this side of Eve?'

'Good folks. I'll introduce you. A couple – I guess they're both divorced from other people. He's from Boston, works in a bank. She's a local, you'll find her in one of the health shops in town. You'll probably see 'em in a few minutes – they've only one car so they go in together.'

I consider this. Wonder what the residents of Robinia Meadows are saying about me, Willow and Rowan. From their perspective, I suppose any new faces here are conspicuous. 'Is it not claustrophic, like a fishbowl, living here, Dale? Everyone knowing everyone's business?'

'We all look out for each other down this end, and when you think about it,' he grins, 'there ain't many of us'd fit in anywheres else. Folks come, folks go, folks divorce or retire, folks downsize for a quieter life. We're most of us come here from changed circumstance, sure enough, but we stay here from choice. It's a community thing. As for it bein' a fishbowl, you give out as much real information about yourself as you want to, and you can't stop people gossipin' but that's not really a problem. 'Ceptin' for Mary Wu, of course,' he smiles affectionately, 'but Mary's OK. You gotta know how to handle her, that's all, what to tell her, what not to tell her and so forth. She's not the worst. We invite her if ever we have a party or somethin'. Better to have her inside the tent pissin' out . . .'

I look across at him, long legs stretched out, perfectly at ease. Had that been deliberate? Does he know he answered a slightly different question from the one I asked? 'What about crime? Everyone seems very relaxed.

Like, I've noticed you leave your car keys in the ignition and when I woke up earlier, the window in my bedroom was wide open. Was it open all night?'

'Oh, who'd want to steal that beat-up old wagon?' He smiles in the direction of the pickup, parked on a concreted patch among his vegetables. 'And we all leave our windows open as soon as spring is sprung in Sedona. Thievin's not much of a problem here. We have to watch the security on the drugstore, but other than that?' He shrugs. 'Look around! You see rich pickin's here? We're not perfect, of course, and with all the divorces and exes around, you have a domestic now and then but, by and large, we're peaceable.'

'Drugs? They're a big problem in Dublin.'

'Again, who knows? Now and then you'd find folks passin' joints but nobody cares about that.'

'How about yourself? Do you do it?'

'Dope? I'm an addict, Arabella. I can't touch nothin' like that.'

'But marijuana isn't addictive.' Although I'd never indulged in it I'd read the newspaper debates, and in England now they're apparently giving the stuff to people to help with diseases.

He shakes his head. 'Ain't addictive for some. Dangerous for most. Pretty dangerous for me.'

'Good morning, people!' Mary Wu waddles up to the rail of Dale's deck. As she approaches, I can see her lightning-fast assessment of the situation. 'Isn't it a wonderful morning, Dale?' She's addressed him but she's looking at me. 'You guys need anything from the store? Morning, Arabella.'

'Good morning.' I tighten the belt of my robe until it's in danger of giving me a hernia. 'It certainly is gorgeous today. Dale let me use his shower this morning.'

'No business of mine, dear.' She turns directly to Dale. 'You sure you don't want no newspapers or nothin', honey?'

'No, thanks. We got it covered.' Dale's voice is lazy.

'Well, if you're sure – see you guys later.' After another assessing glance at me and a rather strange smile at Dale, she moves off. I'm kicking myself.

'Forget it.' Dale's amused. 'She's harmless. She's just lonely, I guess, she has three kids but, well . . .' he looks off into the distance '. . . as for that deadbeat ex of hers . . .'

The world is full of abandoned people, I think, loosening my belt to a more comfortable tension. 'Do you have to go into town again today, Dale?'

'You want I should take you on a little sightseein' trip some day soon? Maybe Rowan too, although he seems to be doin' a little sightseein' of his own.' He grins.

I grin back. I'm having difficulty (a pleasant difficulty) coming to terms with what's happened to Rowan. We've hardly seen him since he met Gina. I know Eve is disappointed on one level, but I've tried to explain to her how this might be the best thing that could have happened. And of course she's convinced that Willow and I were exaggerating about his lifestyle. 'Thanks,' I say to Dale. 'We'll ask him when he surfaces. If he surfaces.'

'But what about your business?' I return to the point of my inquiry about him going into Sedona today. 'Can you just take off any time you want to?'

Although his posture doesn't change, his expression does. He sharpens. 'You want to know what line I'm in.' It's a statement, not a question.

'I have been curious, yes. But if you feel I'm intruding . . .'

'No intrusion.' He looks away, along the line of mobile homes, towards one of the red cliffs, clear and sharp against the blueness of the sky although I'm guessing it's miles away. 'If I don't want to tell someone somethin' I don't tell 'em.'

'Sorry.'

'Arabella, don't apologise. It's normal conversation, especially here in the States. First question anyone asks is "What do you do?"'

'At home too, but it's the second question. The first question is "Where are you from?" It's like we have to place people on a map to be able to talk to them.' I pause for a fraction of a second to give him an opening but he doesn't jump in. 'Can I ask you about something else, Dale?' Mentally I reserve the right to come back to Dale's 'business'. 'Tell me about being a Jehovah's Witness. I've never talked to one before, not voluntarily, that is.'

He smiles, but not, I think, with amusement, and again I see that shadow of pain. 'It's a long story.'

'Well, what was that about dis-disfellowsomething that happened to you?' I couldn't remember the word.

'Disfellowshipping. It means you've been cast out by the tribe.'

'Why would that happen?'

'Many reasons. Mainly if you ask too many questions. If you're not obedient. If you don't accept instructions. If you're not compliant.' His posture and demeanour have changed radically. He is tense.

'Dale, if you don't want to talk about it . . .'

He's gazing at me, weighing me up. He waves in response to a beep from a passing car, but distractedly. 'I'm obviously trespassing here,' I say, when the car has gone. 'Just tell me to shut up, right? My friend Greta would tell you I'm a terrible nosy parker.'

'How much do you know about the Witnesses?'

'Not a lot. They take the Bible literally?'

'That too.'

I wait. Whatever it is, it's serious. I'm now regretting opening up the subject. I'm also intrigued, but when the seconds run into a minute: 'Look, Dale, forget I asked. You're entitled to your privacy.'

'There's no secret about it, no shame. But the only person on this site who knows what happened is your mom.'

'It doesn't matter, really.'

But he has decided to trust me with his story. My tea gets cold in the telling of it.

Speaking softly and looking straight ahead, he tells me he was born into a family within what he calls the Watchtower Society. Both his parents, now dead, were fervent believers and practitioners, but from his late teens he questioned some of the edicts, such as the organisation being the sole channel of information between God and humanity, the authoritarianism, and most particularly the 'rationalising'.

'Like what, for instance? Could you give me an example?' I don't like to interrupt him, but to fix something new in my mind I'm the kind of person who needs a concrete image.

He glances at me, then looks at his feet. He, too, is barefoot. His toes are long, nails clipped. 'Our leaders and elders would pronounce something as gospel truth,' he says quietly, 'like the end of the world would happen on a certain date or somethin' like that. When it didn't happen, they'd tell us that this was not a problem for the Society. That it was just a matter of interpretation. They'd twist it around. According to them, the fact that what they said would happen didn't was good news as it gave us all a new insight into the Bible.'

I think back to Eve's dissertation on Limbo and the dead baby of her friend, Maura. 'But every religion's like that, surely? The Catholic Church is forever changing things. No meat on Fridays – gone; Latin Mass – gone; stroke of the Pope's pen – no more St Christopher or St Philomena.'

'It's not quite the same. Catholics don't disown you for asking questions.'

'Oh, I don't know about that. Every so often I read about somebody being excommunicated for heresy.' I'm on shaky ground here, because my information on the more lurid side of religion comes from tabloid newspapers: *Bishop Recalled To Rome, Furious Pope Gags Cleric.*

'That's a very different matter. That's not simple questioning.' He pauses and it's clear he's not all that interested in having a theological debate. 'There is one thing you should know about me, Arabella,' he says slowly, watching me.

'Fire ahead?'

'I've been married. I have a son in Chicago and a daughter in Cleveland. At least,' he looks away as if he doesn't want me to see his face, 'I think that's where they are. If they haven't moved.'

I sip my cooling tea. 'How old are they now?'

I hope I'd managed the right tone. Semi-interested. Sophisticated.

'My son is twenty-seven, my daughter twenty-five.' I try to do the calculations but he's watching me again. Very intently. 'That would make me forty-nine,' he says.

I think he's amused but I'm not sure. Under normal circumstances, I would be flustered at being caught out but the hangover is still acting as insulation. 'Did your wife remarry?'

'I dunno.' He looks away again. What's going on here? This shiftiness, if that's what it is, is uncharacteristic. 'And before you ask, the reason I don't know, also the reason I'm not sure where my kids are, or my brother for that matter, is because I've been disfellowshipped. When that happens, there's a consequence, and my kids and my brother have shunned me.' He faces me again and, responding to my expression of disbelief, 'Yes, the JWs have a delightful practice called "shunning". It means, basically, that to them you're dead. Except they don't have the bother of visiting your grave.'

'That's awful, Dale.' I don't know what to say next. Insulation or not, I'm reeling, although why is not clear. Being shunned must be terrible.

Then – Hey! I think. We have something fundamental in common after all. He was shunned. I was abandoned. Same thing, nearly . . . But before I can go too far down this road, I remind myself that I've known this guy for, what, two or three days? He's telling me that he has, or had, a wife and two kids. That's certainly a surprise.

That's all it is, I tell myself firmly. A surprise. This is America. I'm going back to my own life in Ireland. Dale Genscher is a nice, decent, hospitable, helpful guy and it's great to have him around, but after I go home I won't give him another thought.

I realise he's still watching me. I smile at him but he doesn't smile back.

'I divorced her.'

'I see. What was her name?' *Idiot! What does it matter?* 'What're your kids' names?'

'She was, is, Martha. My kids are Janice and Joey. Joe, I suppose he'd call himself now that he's no longer a child.'

Janice. Joe. Martha. Real people suddenly.

'And you truly never hear from them?' *Oh, brilliant! Star question of the week, give the lady a goody bag . . .*

'No.' He shakes his head.

'When you say you were shunned, does that include all your mates from the religion?'

'One stuck with me but, as a consequence, he was DFW'd too.' He looks away, over my shoulder. 'We've lost touch. He's in Europe – France I think, or Germany. There's Eve.'

I look across. My mother is sitting in her chair. She seems to have the oxygen mask on. I'm alarmed. 'Is she OK?'

'I'm sure she is.' He's not bothered. 'The mask sometimes helps with the pain in her side until the pills kick in. She's using it less and less. But we should go say hello. She could probably do with company – and your company at that.' He stands up and waves, then turns to look down at me. 'Feel up to it, Arabella?'

He's back to being Dale, everybody's broad shoulder.

CHAPTER THIRTY

Bella was right when she said they don't like bad language here. Gina freaks when I use the F-word.

Last night, on condition that I watched my fu—

Sorry.

Last night, on condition I watched my mouth, she brought me to one of the places she works. She does shifts in a few places because she says she doesn't want to be tied down to any one job. The place she brought me to is a bar – you couldn't call it a pub – in this town near here called Sedona.

The shops is all these fu—

Sorry.

It's all headbangers selling little pyramids and crystals and herbs and stuff, and bits of art made out of string or old tin, and puppets. There's hippies everywhere and head massage and auras and things like that, but also these huge jeeps and cars the length of O'Connell Street, Lincoln Continentals. A Lexus here is as common as a Golf at home, nothing special. You get to know car marques when you've all day to look at them swishing by, so I can always tell you pretty accurately what's what in the car market.

There's loads of art galleries too, with paintings for megabucks. One I saw was twenty thousand dollars for a fu— Sorry. One was twenty thousand dollars for a white canvas with just a dark blue line across it. It's mad, it is. I might take up painting myself while I'm here. Like, how hard can it be to paint a dark blue line across a white background?

And these red rocks. Gina says there's four special ones in Sedona; they're called things like Cathedral Rock and Bell Rock, for instance, depending on the shape of them, and it's because of these, and the Vortexes, that the hippies and artists and health nuts come here. She tried to explain to me what these things are. It's to do with the earth attracting electricity or sending out electricity, I forget which, but the energy is so powerful you feel mad when you're near them. She says there's nowhere else in the world that there's four of these Vortexes collected in the one place and she's going to bring me around them so I can feel the energy for myself.

Actually, I'm quite looking forward to that.

Anyway, this place that she works, it's a restaurant too but she works in the bar part. The punters were a mixed bag, gangs of bints with spangles on their blouses and hair dyed off their heads, ordinary couples, a few baldies and gummies with string ties, wrinklies with cardigans, and at least a dozen homosexuals – Gina won't wear me calling them 'poofters'. I'm learning that you have to look at the world in a whole different way when you're with Gina. The walls in this bar were rough pink with bits of plaster hanging off, decorated with some of the same type of art I was telling you about, and the doors leading into the jacks had these coy pictures on them called 'stallions' and 'mares'.

I shouldn't be negative. The place was pretty game ball and everyone was real friendly on account of I was with Gina. The problem is that I'm so used to being suspicious of everyone, to them giving me a bad time, to keeping up the hard-man act that it's hard to adjust when people are nice and ask normal questions, you know? For instance, while he was polishing glasses, pulling beers, filling orders from Gina, this barman geezer was chit-chatting away to me, asking me about what kind of sports there are in Ireland and what do people like to do on a Saturday night (get locked, is the answer to that one) and would it be a good place to go for a holiday?

Gina wasn't able to give me any freebies but she kept the pretzels and the peanuts topped up in front of me, and because I was with her, the barman/manager doubled up now and then on the measures I was drinking. The two of them recommended bourbon to me and they were right. Actually it was mega, it was. It tastes soft going down but it's strong.

We had a few laughs. I told them a few Mental stories, like the one about how he blagged his way into a U2 concert by pretending to be a childhood neighbour of Bono's who'd come home specially from New Zealand for the gig and how, amazingly, Bono told the security guys to let him in because he admired Mental's guts.

'For real?'The barman is seriously impressed. So is Gina. In fact, they're both impressed that Bono and the other band members are, according to me, straight-up punters that'd say hello to you in the streets. That Bono himself said hello to me once when I was sunning myself on the steps up to one of those posh clubs on Stephen's Green. I'm enjoying being the centre of attention so I'm exaggerating a bit – it was me said hello, but Bono definitely smiled at me. A real smile, not one of those absent-minded things that you get when people are seeing through you, you know? 'Yup. One of Mental's proudest possessions is the snap of himself and Bono and Larry Mullen with pints in their hands.'

'Must try something like that next time I want to get into a Springsteen concert.' The barman laughed. Then, out of the blue, he asks me if I'm looking for a job.

Well, I'm not, of course, and I told him so. But I have to say I was chuffed. Like, do you think I'd be offered a job in Ireland? Would I what!

So then, because I'm chuffed, I change my mind. I call him back over and I tell him I'm on my holidays now but that you'd never know. That I might be in the jobs market. 'Depends,' I tell him.

'Ever worked in a bar before?'

'No.'

'Well, it's not rocket science. Take a guy like you, Rowan. Two, three days, you're on top of it. You speak English – you're already ahead.' He gave me a business card with the name of the bar and his own name. He's the manager. 'We're real short-staffed right now. You decide you want to try it, give me a call.'

'What about green cards and all that stuff?'

'They don't bother us here in Sedona. Not so far anyhow. Every bar and restaurant in town is in the market for staff. They know that. And it's a small town. They concentrate more on New Mexico and Texas and maybe Phoenix. We're a fair distance from the border here.'

'I've – I've no references. Haven't been working much lately . . .'

'If Gina vouches for you, that's enough for me. I know where she lives and works. You dip, she pays.'

'Taking over my job, eh?' In between serving the customers, Gina had been earwigging on this conversation. But I could tell she was pleased.

I'd surprised myself. A job? In America? It was the last thing I expected. Would I want it if there was no Gina?

That I couldn't answer. It was too soon. But I found myself looking down at the suit: I'd been wearing it since I got here. I'd have to get it cleaned. Actually, I should probably buy a few new duds . . .

The barman kept coming with the doubles. They don't seem to measure the stuff much, just splash in whatever they feel like giving you on top of a lot of ice cubes. If I was going to work here, I'd have to have a word with him about that. How can a bar make a profit that way?

I was getting carried away. Maybe it was the bourbon talking.

I put your man's business card safely in the inside pocket of the suit. I'd decide some other time.

Now I have a hangover.

I'm too hot this morning. She has all the sheets. I've kicked off her furry cover but I'm still roasting. She doesn't have air-conditioning but she's like a rake so she probably doesn't feel the heat.

She thinks my ma is great. I'm wrecked from all the travelling, not to speak of being in a headspin because of everything that's after happening with Gina, so I'll be honest with you, I haven't been thinking all that much about my ma. I don't know what to make of her. She's not what I expected. I thought she'd be a tart, I thought I'd hate her, and I had myself all worked up to give her a piece of my mind and I still might. That's why I came here in the heel of the hunt. I could have used that money for all kinds of things, you know, and I nearly did and all. I even went so far as to go to a dealer I know and ask him, casual like, where I could score a decent amount of blow. He was a bit suspicious, of course: 'Have you got the readies?'

'Of course I have. I wouldn't be asking—'

'Show us, then.'

'I didn't come down with the last shower.'

There was a bit of a row but he calmed down and said he'd ask around. I could be set up by now, I could.

But all the time there was this fucking hammer going in my head telling me to come here. She's your ma, bang! She's your ma, bang! I'm half sorry, but I'm not sorry about Gina.

Fuckit – feckit – I haven't the energy to be dealing with this. She wants to talk to me all the time, my ma, I mean, and keeps looking at me. It's freaking me out the way she looks at me. It's embarrassing.

Actually, it's more than embarrassing. She keeps asking me how am I and I have to freeze her out of it to shut her up; it's the only way I can manage. If I look at her in the eyes I'm afraid I'll cry or something. She has the exact same eyes that I have, and that's freaking me out nearly more than anything.

I'll get round to my ma some time. Before I go home anyway.

If I go home. Hey! I'm a man with a job offer! Fancy that! I'd nearly ring Mental to tell him but I can imagine what he'd say.

Gina used to be a social worker. It's a bit of a head-wrecker to be shagging a social worker because I have my own opinion about them. They're good-hearted and do the best they can with not much resources, but none of them ever did much for me, so thank God she's not one any more.

She still uses the jargon, though. After we got back to her place last night she said I had the attention span of a flea and the emotional age of a teenager. Her exact words. She said it joke-joke, but I could see she meant it. I was having a nice peaceful smoke after we did it in her bed and she ruined it. I got all insulted and I asked her what the fuck she meant.

So then she got all pissy and said she'd already warned me and she wasn't going to talk to me if I was going to use language like that and I could go and find other accommodation for the night.

I said I was sorry and she said, 'That's easy to say, but do you mean it, Rowan? I'm not going to tolerate the language of the gutter. Period.' She has this funny eye, as I think I told you, and she was fixing me with this mental stare. She was dead serious.

'If it's that important to you, I do mean it,' I said. I did too, funnily enough. I find I want to please her. She kissed me and said she forgave me. Then *she* said she was sorry.

'For what?'

'I'm sorry if I hurt you with what I said, Rowan, but we've got to know where we stand, you and me.'

'It's a bit early to get serious, isn't it?' At the same time I'm thinking that I can't remember when someone apologised to *me*.

'I'm a serious person,' she goes. 'I know what I like. Do you know what you like, Rowan?'

'I like this.' I grabbed hold of her.

'No.' She pushed me away. 'You know what I mean. I know it's very soon but, as I said, I have to know where I stand.' I was flummoxed and she saw it. 'You're not used to expressing your feelings, are you, Rowan?'

'No.'

She kissed me, real gentle and sweet, then drew back, holding my head between her hands. 'Do you think, given time and goodwill, we could make a go of this?'

'How do I know? As you said, it's early days – and you don't know much about me.'

'Tell me. I'm a good listener.'

Normally I'd shy away from this kind of thing as if it was contagious. But there were all these feelings stirred up. The kind of feelings I had forgotten I had. It was frightening. 'You're pushing me now, Gina – I don't know what you see in me anyhow. I'm bad news.'

'Not to me.' She sat back and pretended to count on her fingers. 'First of all, you're hot. Really hot! I'm a sucker for tall dark strangers with good pecs. Second, your accent's cute. Third, I think that underneath that tough veneer there beats a soft heart. Fourth, although you do your best to hide it, I think you're seriously bright. I wouldn't be interested if you weren't. And fifth, you're a challenge. I haven't been challenged much lately. Take that look off your face!'

'What look?' I'm *hot*? I'm bright? I'm soft-hearted?

'You look as if you don't believe me.' She laughed.

'I want to.'

'Well, do. Now,' she got serious, 'do you want to tell me a little bit about yourself from your point of view? What happened to you that you're so afraid of revealing anything about yourself? I mean outside of being abandoned, of course. That's a given.'

Next thing, I found myself giving her an edited version of my life to date. Cutting out some of the more grisly stuff, naturally, but including the dead girlfriend and child.

'You poor thing.' She gives me another of those real gentle kisses. 'No wonder you're the way you are. But you don't have to be any way at all with me, Rowan, OK? Just be yourself. I wasn't there when all those horrible things were happening to you and you're in Arizona now. You're in my house. This is a new week. But I agree we shouldn't push things and I'm sorry I frightened you. Let's see how it goes, huh?' She kissed me yet again, sexier this time, and next thing, we were back doing it, but not going at it, if you get my meaning. Sort of deeper. Like it meant something.

Sometimes I can't believe that this is happening to me, Rowan Moraghan.

I'm nearly afraid to say this next thing in case I'll put the mockers on it, but the really mad thing is that I like Gina. I like her a lot. I particularly like how in-your-face she is, you know?

She doesn't play twittery, head-wrecking games like some of the women I've known.

And last night – or, rather, a few hours ago at about half four in the morning, before we fell asleep – she said I was a stud. Straight out.

I told her she was a stud too. Laughing.

But there's more to it. It's scary.

CHAPTER THIRTY-ONE

I rang Willow today. Well, I didn't exactly ring her. At the last moment I bottled out because I knew it would be one of those spiky conversations I hate. And I was in enough misery with the hangover. No point in loading a bunch of emotional shit on top of it, I thought, so instead, I rang Greta, pretended I couldn't get through to Willow and asked her if she would pass on a message.

Selfish of me, I know. Willow has to be suffering and I'd imagine it's worse for her now that she's actually seen Eve. If I were in her shoes, I'd certainly be at sixes and sevens: I'd be guilty that I'd run off like a coward, I'd be feeling everything I imagined Eve would be feeling, I'd be giving myself a hard time. But, then, that's me and not her. Maybe I'm just trying to think of her as soft inside and maybe she's not feeling a damn thing. Maybe she really is as tough as she makes out and has already chalked this up to experience.

Dale offered me his mobile phone but I told him I wouldn't dream of using something so expensive, so he brought me to the site shop to get one of those pre-pay cards you can use on a public phone. The shop, air-conditioned, spotless, smelling of apples, turned out to be two trailers bolted on to each other with a door cut between the join. All four sides were covered with shelving, obviously custom made, and were surprisingly well stocked with all the basics, including bread and fresh vegetables and fantastic fruit. It would be possible to live on this site, I thought, never to leave it except for work, entertainment or emergencies. Hung-over or not, I found myself harking back to the fantasy I'd had in the fields around the B-and-B. Instead of looking for a live-in position as a housekeeper or laundry maid, I could rent a trailer on a site like this and commute. Be my own boss.

As well as the phone card, I picked up two lemons because I'd never seen them that big.

191

The shopkeeper sat at a table just inside the door, presiding over his electronic register and checkout, a smaller version of the checkout lanes in the supermarkets at home. There was a noticeboard on the wall, just to the right of his head, displaying hand-printed advertisements seeking and selling goods, services, even pets: 'Sheri, beautiful Chihuahua, loving companion, 5 years old, owner heartbroken but moving in with kids who are allergic. Also humidifier, barely used. Treadmill, still in delivery box. Knick-knacks, various, including antique lamp. Call at Earl Mills's, anytime before Friday 21st.'

As I paid for my purchases, I found myself worrying about Earl. Why was he living here in the first place if he had offspring willing to take him? Was he just too independent, or did he have a fantasy too? Why had he never used his treadmill? Did his doctor instruct him to buy it, but when the tests came back the news was worse than expected? Is this why he's giving in and moving in with his kids – because he can't fend for himself any more? As far as I knew, although I had lost track of the date, the twenty-first was only a few days away, so who's going to take loving little Sheri?

I had to resist the temptation to rush straight over to Earl's.

'Do people here own their trailers or are some of them for rent?' I asked Dale, when we were crunching along towards the public telephone. (He'd already shown me how to use the card. Very simple, if a bit *leadránach* – you had to punch in what seemed to be dozens of numbers before the one you wanted.)

'Why? You thinking of joining us, Arabella?'

'Of course not!' I was annoyed. 'I was only asking, that's all.'

'I don't know for sure down this end,' he said slowly. 'Occasionally you'll find one or two go up for rent or lease. Most of 'em are owner-occupied, though. Don't make sense to rent, does it?'

We had to step aside to let a huge SUV get by, and it was only then I remembered that to work from here I'd need a car. This was America. I don't drive. End of that particular fantasy.

Although, of course, I could learn. Now *there* was a thought.

Greta was in flying form. I tried to apologise again for the mess Jimmy Porter and I had made of her party but she was well over it. 'Shut up about the party, Bel. Youse were only gone ten minutes and we were all up doing "The Birdie Song"! No tunes like the old tunes, eh? It was great. And thanks very much for your present. I haven't got round to sending out notes yet.'

'Don't bother. Consider me thanked. So, tell us, how's it going over there?'

'Have you a cold, Bel? You sound all nasal.'

Long distance, I wasn't going to tell her about a margarita hangover. 'Nah. Just a reaction to all the flying.' Then, conscious of the units ticking themselves off my telephone card, I asked her to ring Willow and told her in shorthand what had happened.

'Why am I not surprised?' She laughed. 'Don't worry, I'll ring her. I'll tell her youse are all having a ball. Youse are in the casinos day and night!'

'*Greta!*'

'Keep your hair on. I'll ring her and say you'll be on to her soon. Tell us about your ma, Bel. What's she like? Are youse getting on OK?'

'It's too soon to tell, really, but she doesn't have horns. I got a shock when I saw her first. She isn't an old lady like I'd pictured her.'

'But you knew all along she was only sixteen or seventeen years older than you – it is only that, isn't it?'

'Yeah. I did know, of course, but somehow in my mind she had white hair and a stooped back.'

'So how are youse getting on?'

'OK, I suppose, but it's a bit, well, strained.'

'That's not a surprise, is it?'

'Hardly.'

'Have you had the conversation with her yet? About the real stuff?'

'Not yet, Greta.' I was getting uncomfortable with this because I hadn't fully sorted out my own thoughts and feelings. 'I've some idea of what happened – she kept a sort of diary and she's given it to me. I haven't been through it properly yet. I've barely skimmed a bit of it – but look, this is costing me a fortune. I'll tell you all about it when I get home, OK?' I didn't say that the thought of what was in that diary made my eyes jangle. Instead I told her quickly about Rowan and Dale and the others. 'And you'd never believe it, Greta, but there might be a bit of romance in the air with this Gina character.'

'Never! You're right – I don't believe it.'

'God knows what's going to happen. I'll keep you posted. But I'd better go. I don't have much credit left on this card.'

'Before you go, quick, what's he like, this fella? I'm dying to know.'

'What fella? Who do you mean?'

'Jesus, Bel! This Dale fella.'

'He's very nice, actually. I think you'd like him – look, I have to go. I'll ring again.'

'But listen—'

'Out of credit, talk soon. Cheerio, Greta.' I cut across her and hung up.

What was that all about? I'd been exaggerating about the call credit: I'd bought a card with 200 units and I'd been on for less than five minutes so there was plenty of time left to run. Normally I'd be chattering away to my best friend about everything and everyone under the sun, but I was holding back everywhere. I certainly hadn't wanted to talk to her about Dale Genscher.

Before I could analyse it, I saw Gina limping towards me from the direction of the shop. She was wearing a battered cotton sun-hat; chunks of her extraordinary hair shot like flames from around the edges of it, giving the impression that her head was on fire. 'Hi there!' she called, shifting a brown-paper grocery bag from one arm to the other. 'I guess you're wondering if I've kidnapped your brother.'

'Not at all, Gina. I can't help asking myself, though, if we're going to see him any time soon.'

I had meant it lightly but her pale face flushed. 'I can't force him to go see his mom. It has to come from himself.'

'Gina, I didn't mean—'

'This isn't easy for him. He's quite sensitive, you know,' she rushed on furiously. 'You and your sister shouldn't be on his case all the time. Give the guy a break.'

I gaped at her. Rowan, sensitive? 'Gina—'

'I think your brother's had a raw deal.' Then she seemed to realise she'd gone a bit too far with someone she'd just met and her tone softened. 'Cut him some slack, Arabella, you and your sister both. He needs a little R and R. He's wound up like a fishin' line.'

'Of course.' I was still gob-smacked. There was no doubt about it: this girl cared for our Rowan.

She took a couple of steps forward. 'You goin' back toward your mom's? I'll walk with you.' She set off, leaving me to follow meekly.

'I don't mean to give the wrong impression, Gina.' I adjusted my pace to hers. 'It's great you and he have hit it off.'

'Yeah. And I gotta tell you, Arabella, we're good together.'

She smiled like a cheeky elf. She has a lovely smile, impossible to resist. 'Good together?' I smiled back.

She laughed outright. 'Use your imagination!'

I did. It produced images I didn't want to dwell on. The proper thing to do, I thought, was encourage this. Or should I warn her? 'He has told you about his lifestyle, has he?' I asked carefully.

'A little.' Her tone became prim: 'He told me about his lost girlfriend and the child.'

'What lost girlfriend and child?'

'You don't know?'

'No.' I was flabbergasted.

'Then I'd appreciate it if you wouldn't mention it to him. Please, Arabella. Do you promise? He told me in confidence.' She looked so anxious that I agreed. 'Anyhow,' she resumed, 'his lifestyle back in Ireland doesn't concern me. That was last week's news. All that concerns me is that he's a nice guy. And in case you think I'm snowed by good looks, although he is a good-looking guy, it's not only that. He's special in other ways too. There's a lot there, buried deep.' She stopped dead and adjusted the brim of her hat to shade her eyes while she looked up at me. 'But for the moment we have to persuade him to clean up his tongue and to open up a little so he can expect a bit more out of life than he seems to expect right now. Deal?'

'Deal,' I said faintly. 'I have to admit, Gina, that we're all surprised at this development.'

'Eve too?'

'I don't know – she hasn't said.'

'So you're talking about you and your sister, yeah?'

'I suppose so – I suppose we see him differently than you do.'

'That's for sure,' she said earnestly. 'It's sure plain to see that you all are waitin' for him to do something dreadful. He's done nothing dreadful since he's been with me, Arabella. He makes me laugh, telling me all about things that happened to him on the streets – bad things, a lot of 'em, but he tells them in a sorta funny way. For instance, that friend of his, Mental, sounds like a gas. Rowan has that good Irish sense of humour, you know. Even if a lot of it is turned against himself.'

We moved off again. Just as well, because as we walked along under the baking sun, our feet scuffling in the gravel, I was feeling quite peculiar. This was amazing. Rowan had had a girlfriend and a child? Rowan makes her laugh? I'd never been treated to Rowan's humorous side – and who was Mental?

'Don't feel too harshly about what your mom did.' She broke into my ruminations. 'She's a real good person. She helped save my sanity, you know.'

'How's that?'

'I was pretty screwed up when we met. My ex was seriously messing with my head. He's a musician, you see,' she explained, 'not a bad one, but a control freak and a user.'

'You feel he used you?'

'He's a user of cocaine,' she corrected, 'and when we were together he wanted me to do it too, and when I wouldn't he'd get nasty.'

'Violent?'

'Among other things – I don't like to talk about it. So, as I say, when I met your mom and Dale I guess I was on the verge of a breakdown. She rescued me. To this day, I don't quite know how she did it. She sort of put herself around me, you know? Kinda like she has an aura or something? Without her even touching me, I felt hugged any time I talked to her. I talked to her a *lot*. I found myself telling her everything, deep down thoughts I didn't even know I had.

'She shoulda been a shrink. It's something to do with her eyes, I think. A kind of wide-open stare she does, real sympathetic or somethin'. Anyways, even though she never once gave me advice or told me what to do, with all the talkin' I began to see there was more to life than following that dumb-ass around from state to state. Well, I guess that's enough about me,' and for the next couple of minutes, she chattered on about her plans to show Rowan around the area, something about bringing him to see a vortex. I barely registered. I was listening out for confirmation of the seriousness of this relationship, if that was what it was. I picked up phrases like 'Rowan thinks' and 'Rowan says'.

Rowan thinks? Rowan says? Since when did my brother have anything to contribute to general conversation? As far as I could remember, conversations between me and Rowan, or me plus Willow with Rowan, were one-way: the two of us women pleading, begging, threatening, wheedling; him grunting, yelling, or telling us to F off and mind our own business.

Willow and I could be accused, correctly, of assuming that Rowan would never break out of his destructive situation, that he was incapable of it. Willow anyhow: to be fair to myself, I had maintained one small candle of hope that Something Would Happen.

Please, please, let him not do something stupid and wreck this.

'Here's where I leave you,' she broke in again, indicating a turn-off. 'See you tonight, OK?'

'Are you not working?'

'I've called in to say I'll be late. I wouldn't miss one of Mario's cook-outs. I've been telling Rowan about the buffalo wings – you'll enjoy this evening, Arabella, I promise. But not a word to your brother about the other thing?

'OK.'

'Thanks.' With a cheery wave she limped away, leaving me thinking that in one short walk I had learned more about my brother than I had in my previous lifetime. I certainly had cause now to watch him . . .

It's evening now and here we are, Gina, Eve, Rowan and me, dressed and ready, sitting on Eve's deck, waiting for the kick-off of Robert and Mario's barbecue. We're a mixed bunch to say the least. In Rowan's case, being dressed means he's still wearing the suit but has combed his hair – and is it my imagination or has his beard been trimmed a little? It's certainly neat. And, yes, he *is* a looker. Why didn't I see this before?

The answer is, of course, that up to now I saw only the negatives.

Gina has changed into what look like combat fatigues. As for me, I could be going to a funeral: I'm wearing my 'good' knee-length black dress teamed with my 'good' piece of jewellery, a jet necklace I found in a charity shop. It had needed restringing but the nuns in the orphanage had taught me well and, although tedious, fixing it up had been a doddle. Eve, though, is the star attraction: she has dressed for the occasion in a silvery kimono, embroidered with brilliantly coloured birds.

The sun has recently set, and its rosy tails are being dragged behind it into the deepening blue of the sky. Ours will not be the only outdoor cooking event this evening, it appears: the dusk is infused with meat-scented smoke. I realise I'm very hungry and wish we could get a move on.

As a group, we've exhausted all chat about the beauty of the evening and what great barbecue sauces Mario's going to give us and we're now silent. It's not a comfortable silence. In fact, there's an underlying tension I don't understand. Rowan is chain-smoking but, watching him closely, I haven't detected any hostility and, as a matter of fact, a couple of minutes ago I intercepted a private, knowing grin between him and Gina.

Right now, though, Gina is continually looking at her watch. So is Eve. Is Mario such a stickler for time-keeping?

I haven't the energy to worry about it. I'm at present in that transient state, where the hangover aches are no longer acute but shading towards crippling tiredness. At the same time, this strange tension is getting to me. 'Tell us one thing, Eve . . .'

'I'm all ears!' She seems as eager as I am to bridge the silence.

'Why did you name the other two after trees and not me?'

'Are you sure you want to know? You won't get all upset?'

I look at Rowan. 'Will you get upset?'

'Don't worry about me.' But his knee jigs impatiently.

'All right.' Eve hesitates a little, then, 'At the risk of being controversial,' she says, 'it was because I loved the Botanic Gardens.' She does a quick check to see how Rowan and I are reacting. I keep very still. She seems reassured. 'It was my sort of refuge in bad times. I went up there with you, Arabella, in your go-car, the day I found out I was pregnant with Willow. You see,' she hesitates again, 'things weren't – well, Petey and I—' She coughs. 'I knew he wouldn't be all that pleased. In anyway,' she continues quickly, 'I crossed the bridge into the rose garden and sat beside the river. You were whingeing so I wheeled the go-car back and forth and you went asleep.'

Rowan has stopped jigging. Eve's gaze has slipped upwards and I can see she's away in a different place. 'Then there was one of those things that happen unexpectedly in life that you never, ever forget. You see, even though it was the autumn, it was sunny, one of those pet days of Indian summer. There was a really beautiful weeping willow beside where I was sitting, a huge one, trailing down into the water, and still green, although there were a few yellowy tips to some of the leaves. The sun was on your face, Arabella, no matter which way I turned the go-car and I decided to push you underneath this tree for the shade.

'As the leaves and branches closed around us, like thick green curtains,

I discovered it was enormous in there, a big shadowy cave, another world, hushed as a church. No grass on the ground, just a quiet carpet of browny-black stuff that felt soft under my feet. The light from the sun outside was twinkling through the leaves on the long branches as they moved in the breeze, making this rustling sound. I could hear nothing else from the outside world, no traffic, nothing except this rustling and the river rushing by and, Arabella, it felt like you and me and the tree were the only living creatures in the world and that no one could ever disturb us. I could have stayed there for ever.'

She darts an embarrassed look at us. 'Sorry, I was away with the fairies there for a minute.

'In anyway, I'm not religious, as you know, but the finish up of it was, that afternoon I guess I promised someone or something, the god of the trees or the river, the sun, moon, the universe, the Catholic God, everyone and anyone that I could think of that if I got through this without – without too much trouble, I'd call my new little baby Willow. The reason was because this tree looked and felt as if nothing, not even a big storm, would ever hurt it and that was what I wanted for my baby. I suppose I was being superstitious and fearful all at the same time.'

She seems to think she has said too much now because her tone changes, becomes brisk: 'As for you, Arabella, I called you that because it was lovely and romantic, very different from all the Marys and Joans and Paulines I knew at the orphanage.' She smiles. 'You were going to be Winston if you were a boy.'

'Thank God I wasn't! But that's a lovely story. What made you think it would upset us?'

'Well, you know, the Botanics and all . . .' She stops, embarrassed again.

More than anything right now, I wish, wish, *wish* that my sister could have been here to hear the story of how she came by her name. 'Did you ever read *The Wind in the Willows*, Eve?'

'I'm not a great reader.' She's uncomfortable.

'No problem,' I say hastily. 'Maybe I'll buy it for you some day. But, more importantly, did you get through that second pregnancy OK? You must have if you kept your promise about the name.'

Something about her nails demands her urgent attention. 'It wasn't too bad. In anyway, the name was fixed in my head by the time she was born.'

'What would have happened if Willow had been a boy?' This is Rowan. Fully engaged.

She looks him straight in the face. 'Willow could be a boy's name too.'

'Was I named after a tree in the Botanics as well?'

'With you it was just a coincidence. My friend Maura always loved that name. She read it in some book set in Scotland so that's why I gave it to you. And before you ask, if you were a girl, you were going to be Rebecca. I liked the idea of three little girls called Arabella, Willow and Rebecca.'

'So you're sorry I was a boy.'

'Shut up!' This is Gina, but tenderly, brushing his knee with a hand.

'I was only asking,' he mumbles, glancing at her. Then, to Eve: 'Sorry. Really.' He and Gina exchange another smile.

The next question begging to be asked is about my father. But not in front of Gina. The sooner we get to that barbecue the better, I think, followed immediately by the wish that Dale was here so we could all focus on him, but no such luck. Apparently he's going to be late and we're under orders not to wait for him but to go on to Robert and Mario's without him. It strikes me again how this man seems to be central to the running of this odd gang. It seems everyone now accepts without question that I am Dale's houseguest, although there was a small ripple earlier when Eve appeared to be miffed. 'If she's not going back to the bed-and-breakfast, why can't she stay here with me?'

'You've only one bedroom,' Dale pointed out.

'Yes, but my couch opens out into a bed – it would be fun.'

'She wouldn't sleep properly with you clumpin' in and out to the bathroom. Have you heard the noise that cast makes on the floor of your trailer?'

'Well, I could give her my bed and I'd sleep on the couch – she's *my* daughter after all.'

'If you were on the couch, *she*'d wake *you* up, goin' in and out to the bathroom. You need your sleep too. She can have the main bathroom in my trailer. My bedroom has its own shower room.' My fate revolved around bathrooms, it seemed, although I was to be given no part to play in the contest. In any case I was too frazzled and sick to want one, and while the argument crackled on, I was struck by how quickly I had adjusted to Dale's speech patterns: those slow relaxed tones, so foreign when I'd first heard them on the phone, now sounded commonplace to the extent that I barely noticed the form any longer, only the content.

Eve gave in with good grace. 'Oh, you!' she said to him. 'I always knew that sooner or later you'd need a woman in that trailer.' Then, turning to me: 'Not a cushion, not a snapshot, it's like a monk's cell. Isn't that right, Arabella?'

I'd smiled at both of them, hoping they'd take my expression to be enigmatic. Mona Lisa Moraghan. What had surprised me was the degree of animation Dale had brought to the discussion. He seemed to want me in his trailer. (Nothing in it. I'm only remarking.)

It's very still on the deck, so still I can hear the soft *whish-whish* of the fabric in Rowan's trousers as he is again jigging one knee. It's been a weird, lost sort of day. The hours had seemed to drain away without my noticing. For instance, as one by one the outside lights on the trailers around us are coming on, it seems only seconds have passed since sunset: darkness falls swiftly here.

Now the standard lamps up and down the street pop into life: faint red glow at first, then a burst into orange. Ginger, mewing and purring, makes his appearance and rubs against Eve's legs. 'Don't be a baby.' She leans down to stroke his head. 'You've already been fed. I'll bring you back some of Mario's delicious chicken, OK?'

Gina looks at her watch yet again. 'We should go, people.'

Rowan springs to his feet. I go to help Eve, but she waves me away, quite irritably. 'I know I'm an invalid but I'm not helpless, Arabella.' It's the first time she has spoken to me with anything less than sweet-talk and I'm taken aback; then, when I think about it, I'm glad. It's normal, I think, for a mother to snap at a daughter, more normal than for all conversations to be conducted at the guardrail around no man's land. To progress like this will make it easier for me to have 'that' conversation with her.

CHAPTER THIRTY-TWO

'HAPPY BIRTHDAY TO YOU!' They explode from the dark trailer on to the unlighted deck.

'HAPPY BIRTHDAY TO YOU!' A flashbulb pops. Mario, Robert, three people I don't know.

'HAPPY BIRTHDAY, DEAR ARABELLA!' Mary Wu and, lastly, Dale, carrying a huge cake with three burning candles.

'HAPPY BIRTHDAY TO YOU!' Lights come on everywhere, hundreds of them, tiny white fairy-lights strung round the deck and under the canopy above it. Then there's a loud fanfare of trumpets. I burst into tears.

Seconds earlier, when our strange procession – tall, bearded man in wrinkled suit leading three females: limping combat veteran, limping refugee from *Madame Butterfly*, able-bodied but unfit Irishwoman dressed in mourning – had arrived at the trailer, everything had been dark and silent. I'd turned to Eve: 'Are you sure this is the right trailer?'

Now, faced with a birthday cake and surrounded by people clapping, cheering and patting me on the back I am so overwhelmed I can barely muster breath. Of course I'd known my birthday was coming up but I'd been so preoccupied that I'd lost track of time; it hadn't occurred to me that it had arrived. 'Whose idea was this? Who told who it was my birthday?' Dazed, I look at the celebrants, beaming as if they'd won a lottery. Even Rowan seems to be in on it. With one arm round Gina, he's grinning with the rest.

'I did, of course.' This is Eve. 'I told Mary here, to make sure everyone knew.'

'Thank you *so* much.' Mary, grinning, doesn't seem insulted.

'I'd hug you,' Eve humps herself across the deck, 'but I'm hamstrung.'

'Thank you.' I throw both arms round her, not caring whether my damned dress rides up, rides down or rips itself apart.

'You're welcome,' she murmurs into my ear. 'You don't think I'd ever forget the date of my first baby's birthday?'

I hug her again, then disengage, wiping my eyes. 'I hope this isn't a trap, Eve Moraghan.' I raise my voice to include them all: 'I hope when I blow out these candles, some gangster's not going to appear with a machine gun—'

Only Dale, Mario, Robert and one of the three I don't know laugh at this – so it falls a bit flat. I wouldn't have thought anyone on the planet could be unfamiliar with *Some Like It Hot*: it's the gabbing again, saying the first thing that comes into my head.

'Come on,' Dale brings the cake to within six inches of my face, 'this is heavy. I'm getting a pain in my arms, blow out your damn candles, Arabella, and let's eat.'

I blow hard, and the candles go out.

They light up again.

Huge hilarity. They're trick candles.

'Here, Mario, take it.' When the jollity dies down, Dale hands over the cake. He's wearing last night's fringed suede jacket, now teamed with pale chinos and a cream T-shirt. The pony-tail is neat. 'Hope we didn't scare the daylights out of you, Arabella.' He smiles, delighted with himself.

I'm still coming to terms with this. 'I don't understand. Where's the barbecue?'

'Barbecue, shmarbecue.' Robert is clicking and flashing with a big camera. 'That would have spoiled the surprise!'

'Yeah!' shouts Mary Wu, whose hair has been backcombed into a huge beehive – Marge Simpson has nothing on it – and who has (unwisely) elected to wear jeans decorated with glitter. 'We wanted you to think we'd all forgotten about you!'

'Here you are.' It's Robert, giving me a Polaroid picture of myself. 'Souvenir of the moment.'

'That's horrible!' I'm appalled: in the picture, my mouth is hanging wide open and from the effects of the flash, my eyes are like red coals.

'Well, you don't have to hang it in a gallery!' He laughs. 'It's just a memento.'

'Thank you. Thank you all.' Now I understand the high tension back at Eve's while we were waiting to come here. 'So all that about buffalo wings and delicious chicken and Mario's brilliant barbecue sauces,' I gaze round them all, 'that was a con?'

'You bet!' It's Gina who answers. Her 'bad' eye is catching the light so she looks slightly deranged. Deranged but happy.

Mario, whose own eyes are glittering as if he's already been at the sauce – or something else – comes back out from the trailer with the cake, minus the candles. I notice for the first time that the icing seems to be a delicate shade of green, probably in my honour. 'That cake looks gorgeous, did you make it, Mario?'

'Sweetheart, you're worth it, but you're not *that* worth it. You can thank Karly's Konfectionery – that's with a K, like the Klan.' He clicks his heels and gives a little bow. 'Special order.'

'Thank you so much.'

'No. Thank *you* for being so special. But why is this not a surprise? Like daughter, like mother.'

'Take a load off, Eve. Arabella, since you're Queen for a Day, you get to sit too.' Robert brings two chairs from inside the trailer and plonks them beside us.

Eve and I sit, triggering a flurry of fuss and business. Dale and one of the unfamiliar men set about unfolding a stainless-steel serving table on collapsible legs while Mario and Robert bustle in and out of their trailer with place settings, condiments, cups, glasses, linen napkins, a pair of modern metal candelabra, banked like ski slopes, and two bottles of champagne.

Robert comes over to me and pops a cork with such ease it's clear he's well used to the operation. 'Here, birthday girl, you first.' He pours me a glass. 'It's not French, I'm afraid, but another few years and the fizz from California will even be drinkable. Chris and Mandy are Californians, poor things,' he fills the two younger strangers' glasses, 'but we don't hold it against them, even if they are guilty of doing something in computers. They live opposite. This here is John. He's our neighbour, right next door, he does very little.' The three laugh at some private joke while he pours champagne for the man who's been helping set the table.

The couple are young, blond, maybe in their twenties, and to me they look bemused to find themselves here and in such company. John, middle-aged, unmistakably kicks with the same foot as Robert and Mario. 'How do you do?' I shake hands with the three. 'Forgive me if I seem shocked. I've never had a birthday party in my life. This makes up for it. I hope I'll remember your names.'

'Oh, by the end of the night, dear, you won't be able to forget any of us.' Mario trips past with an enormous tray of serving bowls and platters heaped with food.

'A toast!' Robert raises his champagne flute. 'To the birthday girl! And reunions!'

'Wait for me!' Mario unloads his dishes so that the table is now laden with lasagne, several different types of bread, salads and dressings. Helped by John, he uses tapers to light the banks of candles, and when they are all blazing satisfactorily, he seizes his drink. 'Houston, we are go for lift-off!'

'To the birthday girl and reunions!' They all raise their glasses. Eve toasts with orange juice, Dale lifts a glass that's empty.

Instinctively I search for Rowan's toasting hand but it's hidden behind Chris's head. 'Speech!' This, unbelievably, has come from him. He is definitely a new person.

'Rowan! You know I can't.'

'There's always a first time.'

I look at them all. It doesn't really matter whose idea this was originally because they've all participated, and I'm so happy I could weep. Again.

Speaking quickly to get it over with, I thank them 'from the bottom of my heart', assuring them that the surprise element certainly worked: 'You only have to look at my reaction!' I run out of things to say. I had been speaking for approximately seven seconds. Maybe half that.

'Hooray!' Mario claps furiously, glaring at the others to join in, while I glug what's left in my champagne glass. Robert rushes to refill it; I drink immediately, as if I haven't had a drink for – oh, at least two minutes . . .

'I'd like to say something.' This is Eve, her tone commanding attention. She is composed, her expression unreadable. Everyone turns to her.

'I won't stand, if you don't mind,' she says calmly, 'but in welcoming Arabella, my first-born child here, and Rowan of course, I would like to say, in the presence of you all, my best and dearest friends, that this is the happiest day of my life.' She looks directly at me. 'Birthdays are special for the person celebrating, Arabella. And so it should be. But they are very special days for mothers too. I will never forget the day of your birth, when in a few seconds nothing mattered except the suck of your little mouth on my breast. You were the whole world to me from then on. And before Willow was born, and then you, Rowan,' she directs her gaze at him, 'I worried that I wouldn't have enough love in my heart. That I had used it all up. But my love for each of you expanded me and filled me up and made life bearable until – until—' She looks from me to Rowan, and under fairy-lights her eyes seem to glow like a cat's. 'I have a broad back, children. Feel free to punish me for what I've done.'

On the deck, the silence is pin-sharp. She turns to Robert and Mario, still cool or seeming to be. 'Sorry, guys, I don't mean to hog your party or bog it down in mush so I won't say any more. In the meantime, thank you, Arabella, for coming. You too, Rowan. And Willow.'

'You're welcome.' I don't quite know where to look.

Robert crosses the deck and plants a large kiss on her cheek. 'Bravo! We love you to bits, honey.'

'We love everybody!' Mario rushes to the food table. 'Eve, you're so *honest*! Too honest for your own good. Now, for God's sake, let's eat.'

'This looks real good.' Dale strolls over and picks up some skewered meat.

The man named Chris approaches me with Mandy. 'I don't know her that well, as it happens, but you have a real, ah, interesting mother, Arabella.'

'You could say that.'

'Have you seen much of Arizona?'

Now it's as if nothing had happened: as if my mother had not ripped herself open in public. 'Not really, it's been such a rush.'

'Oh, you must!' Mandy chips in. 'We're not that far from the Grand Canyon. It'd be a shame for you to be so near—'

'Come on, come on, talk later. Now it's chow time!' Robert, who has heard the last part of this conversation, claps his hands at us. 'And of course you should see the Grand Canyon, and Monument Valley – and our own local sights in these parts too, Arabella. You tell Dale he should take you on a little trip. And tell him I wouldn't mind tagging along – I'll tell him myself. It's been a long time since I did some sightseeing around here.'

'You want I should say grace, Robert?' As movement starts towards the buffet, Mary Wu puts a hand on his arm.

'Sure, Mary.' He places the champagne bottle at his feet, takes her hand in his and searches with his free hand for someone else's. To my aston-ishment, everyone in the group moves to join hands; even a surprised

Rowan finds himself playing 'Ring a Ring o' Rosie' between Gina and Mandy. He doesn't resist.

Because I'm so close to Eve, it's her hand I take. Also Dale's, because he happens to be standing on my other side.

When the circle is complete, they all bow their heads. 'Lord,' Mary intones, 'thank you for this wonderful food and this gathering of friends. Thank you for bringing us all together from the four corners of our great nation and the world. Amen.'

'Amen,' goes the murmur, and I hear myself saying, 'Amen,' too. This public grace is outside my experience and I think that if it happened at home I'd be uncomfortable. Greta and I have discussed this weird thing about Irish people. We're supposed to be a religious nation, even if a lot of us of us are now unofficially lapsed (I suppose that would describe me) or else picking and choosing what rules we will or will not follow. Our deeply personal beliefs are rarely discussed or displayed. And if they are – say, by the people who picket family-planning clinics, or wear scapulars, or go every year to do penance at Lough Derg – we half-Catholics privately think they're a bit extreme.

These people here are unselfconscious about it, though, so the communal prayer was touching and simple and I liked it – although on the 'Amen' I immediately broke the contact with Eve and Dale.

After we've all been served, Robert refills the glasses, including mine (mysteriously empty again), and conversation dies down as everyone settles to eat. Before he picks up his own plate, he presses a button on a remote control and classical piano music filters through a pair of speakers hooked under the canopy.

As I take the first mouthful of my third glass of champagne, I remind myself to be careful. This is the last drink for sure. It may be a coincidence or not, but there are two confirmed alcoholics on this deck and one is my mother. My brother is a possible, if not a probable. Alcoholism is hereditary.

I know deep down I don't have this problem, but since I came here and met Eve, I have become acutely aware of it. No point in flirting with it, I think, and resolutely put my flute on the deck beside the leg of my chair.

Since, for the moment, no one is paying me particular attention, I don't dive into my food straight away. I want to concentrate on fixing into my memory every detail about this evening: the warm, flattering hospitality, the gentle piano music, the balmy air against my bare arms, Mario's candles, outshining the glow of the storm lantern fixed beside Chris and Mandy's door across the way. This trailer is at the end of its row, and further down the empty street I can see, through the windows of other mobile homes, the grey and white flicker of television sets, while several dark plumes, obviously from barbecues, punctuate the air. It's dinnertime all over the site and the meaty tang I'd noticed previously has become even stronger.

Over us all is the high, silent, starlit sky.

Is this me, bare-skinned at this time of night yet comfortably warm? Is this me being fêted like a celebrity at a party in my honour? Is that my mother over there? Is that my delinquent brother and has he genuinely transformed? Have I died and gone to heaven?

There is a pause in the music and I close my eyes to wait for it to start up again – then open them quickly in case someone thinks I'm not enjoying myself, or maybe falling asleep. And, in truth, the champagne, probably working on what's in my system from the previous night, is making me dozy. I meet the gaze of Dale, who is perched on the side of a lounger occupied by Mary Wu. 'You like music, Arabella?' he asks quietly.

'I'm a bit of an ignoramus there, I'm afraid. I think I've been to maybe two concerts in my life.' I don't mention that both concerts were given by amateur brass bands run in conjunction with Jimmy Porter's union. Dale continues to watch me. His eyes are in shadow.

'We've a symphony orchestra in Phoenix,' Robert butts in. 'They're giving the "Eroica" a week tomorrow. I could get tickets, if you're interested.'

'Oh, no – I mean, thank you very much.' I'm terrified they'll learn the extent of my ignorance. Whatever the 'Eroica' is (I *think* that's what he said), it sounds obscure and difficult. 'You've done too much already – you've all been too kind. I'll be gone home by then. Or I'll certainly have worn out my welcome. Dale, for one, will be sick of me.' I glance at my host, who is busy spearing salad on his fork.

'Whatever.' Robert shrugs. 'If you change your mind, the offer's open. It's a good band.'

'Are you leaving so soon?' This is Eve, forkful of salad suspended in mid-air. 'I thought you had an open airline ticket.'

'I have, but I have to get back to work.' I don't want to be discussing this in front of everyone, and I don't want to think about the bloody Leicester tonight. I'm the birthday girl, I'm Queen for a Day.

But the magic has been diluted, if only temporarily.

'What about you, Rowan?' Mercifully Eve turns her attention to my brother, who is eating from his lap while sitting on the floor of the deck with his back to the rail.

'I dunno. I'm in no fu—' He swallows. 'I'm in no rush, actually.' He turns to Gina. 'Can you put up with me for another little while?'

'We'll see how you behave.' She laughs and he joins in, and I think that maybe the magic hasn't entirely lifted.

I turn back to Robert. 'I'm sorry now I won't be able to take up your invitation. Do you know a lot about music?'

'Does Robert know about music!' Mario smiles brilliantly at his partner. 'This guy – I tell you—' He nudges him extravagantly. 'Tell 'em about the musical!'

'Shut up, Mario!' Nevertheless, Robert grins indulgently.

'Robert is writing a musical,' Mario turns back to me, 'a fantabulous work, satirical, based on that lemon of the last century *Of Thee I Sing* – you know it, Arabella? Well, we're going to *bury* that thing.'

'I don't know it.' I shake my head. I'm sorry I asked.

I get sorrier because, drowning the quiet piano music, Mario, who *has* to be on something other than simple champagne, bursts into song. With his glass in one hand, he cavorts and prances around the limited space, singing, in an exaggerated falsetto:

> My country, 'tis of thee,
> Sweet land of liberty,
> Of thee I sing;

To my astonishment, the words are set to the English national anthem. It's following me around.

Mario sits down again.

Through the restored piano music, Robert's voice is quiet. 'He's right, Arabella, I am scribbling a little. It's about gays and Aids, Lord help us.'

'Should be great.' I can't begin to think about a musical based on Aids. But, I remind myself, this is America . . .

'It certainly is gonna be great.' Mary Wu uses her napkin to wipe a dribble of cheese from the corner of her mouth. 'We're all goin' to the prem-ieer. What do you do, Arabella?

I turn gratefully towards her to answer, but have to turn away again and pick up my glass because I might laugh. Her Marge Simpson hairdo is leaning sideways and is in danger of collapsing. 'Oh, I'm only a wait-ress,' I tell my plate.

'What's with this "only"?'

I risk another look to find Mary wagging her finger at me and the beehive shifting another couple of inches. 'A good waitress can travel the world.' Still wagging. 'Europe, America, Asia, food's food. It's a worthy job. It says so in the Bible. There was waitresses at the weddin' feast of Cana, ain't that right, Dale, honey?' She realises what's happening with her hair and shoves one hand into it but when she takes it away, it sags further. It's now listing at a serious angle.

'You bet, Mary!' Dale raises his eyebrows in my direction. He must want to laugh too.

But now I love Mary's hair. I love Mary. I can go home to Ireland with my head held high. My career is global. It's just that no one has endorsed it before.

'You got a boyfriend back home, honey?' Having rocketed me to the sky, Mary brings me crashing back to earth. In sympathy, maybe, her bee-hive crashes too, but no one's watching that because they've all heard the question and they're all watching me. Dale's watching. Eve's watching.

The piano music flows on.

Lightning-fast, I make a decision. 'No,' I say.

CHAPTER THIRTY-THREE

God, it's great to lie in a real bed . . . with a full belly and a nice fucking buzz.

Yeah, I've had a few drinks. So fucking what? I'm on my fucking holidays, amn't I? And by the time Gina gets home I'll be asleep and what she doesn't know won't hurt her.

She wanted me to come with her again, and I said thanks but no thanks. That I'd had enough of fucking cowboys for the moment – except, of course, I didn't say it like that: I said that I was knackered from all the excitement.

Yanks are a howl. They invite you to a fucking party and then it all breaks up at half nine and everyone fucking goes home to bed! All right, the food was good (although I would have liked a bit of roast beef) but I ask you: two fucking bottles of champagne? For eleven people? And this is supposed to be a party?

Nine people, really, I suppose, because my ma and Dale weren't having any. I'm not surprised at Dale. Nothing that geezer would or wouldn't do would surprise me but I'm beginning to wonder is my ma an alky? Like, would you go to a party in honour of your long-lost daughter and drink fucking orange juice if there's champagne going?

I don't like champagne, not that I'm what Mental would call a connofuckinsoor or anything like that, but I like my booze honest. I drank it, though. I'm not a total eejit. The point I'm getting at about this party is, when the drink ran out, you had to ask them if they had a beer or whiskey or anything. They didn't. Only wine. That's homosexuals for you.

I suppose any fucking port in a fucking storm.

Port. Wine. Geddit?

It was a good party for Bel, though. I'm glad. She's a decent skin, Bel. Out here she's even human. Not always riding me and giving out.

211

And thank God Willow went home. Maybe I'll be able to relax a bit now.

Was I dreaming it or did Bel say she had no boyfriend? What was that all about?

I wonder, does Gina have any booze in the place?

CHAPTER THIRTY-FOUR

Dale, Eve and I are the last to leave the party. Gina went first, about half an hour ago; she had to go to work. She took Rowan with her. Mary Wu left too: she has an early shift tomorrow morning – apparently she does two days a week as a volunteer nurse's assistant in a local hospital. Then the neighbours left, and next thing there are just the three of us with Mario and Robert. 'Can I help clean up?' I survey the debris left after the celebration of my birthday. Compared to what I normally deal with at the Leicester, this would be a task so genteel it would take me perhaps five minutes.

'Absolutely not.' Mario won't hear of it. 'But would you guys like another glass of wine?' It's offered generously but it's clear that he and his partner would like us to leave now: they've both been yawning discreetly behind their hands.

'C'mon, Eve, time to say goodnight.' Dale takes the hint and, having fetched my mother's crutches, hands them to her and watches while she struggles to her feet.

'Mario, Robert,' I pick up my handbag and slip the Polaroid photograph into it, 'I can't tell you how grateful I am to both of you. It was such an incredible surprise.' I'm momentarily stuck. Do I know these people well enough to hug them?

'Oh, phooey!' Mario kisses me on both cheeks. 'It was such a pleasure. And it worked so well. You should have seen your face!'

'Unfortunately I have seen it! Robert and his camera made sure of that and I'm not all that sure I want to see it again. But thank you again for everything.' Robert shows no inclination to kiss me so I shake his hand. With further thank-yous and goodnights, we leave.

Having taken a few steps, I look back to wave but already the two of them are whizzing about the deck picking up glasses. Parties here end early, I think, as the three of us make our way towards Eve's trailer. If this one was typical, they're very orderly too: you get there at the right time, you have the party, you all go home within a few minutes of each other – none of your sprawling, open-ended, all-singing, all-dancing, all-drinking affairs like we have at home, where the stragglers stay all night and sleep on the floor of your sitting room; no one throwing up either, or breaking glasses, picking fights; no one doing dodgy joke routines. Have I just discarded poor Jimmy Porter?

We're at Eve's trailer. 'Come in for a cup of coffee.' At the bottom of her steps, she turns to us. 'You and I have so much to talk about, Arabella.'

'To be honest, Eve, I can't keep my eyes open.' This is true, but the real reason for my reluctance is that having had such a pleasant evening I don't want to spoil it.

In principle, of course I want to talk to my mother to get to the bottom of what happened and to try to build some kind of realistic relationship with her, but not tonight. I've just broken up with my boyfriend. I'm free. He doesn't know yet. I'll deal with the guilt of that some other time. With stars overhead and champagne in my blood, I'm in no mood to dive into anything difficult, least of all into a scene with my mother . . .

And, if I'm being honest, the prospect of a one-to-one chat with Dale over a nightcap is also tugging pleasantly at my consciousness. *Stop that, Arabella Moraghan. This man has tattoos.* 'I'll come over here bright and early tomorrow morning', I say to Eve. 'We'll have breakfast together, just the two of us. You're right, it's time we talked properly. So we can have a real chat, I'll have read your diary by then – I promise. I've already read your letter to Maura. She sounds really nice.'

'You read all of them?'

'Only one. The first. You had a hard life then.' I glance at Dale to see how much of this he is taking in. He is staring at the face of his mobile phone as if checking for messages. Tactful.

'Sure.' Eve's face tightens – or I think it does: the light cast by the nearby streetlamp is dim. She teeters a little on her crutches as though to kiss me, but pulls back. 'Goodnight, Arabella. You too, Dale.'

Dale puts away his mobile as the two of us oversee her laborious climb up the steps. 'Don't forget your medication. You cutting down?'

'Sure thing, don't need it as much. I'm sore, but definitely not as sore as I was.'

'Now don't be saying that too loud, Eve. Don't tell that to the guy from the insurance company. He's coming tomorrow, ain't he?'

'Yeah. Don't worry. Meryl Streep won't hold a candle to me tomorrow.' She doesn't look back and suddenly, while watching her go, the brave blonde hair, the bright kimono, I'm assaulted with such tenderness for her that it's like a physical blow.

When picturing the reunion with my mother, I'd painted it as tense and full of screaming. It's been tense, all right – Willow's departure is testament to that – but not all the time, and this unexpected wash of feeling is to be welcomed. I remind myself not to get carried away, that this softness may have no basis in reality: it could simply be a combination of champagne, starlight, and being Queen for a Day. The champagne is certainly a factor: although it's not a repeat of last night, when I was definitely and disgracefully pie-eyed, I couldn't say that right now I'm a hundred per cent sober.

When we reach Dale's trailer, I hesitate for a moment before going into my bedroom. Instantly, he picks up on this. 'You're tired, I guess, but would you like something to drink? A margarita perhaps?'

'Dale!'

He grins widely. 'A cup of tea, then? I know from your mom how you Irish like your tea – and, as you've seen, I've stocked up. Don't wanna waste it!'

'You didn't buy all that tea for me, surely.'

'There were to be three of you, Arabella, don't forget.'

'You'd planned for all three of us to stay here?'

'No. I didn't know if any of you would be staying here. So, would you like tea or not?'

'Sure. But don't ask me to make any decisions. You choose the type.' There's a feeling of unreality about this now, I think.

'Excuse me a moment.' Having filled a kettle and put it on the stove – I haven't seen an electric kettle since I came here – Dale goes through the doorway that leads, I presume, to his bedroom. He has lit two white-shaded table lamps, and although Eve's description of the living room as a tidy monk's cell is accurate, it feels cosy. Spartan, but cosy.

Now that I have time alone in here, I take a sneaky look round, searching for Dale's books – always a good indicator of someone's personality and taste. If he catches me mooching, I can always say I was looking for something to read in bed. Surprisingly, I can't see a single volume. Or a magazine. Not even a newspaper. The surface of the coffee table between the two cream-coloured couches is bare except for a heavy glass dish filled with smooth pebbles, grey, laced with white; the counter tops in his kitchen area are pristine and also naked.

A glass-fronted cabinet mounted in one corner displays the only personal items, if you can call them that: a large white jug with a blue rim, a piece of red rock on a little plinth, and an ornate clock: of gilt and some sort of ceramic, it's a riot of colour and textures, in bizarre contrast to everything else in this immaculate place where almost everything has either a specific function, or four corners, or both. The face of this clock is held between the hands of two china figurines, a crinolined lady and a gentleman wearing a frock coat, long wig, tights and buttoned gaiters, characters you'd like to meet in a novel by D. K. Broster or in *A Tale of Two Cities*. Additional figures and carvings, of cherubs, flowers, leaves, berries, coils of ivy, are so entwined that it's only when you peer really closely that you can separate them.

From behind me, I hear the whistle of the kettle but as I turn to take it off its burner, I'm startled to find Dale standing at the stove and already doing this. 'I see you're admiring my clock.' He starts assembling the tea things.

'You gave me a fright. I didn't hear you come back in. Yes, the clock, it's extraordinary. Is it a family heirloom?'

'Sort of. Now let's see . . .' As he had done that morning, Dale pops open his cupboard full of his neatly filed tea.

'Did it come from your great-grandparents or something? It looks very old. An antique.' Reckless on champagne, I'm not going to be fobbed off, however politely.

He turns to face me. 'It was the only item I took from our home when my wife and I divorced. It seemed appropriate somehow.'

'Sorry – I didn't mean . . .' I feel disgraced. Like a peeping Tom.

'It's a legitimate question.' He selects two tea-bags and drops them into mugs. 'It probably is an antique. My ex-wife has a good eye. Or had.'

'I think that's why I asked. It didn't look like your taste.'

'Maybe that's why I took it. As a reminder of a badly chosen marriage.' He pours hot water into the mugs, replaces the kettle and comes towards me. 'There you go. I'm assuming it's not lemon.' He hands me a small oblong tray with milk jug, sugar basin, spoon and a white mug filled with tea.

'Thanks. That's perfect. Look, Dale, I don't know what to say. I certainly didn't mean to rub salt into old wounds.'

'Old wounds well healed by now. It was a long time ago.' He sits opposite me, kicks off his flip-flops, then dunks a slice of lemon in his own tea.

I'm stymied as to where next to take this conversation. There's something too controlled and unconcerned about the way he's talking. I'm finding it hard to believe the cool.

It's none of your business. Drink your tea.

I concentrate. 'What was your wife like?' Blame it on the booze.

Dale gazes at me. He had removed his jacket in his bedroom; in the quiet light from the table lamp beside him, the tattooed vines and flowers on his upper arms and neck stand out under and over the sleeves of his T-shirt as if they've been carved out of his flesh. 'Let's trade,' he says softly. 'I'll tell you about my ex-wife and family but only if you tell me about your ex-boyfriend.'

'What?' I'm goggle-eyed. How could he possibly know anything about Jimmy Porter? 'What – what ex-boyfriend?'

'The boyfriend you dumped when Mary Wu asked. Does the guy know he's dumped?'

My heart and stomach change places. 'By the way,' I say desperately, 'now that you mention Mary Wu, I've been wondering. What's her real name?'

'Montgomery.'

'I see. Mary Montgomery. Nice name. Does she know how much people talk about her behind her back? Does she know what her nickname is?'

'I think she does. It don't bother her.' He smiles. He knows I'm stalling.

'All right. His name is Jimmy Porter and he doesn't know.'

'So why'd you disown him?'

'I – I—' I cast around for something uncompromising, something that could even be true, or at least convincing. 'I think probably it was meeting Eve.' I'm relieved. 'Yeah, that's it. I think that when I met her I realised what a rut I'd been in and—' I trail off. He's watching me so intently now he's making me very nervous. 'What? Why are you looking at me like that? Do you not believe me?'

217

'Are you sure it was meeting your mother? Sounds a little unlikely to me.'

'No. I'm not sure. Me and him were doing fine until this trip. But what else could it be?'

'You tell me.'

'Well, I can't think of anything. Or maybe I haven't had time to work it out properly yet.' I can't look at those eyes, so I find a speck of leaf on the surface of my tea and try to fish it out. 'Oh, by the way too, and speaking of Eve, you mentioned something about an insurance company to her back there. Is this because of the accident?'

'She won't get rich, if that's what you mean.' As if it's irritating him, he pulls at the scrunchie confining his pony-tail, then takes it off altogether. His hair cascades around his shoulders. Impatiently, he brushes it back.

'I didn't mean that. I hope you don't think that this is why I—'

'I don't.'

'But she is due some compensation, surely – was the driver of the car that hit her insured?' I become extraordinarily conscious of the heat of the mug between my hands.

'He was indeed. That's what we're talkin' about here. Motor insurance.'

'Was he from the site here?'

'Uh-huh.'

'Because that could be awkward.'

We watch each other. 'Arabella—'

Then, far away, but near enough to be identified, we hear a woman scream.

Instantly, Dale springs up from the couch. 'That's Mary!'

'How do you know?'

'I know. Stay here.' He grabs the flip-flops, shoves them on, and before I know what's happening, he's left the trailer. I hear his running footsteps on the gravel, and although he has ordered me to stay, I run out after him.

It's not hard to follow his progress: the streets are so well lit I can even see the little cloud of dust rising from his heels as, just past Eve's trailer now, he sprints towards the front of the site. My 'good' black shoes are unsuitable for running but I do the best I can, and when he turns left to dart between two trailers, I'm not so far behind that I can't

218

mark the spot and turn after him. Mary – if it is Mary – screams again, long, ear-splitting. It's such a quiet, windless night that I can now hear an angry male voice too. The doors of other trailers are opening and people are peering out . . .

A crowd has gathered at the plastic picket fence surrounding Mary Wu's plot. She doesn't have a deck but her garden is lawn, well tended and outlined by painted white stones. In her trailer, she – I'm assuming it's Mary – is continuing to scream. The man is continuing to roar. The trailer is rocking a little because something is thumping, or being thumped, against its walls.

Dale is hammering at the door. 'Mary! Eddie! It's Dale Genscher. Let me in!'

In response, the back of Mary's head crashes against one of the trailer's windows; the glass bursts, showers like bright confetti on to the little lawn and liberates the man's yelling. 'Bitch! Whore! Slut!'

'Eddie! Open this door.' Dale hammers and hammers.

Now there's furniture breaking. More screaming, crying, begging: 'Eddie, don't – don't – please don't!'

Dale turns to one of the men in the crowd. 'I don't have my cell. Call 911.' Then, with both hands, he catches hold of the banisters running up the sides of the steps and, arching his torso as though it is the elastic of a catapult, projects himself against the door. It is designed to open outwards, of course, and all he achieves is the probability of a bruised shoulder.

'Anyone got a garden fork or a spade? Quick.' He turns to the crowd. 'We'll have to lever it open.'

'We do. Go get it, Harry.' A woman shoves at a man.

Meanwhile another man is giving out the address of the site into his mobile phone. 'Yeah, three forty-seven Robinia Meadows. On County Road. And hurry. He might kill her this time.'

Banging and crashing from inside. Another piercing scream.

I feel helpless, fearful for Mary, yet the awful thing is that I'm fascinated too. I hate to admit it but it's true. You see, we get to know America through TV and I've watched scenes like this so often it feels familiar. I half expect a stuntman, representing the lead detective, to come flying round the corner on two screeching tyres.

This, though, is happening to a real person. The real Mary Wu. Mary Montgomery, the nurse's aide, whose hairdo I was laughing at less than three-quarters of an hour ago. A person I know is getting killed, blow by blow, less than eight feet from where I'm standing.

The man dispatched to get the spade returns with it and, as the fracas inside reaches new heights, more screaming, splintering of furniture, he dashes up to Dale. 'Here you go, buddy.'

'Help me.' Dale toggles the blade, working it between the door and the frame of the trailer. The spade's owner manages to get his hands into the gap and, together, he and Dale break the lock, springing open the door.

Dale pulls it wide and goes to step inside. He holds both arms out from his sides as if to show he's not armed (*is this really not TV?*), then comes flying backwards through the door again, almost taking the spade man with him as he tumbles down the steps, managing – just – to stay on his feet. All this happens so fast he has righted himself before anyone can rush forward to help him.

There is a brief pause. Mary has stopped screaming. She is weeping now.

A man, panting, denim bomber jacket spattered with blood, comes to stand inside the doorway and looks out at us all. He is small, a runt, maybe only five feet two or three, and bullet-headed, peanut on sticks, shoulders and chest bulging way out of proportion. He is also quite young. 'Stay out of this.' He glares down at Dale. 'This is not your concern.' His eyes are darting all over the place, almost rotating, and I notice that there's a dribble of white stuff coming from his mouth.

'We've called the police, Eddie.' Speaking quietly, Dale takes a few steps forward. 'They're on their way.'

Indeed I can hear a siren approaching at speed.

The man – Eddie – looks towards the sound. 'Bastard!' He reaches for something inside the trailer and – again before any of us can react – launches himself down the steps and against Dale, who goes backwards. This time he does fall. The man, though, is upright and running. Two of the male onlookers sprint after him but he's too quick, and before they can reach him, he has jumped on a motorcycle parked about fifty yards up the street. He kicks at the starter. The bike snarls into life and jumps away from its pursuers on the back wheel. The front comes down, then man and machine roar away.

The two men follow for a few yards and give up. The siren gets nearer.

All this happens within fifteen seconds. On TV you get different angles and slow motion. Not here. My brain is at last forced to make the transition from TV to reality.

When I turn back from watching the man's getaway, I see that several people are crowding around the door of the trailer. Dale is lying on the lawn below it. The spade man and his wife are kneeling beside him.

'Dale!' I run towards them. 'What happened to him? Why is he lying there?'

The woman, pale, looks up at me. 'I think he's been stabbed.'

CHAPTER THIRTY-FIVE

There's an awful lot of shouting . . .

Next time I see that no-good from the management office I'll give him a piece of my mind. There's rules in this site and one of them is no disturbances.

Them transients, probably. On the other hand, it does sound a bit nearer than them up at the front, although that could be an illusion. There's not a puff of wind tonight.

As far as I'm concerned, they can brawl themselves silly up there. Here's one girl that's not going lollapaloozing along to find out or to do anything about it. She's taken her little white pills and she's comfortable and sleepy and it's too much trouble to get out of this bed and kit out again with those goddamn crutches. What is it Dale says? 'Let the world turn without you tonight.' I love that idea.

So. Arabella's taken with Dale and he's taken with her, any fool can see that and it's great, but what about me? She came here to see me, dammit . . .

Jealous, Eve?

No, I'm not jealous. Of course I'm not jealous.

All right. I'm a little bit jealous. Because it's not only her, it's Rowan too. What are they here for, the two of them? I've hardly seen him at all. Gina's got him held tighter than a hoop on a barrel.

Deal with it. Don't blow it. For God's sake, whatever else you do, don't do the drama queen. Dale's already told her you're a drama queen – that first day they came when you couldn't deal with the real drama and you semi-passed out and you pretended you were dead asleep. So play it straight. Don't prove him right.

Now here comes a siren. Cops? This place is getting as bad as the bad old days in Queens.

Maybe it's not transients. That siren really sounds nearer – hey, here's a thought. Bear?

Keep taking the pills, Eve! We've never been troubled by bears here because we're surrounded mostly by desert, but further up north I hear they're a real problem around trailer parks and campsites. They're getting bolder and closer each year and some say it's only a matter of time until they spread down this far. I hope it's just not a matter of time until they discover the garbage routines at Robinia Meadows . . .

Snakes, now. That's a different story. We do have snakes. I'm always real careful going out on the deck in the morning because sometimes they curl up there; it's probably because it's warmer on the wood than in the dirt under the trailer. At the beginning, when we came here first, I was petrified thinking I'd meet a snake but Dale convinced me early on that most of them are harmless and that they're more frightened of me than I am of them. I won't be testing that any day soon, though.

I guess the SUV that hit me did me a favour in a way. Since I'm not exactly mobile right now, that wreck forced a sort of interval in my life. Made me think, gave me plenty of time to take a survey, if you like.

God, I can't stop yawning. That was a good one. Nearly dislocated my jaw.

Yeah, I would most likely not have gotten round to contacting my kids if that SUV hadn't hit me . . .

When Dale told me he'd found Arabella and it was easy because she was in the phone book, I didn't get excited. Not right then. That's la-la, ain't it? Wouldn't you think I'd get excited about seeing my kids after all these years? Lord knows, I've been dreaming about it long enough. I guess I didn't think he'd find them and the reality came as a shock.

Instead of excitement, my immediate feeling was guilt. I started to think of all the bad things, the resentment and even hate that they'd have for me.

I must ask Arabella how long she's been in the phone book. She must have been ex-directory or something when I was looking for her before. All these years when I was dreaming up real complex ways to contact them, through the Irish radio stations here and that kind of thing, it never occurred to me to try the Irish phone book again. It's probably hard to believe but so was the discovery that the earth wasn't flat and they're both true . . .

Oooh-hoo, yawn, yawn, yawn! I love this feeling of being drowsy and cosy. Like you're lying under a warm cloud and it's tucking you in . . .

What'll I give her for breakfast? I wonder, does she like scrambled eggs? Have I enough oranges to make decent juice for her? This is going to be the most important talk I've ever had. I'm real anxious about it, but I'm just so sleepy . . .

An ambulance now?

CHAPTER THIRTY-SIX

It was dark when I got out here on to the deck but that must have been two hours ago. It's just before dawn now, and misty: another pet morning like the one when I watched the horses.

Given the avalanche of happenings since, that morning seems as though it dawned some time in the last century, and today I couldn't care less about the earthy smell from Dale's vegetable patch. I'm not admiring pearly skies, redness of rocks or birdsong, I'm listening out for Dale, still asleep, probably because of the painkillers. He has looked after me and now it's my turn to look after him.

I have Eve's diary here beside me. I brought it out intending to read it – there's an outdoor lantern attached to the wall of this mobile home that gives plenty of light – but I was too uptight to concentrate. I still am. I have to read it, though: I promised Eve I'd have done so before we talked, and no matter what has happened to Dale or Mary or anyone else, that promise has to be kept.

I do ask myself where Rowan is in all of this. Surely he wants to talk to her too. As far as I can see, though, his only interest since he came here has been Gina. I suppose I could be grateful: after all, I do keep calling it a miracle. How would I cope if he were causing mayhem? But I think the situation between Eve and her prodigal children could not be more weird had it been written by the author of a mystery novel. So far, there's been no sign of life from her place and, as far as I know, she's still unaware of what has happened.

I'm not sure whether Rowan knows either, or Mario or Robert or Gina – by the time she was due back from work we were all well installed in A&E at the hospital. The absence of Dale's pickup might have alerted her that something was wrong, but clearly she didn't check – and why should she? They're all pals here but they don't live in each other's pockets.

So where is Dale's pickup? I hear you ask.

Dale's pickup is parked near the entrance to the hospital. I drove it there. After the fracas, without a second's thought about what I was about to do, I ran from Mary Wu's back to Dale's, got into the cab of that pickup, started that engine and drove.

I don't have a licence. I don't drive. But I drove as part of the hospital caravan: ambulance, police car – both sirens blaring – Spade Man and wife, hair blowing in their mile-long convertible (gold and white with two huge shark fins, something Elvis or Bono would drive), then me. Driving. On the right-hand side of the road. When it was pitch dark. No bother. Not then.

But then we got into the Emergency Room and after the shock of seeing Dale and Mary on the trolleys, covered with blood, full Technicolor, the second whammy was the realisation that *I had driven a van twenty miles with no licence or insurance! Behind a police car!* I shook so hard the staff wanted to give me a sedative but the last thing I needed, I thought, was to be out of it if there was really bad news about either of the patients, so I refused.

Arriving into that A&E wasn't quite as dramatic as you'd think it'd be from watching *ER*: just as in the series, everyone seemed to walk around carrying a clipboard but it was a calm place, with no dashing about – although there was a bit of shouting from some doctor who, as we arrived, was lashing out at a snacks machine.

While Dale and Mary were transferred from the ambulance stretchers on to the hospital trolleys, we three civilians, Spade Man, Spade Wife and Jellywoman (me), were approached by a girl bursting out of her blue over-alls, clipboard in hand: 'Health plan?'

Dale overheard: 'I got Blue Cross.' His voice was weak but clear. 'And I'll personally cover for Mrs Montgomery. Got my credit card in my wallet.' A nurse immediately winkled it from the hip pocket of his jeans and Michelin Girl bore off his card to a machine behind the reception desk.

The waiting room where we three sat was comfortable and airy, painted in ochres and creams and decorated with prints of the local landscape so we had something nice to distract us. Plus, we were all bathed in soothing classical music and our seats, unlike the crowded, sweaty rows of plastic chairs we're used to in Dublin, were upholstered and placed in groups around little coffee tables. The time, though, didn't pass any quicker than it does at home and we remained there in silence until I grew uncomfortable. 'Does Mary's ex-husband often come round like that?' I asked Spade Man eventually.

'Son.' This was the wife, who had a gorgeous southern-belle accent. 'If he were mine –' she pronounced it 'ma-ahn' '– I'd have turned him over to the po-lice long ago. He comes around only when he needs cash. He's a no-good person.'

We introduced ourselves but I immediately forgot their names. They had come originally from southern Georgia, had respectively retired from the post office and an insurance company, and had immigrated to Arizona because the lack of humidity was good for Spade Man's arthritis. They were saving to go to Europe on a vacation in two years' time, and because they knew Eve they were sure going to include the Emerald Isle. This would be their first trip abroad, outside Hawaii, 'But that's part of our country, of course.' They told me that their own son was a diving instructor in Australia. They 'appreciated' what George Bush was trying to do for the world.

Then they turned to the subject of Eve. She was one of their favourite people, they said, and hoped that this 'li'l incident' tonight wouldn't ruin my visit with her.

'We love Eve,' said Spade Wife.

She glanced at her husband who nodded emphatic agreement. 'Eve sure is special. She's had all that pain in her life,' he goes, 'but it's not jest that. We've all had things in our lives to worry about. It's somethin' about her.'

'Yeah,' chimed in the wife. 'It's somethin'. An aura. Sometimes you wanna stare at her, sometimes you jest wanna wrap her up and put her in a candy box.' None the wiser, I smiled, and we all returned to contemplation of the spotless red lino on the floor.

It turned out that, despite all the blood, neither of our patients had suffered anything major. Mary's nose was broken, she had bad bruising to her arms, back and side, her lower lip was badly split, and by the time she was wheeled back to us, both her eyes were swollen, concealed under a welter of black, blue and purple. Some of her hair had been shaven off because glass splinters had been removed from a deep cut on her scalp.

Probably because she was bigger than Eddie, said the doctor who came with her to us, she had defended herself well from more serious injury. She was being admitted for the night but should be released within twenty-four hours.

'I'm so sorry,' Mary pushed words at us through her poor, swollen mouth. 'Eddie's not a bad boy, really. It's just that he's had a run of bad luck.'

I felt so sad for her. No sign now of Mrs Wu, this was Mary Montgomery, mother, pathetic in her loyalty. 'Don't worry about it, Mary.' I gave her a gentle hug. 'It seems everyone's survived. A few days and everything will be back to normal.'

'Have the cops talked to you yet?' She grabbed my arm.

'No. And don't you worry about things like that tonight. Get yourself a sleeping pill and try to rest. Tomorrow is another day.' What a cliché, but it was the best I could come up with. I knew, because I had seen them go into the examination room, that the police were now talking to her son's other victim.

'Look after Dale, won't you?' Tears squeezed themselves somehow from under the bulbous, gaudy mussel shells over Mary's eyes. 'I don't know what we'd all do without him.'

'I will.'

'See you tomorrow. Happy birthday again!' As she was wheeled off, she attempted, horribly, to smile.

Shortly afterwards, when the doctor in charge of Robinia Meadows's saint incarnate came out to talk to us, he told us our hero would be with us shortly and had refused to be admitted. He was a lucky man. He had indeed been stabbed but the knife had glanced off his collarbone so the wound was superficial; most of the blood we had seen had come from where he had hit his head against one of the painted stones on Mary's lawn. 'Again, it's superficial – head cuts bleed a lot – and although he lost consciousness for a few moments and we'd like to keep him in for observation, he's the boss.'

What is it with me and head wounds? Jimmy Porter, poor old Mary and now Dale. Well, three and it's over, as we say. No one need fear being near me from now on.

'Will you be with him during the night, Miss . . .' The doctor scanned for my name on his clipboard.

'Moraghan. Yes, I will. I'll look after him.'

'Are you Irish?' The face of the doctor, an Oriental, creased into a smile.

'I am.'

'Isn't that accent darling?' This was Spade Wife.

'I love Dublin.' The medic was writing busily. 'I trained in St James's. That Guinness! Here's our emergency number.' He tore off a piece of paper and handed it to me. 'If there's any nausea or vomiting, call an ambulance first, then us immediately after so we'll be waiting. Do you have far to travel?'

'Twelve miles.' From Spade Man.

We're always reading in our Irish newspapers about the high cost of medicine in America and I suppose this was the proof: obviously you get what you pay for – in advance – and only that. I have to say, though, that whatever Dale paid for bought a lot because the treatment he and Mary received seemed quick and comprehensive, X-rays, scans, repair work, the whole caboodle, all done in a quietly flowing, no-nonsense stream. When Dale came out, like Mary, he had a bald patch darned with stitching. His right arm was in a sling.

'Well, Arabella,' he smiled down at me, 'sorry about this, you sure are gettin' some introduction to the good ole USA.'

'Yeah. Never a dull moment.' More cliché. Funny how people say the first thing that comes into their heads when they're emotional. And seeing Dale upright and wounded made me emotional. It made me think of what could have happened. Lord, I thought, what a group our party would make now! Eve, Dale, Mary – all walking wounded. Custer's last stand wasn't in it . . .

I was not willing to do another Eddie Irvine so Dale and I had to come home by taxi. He fell asleep beside me in the back seat, and as we sped along the empty highway I took the opportunity to study him, peaceful, mouth slack, fingers at the end of the sling twitching a little as he dreamed. It was odd to see him so open and vulnerable and I had the strongest urge to put my arms round him and cradle him, stroke his hair, soothe his tortured scalp . . .

Of course I did nothing of the sort, but Florence Nightingale wasn't in it when we got back to the trailer. Greta, who's a natural at this kind of thing, would have been proud of me as I bossed Dale around and helped him to bed.

229

Here comes the sun, a pulsating, blinding white crescent growing larger by the second in the V between two peaks to the east. Still nobody moving around the site; the birds and I might have the world to ourselves.

Unlike the birds, though, which no doubt live their little bird lives minute by minute on the wing and take every new day as a fresh bird-opportunity, my brain and stomach are churning people and events, past and present, out of sequence. It's only now that the impact of the previous evening (and of the rapidly blurring days since we got here) is fully hitting me. I feel like wastewater, swirling towards the plughole.

Happy Birthday to you.

Willow: gone.

Jimmy Porter: shed.

Mary's leaning beehive.

Gripping a steering wheel – *driving*.

Eve's grip on my arm.

Piano music.

Dale covered with blood.

Fantastical figurines on a clock.

Rowan – champagne?

Dale's hair when he pulled off the scrunchie.

Motorbike wheelies.

Tea, lemon, sugar basin, china cup.

Cake candles relighting.

Peanut Eddie lunging at Dale.

RowanGinaRowanGina.

Dale.

Blood.

Eve asking something I probably can't give.

The charged silence between Dale and me before he said my name – and then Mary screamed.

CHAPTER THIRTY-SEVEN

Do you know what's extraordinary? I was checking in my handbag and I still have eleven cigarettes left in the current pack. And I know that in my bedroom I still have eighteen of the twenty packs in the carton I bought in duty-free. With all that's going on I should be smoking like a chimney, but I'm not. I kind of forget sometimes that I'm dying for one. Maybe coming to Arizona was my golden opportunity to quit, although right now I'm dying for one, big-time. That could be stress: I'm looking ahead to the coming day, in which every single thing seems out of my control with a 'should' or a 'have to' attached. So, short of pulling a Willow and running away, I'm in for a rocky ride. I'm nearly sorry that I didn't accept last night's offer of a sedative: I could have pretended to take it at the time but saved it up.

The police are coming to take statements. That's going to be a blast, isn't it?

I have to have a tête-à-tête with my mother so I have to know what's in her flaming diary. I fecking promised, didn't I?

I have to ring work. Although I'd left it vague as to what day I'd be back, I promised I'd let them know within a couple of days so they could cover my shifts. It's certainly more than a couple of days now. So much for fantasies about staying in America! I have to make up my mind about when I'm going home.

Let's see, what else? I can't shirk ringing Willow for much longer. I should – I *have to* – ring her today. In addition, I should be with Eve when that insurance bloke comes to talk to her; after all, I am her elder daughter.

Taking everything into account, it feels as if I'm keeping the world balanced in my painfully stretched arms, and if I relax for even a millisecond, civilisation will end. All in all, the holiday deluxe is *finito*. Serves me right for not staying on guard. The only exception to this list of 'haves' and 'shoulds' is Dale. I don't have to look after him: I want to.

So, my dear Hamlet, should I have a cigarette or not? That is the question.

OK. I won't. I'll wait a bit.

Yeah. I'll wait ten minutes. One of the ads on the telly at home says that if you wait, the bad part of the craving eases after a few minutes. Wouldn't it be great if I could quit altogether – if this was the net result of coming out here to see Eve? She'd have done that much for me at least.

I don't know what I think about Eve. I'm still drowning in contradictions, tender one minute, furious the next. Still trying to see this specialness that everyone else sees in her.

Ah, shag it, where's those cigarettes? And no more excuses. Open that bloody diary.

For the hour that follows, sometimes stopping to listen for movement inside the trailer, other times distracted by someone going by as the site slowly rouses itself for the day, I smoke my head off while living in my mother's life. Her years in the orphanage, uncannily like my own, her getting pregnant with me, her life with my father – I skim that part quickly because it's too painful to absorb in detail just yet.

There's a great lot about this woman Maura, who emerges from Eve's blotted, multicoloured and misspelled script as a wonderful friend. Wonderful woman, period.

I skip the bit about that crucial Christmas Eve in the Palm House. To read that I will need to be stronger emotionally, although I do manage a passage about her sitting beside the Tolka river immediately after she left us. I know that river; I probably know that very seat. Apparently, while we three bewildered kids were being shepherded out of the Palm House by what seemed to me to be a giant in a navy suit, my mother was half considering suicide.

I follow Eve's flight to America, her skivvying and the other jobs she had, her highs and descents, her drinking, the priest who rescued her, the car crash, Dale, AA meetings, their southward meandering in Dale's van, meeting Mario and Robert in a small town in Alabama.

It is strange to read her unemotional, non-judgemental spinning of the story of these two gays. I suppose I hadn't expected my mother to be a liberal. She corroborates the remarks Dale had made to us in the cab of the pickup. Apparently Mario and Robert had just got together. Robert, recently out of the closet, had just left his wife for Mario, who was by day a clerk in a dry-cleaner's, by night a part-time barman and waiter. Their town, 'Rednecksvill' is how Eve describes – and spells – it, was agog with the scandal.

One night, Dale, Eve and Gina, just passing through, had happened to go into the bar/restaurant where Mario worked and found him being baited by two heavyset punters a little the worse for wear. He put up a spirited defence, but things started to get nasty. Then one of the men reached over and grabbed him by the front of his shirt. Eve describes it calmly:

> . . . he caled poor Mario an ashole and wors (that I wont go into here) and I felt so sory for Mario. He looked like a lovely boy. I got real indignant and I said to Dale that this has to stop. He tryed to stop me innterfeering but I said I woud be alright and he said on my own head be it. So I just went up to these two rednecks and pushed myself in between them and I told the one holding Mario to pick on me instead of an inosent young man. I sqared up to him with my chest nearly in his face and I looked at him the way I used to look at Petey when he was thretning me and that usualy workd with him and what do you know it worked with this guy too. He let Mario go but wasnt plesed about it and he and his pal left the bar nearly imeedatly. I think it works with guys Maura because they are afrade that if they hit you they will damage your breasts or somthing like that. Maybe they think about there own mothers.

Robert and Mario had decided to get out of Alabama altogether and it was these two who set the course for all five of the core group, declaring that the future lay not in California, as one might have expected ('too queer'), but in either Montana or Arizona where personal freedom was respected. Arizona won out because of the kinder climate – and because Gina's husband, at that time in Toussaint, had bought her a trailer to live in as part of their separation agreement and wanted a swift decision as to where to have it delivered.

As for Gina, she had been gathered up some weeks previously, in the reception area of a motel where she was fighting with the clerk about the bill; apparently her husband was supposed to have taken care of it and hadn't. Dale, of course, had stepped in.

All five had kept in touch by telephone, and when Gina's trailer had been delivered and installed at Robinia Meadows, the other four straggled in to visit. None of them had expected the arrangement to become permanent. From what I gather, Mario works all over the place, in the gallery, taking occasional shifts in bars in Sedona, but he loves to cook so, as far as I can see, most of his life is spent as chef-companion to Robert.

Naturally Dale features a lot in the repetitive, forwards-and-backwards stories of Eve's adventures and traumas. His kindness. His generosity. His patience. Always, however, as it affects Eve herself. In the diary, Dale is a guardian angel. Came from nowhere. Going nowhere. No desires or plans of his own. No mention of his family, his past, his being a Jehovah's Witness. He simply 'is'. Hovering over Eve's life.

I light another cigarette and go back to the bit about the Palm House. I can't resist it any longer. I'm used to Eve's handwriting by this stage and can read it fairly quickly. There are far more crossings-out and rewritings in this section than in any other part of the diary; she has worked and reworked the words here to get the feeling right. This part of the story must be the most important to her. The writing is almost lyrical in some places as she struggles with how best to describe what happened. For instance, 'the rot on my coal black soul', near the beginning of this Palm House entry, started out as 'the stane ("stain" presumably) on my rotten heart'.

All for whom? For us? For me?

I won't repeat the mis-spellings here, it would make me feel even worse than I do; I'll give it to you straight as if I'm reading it out loud. There's little or no punctuation.

Always there is that Christmas Eve my day of judgement the rot on my coal black soul. The three of them looking at me through that hazy wet heat Rowan swinging his heels kicking against his go car then leaning against his straps to examine his feet sitting back up again and smiling at me making goo noises as if I am his best friend and I have just given him the best Christmas present in the world. Willow sulking and turning her back on me because she didn't get a tin box and Arabella did and Arabella with her little arms tight around the tin box and frowning because I had told her to be a good girl and to stay there beside the lily pond for a while. I told her she had to mind the others for me. They were good children they did stay where they were and didn't try to follow me while I walked backwards out of the Palm House holding on to the sight of them for as long as possible. To this day I can remember everything about that place the way the damp made little bits of sweat drop down from my forehead the kind of sharp smell of the huge high plants the trickling sound of water and the shine off of the green lily pads. By the time I got to the door Rowan was on to the next adventure and wasn't even thinking of me instead, he was looking up at the glass roof and giving out short little screams then he was cocking his head to listen to the echo delighted with himself. Willow didn't seem to care either, but that was probably an act. A little green coat she had on that day with a black velvet collar and a green beret. Even at that age that little girl loved her clothes and she was always a little madam and a holy terror to get dressed. Everything had to match. She still had her back to me but she was picking up something from the ground a leaf or a cigarette butt or something and she was holding it up to her face and examining it. Arabella though was the one that put the knife in me. She was the one kept looking after me all the time. When I got to the door she put her hand up and gave me a bye-bye wave or a kind of a half of a one she looked puzzled and brave. I didn't wave back. I couldn't. I didn't look back either when I got out into the open. I wanted to scream out loud but I had to continue with the plan. So I forced myself to stay steady while I searched for someone anyone the plan was to buttonhole the first person I saw. I had practised. The plan was that I was going to say excuse me I was just in the Palm House there behind me and I think someone better go in to have a look. I have to leave I am in a hurry I have an appointment but I would say there might be a problem in there because there are three small kids standing there beside the lily pond and they don't seem to have anyone with them one of them is only a baby. The Botanics seemed to be empty that day. Christmas Eve. It was all going wrong they'd be there all over Christmas. I had put a bottle and clean nappies into the go car and a couple of bananas for the girls but I had used up every single penny of my savings and what Maura gave me on the ticket and the money you have to have when you are going into America or they won't let you in and there was only enough left for the bus fare to the airport and a cup of tea if it wasn't too expensive. I was counting on the three of them being found quick and that the people who would find them would give them food and make sure they would not go hungry. I panicked I would have to go back and forget about the whole thing. Then I saw a keeper or a gardener a man in a uniform in anyway walking towards the glasshouses. He was jingling a bunch of keys in his hand. I pretended to be looking at a flowerbed checking the labels. He said to me we're locking up Miss did you not hear the bell. I said I was sorry and that I was just leaving in anyway. He said right so or something like that and he wished me a Happy Christmas. I wished him a Happy Christmas too. I had no choice then. I walked very slow and every step was a nightmare. When I dared to look back I saw the door of the Palm House open.

I stop. I'm blind. I can't read any more. I remember every minute of that. I was old enough to record it, to commit it for ever to memory, and I have. Not from her perspective. From my own. There's a detail here I'd missed. I hadn't remembered that I had waved.

Additionally, what I can't cope with is the scoring-out, the word-changing, the huge effort my mother has made to get the story right for me. As for the language she uses: not much 'feistiness'. Not much trace of the way Eve now speaks or presents herself. But I know in a way I can't explain that, for sure, my mother is buried within the woman living in that trailer across the road from where I'm sitting.

Now Dale is standing beside me, blinking in the glare. He's bare-chested, his hair is all over the place, and because of the angle of the sun-light shafting into it the stitching on his head wound stands out, a range of microscopic mountains against the bald shine of his shaven scalp. He's holding the bad arm with the other; the stitching on his shoulder has sundered the skeins of tattooed ivy. He's pale. He looks awful.

'What's wrong, Arabella?' He hunkers down. 'Why are you crying?'

'No why,' I say, stubbing out the latest cigarette, only half smoked. 'Listen, you're the invalid. You sit down here and take it easy. Would you like me to make you eggs or something?'

CHAPTER THIRTY-EIGHT

I've fucking blown it. I was tanked last night when Gina got back from work and she wasn't having it. She threw me out.

Well, that's according to her, but nobody throws out Rowan Moraghan, right? I left of my own free will, right? No way was Rowan Moraghan going to stand for all that fucking whingeing and yelling. Who did she think she was talking to? If she didn't want people to skull her fucking booze why did she leave it where people could get it? I was supposed to be a fucking guest, wasn't I? Nice way to treat your guest: fuck them out because you leave them alone and they help themselves to a little refreshment.

Oh, Christ, I don't mean that. I don't mean any of it. I've seriously blown it. She had every right to throw me out.

Whatever way it happened, at half two in the morning I found myself outside in the freezing cold with only my smokes and lighter as luggage. Yeah, it was cold in Arizona, which surprised me. I'd no alternative but to go knock up my ma.

As it turned out, it might not have been the ideal thing to do. I'm knackered. I don't think I got a wink of sleep and it wasn't only the emotional stuff she laid on me (of which moreafuckingnon, as Mental would say), although it was a bit of that, I suppose: it was also that I was pure disgusted with myself and this whole livelong night kept going round in my head like it was postcards nailed to a wheel. Plus I suppose it was the lack of smokes. Bad and all as I wanted one, I hadn't the nerve to light up inside my ma's trailer. It wouldn't have been fair, like.

Anyway, here's the way it happened. First of all, I can't remember much of what happened with Gina. Much of what was said, I mean. It just blew up out of fucking nowhere. She comes in from work. I say hello. I jump on her, kind of playful, like, and I go to pull her down on the couch with me. She goes spare, gives me a slap, yells and shouts and roars at me about how dare I and I'm a drunk and I smell like a skunk and next thing I'm out.

My ma is gob-smacked when she answers my knock. 'Rowan! What a surprise! Come in, honey.'

Unfortunately, I have a small bit of an accident on the way in: I hit a corner of a press, or a counter or something, and next thing there's this big fucking crash and I'm up to my knees in fucking broken glass. 'Don't sweat it.' It doesn't seem to bother her. 'It's only an old thing.'

'Sorry.' I bend down to pick up one of the pieces and next thing I've cut my fucking hand and I'm bleeding.

'Don't worry, Rowan.' She's holding my hand and doing the Florence Nightingale. 'All you need is a Band-Aid. You go on down there and make yourself comfortable. I'll find one and then I'll put on the kettle.' I didn't want tea or coffee or anything. All I wanted was to lie down and shut everything out, but I could hardly say that to her, could I?

It was hard to find a place to sit. She has a big armchair but with tubes draped all over it from an oxygen bottle. And the woman has so many fucking cushions on her couch it's like a bordello.

You're asking now, 'How does that geezer know what a bordello looks like?' Well, when Mental was younger, he lived in Berlin for a while, working on a building site or something, and he's always telling us about the bordellos there. 'Women and artefacts from all over Europe and beyond, my friends. Georgians, Turks – and don't you believe what you hear about the frozen north. Among the silk and satin cushions of Persia, I've had many a romp with a buxom Scandinavian.'

Sometimes I don't know whether or not to believe the things Mental tells us.

So, anyway, I clear a space for myself on the couch, sit down, and my ma comes back in, hopping and dragging and thumping on a crutch. She's carrying a blanket that she drops over the broken glass. 'We'll sort that out in the morning,' she goes. 'I'd be afraid the cat might injure himself.'

'Clean that cut.' She holds out a bottle of some stuff and a lump of cotton wool.

'It's all right,' I go. 'I don't need to clean it. The plaster'll be fine.' No way am I going to torture myself with disinfectant. Pour acid into an open cut?

'Whatever you say.' She gives me the plaster, then sits down beside me and watches me while I put it on.

I hate people gawking at me. I *hate* it. 'I could murder a rasher and a fried egg,' I announce, because it's the first thing that pops into my head, but then I realise it's true: I have a desperate dose of the munchies. I always get the munchies after a skinful.

I don't expect her to do anything about this – it's just something I said – but what does she do but pick up the crutch and hopalong back to the kitchen. 'No rashers, I'm afraid,' she says, 'but I'll see what I can do.' Then doesn't she go and make me scrambled eggs and beans on toast? Two o'clock in the morning, three o'clock nearly, and my ma is making me a feed. Fucking A.

However, there's no such thing as a free fucking lunch, as Mental would say. On principle, Mental boycotts soup runs and Lions' Club Christmas dinners and all the rest of the freebie bunfights because of it being the System that's wrong. 'It's not the charities that should be looking after our basic necessities, citizen,' he'll say, 'it's our government.'

In my case, the downside of my ma's free meal is that she gets to watch every bean I put into my gob. 'Did you have a row with Gina?' she asks, out of the blue, real quiet, and for some reason, probably because of the way she asks, or it could be the booze making loose with my tongue (or even the way she's looking at me with those eyes of hers), I tell her the whole story.

Even while I'm going on about it I know it's not the kind of thing a grown man should be talking about to his ma. But, then, what experience do I have with that? I finish the story anyway. 'So that's how I ended up here tonight. I hope you're OK with this.'

She gives a little smile. Like the Sphinx. Then she asks me straight out: 'Do you drink a lot, Rowan?'

I've a mouth full of food and I nearly choke. 'Depends what you mean by "a lot".' I'm on the *quifuckingvive* now (Mental again: he's an influence on us all). 'I like a few bevvies,' I say. 'Who doesn't?'

'Some of us like them a little too much. I understand that, better than most.'

I stare back at her. 'You an alky?'

'I am an alcoholic, yes. I haven't had a drink for many years, but I'm just one drink away from it right this minute. Every day is a new test.

Tell me about yourself, honey. What's happened that you made booze your best friend?'

She's eating me up with those fucking eyes of hers. I did tell you about them, didn't I? 'I don't know what you mean.'

'You know what I mean. I'm not giving out to you, Rowan. I'm the last person with rights to give out to anybody, certainly to you. I just want to know what happened. In addition to all the damage I caused you, of course. The girls told me a little, but could you tell me yourself?'

I want to stand up from the fucking table and throw things. I want to splatter my mother's calm, quiet face. I want to gouge out those lamping eyes, and as for Bella, it's that bitch has me in this condition, I think, and next time I see her I'll ram a plateful of fucking eggs and beans down her throat.

I can't control myself. I split open. I give her the dibs on the institution she left me in, the mouldy bread, the lumpy porridge, the grey, slithery fish on Fridays, the cold, the bed-wetting, the beatings until you couldn't see but, worst of all, being forced to watch other fellas, little fellas, being half killed. The education, so-called, that filled your head only with fear of the belt or the strap or worse. I don't have to think or remember. It spills out as fast as Niagara Falls.

I can see I'm getting to her so now I lay it on, punishing her. I tell her about the filthy squats where you have to be careful where you lie or you'd be stuck with a used syringe and maybe get HIV; I tell her about the streets, the wet, the cold, the spits, the coughs, the pain in your belly because it's empty and you've drunk cheap beer, the blisters on your feet because you've no socks and because your shoes are two sizes too small, the hatchet in your head because you always have a hangover or you're so hungry you're seeing double. The fights. The cuts. The bruises, black eyes, broken fingers. The shitty smell off your sleeping-bag that comforts you at night because it's your own. The hospitals where they wrinkle their noses at you when they think you're not looking. The shame.

Mental.

I tell her about Mental. How I'm afraid of him but that he's probably the only person on the streets, in the whole fucking world, that I can call my friend. He doesn't seek my company and he's off his head a lot of the time (and I've the scars to prove it) but he wades in on my behalf if he feels I'm getting a thumping I don't deserve . . .

'And that's only the physical stuff. People like you can't fucking begin to know about the hole in your chest, the hole around you, the hole everywhere you look . . .' I can't stop. It's like I've been saving up for this since the day I was born. 'Why did you do it, Ma?'

What?

Where had that come from?

Horror. I'm snivelling. I can feel the tears coming like I'm a fucking baby. I stop them. Rowan Moraghan doesn't *do* baby. Not any more. The last time I cried was when my foster-family sent me back to that con-centration camp because they said they couldn't handle me.

But the tears are pouring down her face now. Christ, I hate to see a woman cry. 'Shut up! Shut up!' I jump to my feet. 'Stop it. Stop crying. Stop feeling sorry for yourself. You asked me. And you put me in that institution in the first place.' I won't let her do this. It'd be too easy to cry together and then everything'd be all over and everything'd be sugar and kisses. Boo-hoo – boom! Magic. I won't let her do it because crying doesn't change a damn thing.

She's standing too now. I didn't see her get up. She's caught my face in her hands. She's holding it real tight. Her hands are very warm. They feel strong.

I don't know what to do. I can't struggle. She's an old lady. I might hurt her. She's my mother. She's telling me she loves me. 'My poor little boy . . .'

Next thing I'm on her neck. Me, Rowan Moraghan. I'm on my mother's neck and I'm crying like I'm two years old.

Somehow or other we get control of this situation. We sit down and she hands me a box of tissues. I blow my nose. She's looking at me but I can't look at her. She doesn't say a word.

I can't honestly say I've spent much time in my life dreaming about meeting my mother. Maybe at the very beginning, as a nipper, very small, when all us boys talked about was what it was going to be like when our mas came to take us home – the toys, the food, the quiet – but I gave up dreaming about anything long ago. And after decades of doorways and fights and ruined feet, my mother, as I think I told you, became the face of every street whore I saw.

I have to snuff out those words she said to me, that stuff about 'poor little boy'. They're too dangerous. 'I don't even want to know why you did it,' I say to her. 'You did it. That's enough. I'm not going to forgive you for it. Ever, ever, *ever*.'

'I don't expect you to. And I'm not going to insult you by making excuses.' She waits. I say nothing. What's to say?

'Tell me about you and Gina,' she says softly. 'You told me about the row. Tell me about the feelings.'

I want to tell her diddly, right? But I hear myself telling her anyway. Is this what mothers do? Have they got some sort of laser thing in their brains as a result of you having half their blood or something? Whatever, I hear myself telling her that it's typical of my life that I blow something I don't want to blow. I hear myself revealing little things about Gina. Crappy little things that'd make anyone smile. Like how sometimes Gina goes to pick up something off the table, maybe, and misses because of the bad eye, but how she makes a game out of it, closing the eye and laughing at herself. 'And would you believe I even thought—' I stop. This is taking it too far.

'You thought you might have a future?'

Bollocks! That laser thing again. 'Yes.' I'm nodding at my shoes.

'And what does she like about you? Has she told you?'

I can't tell my mother that stuff. I've had years and years of practice at hiding things. Things that matter. 'No,' I say flatly. Which is a lie, of course, and suddenly it becomes very, *very* important to make things right with Gina.

'Gina's a really good person,' my ma says softly, lasering me again. 'Why don't you go and apologise and see what happens?'

'It's too late. I've blown it.'

'You don't know that. She likes you. I can tell. I've known Gina for a few years now and I've never seen her smile so much as she has in the last few days. Go say you're sorry. Mean it, Rowan. She'll know if you don't.'

'You really think she might give me another chance?' I look at her, take the risk.

'I think the odds are fairly good if she believes you,' she says, 'but she won't give you a third.'

'So I should go over there now? At this hour?'

'No, of course not.' She smiles. 'First thing in the morning. You'll never know unless you try.'

I think about this.

'So what about the booze, Rowan?' She has this voice as well as those eyes. It's soft and soothing, makes you want to swim in it. 'Even if Gina and you are not to be as a couple, there's still you to consider. You and your own life.'

I start rearing up but she's doing the quiet laser thing again and it fizzles on me. I hear myself saying I'd think about it.

'Do you mean it?'

'All right, all right, I fucking mean it. I will do something about it.'

'Please don't use language like that in my presence. It's not appropriate.' The voice stays at exactly the same level. 'There's a good AA meeting in Sedona. You could come with us. It can be fun. Your choice. No pressure.' She pushes herself to her feet. 'See you in the morning. Get some sleep – that sofa pulls out, there's a comforter and pillow in it.' She collects her crutch and goes off into the bedroom without looking back. The minute she closes her door, I dive to the nearest window and scrabble at it to get it open so I can light up and blow the smoke outside.

As I took that first deep, lovely drag, the main feeling was relief. It felt good that someone (other than the blisters, of course) had brought up the subject of booze. And she was so matter-of-fact about it. Maybe, I thought, I would give it a go with AA. I'd been doing so well since I gave it up. Maybe trying to do it on my own without AA, or some other kind of crutch under me, was too difficult.

She must have used some psychological crap on me, though. I went soft. It's *years* since I went soft. I didn't even go soft when I had to go up to the Mater Hospital to identify my dead girlfriend – although I have to admit I was near the edge because I couldn't stop thinking about my son or daughter dead inside her belly. I met Caroline's mother for the first time at the removal, and that was hard too. The poor woman was small and frightened and looked about a hundred years old, although she couldn't have been more than forty-five or fifty. She seemed afraid of me, and that was terrible to see.

I went on some bender that night.

The fucking birds are starting to twitter outside. It's a sound I hate. I could get up, I suppose, and go outside for a smoke but I'm nearly afraid to stand up out of this bed-settee thing in case I break something else. No wonder I smashed that glass bowl or whatever it was – there's enough gewgaws and fucking ornaments and little tables in here to set up a stall in the Liberty Market. The place is a fucking pharaoh's tomb.

You know the maddest thing? I hated it but I liked it when my ma told me to mind my language. It was like what I've always imagined a ma would tell her kid. Whatever. This has been the maddest night of my life.

I shouldn't have drunk so much. And I will do something about it. I sure am paying for it now and not just with a blazing hangover . . . I can handle that, I suppose, but I could do with a hair of the dog . . .

Try an apology with Gina, she said. She's big into apologies, it seems.

I wonder, is Gina awake yet? Like, if she really meant it, she would have thrown out my gear after me, wouldn't she?

CHAPTER THIRTY-NINE

I'm not a great reader. I think that's something you get into when you're young and I sure never got the opportunity to develop any nice habits like that. Lately, though, I did read somewhere, maybe in a newspaper or magazine, that poetry is about what you can't express.

Dear God, I wish I could write poetry because I can't express how much I love my son.

This has to be a secret between us because mothers shouldn't play favourites. There's Arabella, so good, so decent and generous with her sympathy. Of course I love her – she's very easy to love and it isn't fair that she isn't the favourite. I could go travelling with her, I think, and we wouldn't have many cross words.

I love Willow too, but in a different, sadder way. I need more time with her to win her round.

After tonight, however, I can see that the more ornery Rowan behaves, the more he effs and swears, the more I'm going to love him, even though it's a love that doesn't make sense and that might break my heart.

Is it because he's a boy? The only son and that mother-son thing is kicking in? Is it because he's my baby? Or is it that he's the black sheep – I sure know that role, so maybe it's because I'm identifying with him.

I'm able to split myself in two where he's concerned. In my head I'm a hundred per cent disapproving of the way Rowan has lived his life and would agree with anyone, Willow, cops, social workers, the whole kit and caboodle, that my son is a reprobate and should be given a good roasting, if not kicked out to fend for himself. No matter how much my head drums on about this, though, my heart remains wide open and soft for him.

Last time I went out to the john I took a quick look at him down there on the couch. There was only one lamp lit so I couldn't see very

245

well (and I didn't want to risk waking him by going all the way down there – this cast makes a helluva lot of noise) but he seemed to be sleeping peacefully on his back. I nearly died from tenderness when I noticed that one arm was thrown across his eyes as if he was trying to shield his face from an enemy blow.

It would be wonderful to go right down there, I thought, to sit in my chair and do nothing but watch my son sleeping. I would spend the night scheming for his happiness, for his meals, his clothes, his children. For conversations we would have when I get old.

I did nothing of the sort, of course. After I'd done my business in the bathroom, I went back to bed, where I've been lying awake, reliving, thinking. Not planning – no point in planning – and mentally apologising to my sweet Arabella for not choosing her as my number-one child.

This is a strange business, this reunion stuff. You know, over the years people like Dale have asked me why I never made much of an effort to look for my own kith and kin. The answer to that is complicated. In the orphanage we all painted pictures of what our parents looked like but a lot of the other girls had an advantage over me because they were orphans, and some, if they'd been old enough before their parents died, had proper mental pictures of their mammies and daddies, frozen in time. To me these were the lucky, even superior ones. Others were 'in care' and got to see their parents from time to time under supervision; many of these would use a lot of black and dark purple or grey and brown in their portraits, sometimes they'd paint devils, demons, animals with horns and snarly teeth. You'd hate to think what happened to them before they were taken in, wouldn't you?

There were only a few of us foundlings, as we were called. In the mammies-and-daddies stakes, we were the most pitied, but also free to choose any parents we liked. They could be Bing Crosby and Ava Gardner, John Wayne, Maureen O'Hara, Marilyn Monroe . . .

My main focus went on my mam. While Daddy was a careless, dashed-off stick figure, I spent ages drawing and painting her, lashing on the vivid colour. Mostly she wore a button-through dress, pink, blue or yellow, with a Peter Pan collar over her luscious curves; she had bubbly golden curls, red lipstick outlining a smile that covered half her face, and eyelashes like hearthbrushes. Curiously, she always carried a very large brown handbag.

I don't know what was with this handbag, but when one of the teachers asked me why it was so big and what was in it, I told her it contained toys and sweets for me. Until she asked me, it had never occurred to me to wonder about its contents – it just completed the picture. Perhaps I was influenced by the newspaper photographs of Queen Elizabeth of England who carried one everywhere she went. One of our nuns loved the British Royal Family, kept an album and absolutely adored 'the two little Princesses', as she continued to call them, even after Elizabeth was married and crowned. If I ever went to a shrink – chance would be a fine thing – I'm sure that first on the agenda for him, if he got that far, would be some sort of discussion about my imaginary mother's handbag.

Nothing that was left with me at that orphanage door gave even the smallest clue as to my parents or where I came from. So, yes, I have wondered, and maybe if I'd stayed in Ireland I might have done something about searching. Dale says a whole international industry has built up around 'tracing', but what would be the point, even if they were still alive? None of us can change the past, and what good would it do me?

There were social workers around from time to time, but now that I think about it, I don't remember none of them putting it up to me – and I was so busy trying to survive in the early years, first in Dublin and then here, that finding real family was the least of my concerns. I didn't have time to be lonely.

At least I left a photograph of myself with my three. I knew enough to do that much. Small consolation to them, no doubt, and Rowan yelled at me out there about how I couldn't know nothing about the hole at the centre of his chest. I know about it, all right, but from all kinds of different viewpoints, especially when I was a very little girl in the early years and in trouble, or getting whipped and had no one to soothe my pain. There were also times, I suppose, especially when Petey was bashing me around and treating me mean, that I did cry with rage that my mother had left me to this fate (a bit like Willow feels about me, I think) but I don't spend my life feeling hard-done-by. Not much point, really. *Get on with things* seems to be my motto.

I still do fantasise about my mother occasionally. To go back to that 'Old Woman of the Roads' poem I told you about, I sometimes transfer the fantasy to her so now it's her who's sweeping the hearth and sitting on a little stool on a cold, windy winter evening. She's a bent-backed crone with a kind face; she no longer wears a pretty dress but has covered herself in a big thick shawl. As for the goldy curls, they're history. Her hair is pure white, pulled into a tight little bun. She's traditional Grandma in an old schoolbook. (In the twenty-first century? I told you I don't have much imagination. At least I've had a lifetime's value out of the images that did stick.)

When I think about it logically, I should be mad as hell with my mam but I'm not. I guess I'm either desperately practical or desperately shallow, but after a lot of distress, at least I've managed to scratch out a flat, quiet place for myself and that's enough. If I can get a relationship of some sort going with my kids, that'll be a bonus.

So that's all a roundabout way of telling you that I do know about Rowan's hole at the centre, but sadness comes in waves as you get older and what was the chewing of a tiger at your insides shrinks to the nibbling of a mouse. I'm not even bitter about it. We're all born alone and we'll die alone.

To tell you the truth, I don't even miss Ireland any more. What's to miss? It's not as if I had a great life there, is it? Oh, like all the Irish I've met over the years, first, second, even third generation, I can talk big about the old country, O'Connell Street and turf; I can sing 'Danny Boy' with the best of them on Paddy's Day. When Arabella was telling me back there about Dublin and the new Spire and all the changes Dublin's gone through since I left, I'll admit I suffered a few twinges, but they soon passed. She's a great story-teller, really brings things alive. You can tell *she* reads a lot.

Since I came to America, apart from my kids – or the image or idea of my kids – the only person I've really missed is Maura. I do miss her terribly, flesh and blood. Dale is fine as a friend, so is Gina, so are the others, but she was my heart's companion, the sister and mother I never had.

At four or five in the morning you start asking yourself petty depressing questions, don't you? Like, if things were chugging along, why the hell did I start this train going with Arabella, Willow and Rowan?

On one level, I'm really, *really* glad them and me finally got together, but does it change anything for the better for any of us? Willow ran as fast as her feet could carry her. Rowan has already said he won't forgive me, ever, and while he might have been shooting his mouth off because he was in a temper, it's quite possible he never will. As for Arabella, I think there's a part of her that will continue to struggle with the task of building some kind of relationship with me even after she goes home. That's little to do with me: it's because of her loving nature.

So, have I done something really selfish? Thrown a bomb into their lives?

As for myself, the truth is that although I know them now, although two of them are still here and I'm nearly sick with love for them, the nibbling of my mouse is getting more painful, and I'm lonelier now than ever I was.

They won't see that. I'll do that much for them at least.

CHAPTER FORTY

An electrician's van cruises along the gravel, its driver peering at names and number-plates on trailers. The site is well awake now, people driving by, strolling past on foot, or – if they're one of our seniors – scrunching by in their brightly coloured electric buggies, which look like lawn-mowers without blades. Almost without exception they wave or say a cheery 'Hi' or 'Hi there!' or 'Have a good day' – and you feel they mean it. From up near the transients' area, I can hear the screech of a buzz saw tearing into metal.

I already fancy I can tell the difference between one of 'us' and one of 'them' up at the front. I think the main difference is age. Down here, I'd say the average age would be forty-five or more; up there nearer the entrance, they have kids. They're much younger.

Funny how quickly you settle into the rhythms and routines of a place. When Greta and I are in Tenerife or Lanzarote, by day three of the holiday we refer to our apartment as 'home' – and it feels that way – while on the beach we watch out for regulars and have names for them: Miss Chest, Slinky, Mr Wobble, Baldy, Tomato Face and so on.

What names would we give our regulars here? 'Hopalong', for either Eve or Gina is just too easy; but Robert could be Mr Cool. Peter Pan and Tinkerbell for Chris and Mandy? Bali Hai for poor Mary? The Dancer for Mario?

And what would Greta and I call ourselves if we met us? Plink and Plonk, probably.

What would we call Dale?

The Cowboy? Mr Tattoo? Too clichéd. Dale defeats me. The Enigma? That's better, although now I think of it it's too Sean Connery. Greta would come up with something perfect. Suddenly I wish she was here. I want to talk to her about Dale.

250

No, you don't. When you had the opportunity you closed her off.

From here, on Dale's deck, I can see that Eve's doors are still closed. The conversation I have to have with her has built up in my mind to such a degree that I feel like I'm a world leader approaching a summit. I should be nervous about giving my statement to the cops this morning, but I'm far more worried about breaking open the shell between Eve and me.

At least I'll have a story to grease the first few minutes. I'm sure she still doesn't know what happened last night. If she did she would have been over here like a light.

The fact that, because of the bloody diary, I know what she suffered, or that her suffering made me cry earlier, doesn't take away from what she did, dammit. I've been trying to figure out – again – what inspires so many people to help her and surround her and think she's terrific. There's no hint of it in that diary: she's very hard on herself. Maybe that's it. Her honesty.

Speaking of terrific, Dale was very good about finding me crying like that. If it was me who had been stabbed, I'd be feeling pretty sorry for myself, putting myself first, but his behaviour couldn't have been more appropriate and tactful. While he didn't ignore the tears, he didn't make a big deal of them. Offered me a cup of tea, which was exactly the right thing to do. Saved my dignity.

And then I went and blew it.

Because of his injury, he agreed that I should cook breakfast. I didn't make a great fist of his cooker: I'm used to electricity, and for a bottled-gas novice, all that popping and hissing and naked flame is frightening, but I managed to scramble a few eggs and grill bacon without setting the place on fire.

'How are you feeling?' I asked, when we sat down to eat. 'Are you in much pain?'

'I'm fine,' he said, in a way that invited no follow-ups. So I didn't follow up. Particularly when I saw he was holding his head low over his food and realised, once again, that I could never get a real feel for what goes on in that mind of his. He isn't the chattiest person in the world, yet most of the time I think we're grand and easy together. Sometimes, though, there's this really severe tension.

This morning, lorrying into my rashers and eggs as I was, I was ultra-relaxed, despite what I'd witnessed the previous night and the living proof of it sitting opposite me at the table. (I've found over the years that the more fatigued I am, the less I'm stressed; it's as if I haven't the energy to obsess. And, of course, I probably still had champagne bubbles in my veins.) Nevertheless I felt, vaguely, that Dale and I were straining against a rubber band stretched between us.

I'm not being naïve here: although I could hardly claim to be wildly experienced, I do know about sexual vibes (sadly absent with Jimmy Porter) and from time to time I think they're the cause of the intermittent pull between Dale and me. If they are, they vanish as quickly as they occur. That's what's odd. He's very attractive but not all the time. It's something I haven't come across before.

This morning I decided that, rather than agonise or get all funny, I'd keep my trap shut and so I did, but when the stiffness on his side of the table eased a bit, I asked him a question that's always fascinated me about the Jehovah's Witnesses: 'You bled a lot last night, Dale. If you'd needed a blood transfusion, would that have been a problem for you? Would you have refused it?'

'I'm no longer a JW,' he pointed out.

'I know that. But that's the kind of thing we read about. You know, "Parents Allow Baby to Perish Because of Religious Conviction", that sort of thing. Where does that come from?'

'I'm not sure you'd understand.'

'Try me.'

'Well,' he said slowly, 'I'm not going to diss the Witnesses, because I still hold some of their beliefs.'

'Like what?' I bit into some crunchy bacon.

'Like I'm against abortion,' he was watching closely for my reaction, 'and killing animals for pleasure, hunting and shooting and so on.'

'In America? Land of fifty billion guns or whatever it is?'

'In America.' He remained patient. 'Hey, we weren't all born wearing coon-tail hats, you know. Anyways, it's permitted to kill animals for food or clothing or when they threaten you.'

'I'm with you so far.'

'And we – the JWs, I mean – forbid violent or dangerous sports, like boxing.'

'Ugh!' I shivered. 'I hate boxing.'

252

'And it's also forbidden to partake of any drugs – like cigarettes.' He grinned.

'Listen, Dale,' I felt myself going red, 'enough's enough. I asked you about blood. Stick to the blood.' I made a mental note to ask him about the tattoos – when and why? They certainly didn't fit with what I was learning about Jehovah's Witnesses.

He got up to pour himself more coffee from the percolator. He had put on an overshirt checked in red and black. It didn't suit the grey hair.

'OK. Here goes.' He came back with his fresh coffee. 'For Witnesses, God's law states that the soul, life itself, if you like, is in the blood. And therefore it follows that it's wrong to take others' blood into your own body, to eat the life of another.'

I thought about this. 'Cannibalism? You think that having a transfusion is like cannibalism?'

'No. But the Scriptures contain passages about it and, as you know, for every scriptural religion, it's all about interpretation. The Witnesses are big on interpretation, as I told you. In accordance with the Bible's instructions, abstaining from blood would be morally in the same league as abstaining from fornication, or pre-marital sex. So, to force blood on a person against his will might be seen as rape.'

'I could argue with that.'

'It's complicated.'

'Yeah, but isn't there a way round it? What about using your own blood? Couldn't you have some taken and store it frozen in case you needed it? Surely that's not eating somebody else's soul?'

'This is where it gets real tricky. I'm sure you don't want me to quote chapter and verse of the Bible at you,' he smiled, 'even if I could remember the specific bits, which I don't. But blood, once removed from the body, must be disposed of. Buried or burned or whatever. You're making things too black and white, Arabella, although I will admit that the Watchtower Society runs a very black and white religion. It's one of the reasons I left it, if you remember.'

The whole blood thing still didn't make sense to me. 'Sorry, Dale, I don't mean to be rude or anything but if a transfusion would save your child's life, have you the right to speak for him or her?'

'I don't want to be put in the position of defending these doctrines because they're a cause of concern to me, Arabella,' he sighed, 'but I do

know that the medical profession is developing all kinds of new therapies all the time. Even bloodless surgery is now possible, using new tech-
nologies. Look,' he ran his fingers through his hair in frustration, 'every
religion holds beliefs that don't make sense rationally. Do you really want
to go into all this? I could turn this whole thing on you, you know –
make you defend transubstantiation.'

'What's that?' I was foxed, although the word did ring a distant bell
about something I'd been taught in childhood.

He laughed. 'It's where Catholics, unlike other Christians, believe that
when they take Communion they are not only commemorating the Last
Supper, they are eating a piece of the real Body of Christ, physical and
present, transubstantiated by the priest during the Mass. Now that's what
I call holy cannibalism. That's *really* weird.'

'*Touché.*' I laughed. 'Would you accept blood now?'

'I would. Now, if we're done, would you like more tea?'

'Yes, please, but I'll get it myself.' I popped in the last lovely morsel of
blackened rasher, and went to put on the kettle again. Being me, I couldn't
leave well enough alone. 'While we're on the subject, do you think we
should try to contact your kids? I know it's been a while since you heard
from them, but I'm sure they'd be concerned if they knew you were injured.'

'No.'

Even at a distance of twenty-five feet or more, I could feel his attitude chill by several degrees but I was still so relaxed I pushed on. 'Why
not? This thing you have where they don't see you—'

'It's called shunning, Arabella,' his attitude iced some more, 'and in the
politest way possible, could I ask you to butt out?'

'Are you sure?' I gave it one more go. 'You're a really nice man, Dale,
and I'd bet you're a great father. It's such a shame. How do you know
they're not secretly pining to see you?'

'Please don't talk about what you don't understand.' His mouth tight-
ened into a stiff, thin line. This was a side of Dale I hadn't seen up to
now, and in a novel it would say here that I suddenly lost my appetite.
And, yes, his cold silence might have been intimidating on any other
morning but I was in Cuckoo Land, didn't care about moods, my own
or anyone else's. (He was entitled anyhow. He was the one who'd been
stabbed and I was the one who'd trespassed.) So it was no hardship to
give in. 'OK,' I said meekly. 'You're right. It's none of my business. Sorry.'

'No need to apologise, but could we drop the subject now, talk about something else?'

'All right. Let's see. I know – what kind of music do you like?'

'You wanna hear some music?'

'Sure. Music while you work.'

'What?'

'It's just a phrase we use in Ireland. I think it's from an old radio pro-gramme. We're all pretty big into radio over there so it'll be nice to have music while I do the washing up.' I turned off the kettle. I'd lost my desire for more tea. Maybe the novels are right.

'No need to wash up. I do have a dishwasher, Arabella.' He got up and walked the couple of steps towards his stereo.

As it happens, I quite enjoy washing dishes if it's not for work: it's soothing, and I told Dale as much.

He selected a CD from a wall rack. 'Whatever turns you on. You like country music?'

'Sure.'

'John Prine, then. OK?'

'Perfect.' I'd never heard of John Prine but it was great that once again we had *glasnost*. I paid no attention to the lyrics but the music Dale put on was pleasant and undemanding.

The mobile phone rang while I was doing the washing up. More pre-cisely, while I was in dreamland, watching a succession of fat little deter-gent rainbows stretch, then burst between the fingers of my rubber gloves. I was entertaining thoughts about what it must be like to be one half of a domestic partnership: performing pleasant, homely tasks like this, eating breakfast together, listening to mutually acceptable music and one half caring for the other when sickness or injury occurred. I was so lost in these imaginings that I didn't hear Dale speak to his caller and was star-tled when I felt him standing beside me, holding out the phone. 'It's for you, Arabella.'

'Who is it?' I snapped off the gloves. It wasn't a shock that it was for me: Willow and I had left Dale's number as a contact. It had to be her, but there was something about Dale's expression that made me uneasy. Had something bad happened?'

He shrugged as I took the phone from him, about-turned and went outside.

'Is that you, Bella?' It was Jimmy Porter.

The dreaminess evaporated sharpish. I haven't said anything yet, I thought, I can hang up. But I wasn't up to conflict today. Anyway, hanging up would be cowardly and no use: he'd just ring back. I did a fast calculation: he must still be with his cousin in the North of Ireland on that trip we'd both planned: that'd be safe territory. 'Hello, Jimmy, how are you?' Jolly hockey-sticks. 'Are you having a good time? Have you been to the Giant's Causeway and is it fantastic?'

'We're doing that today. Everything's fine here. I explained about your predicament and everyone here understands.'

'How's the weather over there?'

'It's raining and foggy. The forecast is good, though, if they get it right, of course.'

I'm sorry, but it's all off . . . Too brutal, especially on a mobile phone. And what about the time Jimmy searched every sweetshop in the city because you'd said you'd like to try a brand of chocolate because you'd read it was supposed to give you a 'natural high'?

'That's great. The weather here in Arizona is very hot. It's hot every day.'

'Of course it's desert there, isn't it? I looked it up in the atlas.'

'That's right. Desert.'

Silence.

Say it, say it.

'I thought I'd ring you, Bella, just to see how you are. I spoke to Willow and she says you're getting on fine with your mother.'

'Thanks, Jimmy.' I didn't dare imagine what Willow had told him about me 'getting on' with Eve. 'Yes, things are grand here. And how are you?'

'I'm fine.'

'Where are you ringing from?'

'I'm on the house phone here.'

There's the get-out. 'Oh, God, really? We shouldn't stay on too long. This'll cost them a fortune.'

'They don't mind. And of course I'll pay them.'

'Of course.'

The line was free of atmosphere or static of any kind. I could hear him breathing.

Jimmy, I'm terribly sorry but I think we should take a break from each other for a while.

'Listen, Jimmy—'

'Arabella—'

We had spoken together through the silence. 'You first,' I said miserably.

'All right. I'll go first. We had a bit of a tiff the last night, Bel.'

'Yeah, you could say that.'

'I'm sorry I ruined it for you.'

'Jimmy, you didn't.'

Why are you letting him off the hook? Tell him the truth. 'It's water under the bridge.'

'But I did ruin it. I know I did, I know I did,' he was all in a rush now, 'and I'm sorry, I really am, Bel. Can we be friends?'

'Of course.'

Now's your chance. He's given you the opening. Friends. Tell him that's all you can be in the future. 'Of course we can be friends, Jimmy.' *Go on, go on!* 'But—'

'And listen,' he broke in eagerly, 'wait'll you hear what happened last night. I was in a pub here with the others, we went at about eight o'clock – I know it was about eight o'clock because *EastEnders* was just over and by chance, wait'll you hear this, just by chance wasn't there a karaoke competition on? And didn't I enter? And didn't I get second, Bella? Second! There was twenty-seven people in for it, and some of them were really good. Youngsters, you know. And I got second.'

He sounded so bubbly and happy. How could I rain on his parade? 'That's great, Jimmy. Was there a prize?'

'Fifty pounds. That's the guts of seventy-five euro, Bel. Can you believe it? Are you proud of me?'

'Very.' *Shit.*

'So I've decided to concentrate on karaoke. The comedy routines weren't doing much for me anyway, were they? They were just getting me into trouble.'

'No, I suppose they weren't. I mean yes – whatever.'

'You know, I think you're getting a bit of an American accent.'

He's teasing me now. He sounds proprietorial. Shit, shit shit.

He chuckled. 'Don't let me see you come back as one of those Yanks, throwing your weight around, right?'

'Don't worry about that, Jimmy.' I attempted to chuckle back but it went wrong.

'So look, that's enough about me. Sorry I interrupted you back there. What were you going to say? Tell me all about what's going on over there.'

I can't face it. 'Ohmigod, Jimmy, did you hear that bleep?'

'What bleep?'

'I think the battery on this phone is about to give up. Listen, we'll talk again, OK?'

'When are you coming ho—'

But, yellow, gutless, lily-livered, spineless sleeveen that I am, I'd pressed the off button.

I went out to Dale and gave him back his telephone. 'Everything OK?' He didn't look at me as he took it.

'Oh, fine. It was just one of those check-in calls. You know.'

He glanced sideways at me, his expression blank. 'Well, I think I'll take a shower. Aside from the cops when they come, you got any plans for the day?'

Was he suggesting I'd worn out my welcome? I was so mad at myself I wanted to challenge someone. Anyone. When it was too late. 'You're probably sick of having me here, Dale. You're used to your space. I think I should probably move back into a motel. What do you think?'

'I'm not sick of having you here, as you put it, but,' he shrugged, 'you gotta please yourself, Arabella.' He went inside and a few seconds later, through the open bathroom window, I heard the shower start up.

So here I am on Dale's deck, listening to the shower still running, furious with myself for being such a nellie, furious at myself for giving myself a departure ticket from the trailer, furious, period.

Now, double dammit, Eve's door is opening and there's Eve herself, yawning and stretching in front of her crystal curtain. She's carrying her cat. She's still in her dressing-gown. Now she's putting the cat down and filling a bowl with something from a tin . . . She's looking across. She sees me. She's waving, beckoning me over.

I panic. It's all very well telling my sister how she should feel and to give Eve a chance and all the rest of it but now that it's my turn to have a heart-to-heart . . .

I mime that I have to get dressed first.

'Don't be silly,' she calls. 'Look at me still in my robe.'

I can't put this off any longer.

CHAPTER FORTY-ONE

I suppose Arabella and her friend Greta would tell me to relax and enjoy this. But how can I relax? (Although I have to say that the girl applying my makeup has a feather-light touch. She seems to have understood, too, that I am not one for small-talk and is leaving me to my thoughts.)

I hope I have made the right decision in agreeing to go on this programme, but as everybody keeps telling me, it will be the quickest way to get results. So why am I doing it? Some deep down madness, I suspect . . .

Perhaps it was those British Airways martinis that gave me 'a rush of blood to the head' that night, but after two, I couldn't sleep after all. Instead, the contents of our mother's tin box danced around in my head like an extra scene from Disney's *Fantasia*. Of special prominence were the photographs. Of our mother with the woman Maura. And with the girl Philomena.

And the note that was left with her.

We were somewhere off Greenland when I realised that these images were not easily to be shrugged away so, rather than allow them to fester in my mind, I decided to *do* something about them.

Next thing: what?

That was relatively easy. Both photographs should be published – on a website, perhaps, or in a newspaper – with a request for Maura or Philomena or both to come forward. My main target would be the former, because she would have known my father and – after my mother abandoned us – might have had some contact with him. She might even be able to give us some lead as to where he is now.

In fact, as I worked it out, I realised that Philomena, whoever she was, was a red herring and it was only Maura who interested me. Let our mother advertise for Philomena, should she be so inclined. I could suggest it to her. Some time in the future.

The next question was how to go about it. Advertising in newspapers can be expensive; I know this because I serve on the fund-raising committee at the children's school, and to publicise our annual concert and tombola in the local rags puts quite a dent in our badly needed funds. The 'Personals' on the *Irish Times* back page, my personal preference, have always been prohibitively costly for a small group like ours.

Then I remembered the journalist-mother of Aoife, one of Maeve's schoolfriends. This woman works on one of the tabloids, I am not sure which – the *Star* or the *Herald*, maybe the *Irish Mirror* – and apparently she is quite famous. She would be able to advise me on how best to go about it, I thought, with the added attraction that she might be able to get me a discount if I advertised in her newspaper.

Decision made, I dozed off.

I was seriously jet-lagged when I got home, of course, and after the children had been borne off to school by Paddy, I went to bed but did not drop off straight away. Instead I lay there, forcing my tired mind to test the decision this way and that. It seemed to stand and I saw no point in procrastination. I would telephone the woman at tea-time. I slept like a baby.

To say that the mother jumped at the idea would be a major understatement. 'You mean you were abandoned? And your mother was too? In the Botanic *Gardens?*'

Her excitement unnerved me. I had had to tell her about the background, you see, or she drew it out of me – I forget which. 'Yes, but my mother wasn't abandoned in the Botanic Gardens.'

'Both on Christmas *Eve?* On the exact same day?'

'That's not the point, really. The reason I rang you, what I'm asking about—'

'Willow,' she interrupted me again, and I got the impression she was no longer listening, 'I had no idea. Poor little Maeve. She never let on a word about this to our Aoife. This is a *marvellous* story, Willow. It's fantastic. I can only *imagine* how you must feel. I don't even have to run it by my editor because I *know* he'll jump at it. I can tell you now that we'll run it big. *Really* big. We'll splash it. I'm coming over to talk to you. Right now. See you in ten minutes flat.'

'But—'

Too late. She had gone.

Thank God for Paddy. He was in our much-patched and caulked shed in the back garden, checking what needed repairing and so forth before the coming summer. Panicked, I ran out to him and spilled the whole story. 'She's on her way over here. She's a reporter, Paddy. She says she's going to splash our story all over the newspapers—'

'Calm down, Willow.' Paddy is an ideal civil servant. He never jumps into a problem, but sorts it out one step at a time. 'Let's look logically at this. First of all, you didn't invite her to drive over here – or did you?'

'No, I didn't.'

'Then the first option is, when she arrives, you say you're sorry she's had a wasted journey, but that she has misunderstood. All you wanted was advice about the most efficient and cost-effective way to find the woman in the photograph.'

'But she knows now. She can write about us.'

'Not if you tell her she can't. I can ring her editor if you like. I'll do it first thing in the morning.' He turned off the light, one of those old flexi-armed desk lamps with a shade shaped like an elongated shell. Paddy hates waste and had rescued this from a skip in the basement of the department. He took a last look round the dim, cluttered interior, then took my arm to usher me outside. I was feeling better already. He has a calming effect on me.

'Well, maybe you're right. And maybe when she gets here I can still ask her to help.'

In the kitchen, I flew around, dumping the tea-things in the sink and covering them with sudsy water – I hadn't time to wash up – but he stopped me. 'No. Don't let her see you're intimidated. This is our home, Willow. She takes us as she finds us. Now, sit down there at the table and let's go through this.'

Once we were both seated, he pointed out that the situation could be turned to our advantage. 'You were prepared to pay for advertising, right? Publication of the photograph?'

'Yes, I was.' I nodded miserably. I was sorry I had ever thought of going this route. If I could have turned the clock back, I would not have had those martinis.

'Well, then, here's another possibility. Why not take it a step further? Let her do the story, but in a form controlled and dictated by you. That will be *free* publicity. But you have to make sure she accepts the rules you make, like how much of your story she may reveal and what's off limits.'

'You mean really co-operate? Let her do the story?' I was not convinced.

'Did you listen to what I said, Willow?' He was getting a little irritated. 'She can do it, but in a limited way. She'll have to write the story your way. They do this all the time. There's nothing shameful in it, anyway. We've been over this many times. What did you or any of us in this family do that was wrong?'

'Nothing, I suppose.' Leaving out Rowan.

'All right so,' he remained patient, 'if you really want a short cut to finding this Maura, she's offering you a ready-made way to do it.'

While I mulled this over, he got up, filled the kettle and plugged it in. He was thinking too. Then, leaning against the sink: 'It's not beyond the bounds of possibility that there could be money in this – you might even make back the cost of the trip.'

'No!' I was adamant. 'No money. I'd feel like a prostitute.'

'Are you sure? Newspapers pay big money for stuff like this.'

'No, Paddy. Definitely not.'

He saw I was serious and conceded. 'Fair enough, it was just a thought. But if you change your mind . . .'

'I won't.'

He reached into the cupboard above the sink for fresh cups and saucers. 'You take a few minutes to think what you want. I'll leave you alone with her but I won't be far away if you need reinforcements.' He busied himself with the tea caddy, sugar bowl and milk jug. Brought up in a large, impecunious family on a small farm where it was every person for him- or herself at the table, he cannot abide sloppiness at mealtimes and always insists on the proper setting of a table for the most minor meal or snack.

'Should we give her biscuits?'

'Will we hell! She's going to be getting enough out of us without biscuits!' Quickly, he removed the canister from its normal place beside the bread bin and put it under the sink, just in case.

The doorbell rang as the kettle came to the boil: she lives less than half a mile from us. I panicked again. 'So, have you your thoughts in order?' Coolly, Paddy unplugged the kettle.

'I know what I want – that picture disseminated as widely and quickly as possible, with as little fuss as possible and breaching as little of our privacy as possible. After all, it's not only Arabella and me. There's Maeve and Dermot to consider. And you. And your family. And the school. And the department.' I still could not bring myself to mention Rowan.

'Jaysus,' he went towards the door, 'you don't want much, do you? Stay there now at the table and try to look as if you do this kind of thing every day of the week. Don't let her see the whites of your eyes. All right? And whatever you do, don't mention Rowan. That'd be meat and drink to someone like a tabloid journalist.'

Paddy has the knack of picking up my thoughts. I suppose it comes from a long time of living together.

I had to be still suffering from that disorienting jet-lag because as he went to open the door – probably because I've seen this woman's state-of-the-art kitchen – I found myself thinking not of the ordeal to come but that our own kitchen could do with upgrading. Instead of cream-painted walls, it could be a more vibrant colour, yellow, perhaps, or green. And I would love a streamlined run of countertops, and a double sink, like she has, and a dishwasher.

Yet I like my house: it is familiar and feels safe. I like the muffled sound of the television in the living room where, at that moment, Dermot was watching something; and I like the rhythmic thumping of Maeve's ballet practice in her room, which is above the kitchen. We have installed a miniature *barre* on one of her bedroom walls. It is only two feet long but it's sturdy enough to support her. She is never going to be a prima ballerina, but she is agile and neat and has passed all her exams so far, one or two with honours. She did not get her interest in dancing from me. Maybe from Arabella, who does enjoy it.

I snapped back into reality. Preliminaries at the hall door over, Paddy and the journalist were coming into the kitchen. I stood up. I prepared my face.

'Hello, hel-*lo!*' she gushed, as she walked through the door. She was carrying a tape recorder.

A tape recorder?

'The kettle is just boiled,' I said idiotically. 'We were just clearing up after tea. Will you have a cup in your hand? Sit down, won't you?'

'No cuppas, but thank you very much. I'm up to my tonsils in tea and coffee. I try not to have any caffeine after four o'clock.' Still standing, she looked around. 'Isn't this lovely? So homely and *original*. I think you made

263

the right choice in not modernising. These houses are like *gold dust*, these days. So well built – much better than the flimsy rubbish they're throwing up everywhere now. It's a shame to tamper with them.' At last she sat.

We sat too. 'Well now,' Paddy began, 'we don't want to detain you but we're very grateful you've offered to help us find this woman through the photograph. Thank you very much. We really appreciate it.'

'Oh, don't *thank* me, please! This is a win-win. We help you find this woman, we get to tell Willow's story and everybody's happy. Isn't that right, Willow?'

She is a large woman in every way: wide body, big hennaed hair, deep, almost mannish voice, large features, especially her plump, lipsticked mouth; she favours very bright red lipstick, and was wearing a bright red trouser suit. She looked like a fire engine. Her very loudness steeled my resolve. 'I think we'd better set a few ground rules. Could we decide in advance what you won't report? What's off limits?' I glanced at Paddy, who raised his eyebrows in approval.

'Of course. Of *course!*' She could not have been more accommodating. 'I'll just switch this on, shall I?' Deftly she positioned the tape recorder right under my face.

'I'll leave you to it. I'll be in the sitting room,' Paddy looked mean-ingfully at me and exited, leaving the door ajar.

She barely noticed his departure as she leaned towards me. 'Now,' she said, 'all you have to do is say, "This is off the record," when you find yourself slipping into dangerous territory. Okey-dokey?' Her heavily kohled eyes took on an expression of deep sympathy and her voice dropped so it was low and thrilling: 'Tell me, Willow, you've been searching the world for decades to find your mother, is that right?'

'Well, that's not strictly—'

'Let me get this straight. You're just back from Arizona, right?'

'Yes, that's right. But—'

'You can tell me about that later. First, though, in your own words, tell me what it's like to have lived all these years without knowing who you are.'

'But I do know who I am. And don't you want to see the photograph I'm talking about?' I glanced down at the tape recorder, turning and turning.

'Sure, of course I do.' She touched my arm, holding her hand there for slightly longer than necessary. 'We'll get to that later. I'm just looking for a bit of background here, Willow.' I noticed she used my name a lot. 'Now, did you always feel empty? Always wondering "what if"?'

We stumbled along in this manner, she asking her questions and many times answering them, merely inviting corroboration. There were surprisingly few 'off the records' however: somehow, the woman's big personality radiated an aura of trust and I found myself opening up more than I had anticipated.

Looking back on it, I can now see that, while that tape was turning, she left most of the talking to me. That's probably the skill they learn. Or maybe she didn't want to push her luck. It was obvious she did not like my saying 'off the record' on the few times I did say it, but each time I did – for instance, when I found myself telling her who Peter Moraghan was in one of the photographs – she ostentatiously pressed the 'pause' button on the recorder, which reassured me, to the extent that I found myself showing her the tin box and its contents.

The sight of this sent her almost into orbit. 'Oh, this is so *moving*, Willow . . .' Delicately, with the tips of her fingers, she sifted through it. 'Ooh, look at the little locks of hair. But there are *three* – look.'

'If you check,' I said quickly, 'you'll find two are the same.' Remembering Paddy's warning, and my own instinct, I could not bring myself to go into the story of my black-sheep brother.

She did not pursue it anyhow because she had found the note left with Eve and had scanned it. 'Oh, my Gawd, Willow! Look at *this*! "Curiouser and curiouser," as Alice said to the White Rabbit. Or was it the Queen? It doesn't matter.' She was now all business. 'Can I borrow this tin box? I'll take *very* good care of it, I promise. What's in here will *really* do the trick. It's so precious. And I'll bring everything *straight* back after we've photographed and scanned. Oh, Willow, thank Gawd you phoned me. This is so *wonderful*.'

'I think I should ask my sister before I let you take the box.' This was spiralling out of control and I was about to call Paddy, but almost as if she knew this, she put her hand on my wrist and dropped her voice: 'Speed is of the essence in these things. You don't want some *unscrupulous* hack to get hold of this, now, do you? You're not to worry about a thing, Willow, you're in good hands, I promise. Trust me. And in case you're worried about any scandal attached to this note left with your poor ma, times have changed. And thank Gawd for it.'

At that point, Paddy popped his head through the doorway. 'Everything all right, girls?'

'Abso-*lutely*, Paddy,' she smiled brilliantly at him, 'it's been *won*-derful.' She turned back to me. 'Now, I'm willing to bet you anything you *like*, Willow, that *somebody* will come forward for you. Oh, Willow, Paddy, this is so *exciting*. Are you excited?' Then, turning to Paddy, chivvying, 'Aren't you excited for her, Paddy?'

Paddy looked at me for guidance.

'We're both excited,' I said, in as flat a voice as I could find. It did not deter her.

'And are you *absolutely* sure you don't want me to publish poor little Philomena's photo as well?'

When she left shortly afterwards, taking the box with her, she promised once again to return everything safely 'within twenty-four hours. I know how much all this means to you, Willow.'

She had been with us less than forty minutes, but after we closed the door behind her I felt wrung out. 'How'd it go?' Paddy asked.

'I don't know. I was careful, but I have the feeling that she got away from me. I hope I've done the right thing.'

'Listen, Willow, it's done now. And don't forget the core point. You haven't been guilty of anything at all. I'm going back out to finish up in the shed. Will you be OK?'

'I'll be fine.' We smiled at each other but did not hug or anything like that. It is not our way.

That was the day before yesterday, the day I got home.

I was still on leave from work yesterday and was pottering around when the doorbell rang. It was Aoife's mother again, returning the tin box and its contents. 'And I've great news for you, Willow . . .' My 'story' would be in the edition of the following day – today, this morning – and she had alerted TV3 about it. 'They're very excited. They want you on their morning programme. Isn't that am*azing*? They'll use our feature on you as a peg for the interview – and, believe me, Willow, we're going *big* on this. It'll take a Second Coming to get you off the masthead. I tried RTE first, but they couldn't make up their minds. They said they'd get back to me but they didn't. Anyway, the morning show on TV3 is growing all the time. It's *mega*. Their researcher will give you a buzz some time this afternoon. And our photographer will be round this afternoon to take a few shots. Will the children be here? When would suit you? It will be very informal, nothing to worry about at *all* . . .' She paused for breath, took out her mobile phone and poised her fingers expectantly over the keypad. 'I've to let the picture desk know.'

'Photographer? Television? I don't know – you'd better come in. We should discuss this.' I felt as if I'd been standing under a shower of hailstones. Very large ones. She was the most pushy person I'd ever encountered – we were mere acquaintances, as I told you, and I had not seen her professional side before.

'Thanks, Willow,' she said quickly – actually, she sounded slightly peeved, 'but I'm afraid I'm on the run. You know how it is, you're a working woman yourself, it's bedlam out there these days – and you *did* say you wanted a result from this photograph, didn't you?' She lowered the phone a little. 'Our story and television combined is going to give you the widest possible exposure, Willow.'

She had already given a copy of the snapshot and the note to the TV station.

Normally I would freak at being railroaded like this but Paddy's words came back to me yet again: no one in my family had done anything wrong, not I, not Paddy, not Maeve, Dermot or Arabella. (Leaving Rowan out of it, of course.) So what was I ashamed of? Why was I hanging back? I guard my privacy and I hate what the nuns used to call 'looking for notice' but suddenly, I thought, *Oh, what the hell. Let them do their worst.* I had put it 'out there', as Maeve would say. Now it was time to see what came back and I was being offered a Rolls-Royce opportunity.

Also, I thought, Maeve and Dermot would be excited to see their mum on television. Perhaps it is my age, but lately, as I did on the plane, I have discovered strange, reckless urges in myself. Nothing *outré*, you understand, just a feeling that to put in one's short span of allotted time on earth like a mole or a turtle might not be the most satisfying way to live.

Aoife's mother was watching me impatiently.

'All right,' I said. 'And perhaps as a special treat I could take Dermot and Maeve with me to the television station. Could you arrange that for us?'

'No need.' She was already punching numbers. 'You could arrive with the Russian army and they wouldn't turn a hair. They're very professional.'

I was waiting for Maeve and Dermot when they arrived home from school. 'Come on, chaps, into the bath, and be quick about it. Get your Sunday gear out of the hot press and put it on. I've a surprise for the pair of you.'

'What?' Of course they were intrigued, but I would not reveal anything until they were dressed and ready. 'You remember I told you about maybe meeting Granny in America?' I asked them then. As usual, I was tying tea-towels round their necks so they wouldn't stain their clothes while they were eating their after-school snack, but they were so fascinated that for once they accepted it without protest. 'Of course we remember. So?' This was Dermot. Mr Cool.

I had had barely time to tell them what was in store next day when the doorbell rang. To the great interest of the neighbours, the photographer had arrived. His van outside proclaimed, in huge red letters on its white paintwork, the name of his newspaper.

Next morning, *this* morning, we were up at an ungodly hour. TV3 is out in the wilds of West Dublin but they sent a taxi to collect us at a quarter to seven so I did not have to negotiate the M50 myself. The children were bubbling, as you can imagine. I've always told them the truth about their heritage, the bare bones of it at least, so they were going to get no nasty surprises when they heard the interview. They had been delighted with all the attention from the photographer the previous afternoon and thrilled, of course, to be given the half-day off school today. Dermot was concentrating on the possibility of a trip to America to meet their 'new' grandmother. Maeve was more interested in having Eve Rennick come to Ireland. She fancied herself, I think, as a guide to the sights her grandmother had probably missed by leaving the country so long ago. 'When do you think she'd come if we asked her?'

'I'm not sure.'

'But we'll be going to America to see her *before* she comes here, right?' This was Dermot.

'I told you. There are no arrangements yet. And listen, Dermot, her – her place is quite small, you know, so I don't think she'd have room for us all.' I was not quite ready for everyone in my children's school – and by extension the staff and my own committee – to know that my mother lives in a trailer park.

'Well, if she comes, will she be staying with us in our house or with Auntie Bella?' Maeve takes after me. She needs everything settled and organised or she cannot relax. 'She could stay in my room.' She was already sorting this out. 'She could have my bed. We could borrow a bed from Aoife's house. They have an inflatable that they use in the mobile home in Brittas Bay when they have other kids staying. I don't mind sleeping in that, Mum. I slept in it last summer.'

'That's not fair,' Dermot objected. 'Why do you get her in your room just because your friend has a poxy inflatable bed?'

'Shut up!' She thumped him. 'Mum! Tell him to stop!'

'Shut up, yourself?' He thumped her back.

'Stop it! Both of you! Please! Stay quiet for a few minutes, will you? I've to think of what I'm going to say on the television.'

'What'll we call her?' Maeve was still on the track. 'Aoife calls one of hers Nan. Will we call her Nan, Mum? Do you think she'd like that? We can't call her Granny because that's our County Clare grandmother – we can't have *two* Grannys.'

'That remains to be seen. You can discuss it with her, maybe.' It struck me forcibly that it had been a bad idea to involve the two of them. Willy-nilly now, I was being drawn into a relationship with my mother. I had not *thought*. I had *reacted*. Emotionally too.

And I had not considered my colleagues' reaction. The best I could hope for was that my appearance would not be seen by many of them; I was told I was scheduled on soon after eight o'clock when most of them would be on their way to work.

So here I am, for better or worse. My excited children are in a corridor outside this makeup room, sitting on couches lining one wall. (I was surprised, actually, that TV3 is so small. I was expecting something far grander.) A very nice young man who introduced himself as a producer's assistant, or something like that, has brought them milky coffee and a doughnut each. They're not normally allowed coffee so this is an extra treat.

Almost despite myself I am relaxing in this chair. As the girl gently dusts powder on my cheeks with a soft cotton pad, I find myself drifting away – and reflecting that it has been a long time since anyone patted my face. Now she is using a soft brush to apply blusher. Her breath smells sweet. I suppose they have to be careful with their oral hygiene – after all, they are leaning over you, only inches from your face.

The atmosphere here is sequestered and comforting, like a cloistered convent. People are moving quickly but not rushing. They speak calmly. The two morning presenters on the screen talk quietly, or so it seems. The colours are bright, the teeth are white (they smile a lot), everything is under control and you could lose your sense of the outside world; you could almost forget you are about to be asked about your most private feelings.

'Here's the paper, Willow.' The researcher who is looking after us pops her head in and hands it to me. 'What a fascinating story. Lovely photographs too – you have great kids. Everyone is loving them.

'Weather just wrapping,' she says over my head, to the makeup girl. 'We'll be ready for her in five. Good luck, Willow.' She leaves and the newspaper in my hand makes a rattling sound like a set of dry bones because it is only then that I realise fully what I am about to do.

CHAPTER FORTY-TWO

'Good morning, birthday girl!' Eve is smiling broadly as she greets me from inside the door of her trailer. She hops back and indicates the far end of the trailer. 'Surprise!'

Surprise is right. Temporarily, I forget my own bad humour as I see my brother, stubbled, red-eyed, sitting at Eve's table and munching his way gloomily through a bowl of cereal. A half-eaten slice of toast lies on a plate beside it. 'What are you doing here? I thought you were staying at Gina's?'

'Mind your own business.' He scowls at me.

The second time I've been told that this morning, I think, and turn to Eve. 'What's going on?'

She puts a finger to her lips. 'Lovers' tiff,' she says quietly, 'but he's going to go back there now to make amends.' Then, loudly: 'Isn't that right, honey? You're going back to Gina's after breakfast?' Rowan's attention remains buried in his cereal. She raises her eyes to heaven, then peers closely at me. 'You look real tired, Arabella, didn't you sleep well?'

'Not great.' I rub my own eyes, which feel as bad as Rowan's look, like they've been sandpapered. 'And in that regard I've something to tell you, Eve. Something happened here last night – I hope you're prepared for a shock.' I accept a cup of coffee from her and, leaning against the kitchen sink, summarise the events of the previous evening, emphasising every few seconds that the outcome is benign. Nevertheless, she listens in growing horror.

'Good God,' she explodes, when I've finished. 'I never heard a thing. Did you, Rowan?'

'Hear what?' He looks towards us. He hasn't taken in a word I've said, so I repeat the story. His response is muted, to say the least. As he comes towards us and puts his empty cereal bowl in the sink beside me, he shrugs. 'Too bad. I'm off. See youse later.' The crystals chime behind him.

271

'We should make allowances.' Through the window, Eve watches him shamble off down the sunny street. 'I think he has a bad hangover.'

'He's drinking?' I'm alarmed. I'm not going to be able to handle this. 'I watched him at the party and he didn't seem to be overdoing it.'

'It was a blip.' Her tone is casual. 'We've had a chat about it and I think he listened, but that's not important right now. We should go across to Dale. I'm absolutely shocked about this. As for that Eddie,' her lips turn down in disgust, 'I hope this time they throw away the key. For once I wish this was California. Three strikes there and you're out for good. The guy's not right in the head – he's never been right, if you ask me, but that's no excuse.'

'But why would he do that to his own mother?'

'Why?' She grimaced. 'For money. He's done it before, but from what you tell me, this time it's real bad. Mary covers up for him all the time and she'll never make a complaint about him so it's not for me to say, I suppose. He doesn't need to beat her up, you know. She'd hand it over in any case, so my guess is she wasn't quick enough about it, or she objected, and he lost his temper because he's hopped up on something. Probably crack. There's a lot of it around. He's obviously getting worse. And after all that poor woman did for the kid.'

'He didn't look like a kid – he was a grown man.'

'To his mother even a grown man is still her baby.' She turns away from the window and reaches for her crutch, balanced against one of the kitchen units. For some reason, I feel snubbed. I don't have time to examine this, however, because being mad at myself has lent me courage, and I'm determined to say what I have to say to Eve and get it out of my system.

'Dale's in the shower so we have a few minutes. Could we sit down and have a chat?'

'I thought you'd never ask.' As she replaces the crutch she smiles, but immediately knows the joke has fallen flat: her eyes sort of flatten out. 'Let me get myself a cuppa,' she moves the kettle on to the stove 'and then you'll have my undivided attention. How about yourself? Want a hottener on the coffee?'

'No, thanks. I've barely touched this one.' No hotteners. No blarney. She's not going to distract me from my purpose. She can cry or beg or plead, I'm going to tell her that what she did was wrong, wrong, *wrong*.

While I wait for her to join me at the living end of the trailer, I busy myself tidying a little, no easy task as it turns out. Rowan had obviously slept on her sofa-bed, a spring-mounted affair taking up almost all of the limited floor space. It takes me a few moments to figure out how to repackage it.

I notice as I'm plumping cushions and moving everything back into place that there's a light film of dust covering most of the surfaces. Eve doesn't strike me as a slattern but the accident has obviously got the better of her housekeeping skills. 'Would you like me to do a bit of Hoovering and dusting for you, Eve?'

'Nah. Don't worry about it. You're on vacation, you're not here to skivvy for your old crock of a mother!' Another attempt at lightness but she's not going to get to me that way either. I avoid her gaze by picking up the crumbs Rowan left, one by one.

'It'd be no bother, really.'

'Oh, leave it, girl. Relax. Sit down and drink your coffee.'

Stubbornly, I continue with the crumbs. Something occurs to me: I know she lives on the equivalent of the American dole but would that stretch to buying a trailer? I have no idea how much one might cost; admittedly, this is America where everything, it seems, costs less than at home, but still . . . 'Do you rent here, Eve? Or is this your own?'

'It's mine, but I wouldn't have been able to afford it without Dale's help.'

St Dale again. I straighten up. Then, casually, 'What does that guy *do*? He seems to have all the time in the world and there's no evidence in his trailer that I can see of him being a working man.'

'Oh, we reckon he has a private income. Trust fund, maybe. His parents are dead, you know.'

'He told me.'

'This quick?' Her eyebrows arch. 'My – ain't that somethin'! It was years before he gave me that bit of information.'

'It seems to me, though, that when it comes to information, the traffic with Dale is very much one way. He seems to know everything about everybody else but gives out very little about himself.'

'What's the matter, Arabella?' She stops pouring boiling water on to her tea-bag. 'Do you have to know everything about a person's private life to like him?'

'It's not that.'

'Then what is it?' The expression in the remarkable eyes is alert now.

Shrewd. To avoid it, I pick up the tubes attached to the oxygen bottle and pretend to look for a place to stow them. Eve resumes pouring. 'He does go away quite a bit,' she's thinking aloud, 'sometimes overnight, and never says where. One thing we do know is that he's very generous with his time *and* his money. If you stick around for a little while, Arabella, as I hope you will, one great thing you'll learn about America is that it's big enough for everyone. All types.

'Take me. I'm a gabber. I'll tell anyone anything they want to know about me and sometimes what they don't. But there are so many people doing their own thing here on this site that there's plenty of room for those who like to keep some things private. It's sort of an unspoken rule. Unless someone is being seriously antisocial, you accept 'em at face value and that includes their history, or lack of it.'

'Actually,' I'm still clutching the tubes, 'there is one thing I can't accept at face value – his attitude to his children, whatever has happened in the past. Have you met them?'

'Uh-uh! All that happened with Dale before we hooked up.'

'But don't you think they should be told about his accident? He could have died in that stabbing. Don't you think they deserve to know – suppose he had died? How would they feel then? I know what I'm talking about.' I'm warming up. 'I know how I'd feel about Dale and the rest of them now if you'd been at death's door and actually died and I'd never got to say even hello?'

'You have a point.'

'It's been a long time. Maybe they've changed a bit towards him, but he doesn't even know for sure where they live. I mentioned it, though, and got short shrift.'

'I'm not surprised. But hey!' She thinks for a few moments. Then: 'Leave that with me for a while, OK? You might be right. This might be a good opportunity but it'll have to be handled carefully. He's touchy about his privacy, but sometimes it's better to risk someone's anger – what's that saying? "For evil to triumph it's necessary only for good people to do nothing"?'

'Something like that.' She's not precise but I've heard it often enough from Jimmy Porter, God knows, to get the drift. Jimmy uses it to justify being a busybody on his own road – too much litter in people's gardens, that kind of thing.

274

Oh, God – Jimmy Porter.

I force myself to keep my mind on what's happening here and now as Eve clumps towards me, holding her tea carefully so it doesn't spill, and I notice that, even in the short time I've been here, her posture has improved. When she gets that cast off, I think, there'll be no stopping her. 'Do you need this oxygen any more?' I brandish the tubes. 'Dale says you've been using it less and less.'

'It was a standby. I had to use it for a coupla days when my ribs were sore but they're much improved now. Don't tell me any good jokes, though, because when I laugh it still hurts bad. I'll put all that stuff away later. Better yet, I'll get Dale to – oh dear!' She stops. 'I can't really ask Dale to do anything right now, can I?'

'The wounds aren't all that serious – I probably exaggerated a bit. I'd be more worried about Mary. She's going to look like something out of a horror movie. If you don't think you'll be using it, will I put this equipment outside in that storage-box thingy?'

'Sit *down*, Arabella. That's an order.'

I sit on the reconstituted sofa and wait while she deposits her tea on the side-table, then manoeuvres herself into the big armchair, making heavy weather of it because the cast is at an awkward angle. She thumps it in frustration. 'Dratted stupid thing! Make sure you never break your leg, honey.'

'When are you getting the lighter one?'

'I hope day after tomorrow. I've an appointment at the hospital.'

'Well, at least you'll get some compensation from the insurance.'

'Oops!' Her hand flies to her mouth. 'Senior moment, Arabella. I pure forgot that guy is coming today. Look at me, still in my robe. I'd better get my act together.'

'Would you like me to be with you when he comes? You should have somebody.' This is automatic because it's on my list of shoulds and have-tos. I only half mean it. Then I don't have to mean it at all because she smiles.

'Them insurance boys'd want to get up early to get anything over on me. I'll be fine. Don't worry.' She takes a deep mouthful of her tea.

I follow suit with the coffee. It's still hot and strong; very good, actually. I watch her over the rim of my cup. There is little trace now of the sick woman I saw only a few days ago (how many? I must sit down soon with a calendar to calculate). I think back to the collapsing, the oxygen use, the panic that Willow and I got into when we thought she'd lost consciousness . . . I have to work hard to restrain a hefty surge of fury, a combination of resentment of her and the still-simmering anger with myself, and when I put my cup down, it clatters. 'Tell me something, Eve, in all those years why didn't you make any effort *at all* to get in touch with us?' There. It's on the table.

She's been expecting it. The eyes flicker, just once, and then she tells me about the efforts she made over the years. She and Dale made. 'Did you have an unlisted number, Arabella?' she asks then, as if my not being turned up by Directory Enquiries years ago (*because I didn't have a phone, stupid!*) excuses everything.

'When was this? When you were trying Directory Enquiries, I mean. Actually, it doesn't matter.'

'But it does. It matters very much. What more can I tell you?'

'Let it go, Eve. At least you did make *some* effort.' But I'm seething. 'Everyone here seems to think you're something really special. All your friends. Dale. Them all. I haven't seen anything all that special about you. What *is* so special about you, Eve?'

'Beauty is in the eye of the beholder?' She smiles mischievously. And has got even calmer, if that's possible. I feel as if I'm the one in the confession box.

'There's another thing I'm curious about,' I hurl at her. 'That day when we first came and there was all that emotion and you had to use the oxygen, was that an act?'

'I beg your pardon? What do you mean?'

Hah!

I'm aware this is only a sidebar, as they say in American courtroom dramas, but at least I've punctured the calm. 'You know!'

'I don't.' Bewildered. (Maybe?)

'I mean, was it for effect?'

'You think I was faking?'

If the astonishment is put on, she's a very good actress. 'I'm asking, that's all. It's something I really would like to know. You seem to have made a very quick, even miraculous recovery.' I'm dogged now, driving. 'I'm talking about the fact that as far as I can see you've made a remarkably rapid recovery overall. Could it be possible that you had it all planned?

That you were going for the sympathy vote with me and my sister? Look at you now, hampered by that cast, yeah, but in general pretty hale and hearty, I'd say.'

'You don't know me,' she says softly, almost sadly, after a pause. 'All right, I was desperately nervous at the thought of you girls arriving and that might have made me look a bit dawny. Are you talking about being tucked into a blanket and all that?'

'Yes.'

'That was Mario's idea. Fussing. Trying to be a good nurse, but nearly as jumpy as I was. As for me, I went along with it because I didn't know what to do, what not to do. Nobody's written any manuals on how to behave in this situation. I'm sure you've found that yourself.

'And yes, I can see why you thought it was a try for the sympathy vote, as you call it,' she smiles faintly at the recollection, 'but that oxygen thing was for real. I got hyper. I wasn't able to breathe properly, or I thought I couldn't, and then afterwards I felt completely exhausted. I'm a strong woman, Arabella. I have no need to fake anything and I don't want sympathy. I've survived far worse than a piddling car wreck.

'As have you. I'm sure you have plenty of things you'd like to say to me.' The eyes are so deep and wide I'm in danger of drowning in them. Now that I'm faced with her, all the 'stuff' I've stored for this moment, the accusations and the anger, is jumbling. It's happening not for lack of courage, at least I don't think so, it's that suddenly it seems pointless. She's been flayed by Willow, I'm sure she has. God knows what Rowan said to her, probably more of the same. Is there any point in my repeating the exercise? Yet I can't pretend it was nothing.

'Don't *do* that, Eve.'

'Don't do what?'

'Whatever it is you're doing to me with your eyes. You're not going to influence me. I'm not letting you get away with what you did. What you did wasn't *nothing*!'

'I certainly don't think so,' she agrees.

'Don't bloody *agree* with me. Fight me, Eve. Please fight me. I want a fight – I *need* to fight with you.'

'A fight has to be two-way. What do I have to fight with? Anything you say to me is justified. And I won't blame you for it. Honestly. I don't think there's anything you could accuse me of that I haven't accused myself of thousands of times, but let me ask you something.' She is sad now, even tentative. 'Have you read that diary I gave you?'

'I've read the diary.'

The phrase plops and spreads ripples, small at first, but growing into large waves. 'Ah!' she says, just that – but there's a world within the sound. What is to happen next, what she says next, is crucial.

She puts down her cup on her side table. 'You're very angry with me, aren't you, Arabella? You're all very angry. Can I do anything to put it right?'

'No.'

'Ah.'

A car goes by outside and she looks away for a moment, as if distracted. We both do and I can feel something change between us. When she looks back, she says quietly, 'We are where we are, Arabella,' and I can see clearly the line she has marked. She might have offered herself for crucifixion but it was on her terms. She has now withdrawn the offer. There is something inside her that is never going to give.

I'm not yielding either. My anger has been just.

If she'd gone for sympathy again, as she seemed about to do when she mentioned the diary, or wriggled or prevaricated or made excuses – if she'd dragged me back into her life of forty years ago – I'd probably have got up and walked out. Instead I'm knocked for six. Self-pity, resentment, rage – they all fall away, whether temporarily or permanently remains to be seen. Maybe it'll all pile back again tomorrow but right now, for today at least, I feel physically lighter.

I meet her, stare for stare, and I feel something pass between us, a small starburst, an exchange of respect. We smile at each other, cautiously, me with something approaching relief.

We're only at the beginning, though, and if a relationship is to develop between us, mother-daughter, sister-sister, woman-woman – even friend-friend – from this point on it will be one of equals. No more moral outrage from me. No wheedling, crawling or begging for forgiveness from her. We've been through all that, even if a lot of it hasn't been expressed.

She is relieved too, it seems, because the years fall away and I can see the girl in her: not the sad skivvy arriving in America in wedding suit and borrowed hat, but the girl, Eve, in full young stride. Eve declaring herself at Immigration, full of sorrow about us but also of hope and plans and dignity. 'Do you want to talk about your father?' she asks quietly. 'I should imagine you would. He had some good points. I've been worrying that all you're got about him are the bad bits from the diary.'

'I'd like to hear, yes. And it *was* pretty one-sided about him in the diary but I could read between the lines, Eve. You had a hard time, sure, but he was forced to marry you and that couldn't have been easy for him. It certainly wasn't a good start.'

'It was different times.' She spreads her hands and studies them as if they were a map. 'You girls, anyone of your generation, can't really grasp the shame of being pregnant out of wedlock in them days. You know about the Magdalen laundries, do you?'

'I've seen documentaries.' No one in Ireland could have missed the flurry of films and TV programmes about these punitive institutions where pregnancy was a sin and the sinners condemned for life. 'And I do have an imagination. It was a scandal, what girls like you were forced into.'

'It was different times,' she repeats. 'But about your father . . . He was,' she thinks, 'he was a charmer when he wanted to be. He talked his way into my life in anyway. And he was intelligent – he was certainly that. And very quick with figures. He could do a long tot quicker than a cash register.'

I can see she's dredging. 'How did he feel about me? After I arrived, I mean.'

'He was . . .' again she thinks '. . . he was very busy. Out a lot. You know?'

'Doing what?'

'Oh, you know. Things were bad in Dublin in them days. There were thousands looking for work.'

There seems little point in staying on this road. She is being ultra-cautious while she tries to find neutral things to say but the picture seems clear enough. My father, Peter Moraghan, didn't give a toss about me. Otherwise he would have come looking and easily found me. Found us. For instance, even though it was Christmas, with no newspapers for days and days, the finding of three babies in the Palm House had to have excited some public comment. I had always planned 'some day' to do a search for cuttings of that time. Had even got as far as the door of the National Library in Kildare Street, but, peeking in, had been intimidated by the formal-looking entrance lobby. 'Not for the likes of you,' it seemed to say. Now I thought I would definitely pursue this when I got home. 'Are you bitter about what happened to you, Eve?'

She clenches her fists suddenly and looks at me, eyes blazing. 'Of course I'm not. I was a fool to let it happen to me, society or background or otherwise. I blame myself first, last and always.'

'You were very young.' I'm aware the roles have reversed and I'm the one now making the excuses.

'I wasn't that young.' She remains heated. 'I was fourteen when I left that orphanage. We were innocent in the ways of the world, sure, but we'd been hardened, too, and in some ways knew more about reality than anyone. We'd been through more.

'In anyway, how could I be bitter when he gave me three lovely children? Petey himself is a separate issue. I think he was a bastard – sorry, Arabella, it's probably unfair to say it to you, but that's the way I feel about him. I also feel sorry for him now. He's the one lost out in the end.'

She is gazing at me with such passion it's painful. I attempt a reassuring smile. 'We'll talk about this again, eh?'

'We've a lifetime to talk now. I'm glad to stop for the moment.' She smiles back, and we lapse into quiet conversation about our respective orphanages, hers and ours, discovering few difference in the regimes, except that most of us were eventually fostered – some even adopted – while Eve and her contemporaries usually had to stay the full course before being decanted as maids into the attics of farmhouses or the sculleries of town professionals. There's no point-scoring or self-pity, I'm glad to say, it's a conversation of understanding between equals.

All the time I'm trying to discover what I truly feel about Peter Moraghan.

Very little, is the answer. As I think I told you already, I haven't lost sleep over him and I'm not going to do so tonight. There is a little 'if only', but I feel that about winning the Lotto.

Meanwhile I have a relationship to build with my mother. I'm not silly enough to believe everything is going to be smooth and hunky-dory from now on. Or that we won't refer back. Right now, though, our mutual situation lies between us like a flat sheet of unblemished silver on which anything can be engraved.

It's liberating. I feel high. I should mark this moment in some way, but

I can't think of anything suitable to say or do: that silver is so clean I want to admire it for a while.

True to recent form, Eve and I don't get much time to bask, or even to move towards some practical plans, because now there is a knock on her door and Dale, protecting his injured neck and shoulder with his left hand, clinks in through the crystals. With his right, he's holding out that damned mobile phone again.

Instinctively, I rise from the couch, waving my hands in front of me, whispering urgently, 'If it's Jimmy, I'm not here.'

'It's your sister.'

'Oh! Thanks. I'll take it outside.' Mortified, I take the yoke from him. As I leave the trailer, I hear Eve struggling to her feet to fuss over him.

Outside, the deck is baking, so hot it's hard to stand on it in my thin-soled shoes, and for the first time since I arrived, I'm conscious of the hum of insects. Each successive day seems to get hotter here so August must be cruel. Quickly, I take advantage of being outside to light up. Then I sit and brace myself for Willow. 'Hello?'

'I don't have much time, I'm calling from work.'

'Hello to you too, Willow.'

'I'm sorry I missed your birthday – the time-change, oh, I don't know. I'm not properly organised yet after the trip. I'll have a card and a present for you when you come home, all right?'

'That'll be nice. Don't feel bad, I got confused about the days myself. But they gave me a surprise party.'

'Did they? Great.' The honour obviously doesn't register deeply with her. 'Look,' she says rapidly, 'there've been a couple of developments.'

'Yes?'

'I went through that tin box of hers and . . .' Unusually for her, she hesitates.

'I'm all ears.' I take a lovely deep drag of the cigarette but when I blow out I make sure the mouthpiece of the mobile is somewhere near my hairline. I don't want to pollute the bloody thing.

'Did it ever occur to you that we might have a whole different family out there somewhere? Cousins, aunts, even grandparents. It's not beyond the bounds of possibility, you know.'

'What's in the box that I missed?'

'There's a note. From whoever left her – wherever she was left. It says, and I quote, "We can't look after this infant." "We", Arabella. A group.'

'Are you implying she might have been born into a cult or something?'

'Of course not!'

She's impatient, the old Willow. And she has a point. I'm being affected by the vibes flying back and forth at Robinia Meadows. 'Unlikely,' I admit, 'in Ireland in 1944.'

'But don't you think it's odd? "We"?'

'Now that you mention it, I suppose – but what should we do about it?' I'm intrigued at the notion of a whole new slew of relatives. 'We' could be the parents, but even so, they had to have family too, didn't they?'

'It's not urgent, of course, but in the meantime . . .' She hesitates again.

'Yes?'

'There's something I want you to pass on to her. Do you remember I told you about ringing up all those Rennicks everywhere?' Willow lowers her voice as though someone has entered her office.

'Yeah.'

'And we figured she took the name Rennick because of this friend Maura she's always talking about? And all those returned letters in the box, you know? Well, this Maura, it turns out, moved house shortly after Eve left and the cousin who was supposed to look after her post died at around the same time.'

'How do you know all this, Willow?'

'Well, I got this idea into my head about this Maura and now the oddest thing has happened. To make a long story short, I've located her. Or, to be more precise, she contacted me.'

'That's fantastic!' I forget my prickliness. 'That's wonderful! How on earth did you manage it? Eve'll be thrilled – listen, hang on a minute and I'll bring the phone in to her. You can tell her yourself how you did it. Is the woman in Ireland? You're amazing, Willow!'

I scramble to my feet and move back towards the door but she stops me with what I can only describe as a screech: 'Bella! No!'

'What?' I'm puzzled.

Through Willow's now covered mouthpiece I can hear her muffled voice apologising to someone for the yell. When she gets back to me, she hisses, 'I'm merely passing along the information. You tell her about it, OK?'

'But she'd love to talk to you.'

'I've done my bit. Stop pushing, Arabella – look, I have to go. I've given Maura Rennick the campsite address. Her married name is Lewis. She'll be writing. Our mother can take it from there. I've done my bit.'

'Willow, I can't tell her you rang and didn't want to talk to her. She'll want to thank you at the very least and she'll want to know how you found this woman after all these years.'

'The story's too long to tell on a transatlantic phone call. I'm at *work*, Arabella, and I shouldn't be using this phone for a personal call. But you can tell her I said hello.'

'Hold on – Willow!'

She's gone.

CHAPTER FORTY-THREE

I've found myself a five-star retreat. I'm at the very end of the caravan site, sitting where no one can see me behind a row of skips full of stinking rubbish, sharing my personal space with bluebottles and other things I'd rather not think about, thank you. It's hot. It's hopeless.

Easy enough for mothers to laser you and tell you to go and apologise, and that they're pretty sure if you do everything will turn out all right. Mothers probably hope this all the time. They don't fucking *know* the real world.

Like my world.

Because, you see, the more I think of it the more I think there's no point in apologising to Gina. Certainly not now. She'll only give me a lecture and then probably throw me out again.

Nah. I've wrecked whatever chance I had there. She knows what the real story is with me. There's no going back from this and, cards on the table here, I don't think I have ever, *ever* felt so shitty.

So let's see now, let's get a bit of *perspective* here: on a scale of one to ten where does this morning score?

That night in Arbour Hill when I was put in with all the sex offenders because there was no room in the Joy? That was a seven.

The night of the big snow in Dublin that caught me and Caroline out because we weren't expecting it and we nearly froze to death because we didn't have enough cardboard to put underneath us? That had to be an eight or a nine, I thought at the time, but then, of course, she goes and dies on me so by comparison that night shrinks back to maybe a six. (I wouldn't score the night she died. I wouldn't be able.) It's all comparisons, isn't it? Gangrene in my toe? A piffling four or five.

Mental giving me the hiding of my life so I had to go to hospital? Maybe only a two or three because, in a funny way, being done over by

284

Mental gives you a sort of status with your peers. He wouldn't bother if he didn't care, is the way the thinking goes.

It was maybe a seven or an eight when I took them snowballs and had to have my stomach pumped because the skanger who sold them to me had cut them with rat poison.

A definite nine when I was sent back to the home by my foster-family.

A nine as well for that time Brother Ambrose threw me into the coal-house with the rats.

So. How does this morning compare with that? I'm trying to convince myself that all we're dealing with here is fucking feelings. But right now, with the blazing heat and the smells and the horrible shite feeling that's in my insides, I'd give it – oh – I'd give it the round ten.

Listening to my ma and Bel whispering about me in my ma's trailer this morning was a highlight too. It wasn't just that I'd blown it with Gina, although that was it mostly, I suppose, but it was also that I'd blown it with me and I knew it. And it looked like they knew it too. All that effort getting clean and staying clean gone down the jacksie for the sake of a couple of belts of champagne.

What is it they say, those alkies? *Just one drink away* . . . And isn't that what my mother said, too, in so many words?

You see, when you can blame the System, it's like a little everlasting flame that gives you permanent heat and light. This morning, as I was eating those cornflakes, I couldn't blame the System. No System, no nothing. I screwed it up, this time, every time, all times, and as I was leaving my ma's trailer this morning, I felt not only that I had the hang-over of the century – which I had, because I'd mixed the champagne with quite a lot of Gina's Scotch – but like the smallest, crappiest, wormiest person in the world; a person who deserves Gina to step on him on her way out the door to a proper life.

At the same time I was going to give it a go. My ma said, 'Apologise,' so I was going to Gina's with the full intention of apologising. On my word of honour I was.

I'm sorry I yelled at my ma too, although she deserved all she got and I'll believe that to my dying day. But I shouldn't have been so hard on her. As Mental says, you only have one ma.

Mental's ma lives somewhere down on the Costa del Sol with some gouger who has dosh. She sends Mental three cards a year, on Christmas, his birthday and Valentine's Day (by the way, none of those cards ever has any readies enclosed) and you might think he wouldn't give his ma the steam off his piss. But he's fond of showing you the latest card, carries it around with him. I used to scoff (privately, of course), thinking he was a right sentimental oul' shite but now I see where he's coming from. They might be crap in the maternal department but they *are* the only mas we have. And they have to forgive you and give you chance after chance. It's their mission in life. It's their duty. It's not the duty of girlfriends. Certainly not one that you've had for only a few days, no matter how serious they say they are. They have lives of their own.

So that's the whole story. Hello, crows! Hello, flies and rubbish and flaking heat! At least I have booze. Three-quarters of a bottle of temporary relief, full when I started.

Robbed it.

Robbed it from Gina.

Wouldn't you be proud of me?

CHAPTER FORTY-FOUR

Since I told her about Willow's discovery of her friend, Eve has been as excited as a five-year-old child on her way to Disneyland. She has already made up her mind to cross the Atlantic, but the big question is, should she wait to receive the letter or should she travel to Ireland as a pre-emptive strike? 'But why didn't she give you Maura's phone number? Why do I have to wait for a letter?' She's so focused on joy, I don't think Willow's snub has registered.

'Take it easy, Eve.' I was conscious of a few twinges of (unwarranted) jealousy: I was her child after all. This Maura person was just a friend – but I got over it in the reflection of her pleasure, which was infectious. 'Take it easy, Eve,' I said again, and laughed at her. 'We don't know yet whether your friend is actually in Ireland or where she is. Willow hung up before I could put her through the third degree. But I'm sure that when she writes to you she'll give you her phone number so you can ring her.'

'When that letter comes, that's something for my tin box, eh? I gotta start a new one!'

'Please, God, we won't have to carry around our tin boxes any more – either of us!' I've just discovered another liberation. My tin box has already lost its worth as a talisman. I no longer have to guard it with my life and defend it from all comers. Like ordinary people, I can put it in some notional attic for the next generation. For Willow's kids.

Or even Rowan's. Now there's a thought – and not as far-fetched as it might have seemed as lately as a week ago.

In any event, it's terrific, I think, that for once we can all celebrate pleasant news, uncomplicated by the fear of doing or saying the wrong thing.

Then, naturally, I say the wrong thing. 'Maybe you could come too, Dale. Maybe this is an opportunity for you to look up your old friend.'

287

'What friend?' Immediately he's on alert. Warning me.

'You know, the friend in France or Germany?' Faltering, I glance at Eve. He'd said she knew his whole story so what was the problem?

'I don't think so.'

He glowers but Eve is having none of it. She winks conspiratorially at me, then cracks him on the knee with one hand. 'Oh, for goodness' sake, lighten up, Dale,' she says happily. 'Yes, of course you should come. We'll all go! I'll have money from the insurance. I can treat us − 'bout time too, Dale, after you being so good to me all these years.' Then, to me: 'Do you think Maura and me'll know each other straight away?' The wattage from her smile would power a stadium.

'Oh, I'm sure you will. Why ever not?' I see the eyes react to something over my shoulder and look to see what has happened. Up and down the street, people are coming out on their decks because a bashed-up police car is bumping wearily in our direction. It pulls up in front of the trailer and two exhausted-looking men get out, pulling on their hats. I tighten the belt of my dressing-gown once again. Waynetta Slob, still in her night attire at half ten in the morning.

'Good morning, officers.' Eve's bubbly mood persists.

'Morning, ma'am.' The first policeman tips his cap, then turns his attention to Dale. 'Dale Genscher?'

That wasn't a difficult call. Dale's injuries are obvious.

'That's me.' Dale puts up a hand like he's answering a roll-call. 'I gave a statement last night at the hospital.'

'May we come up?' The second guy, older than the first, has already climbed the steps.

'Sure, officer.' Eve then asks them to sit and offers them coffee. Politely, they decline.

'This injury connected with the incident, ma'am?' Cop number two indicates the cast on Eve's leg.

'Not at all.' She brushes off the question. 'It was just an accident. Are you two perfectly sure you won't have coffee? Iced tea? It's going to be a hot one today.'

'No, thank you, ma'am.' In chorus.

'One or two details that we need to clear up if you don't mind, Mr Genscher.' The first policeman consults a notebook. 'This guy, uh − Eddie Montgomery. Did he say anything to you before he stabbed you?'

288

'I can answer that,' I barge in. 'I was there.'

'We'll get to you, ma'am.' Then the cop grins widely, teeth glowing against the blue-blackness of his skin. 'Is that an Irish brogue I hear?'

'Mmm.' I'm taken aback: I don't think many Dublin people would describe their accent as a 'brogue'. 'My great-grandfather came from Skibbereen in County Cork,' he says. 'You know Skibbereen?'

'No,' I say faintly. 'I've never been to Cork. I'm from Dublin.'

'Some day I'm gonna go there – take my mom. She'd love it. She has such stories in her family.' Laughing and shaking his head, he opens a fresh page in his notebook. 'So your name is . . .'

At this stage Robert and Mario, standing outside the rail along the deck, have joined the gallery of interested spectators. They are both wearing running gear, sweatbands on their wrists and bandannas round their heads. Conscious they can hear every word, I give my statement, pathetically short as it is but including what I remember of Eddie's physical appearance: the wild look, the dribble of foam at his mouth. 'I'm sorry,' I mutter, 'I'm probably not much help. He said hardly anything. Just told us not to interfere. And that one word, "bastard", before he stabbed Dale. The whole thing happened so fast.'

'Don't worry, ma'am, every little helps and your story corroborates everything we've heard so far.' He turns back to Dale. 'So, no row between you, you were just trying to help Mrs Montgomery, right?'

'Right.' Dale remains calm.

'And apparently you're not going to press charges? That the case, Mr Genscher?'

'I'm taking the lead from the guy's mother,' Dale is beginning to sound irritated, 'and, actually, I don't see what it would accomplish. The man needs a hospital, not a jailhouse.'

'If he was put away for a while it might give the lady a few years' peace.' The second cop stares at him. 'I looked him up. He has a sheet.'

'His mother don't want to take things any further.' Dale looks at his feet. I'm becoming familiar with this tactic: as far as he's concerned, the subject is closed.

The policemen exchange a glance and the first shuts his notebook. 'That's all for the moment. You understand that these are preliminary interviews? We'll probably ask you to come down to the precinct to sign formal statements.'

'Fine.'

They ask a few more general questions, then, thanking us for our time, amble back to the patrol car.

As soon as the steps are clear, Robert and Mario rush up to join us. 'We just heard.' Mario is wide-eyed. 'How dreadful. How are you, Dale, you poor lamb? And Mary? Is she OK? Should we send her a bouquet? Is she well enough?'

'We'll go visit with her. Will she be OK with that, do you think?' Cooler, Robert is, nevertheless, just as concerned.

'She'll be fine.' Dale yawns. I'm getting the impression he's not enjoying the attention. 'She's being discharged after lunch. I called earlier and she was already up and about. She won't look pretty, but who does?' He stands up. 'We'll all be fine but if you're going to the hospital, Robert, could I take a ride? My truck's still in the parking lot.'

'Sure,' Robert agrees. 'You OK to drive with that shoulder of yours?'

'It's only twenty minutes.'

'Fine, fine. I hear you, buddy, whatever you say!' Robert makes an I'm-backing-off gesture, both hands pushing at an imaginary wall. 'Here's an idea. We can pick up Mary and give her a ride home. But why don't we all go to town a bit early to show Arabella around a little?' He looks at Eve for affirmation. 'She'd love to see the Chapel of the Holy Cross, yeah?'

'Thanks, Robert, but leave me out of it.' Eve pulls her crutch towards her. 'I've things to do. Busy day ahead.' Again she winks at me.

'And me, Robert,' Mario pipes up. 'You know how much I hate hospitals. I'll cook for her instead, OK? I'll do something really special for poor Mary so she'll know I care.'

'Fine, fine! It was just an idea.' Robert waves at us all. 'Stop by when you're ready, Dale. The offer's open, Arabella, if you want to come along. I'd love to show you my gallery.'

'That would be great, Robert. Thank you.'

Half an hour later, I'm trying to put some kind of *smacht* on my hair with my worn-out hairbrush. Dale, sprawled on a couch, black shirt-collar pulled up to cover the spidery stitches on his neck, is already on standby to go out; we're in the living area of his trailer, windows closed, air-conditioning on full blast. It's approaching noon and outside the heat is becoming unbearable.

As I struggle with the tangles, I notice he's watching me with an intensity I find unsettling. 'Would it be OK if I continued to stay here?' I blurt what's been on my mind. 'That's if I'm not in the way. I said that this morning only because – because—' Then I can't come up with any plausible reason why I'd said it. He's still watching me. 'You're making me nervous, Dale. Did you hear what I asked? Why are you looking at me like that?'

'Your hair.'

Instinctively, I pull it back from my face with my free hand. 'It's too thick. It's always been the bane of my life.'

'It's beautiful.' He looks away, then stands up abruptly. 'We should go. Robert's a stickler for timekeeping. And after his gallery it's a coupla miles up to Holy Cross. We don't want to leave Mary in the lurch when she's expecting us.'

I'm left with my hair stupidly bunched in my hand. *He thinks it's beautiful?* I let it drop, self-conscious now. 'This Holy Cross place, it's worth seeing?'

'It is.'

'So it's OK if I continue to stay here with you?'

He still hasn't looked back in my direction. He is adjusting the temperature on the air-conditioning unit. 'If you want to.'

He goes towards the door, holds it open for me and I'm left with no option but to walk towards him. He waits until I'm out, lets the door swing shut behind me, then takes off like the clappers, walking so fast I have difficulty keeping up with him. We've gone maybe thirty yards and I'm already panting. And blathering some more. 'Do Robert and Mario own this gallery fifty-fifty? Mario doesn't seem all that interested.'

'I don't know what the arrangement is there. I suspect Robert simply gave him a share. I doubt if it was fifty-fifty. Robert's a businessman.'

'Oh, I see. And is it always this hot so early in the year?' Vaguely, it occurs to me that I may have asked this question before but I'm desperate for something safe to say.

'No, average temperature around here this month is mid-seventies, but not always. This is unusual.' His tone tells me that he *has* answered this before and I'm about to apologise when he nods down a side-street and stops. 'But then, with global warming and that, what's usual any more? There's Gina.'

Indeed it is. When she sees us she breaks into a lopsided trot. 'Where is he?' she calls. 'Have you seen him?'

'You mean Rowan?' I try to sound steady and motherly. 'Did you try Eve's? I saw him there earlier. He left when I arrived but he may have gone back.'

'I tried there.' She purses her lips. 'I went there first, naturally, but her neighbour told me that your mom had hoofed it up the telephone kiosk and when I got there she was on the phone. She told me she hadn't seen him for a couple of hours and that she couldn't help look for him either because she had some guy from the insurance company coming.'

'You had a row with him last night?'

'I was horrible to him. But he deserved it – he was out of his brain.' It's only then that she cops the state of Dale. 'Jeez! What happened to you?'

'It's a long story. Mary Wu's still in the hospital.' Dale's tone is calm. 'We're collecting her later.'

'Eddie again? When did it happen?'

'Last night and, yep, he's the one.'

'Why didn't you guys wake me up?'

'Do you want we should help you look for Rowan? He can't have gone far.' Dale does his thing: not answering the question he was asked.

'Oh, I'm sure I'll come across him,' she looks over her shoulder as if expecting Rowan to materialise, 'or he'll come back in his own sweet time. You're right, Dale, he can't have gone far. All his stuff is still at my place. Including his cash. Where could he go without money? Oh, God, I wish I hadn't said some of the things I said,' she says mournfully. 'I called him terrible names and told him I never wanted to see him again.'

'These things happen, Gina.' I patted her shoulder. 'I'm sure he knew you didn't mean it. And now he's probably just making you sweat. You know what men are like.'

'You think so?'

Dale takes her arm and aims her back in the direction she'd come from. 'Best thing you can do is go back to your trailer and wait. I'll round up Robert and Mario and between us we'll find him. As you say, he has no money so he can't have left. There's no way out of here except by car or taxi. Is your car still in your driveway?'

'Yes. But he could hitchhike, couldn't he?'

'I doubt it,' I chime in. 'As far as I know Rowan has never hitchhiked in his life. Anyway, who'd pick him up? When I saw him this morning he was eating his breakfast but he looked like the Creature from the Black Lagoon.'

At least this raises a smile. 'OK, then,' Dale takes advantage of it, 'you go on home, Gina. Turn on daytime TV and give him hell when he does come back.'

'Be sure of it!' She hurries away towards her trailer.

It doesn't take long to find my brother: Robert discovers him, asleep behind some skips at the furthest end of the site. He tells us he hasn't been able to wake him – 'Don't worry, he's breathing!'

Although the skips are covered, the place is buzzing with flies and very unpleasant. I stand looking down at my brother, curled like a hedgehog, hands tucked in under him, one side of his face sunburnt to the colour of a fresh beetroot. That's going to be sore later. *Good enough for him*, I think, with sisterly contempt. 'Rowan!' I lean down and shake him hard. He doesn't respond.

'Oh, dear Lord – you don't think . . . ?' Mario's all of a tizz.

'No, I don't. *Rowan!*' I shake him harder, this time with both hands. When there's still no movement, I hunker down close to his face. His breath stinks of alcohol. I search around him and, sure enough, half hidden under the nearest skip, I see a bottle lying on its side. At least there's still some drink left in it – and some of it may have poured away or evaporated.

I stand up again, torn between disgust and my normal instinct to prevaricate in order to shield my brother from the disdain of strangers. 'He's been drinking,' I say flatly, trying not to load the sentence either way.

'We can't leave him here. He'll fry.' Dale takes over. 'Mario, Robert, take a hand each and I'll get his legs. We'll carry him back to my place. And I think we should call a doctor.'

'You can't carry him,' Robert points out. 'He's a big guy. You'll rip out those stitches in your shoulder. Mario, you go get the car. We'll load him up and drive him.'

Dale agrees to this. I offer to tell Gina the news. 'Which is her trailer?'

'From here it's three streets up and then four across.' Aided, one-handed, by Dale, Robert is struggling to uncurl Rowan and turn him on to his back. 'You can't miss it – the deck's painted bright purple.'

Gina's deck is certainly unmissable, a purple so bright it leaps at the eye from the rows of sober whites, browns and naturals on her street. She is standing at the rail and when she sees me, leaps down the steps. 'Is there news?'

'He's just sleeping it off, Gina. The lads are taking him back to Dale's, but as a precaution we're going to call a doctor.'

'Alcohol?' She snatches my sleeve and half drags me in the direction of Dale's. Partially disabled she may be but I'm having difficulty in keeping up with her.

'Yeah, but I don't know where he got it. He was sober when he left Eve's this morning and, as you say, he didn't have money with him.'

'I know where he got it.' Her expression is grim as she marches me along. 'I'm missing a full bottle of Southern Comfort. I slept late this morning. He must have snuck back after he left Eve's.'

'I'm sorry about this, Gina. I'm so ashamed.'

This draws a look of incomprehension. 'What are you ashamed of?'

'Well, he's my brother. I sort of feel responsible for him.'

'Don't be silly, Arabella. He's not your responsibility, he's his own. I'll kill him,' she adds, and my spirits lift. You don't get this degree of mad at people you haven't an interest in.

Mario is pacing Dale's deck as we get there so the stretcher party must have arrived. 'One thing before you go in . . .' I warn Gina about the sunburn on Rowan's face, or half of it.

'I'll kill him,' she repeats. 'Idiot! Big hairy fool!'

CHAPTER FORTY-FIVE

The doctor was a tall chap who had to keep his head inclined so as not to hit it off the ceiling of Dale's trailer and I couldn't help thinking that since everyone here lives in one, he had chosen an odd place to practise. He tried to remain impassive and professional but, sensitised as I was, I fancied I could feel his scorn as he told us there was little to be done 'in these cases' except to make sure the patient didn't choke on his vomit. For the sunburn, already blistering, he wrote prescriptions for antihistamine and ointments and recommended that we should stock up on Alka Seltzer or our 'proprietory analgesic of choice' for when Rowan woke up. 'Because he will not be a happy man.'

Dale took out his wallet but I paid the 120-dollar fee for the house call and gave Mario, who had volunteered to go to the drugstore, fifty to cover the things Rowan needed. This put a dent in my funds; sorting it out with Willow would be a real treat.

Rowan slept on. The men had taken the precaution of covering Dale's pale couch with a fleece blanket, taken from the boot of Robert's car; its colour (vivid green) and pattern (a Goofy cartoon) were incongruous, to say the least. 'OK, guys,' Gina was dragging a chair towards the couch, 'I'll stay here with him and you go into town to pick up Mary, like you'd planned. Cool with you, Dale?' She sat on the chair and looked down at Rowan with an expression I can only describe as 'angry tenderness'. 'If you like, we could move him to my place.'

'Stay here, no problem.'

'Thanks, hon.' She grinned up at Dale.

Dale, Robert and I are now in Robert's car, me in the front beside Robert, Dale sprawled along the back seat. Mary Wu won't now be discharged from hospital until half past three and, with a few hours at our disposal, Robert has taken the scenic route into Sedona, skirting the town in a big circle and coming back into it via a gorge called Oak Creek Canyon. We're driving on a narrow, twisting road cut into the side of a lush forest rising sheer to a height of many hundreds of feet. Racing alongside is a clear, tumbling river, whose far bank is another vertical mountain: pink and red rock, scrubby vegetation. The sun is not yet directly overhead, so Robert has turned off the car's climate control and opened the windows; the burbling of the water drowns the sound of the engine. 'This is gorgeous, Robert. Thank you very much.'

'You're welcome. The trees here, if you're interested, are mostly cottonwood and sycamore. Very old. By the way I'm sorry that your first visit is proving such a rough experience. It isn't always this hectic at the Meadows, you know – we generally jog along quietly enough.'

'Please don't apologise. I'm afraid my family has done its bit to add to the trouble. But don't worry, we'll all be out of your hair fairly soon.'

'Really? All of you? Gina won't let go so easily.' He chuckles. 'What do you think, Dale? I don't think I've ever seen her so upset about a boyfriend.'

'Uh-huh.' Although Dale is noncommittal, this thuds into me like a missile. It hadn't occurred to me that Rowan might be just one in a long line. But Gina's a free agent, entitled to dally with anyone she likes, for however long she likes. 'She's had a lot of boyfriends, then?'

'Casual.' Robert brakes to let a family of risk-taking rabbits scuttle off the road into the undergrowth. 'Since her divorce from that no-good entertainer there've been a few, but nothing serious as far as I could see. Certainly none that she's ever held hands with in public like she did last night at your party.'

Had the party been only the previous night? I'm quite shocked. So much has happened, it seems like days, even weeks since they all burst out at me singing 'Happy Birthday'. 'Thank you so much for that too, Robert. It was wonderful. You and Mario went to an awful lot of trouble.'

'No trouble at all, sweetie, especially for someone as nice as you!'

The landscape opens out and we come into Sedona and a wide street running between a straggle of restaurants and shops, mostly of the souvenir and T-shirt variety, but also displaying a variety of artefacts and local art – Native American jewellery, dreamcatchers, and other craftwork – including a large display of handmade Christmas tree ornaments. In April! These are interspersed with the 'surgeries' of aromatherapists, herbalists, yogi and practitioners of all sorts of alternative therapies, including something called Metamorphosis.

At a junction – 'This is what we call the Y,' Robert volunteers – we veer left across a river, then right past more of the same intriguing mix of businesses. As we pass a small mall, filled with more upmarket art galleries, Robert slows down. 'We're in here. That's us over there, Bright Sky, see?'

In the row of elegant frontages, Bright Sky stands out: its logo is scripted in blue and silver on one of its vast windows, its exterior walls are burnished like old pewter, and two beautiful bronze statues of deer stand guard at its open door. 'That's a lovely name. Was it your idea?'

'Mario's. He's a Jicarillo Apache. His birth name is Marlon Bright Sky. He doesn't like Marlon so he changed it to Mario a few years back. When we were thinking of a name for the place, we couldn't come up with a better one.'

'I didn't know he was Jicarillo.' This is Dale, his first sentence for some time. 'That explains a few things. How come you never told me that, Robert?'

'You never asked.' Robert has stopped the car. 'Names aren't all that important in Robinia Meadows, are they?' He smiles at me. 'You can be anyone you like in that place, Arabella, but I guess you know that by now. You want we should have a look around, or shall we go to the chapel first?'

'No time like the present!' Although art isn't my thing, he is clearly so proud of his gallery I can see no way to refuse.

Dale, however, has no such qualms: 'I'll stay in the car, if you don't mind. I've a few calls to make.'

The only sign of human occupation in the cool, white-painted gallery is the faint keening of some solo jazz instrument coming from somewhere I can't see. 'Is Mario here today?'

'He's gone to visit his folks for a couple of days.' Robert's face creases with an affectionate grin. He drops his voice: 'It's thanks to your mom we're together, you know.'

I get the same peculiar feeling I'd had when Gina was telling me about Eve's 'helping' her separate from her abusive husband. 'How come?' I ask, although I do know the story.

'I suppose she'd told you how we met in that *shithole* burg in Alabama?'

He shivers with distaste. 'Sorry, Arabella, but that's the only way to describe it.'

'I do know what happened in Mario's bar.'

'Well, I was in despair, you know. I loved Mario more than I'd ever loved any human being in my life. Even my mother. And definitely my wife. That was shocking to me. I'd been married for several years and had never, *ever* looked at a man, or thought I hadn't, until Mario breezed into town.' He smiled reminiscently. 'Anyhow, my wife was OK about it when I 'fessed up, pretty damn good, actually, after the initial kick in the teeth, but even though Mario and I were pretty careful, or thought we were, the story got around and some of the so-called solid citizens took exception. I really felt that Mario's life was in danger. I was about to back off completely, I'm a natural coward, but then your mom did her intrepid umpire act, Mario came running to tell me and gave me an ultimatum – we leave town together or we break up – so we left town. The rest is history. We've Eve to thank for it all.'

'But if things were that hot and heavy in that place, the two of you might have left town anyway?'

'I don't think so. My business was there. As I told you, I'm a natural coward, and so is Mario. It would have been so much easier to let them win. I don't think I'd have gotten off my butt if it hadn't been for your mom's intervention, which led to Mario's ultimatum. It was the domino effect. Her courage.'

I know feck all about art, as I said, and as my host leads me around, I find it hard to make intelligent comments and try to cover my ignorance by marvelling at the sense of peace and order in the place. He's pleased at the compliment. He shows me the specialised air-conditioning ducts and controls and explains that to display the larger works properly they had broken through into the second storey of the original building, then suspended a false ceiling. 'It's just a crawl space above there now – we use it for storage.'

The redesign had been necessary: a number of the paintings are enormous, I would guess maybe ten feet long by eight feet high, and there's one wooden sculpture that has to be all of fifteen feet tall. The names are peculiar: *Apex XIII* is tagged on one work that to me just looks like a dark blue – or navy – slanty line going from the bottom left-hand corner of the white canvas to the top right. *Inertia R* is yellow and grey blobs on a purple background.

Robert hasn't patronised me so I feel comfortable enough to ask him the meaning of *Ergo Est*. This is a sculpture, about six feet across and three or four high. It looks like a puddle of thick grey mud leaking through holes in a metal colander of the same colour, only the colander is shiny, without handles and badly dented. 'The phrase is Latin, Arabella.' He gets all enthusiastic. 'Translated literally, it means "therefore it is". The artist would have to tell you what he's showing us here but to me the piece is kinda witty. You think you see something you know but you can't rely on it.'

'I see.'

He smiles again, probably because he's seen through my bright, *Alice in Wonderland* expression, but he lets me down tactfully. 'I guess everyone's reaction to art has to be individual. We've had a couple of enquiries about this one, as it happens – it's an outdoor piece and to show it like this doesn't do it justice. But, Arabella, try to imagine it spotlit against a shrubbery.' He backs off a little to get a better view of the thing. 'Or as a conversation piece in a summerhouse. If it's acquired by a local collector, imagine it placed in a rockery against all that stunning red rock.'

'Oh, yes. Now I see what you mean.' I nod earnestly. My overriding reaction, however, is that fools and their money are easily parted. The price of this sculpture is twenty-eight thousand dollars. 'You're a very nice man, Robert,' I say impulsively. 'Mario's very lucky.'

'Ah. You got it wrong there, Arabella. I'm the lucky one. He could have anyone he wants. I still pinch myself that he chose me.' Then, maybe a little embarrassed, he bends to remove a piece of fluff from the sculpture. I hadn't meant to trespass that far into his private life so I concentrate again on the art.

I'm still trying to figure out why anyone in his senses would spend that much on something so ugly when a door in one of the white walls opens quietly and a woman comes through carrying a sheaf of papers. 'Robert! I thought I heard your voice.'

Robert's ex-wife is taller than him and towers over me. Dressed in a navy jacket, short white skirt and patent leather pumps, she seems much younger (face lift?) than Robert. He introduces me as a friend of Dale's and she shakes my hand – although not before she has given me a quick up-and-down (fair exchange is no robbery). 'Howdy,' she's pleasant and friendly, 'welcome to Sedona. It sure is a hot one, huh?'

'It sure is,' I agree. I'm getting some education here and not only about art: I can't imagine an Irish ex-wife staying friends and working with the gay husband who deserted her for a Mario/Marlon. Or maybe I'm still living in the last century and things have moved on in Ireland without my noticing. 'Which paintings are yours, if I may ask?'

'Oh, I'm kept in the low-rent section.' She indicates a white screen placed diagonally across a corner of the gallery and hung with eight land-scape pictures, mostly featuring Arizona's famous rocks. 'It sells, however.' She flicks a glance, impossible to interpret, at Robert. 'Nice to meet you, Arabella. I've left someone holding on a call back here. Could you come into the office when you're finished here, Robert? These need sorting – I believe there might be an underpayment.' She holds up the papers.

'Sure, hon.' He shrugs apologetically at me as she closes the door. 'Sorry about this but when duty calls . . .'

'No problem. We've oodles of time before we collect Mary and I don't mind having a look round the other shops.'

'I have a feeling this will take a while. She doesn't come in often but when she does she sure likes to make her presence felt. Stay here, sweetie. Make yourself at home. I'll go have a chat with Dale, see what's best to do.'

Through the windows, I can see Dale leaning against a car and talking animatedly on his mobile phone. As Robert approaches, he finishes up and puts the phone away. Like most people in Robinia Meadows whose outer lives can be peeled off like onion skins to show others underneath, this man definitely has a parallel existence.

Both men look towards the gallery and I wave. Robert raises his hand, then hurries back to me. 'It's all sorted,' he says. 'He'll take you up to the Chapel of the Holy Cross. You really gotta see it, Arabella. You're Catholic, yeah?'

'Mmm.'

'It doesn't matter. That place has an effect on everyone, Hindu, Jew – I've even seen diehard atheists come out with an odd look in their eyes. So off you go. You're going to stop by here to pick me up on the way back into town. By that time I should be finished and the three of us will have lunch together before we go to the hospital. That OK with you?'

'Of course. But is Dale all right to drive?'

'Sweetie, driving my car is a picnic compared to that beat-up old wreck of his. I can't understand why he doesn't get himself a new one. Anyway, mine's an automatic so he'll be OK with his good arm.'

CHAPTER FORTY-SIX

Conversation-wise, the ten minutes between leaving Robert's gallery and arriving at the chapel had been passed with me making the running, some overtures more successful ('Robert's gallery is gorgeous') than others: 'Isn't it interesting that Mario is an Apache? Isn't that what Robert said? And you said, "That explains a lot," or something? What does it explain?'

'Are you always this inquisitive, Arabella?' But he said it with a half-smile so I could ignore the dig. Which I did.

'No problem, I was just interested.'

'Those Jicarillos,' he softened, 'have mineral resources on their lands, and if you're a member of the tribe, you get royalties on the product, whether you live on the reservation or not. As a result there's doormen in Vegas and bartenders in Manhattan who live to a pretty good standard. Mario don't need a regular job, especially with Robert around. That's what I meant.'

Before I can pursue the obvious question – about himself and his own means of support – we're at the chapel and he's parking carelessly across three spaces in the empty car park. We get out and walk the last part of the steep incline towards the chapel door. 'You go on up.' Dale seats himself on a low wall, the only barrier between him and certain death in the ravine below. 'It's good you'll have it to yourself. But be careful. This place can really get you where it stings. Some say it's because it's so near one of the vortices they talk about.'

I already knew about these famous bursts of electrical energy, or whatever they're supposed to be, because everyone here talks about them, but as I cross the wide plaza in front of the entrance, I'm asking myself what the fuss is about. Yeah, the air is sort of tingly and I find I'm walking with a bit more pep than usual, but I could be imagining it because it's what

I've been led to expect – and, anyway, mightn't it be caused simply by the relatively high altitude? We're almost half-way up a mountain, for God's sake. A bit of an exaggeration, but I'm grumpy. Although I appreciate everyone trying to entertain me, I would have loved an hour to browse in some of the more unusual shops in Sedona.

As for the place itself, I hadn't been all *that* impressed as we drove up. From beneath, the chapel had looked to me like a plain, concrete cross, framed in a glass box and set into yet another soaring pile of red rocks, blah-di-blah; I'd oohed and aahed to Dale, getting little or no response, while secretly thinking that all over Ireland I'd seen Marian shrines built into mountainsides of solid rock and, except for the colours, every bit as remarkable. There might be better ways to spend my time in America than visiting bloody chapels.

Inside, however, where the air is infused with the unobtrusive plain-chant of monks and a memory of incense, I'm caught up short. After the sound of the car engine, quiet though it had been, and the *thuck-thuck* of my sandals on the plaza outside, the hush is almost physical.

I sit on one of the hard pews.

Although bare and small, the Chapel of the Holy Cross is a triumph of architecture, construction and engineering but it's not the professionals' achievement and subtlety that get to you as you sit gazing through the floor-to-ceiling windows behind the altar. It's a sensation of being suspended in the sky: of being granted a view of time itself drifting into blue eternity.

Against the right-hand wall, the candle flames burn straight and true; the soft plainchant is almost hypnotic. *Salve Regina . . . Mater misericordiae . . .* Hail, Holy Queen, Mother of mercy . . .

I haven't darkened the door of a church for many years, and the *Salve* is one of the few prayers I remember from my childhood.

Ad te clamamus exsules filii Evae . . . To thee do we cry, poor banished children of Eve – yes, that's us all right.

Now I find myself breathing the Hail Mary, asking for peace for the three of us. For us all.

Then I see the eagle. He banks and glides in wide, unhurried circles over the plain below and, for some reason I can't explain, it comes to me in a rush that my father is dead. I know this as sure as I know my name. My whole body is charged with the revelation. I fight it off but it over-comes me. He's here. He's with me. He's sorry.

He loves me.

Blinded, stumbling, not caring who comes in to see me making a show of myself again, I get up and fumble in my handbag, find a five-dollar bill, rush to the candle bank and bundle the note any-old-how into the slot. Then I light a candle for my father.

When I sit down again, the windows behind the altar are blurred; the circling eagle outside is hard to follow; my candle flame – fourth from the left at the back – seems to leap and grow to the size of a raging bonfire and I can no longer differentiate notes in the plainchant: they band together, rising in volume until all I hear, like a trapped howl, is the clang and reverberation of a cathedral bell. The sound scours me with grief.

The clamour dies down, the plainchant – *O clemens! O pia! O dulcis Virgo Maria* – flows back in familiar sequence to take its place, and as my vision clears, I can see that my candle flame is neat again.

The end of the *Salve*. Now the *Credo* begins. My limbs, though, are weak. I have to wait until they strengthen.

The eagle has gone.

Dale sees me emerge from the doorway but – deliberately, I think – averts his eyes from my red-rimmed ones and looks towards a nearby peak. 'See the golden eagle?' He points to where a bird (my bird?) is flying a little below the summit. 'There's usually two of 'em. They're a pair. It's early, but there could be chicks up there in a nest.'

'I saw it from inside. Or maybe that's the other one.' My voice is croaky. Vegetation here is sparse so there isn't even the sound of a leaf stirring in the warm breeze that is lifting a few hairs off the nape of my neck.

'Yeah.' He keeps his gaze trained on the bird. 'Could be. At this distance it's hard to tell 'em apart. It was Frank Lloyd Wright, you know.'

'Who?'

'The architect.'

'Oh, I see.' I have no idea who he's talking about and I don't know what to say next. I feel it should be something significant to mark the experience I've just been through, but I'm afraid that if I talk about it I'll shatter something new and private. The only way I can describe how I feel is to say that my insides feel snowy white and clean and I don't want to add any marks.

I'm becoming conscious of Dale's smell: lemon, with fresh sweat and a tang of the disinfectant on his wounds. It must be because I feel so raw emotionally that the urge to touch him, to lay my head on his breast, is almost overwhelming.

Appalled, I take a step backwards.

'So! You ready to go?' His voice is gruff, and he's clutching his sore shoulder. He makes no move.

I don't move either. I can't. The soles of my feet are tingling with the effort to lift them. The urge to touch him is getting stronger. He's as tense as I am. I know it: a small muscle twitches in front of one of his ears. What the hell am I going to do?

Move, move! Put one foot in front of the other, blast you! 'This is ridiculous.'

'What's ridiculous?' This brings him round.

'This. Nothing. Something . . .' My voice dies away as I see what is in his eyes. I make one last effort but can manage only a whisper: 'We should go. Robert will be waiting for us. We shouldn't keep him wai—'

I can't describe what happens next without sounding melodramatic or novelettish – but Dale springs at me. 'Your shoulder – mind your—' My voice is swallowed in his mouth as I am kissed.

What does it feel like?

Hard and demanding and rough; every inch of my own body, inside and out, feels hard and hungry too. I'm warm and cold; I'm elated and afraid; I'm bruised with delight, I'm every goddamned sensation you can imagine – and as the kiss ends, I'm so full of desire I'm dizzy.

We stand looking at each other. From somewhere, down below us now in the valley, the eagle shouts, or cries or screams, whatever it is eagles do, but neither of us looks to see why. Dale's shivering. So am I. My shivering is from lust and I don't dare think about his.

'Arabella, I'm—'

I put a hand over his mouth so quickly it's nearly a slap. 'If you say you're sorry I'll kill you!'

I wait a moment then take my hand away.

'You're another man's woman.' He's very still.

I nearly laugh. 'You really think so? After what just happened, you really think that?'

A car is approaching the car park. 'Let's go!' He turns abruptly to head down the hill. I'm left with no option but to follow.

On the way back into town, downhill most of the way, he drives

Robert's car slowly, at twenty miles per hour or less, repeatedly stabbing at the brakes, despite the impatience of the lorry driver tailgating us.

Each time I dare to glance at him, I can see that muscle pulsing in front of his ear.

We're passing the wide gateway of a resort hotel when, without warning or indicating, he pulls in and parks. To my surprise, he returns the finger flashed at us by the furious lorry driver. Then, with his head sunk on to his chest: 'Stop looking at me like that, Arabella.'

'I'm not looking at you any particular way.'

'Yes, you are.' He raises his head again and takes my hand. 'What happened up there happened. And I don't want to put my life on the line,' he grins, 'but I am sorry. I shouldn't have come on so strong but it's somethin' I been wantin' to do since the second day of your visit.'

'Not the first?' *Shut up. For once, no wisecracks.*

But it gets a laugh, deep in his chest. 'Definitely not the first! Tell you the truth, Arabella, first I saw you and your sister at that airfield I wanted to run to New Mexico.'

'Why?'

'Never you mind why!' Stroking my hand now, he gets serious. 'I meant it up there. I don't want to mess with another man's woman. It's sort of a principle of mine.'

'But I've told Jimmy—'

'Maybe you did, maybe you didn't, it's a principle,' he repeats, putting a hand over my mouth, then immediately taking it away. Quickly, he clonks the automatic gearshift into position and we take off towards town with me wanting to kick him to kingdom come but wallowing, also, in the marshmallow feeling in the pit of my stomach.

Our lunch date is waiting for us outside the gallery. Dale lowers the car window. 'We're not late, are we?'

'No, not at all.' Robert's agitated. 'But I think we'd better take a raincheck on the restaurant. I called the hospital to say we'd be there at three thirty sharp but Mary had left just before I got through to her floor. They said her son came and took her home early.'

CHAPTER FORTY-SEVEN

I couldn't say I woke up. More like Gina dragged me up.

'Where am I?' I know it's the oldest line in the book but it was weird not to recognise anything.

'You're in Dale Genscher's trailer, no thanks to you.' She gets on my case right away. 'We gotta talk,' she says, 'but not now. I'm prepared to wait until you're feeling better. Here, take these.' She holds out a handful of pills and a glass of water.

'What are they?'

'The doctor says you're to take them, and you're in no position to argue, Rowan.'

While I'm forcing them down, she goes on about somebody called Mary Wu being attacked last night and now in hospital. Who the hell's Mary Wu when she's at home? I'm too sick to ask. Somewhere in my half-cooked brain the name rings a bell, as if I'd heard something about this before, but I can't get a handle on it. If an old lady's half dead that's awful, but I'm too busy keeping it together for myself to give a shit right now. As well as being sick, my face is fucking killing me.

Gina is now opening a jar full of green gunge.

'What's that stuff?'

'It's a prescription ointment. Hold your face up. Keep it still.' Gently, she spreads some of the stuff on me. It burns at first, then sort of numbs the skin. For which much thanks.

I lie back on Dale Genscher's couch. I'm afraid to say anything. Anyway, what can I say? She'll say it for me, no doubt. And she does. 'You stink, Rowan.'

'Thank you for that.'

She cocks her head to one side. 'Aren't you going to ask me how you got here?'

'How did I get here?'

'You were carried. Can you imagine the humiliation of that – how it looked to everyone? It was the middle of the morning and there were plenty of people about. You were carried out of the trash back there to Robert's car and driven here. Then you were carried into this trailer.'

'I'm sorry.'

'Well, I sure hope you are.'

'I'm sorry, I'm sorry, I'm *sorry*, right?' The effort nearly splits my skull and I have to whisper the next bit. 'What more do you want me to say?'

She glares at me. 'You might tell me why you *stole* my bottle of Southern Comfort.'

I don't answer that. How can I? How can I expect her to believe that the booze was a spur-of-the-moment thing? That I came back to her gaff this morning to talk to her and when she wasn't in the living room, I thought she wouldn't miss just one slug of something to fix me up, hair of the dog. That I was searching for vodka and it was only because she didn't have any, that I grabbed the Southern Comfort. That when I had the bottle in my hand, I thought I heard her getting out of bed and got such a fright, I legged it, taking the booze with me.

'I'm waiting, Rowan.'

'Waiting for what?' As if I couldn't guess.

'I'm entitled to know why you helped yourself to my booze.'

'Gina, you don't want to know.'

What she doesn't want to know for sure is that I'd crawl on my knees over broken glass for another drink right now. It would really help. (It's a proven fact that with booze you shouldn't ease off too sudden. Cold turkey is dangerous.) The pain in my face would ease off a bit too. Fuckit, I *need* a drink. 'Could we discuss this some other time? You have no idea how bad I feel. In every way.'

'All right.' She softens a bit. 'But we will discuss it. You can bet on that.'

'If you're going to take that attitude—'

'Don't come the attitude with me, buster.'

I make myself sit up but when I do, my face feels like it's being hit by two mallets, one on each side, and I have to lie down again. 'Just go. Leave. I'll sleep for a while and then I'll be out of your hair for good.'

'That's not what I want. I don't want you to be out of my hair. I thought we had a good thing going.'

'I thought so too. But obviously we haven't. I'm a bad person. I'm a shite. Blah, blah, blah. I'll say it for you.'

'Rowan. Stop that.'

'Well, *what* do you want from me?' I raise my voice and the effort nearly kills me.

'I want the lovely Rowan who made love to me the night before last.' She raises her voice too, then springs to her feet. 'I want the Rowan who made me laugh with his wild stories, my Irish lover. Not this – this *parody* of a person.'

'I told you I'll go,' I say wearily. 'Please, Gina. Please go away and let me sleep. I can't take this. How many times do I have to tell you I'm *sick*?'

She turns her back and patters up and down the trailer for a while. Then she sits beside me again. 'I'm sorry. I lost my cool.' She's only a few inches away from my face. I can feel her body heat on my scorched cheek. 'Oh, Rowan,' she whispers sorrowfully, 'why do you do this to yourself? It's not the first time, is it?'

'Nope.' I stare at the ceiling. I have no idea which way this is going to go. But there's no point in lying.

'Do you like me?'

'What do you think?' I manage to get it together enough to face her.

'I think you do. I think we might have had something going.'

'But I blew it, right? Listen, thanks for looking after me, Gina, but you'll never have to go through that again. Really. I'm not going to go on about it and I'm only going to apologise one more time. You either fucking believe me or you fucking don't. Sorry about the language but I'm past caring.'

'It's not the language that worries me now,' she says quietly. 'You need help with your drinking.'

I groan inside myself. That's the second time I've been told that in a few hours.

She's looking at me, waiting for some response. I feel safe with Gina, or did. Maybe I could trust her again. Anyway I've nothing to lose now. 'You might have a point.'

'Are you just saying that because you feel awful right now, or to get back with me? Do you really want to sort this out?'

'Don't know to the first. No, to the second, because I know that's not going to happen. Yes, to the third, because I do want to sort this out. My mother said the same thing to me last night. I've said it to myself recently.'

'That's the beginning. That's real good,' she says, in a completely different tone. 'Acknowledging you have the problem is the first step.'

'I know that. I'm not thick. That's social-worker speak. Please don't rub it in.' My face is throbbing again and the bright light streaming through the trailer window is hurting my eyes so I cover them with my hand. 'Now, will you please go and leave me alone? I mean it, Gina.'

She surprises me. 'You have beautiful hands, Rowan,' she says, quiet again now. 'That's another thing I like about you.'

Shocked, I open my eyes again and look at her. She seems to be in earnest.

In all my born days, nobody, but *nobody*, has ever paid me a compliment about my hands. I actually hate the word 'hands'. *Moraghan, hold out your hands* – coming at you, roaring, with the strap or the split cane. One of those skangers had split the bamboo all the way down, then wrapped the tips of it at each end in electrical wire so you were caught both ways – pinched and beaten at the same time. I suppose it could have been called a labour-saving device.

It's on the tip of my tongue to ask Gina what's beautiful about my hands so that I can tell her about that stuff but something stops me. It's her expression. She's looking sad.

Cautiously, I reach out to take one of her hands in mine. I'm self-conscious about mine now, but in a good way. 'Can you forgive me? Can we start over again?' I hold my breath. I really want this, I think. I'm daring to hope that she might be open to it, but she continues to look sadly at me.

'Now's not the time. You were right when you said that.'

'OK. I get the picture.' I let her go.

She takes a big breath, then, looking down at her own hands, 'I don't have the best track record in picking guys, as you know, so I'm a bit wary . . . but yes, I probably can forgive you, if you mean to do something positive about that drinking. You didn't do anything dreadful to me after all, Rowan. The damage you're doing is to yourself.'

'You're right.' I'd nod if I wasn't in such pain. There's something beginning to bubble in the middle of my chest. Hope? 'Can we seal it with a kiss?' I attempt to smile winsomely but my face won't hack it.

'Hey! You think I want slime all over my face?' But she laughs.

We look at each other and know we've taken a few steps back towards where we were. I could sing.

She becomes brisk. 'I don't want to frighten you,' she says, 'but that burn is really bad. I think we should go to the hospital to have you checked out. The medical-centre doctor's visit was fine and dandy, but that needs proper burn care.'

My stomach does the breast stroke at the thought of going anywhere off this couch. 'I'll be grand.'

'You haven't seen your face. I'm looking at it now. Wanna know what it's like?'

'Not really.'

'I can't even see the eye on the bad side,' she continues relentlessly. 'You seen *Shrek*?'

'No.'

'He's supposed to be an ogre and, believe, me you'd give him a run for his money. You look like a jellyfish with boils.'

'Thank you for that.'

'Listen to me, I'm afraid those blisters will burst and get infected.' She gets up and goes to the little hook inside the door where she keeps her keys and takes them off. 'So I'll give you a choice. You either let me take you to the hospital, or I call in the paramedics, say where they can find you and you make your own arrangements. I can't be responsible for you, honey. My training is as a social worker, not as a doctor. On the other hand, I can't have you on my conscience.'

'Gina, I'm too sick. Suppose I spew all over your car?'

'I'll drive slowly. We'll stop if you have to get sick.'

Somehow, I pull myself into an upright position, and when the trailer stops spinning, she's there in front of me, handing me a small glass full of pink gloop that the doctor recommended. It tastes like toothpaste but I get it down. 'And now drink this as well.' She hands me a large tumbler full of cloudy water. 'There's salt and sugar in it. You need to rehydrate. I'll put some in a bottle we can take with us and you can sip it in the car.'

'Gina?'

'Yes?'

'Can we please start again? I'm so sorry.' We're standing very close to each other and I'm in physical pain. I'm full of shame and embarrassment and remorse, too, but there is also the return of that piercing, half-giddy feeling under my ribcage that probably means I'm in love with her, although as of now we're both skirting around that word.

'And the booze?' She frowns.

'I told you I'd get help. I meant it.'

'You know, I'm beginning to wonder if it's such a good idea that you take a job in a bar.'

'Whatever you say.' I'm a beaten docket and I'll do anything she asks now to get back with her.

'On the other hand, bar people are probably the best at watching out for signs.'

'You're dead right.'

'Stop agreeing with me, dammit!'

'You cursed!' I summoned all the energy I could find. 'I don't believe it, Gina swore!'

'Shut up, stop it!'

But I know the initial battle is won. I want to scoop her up off the floor and hug her little body to pieces, but in my present state, the effort would probably kill me so I have to satisfy myself with just crushing her to me in a bear-hug. 'Rowan, let me go, you're smothering me!' She wriggles in my arms, and when I let her go, she's red-faced, but smiling. 'You're too strong for your own good, Rowan Moraghan.'

'And that's with me sick! Imagine what I'm like in the whole of my health.'

'I'm imagining!'

'Am I really forgiven?' I touch her cheek.

'For now. But don't think that's the end of it. We're going to have a real, downhome chat some time not too far away.'

'Thank you, Gina. I don't deserve you.' I hug her again, more gently this time, and I feel that giddy, piercing feeling spread through my whole body.

I loved Caroline, but I never felt we completely trusted each other. We were both on edge all the time, not knowing what the next minute held. We made plans, sure, but although I thought and spoke enthusiastically about them and did the best I could to make them happen, I never visualised them coming to pass. That wasn't surprising, given the flaky way we lived. We knew the worst of each other in an accepting, flat way. We had few expectations.

This relationship is different. Already it feels deeper and more honest. Gina sure knows the worst of me, or most of it, and is disappointed. She will expect more of me than I've delivered so far in my life. She will give me something to aim for.

And she's giving me a chance . . .

None of this makes sense to you, probably, because we're so new together, but it makes sense to me. She's making such generous efforts that it must make sense to her too. She picks up my hand and kisses it. 'Don't expect me to kiss that face. Now, come on, let's hit the road.'

When we leave the air-conditioned trailer, the heat outside hits my face like someone is slamming it against a fu– against a bloody anvil, and when the air-conditioning in her car gets going, the cold feels nearly as bad. However, she's as good as her word about driving slowly, creeping along at about ten miles an hour, but then, out of the blue, she hits the brakes so violently that, even at that speed, I nearly hit the windscreen. 'What the—'

'What's going on over there?' She's looking across me through my window.

All I can see is a bunch of mobile homes, a man washing his car, a few other people doing ordinary things, a taxi with the back door half open and a guy paying off the driver through the window. 'What do you mean? I can't see anything.'

'That's Mary getting out of that cab. And that's Eddie paying the driver. What's he doing back here?'

The woman moves away from the taxi now and I recognise her clobber from Arabella's party. You couldn't forget it: it's kind of a tent top with big flowers on it over huge jeans with spangles all over them. It'd be hard to recognise her from her face, though: it looks like it's been put through a mangle – exactly like mine feels – and her hair is all long and scraggly. You'd feel real sorry for her. 'Mary? That the woman you said was nearly dead?'

'I never said anything of the sort.' Now Gina's out of the car and running towards the taxi, her bad leg dragging a bit. She's waving and shouting.

I don't know why I do it but, crap and all as I feel, I get out to follow her. Naturally I don't run, I can't, and by the time I get up to them, the taxi is driving off and Gina's going at it hot and heavy with Eddie and even using bad language: 'Get out of here, you bastard! You've no business coming back here and if you're not gone in thirty seconds I'm calling the cops. I'm calling them anyway.' She goes to move away but this guy, Eddie, stops her. He pulls at her quite roughly, and although she struggles a bit, 'Let me go! You're hurting my arm!' she can't get out of his grip. Her top is all bunched off her shoulder in his fist.

Well, I'm not going to have that, am I? But at the same time I'm in no condition to start a mill. 'Leave her alone, friend,' I say, quite reasonably, going right up to him and putting a hand on his shoulder. It feels like a piece of street furniture. This character is not to be underestimated, I think, but I'm taller than he is by about a foot, and I've the advantage of being a Dublinman. Also, where street fighting is concerned, I learned at the feet of a master.

'Who the hell are you?' He keeps his hold on Gina. 'Who's this sideshow freak?'

Before she can answer, I take my hand off his shoulder but move in a little closer so we're almost touching each other, the three of us. 'I'm a friend of Gina's.' I pull myself up to my full height, hard to do because my stomach starts to slosh around. The adrenaline is kicking in, though. 'If you know what's good for you, you'll take your fucking hands off her. Right? You're not dealing with an old lady here, you've me to deal with now.'

The old dear who, in addition to her multicoloured physog, has a bandage round her head, starts to cry. 'Eddie, let's go inside. Please. No more trouble – please.'

Gina goes to say something but suddenly I don't feel sick any more. 'Shut up, Gina!' Even my face has stopped hurting. It's a good – no, it's a *great* feeling to be in charge. All the troubles and upsets of my whole life have come down to dealing with this one scumbag in front of me. I haven't really got a handle on what he's done, I was too sick to take much notice when Gina told me, but if he did it to that old lady and if Gina doesn't like it, that's enough for me. And the old dear is crying openly now. Nobody should make an old lady cry.

The guy's frowning, trying to figure out what to do next. He's quite young, with little piggy eyes: Mental'd have him before breakfast and I would too. 'I'll handle this,' I say to Gina. Then, to him: 'Eddie, is it? You heard the lady. Just back off. Take your hands off my girlfriend. Go inside. No. Here's a better idea.' I'm feeling really on top of things now. 'I get the impression you're not welcome here, so why don't you just turn round and go while you still have your health. You'll be picking your brains out of your teeth if you don't.'

We stand there, the four of us, our own little mob, in front of this trailer, presumably the old lady's, while the skanger is making up his mind. I can see the brain rolling around behind his little eyes. We have an audience now too, people out in front of other trailers, but I don't give a shit. The world, as I've said, has shrunk to us four and this hot gravel under our feet and I'm top banana.

The guy lets Gina go and I relax. I'm congratulating myself for handling that really well. I'm even reaching to take Gina's hand.

Then something happens and, to my dying day, I will never be able to give anyone a proper blow by blow about what it is.

Out of the corner of my eye I see a flash, the sun on metal. Something new. The guy has pulled a gun.

A fucking gun.

Next thing I'm on him and the gun is in my hand and he's on the ground, bleeding and screaming, and Gina is screaming and the old dear is screaming. It's bedlam. But I have the gun.

Unfortunately, I get sick then, and because I'm holding this gun the sick goes all over it. I'm getting sick and sick and sick – there's a bottomless pit in there – and all the pain is coming back into my face and now Arabella and this geezer Dale and other people are all around me and people are holding me and trying to give me water and Dale is taking the gun out of my hand, even though it's all slippery and gungy with sick, and I hear a lot of shouting and people yelling, 'Nine one one,' or something and Gina's face is a big round white plate that goes all fuzzy and then I pass out.

CHAPTER FORTY-EIGHT

My son, the hero? The talk of the Meadows? Can you believe it? I missed it all, dammit – nobody tells me anything these days!

What happened was, I'd written a letter to Maura and was thinking of schlepping it down to the telephone to call Willow for her address. Good excuse to talk to her as well, yeah? Then I heard the sirens and at the same time Arabella arrived with her breath in her fist to tell me what was going on over at Mary's. I could see something going on with her too, outside the immediate drama, but I couldn't put my finger on what it was. 'Are you all right?' I asked her.

'Why?' She didn't quite get on her high horse, but nearly.

'You look – I don't know. A bit flushed?'

'It's a hot day, Eve, and I've just run over here, for goodness' sake. Here, take these.' She handed me the crutches.

'Fine!' I didn't press it.

By the time we got over to Mary's trailer, the police and paramedics had left and everything was quiet, except you could nearly feel the buzz of excitement up and down the roadways. Folks who barely say hello to each other on a normal day were nose to nose in little bunches, yapping like poodles. Mary's son had already gone to hospital – under arrest – to be checked out. Our hero decked the guy good. Rowan himself is apparently suffering from sunburn and had also been taken there. Dale had handed Eddie's gun to the cops and was inside the trailer with Mary.

The woman was in bits. This was the first time I'd seen her since the party and Arabella wasn't exaggerating about the way she looks. The poor old thing. It isn't bad enough that she's injured – and by her own son – but now that son is in very serious trouble. Talk about emotional tangles! I bet she won't want them to charge him but him having the gun changes things: it puts it up to the cops, and Dale said to me quietly, when she was in the bathroom, that he didn't think they'd even need her to make a complaint: they could charge Eddie directly.

Nobody knows what's going to happen. We don't even know yet if Eddie had a gun licence. Probably not, I'd say.

Yeah, poor Mary. What was I saying earlier? Your son is your son even if he has a drink problem like mine, or is a vicious psycho drug addict like hers. We'll all have to rally round. Maybe she could come to Ireland with us. Take her mind off her troubles. There'll be more than enough money – the insurance man told me this morning that the SUV driver's insurance company isn't fighting our claim. (I'd like to see them try!)

Well, maybe we won't go as far as inviting her to Ireland with us. Me and Mary aren't *that* close.

Oh, God, I'm so proud of Rowan.

I'll murder him first, of course. I gather he looks like something from one of the alien planets on *Star Trek*. Arabella told me why, too. If I was Gina's mother, rather than Rowan's, I'd tell her to run a mile, so thank God I'm not. Nobody knows better than me that the only person who can 'cure' you of the drink is yourself, but with Gina around my son has a solid foundation to stand on and it doesn't take an agony aunt to figure out that she adores him, and thank God for that too.

He has a great chance now, with Gina, and if he blows it—

Yes, I'll definitely murder him when I get my hands on him.

On another matter, me and Maura is not the only reunion in the pipeline – I hope. This is for your ears only, it has to be kept as a surprise because, number one, you never know how Dale will react and, number two, it's still a bit iffy . . .

I managed to find the daughter. Janice.

How'd I find her? Easy in the end. If there's one thing that works in the States it's the Telephone Information Service: for a good old American quarter you can get nearly anyone's number anywhere in the country.

Dale mentioned at some stage that she was living in Cleveland but no 'Janice' or even 'J' Genscher came up there, so on a whim I tried California. Well, everyone ends up sooner or later in California, don't they? I wasn't going to stop there, of course. I was going to try every state in the union, if it came to that – I'd bought a 250-unit telephone card.

In fairness to Ma Bell, the operator I got was very helpful. She tried every town and city in California, from Fresno to Los Angeles. Then she found two Janice Genschers in Santa Barbara; the second was Dale's. I was lucky she hadn't married so the surname had held.

Goes to show that when it comes to this shunning business, Dale's as bad as they are. All along he could have found her as easily as I did, if he'd wanted to. In his own way, he can be a stubborn cuss.

In anyway, as you can imagine the daughter was gob-smacked when I told her who I was and why I was calling. She thought I was some mad-woman, I think, and at first I was afraid she'd hang up on me. But with the units clicking big-time off the card, I managed to keep her on the line and by the end of our conversation she was even a little friendly.

She's thinking about it. But the reason I'm not to tell anyone is that she's not a hundred per cent convinced she'll go with this. 'I don't want to raise his hopes,' she said. 'It's a big step for me.'

'How about your brother?' I pushed my luck a bit. 'Should we tell him too?'

Silence on the line and I thought I'd lost her. Then she came back on. 'Under no circumstances is Joseph to know about this,' she said, and you could cut the atmosphere into little pieces with the tone of her voice. 'If there's any question of that—'

'Forget it,' I interrupted her. 'Forget I even *thought* about it. This is just between you and me. I promise.'

That's how we left it. I've to call her back tomorrow. I'll do it after I call Willow – I'd been on the phone for so long, with people waiting behind me in a line, that I didn't want to hog it any more with a call to Ireland. I'm tired now. Enough excitement for one day.

Wouldn't it be great? Maybe I'll get to talk to Maura tomorrow. Tomorrow's going to be a great day. This blooming heavy cast off, Maura – maybe, even, me and Willow can move things forward a bit.

The only thing to worry about is poor old Mary and she's not part of my family, after all . . .

I have a family!

Jeez, it's all happening at Robinia Meadows, isn't it?

CHAPTER FORTY-NINE

Despite everything that's happened with Rowan, Mary and that Eddie, all I can think of is being kissed by Dale Genscher.

All right, I know I'm the age I am and that I was feeling really strange and emotional up in that place (I'm beginning to think there might be something in this vortex stuff) but I wasn't imagining what happened to me with Dale. I have never in all my born days been kissed like that – or felt like that afterwards.

I know, I know, one kiss doesn't a romance make but, honest to God, it did feel as though our bones melted into each other's.

Yeuch! But it's really what it felt like. I can't help it. I want *more*.

Of course I had no opportunity to bring it up again with him after the shock of Robert's news. After the hoo-ha back at the site, when we were all sitting with Mary in her trailer and trying to console her, he was as solicitous as any of us with her, but with me he seemed to have placed a cone of silence around himself: he didn't address me, didn't glance at me; it drove me mad. 'Have you plans for the rest of the day, Dale?' I challenged him directly.

'Nothing firmed up, Arabella.' At last his eyes flickered in my direction, then flickered away again. I decided that, to get out of there, I'd go and ring work. It was something I should have done already. I'd told the Leicester's management that I'd be away for a week or so and I was getting dangerously near borrowed time. By my calculation I had at least five working days left on my leave card but I had to keep those for September in the Canaries with Greta.

I thought I'd melt under the Perspex canopy over the booth while I punched in all the numbers. The phone rang for ages. They must be short-staffed on the front desk as usual, I thought, and entertained myself by reading the little cards that advertised taxis, massages, ayurvedic healing, dog grooming, car repair, pizza delivery and so on. When my call was answered, I asked to be put on to Greta in the kitchen, reckoning I'd catch her just before she started serving breakfasts. I'm obviously getting good at this time-change lark because when she came on I could hear that she was right in the thick of it: 'Howya, Bel, can't stay on long but it's great to hear from you. How're things? What's going on?'

'Hiya!' I said, as jauntily as I could. 'Nothing much to report,' yeah, right! 'but we'll have loads to talk about when I get home. I thought I'd stay an extra few days,' *what?* 'so will you tell the powers-that-be? I can't face being put on hold for ages and listening to bloody Irish dance music on the tape. Tell them I'll ring again when I have my flight booked. I should have at least another five days' leave owing.'

'You lucky so-and-so.' Greta didn't react to the possible ditching of our holiday.

As for me, I was shocked I'd said that because I hadn't known I was going to. 'Listen, Greta, I'll take a few days unpaid for Tenerife—'

'Would you ever shut up? That's a minor detail. We can sort it out later, but lookit, for God's sake, will you ring Jimmy Porter? He has me haunted. "When's-she-coming-home-when's-she-coming-home?" Did youse have a row or something when youse spoke the last time?'

'Of course not. But what's he ringing you for? Why doesn't he ring me himself? He has Dale's number.'

There was a short pause. The line was very clear and in the background I could hear the mixer grinding away on batter for pancakes. 'It's that Dale fella, isn't it?' Greta was half accusing, half triumphant.

'Ah, you know Jimmy,' I carried on, as if I hadn't heard her. 'It's probably the money. Him ringing an American mobile and having to pay for it?'

'Bel Moraghan! Don't make me lose me rag. Answer me. What's going on between you and this Dale?'

'Nothing.' But I couldn't keep it up and went on, in a low, slightly shamed voice, 'Well, nothing much.' Then, despite myself, a sort of thrill broke through. 'He says he won't mess with another man's woman.'

'You're joking! That's what he said? Those words?'

'Those words exactly.'

'Who is this guy? Clint Eastwood?'

'He's not like that, not really, although I do have to admit there's a bit of the strong, silent type there.' At her end I heard a loud crash – I guessed

319

a full tray from the dishwasher – she let out a string of curses and I heard the receiver bang against the tiles as she dropped it. After a few seconds she was back: 'Bel, I'm going to have to go. Come back soon, for God's sake. It's like a cage of monkeys in here. In the meantime, give us another bell whenever you get a chance – *Dilip!* Not *there!*'

'Be sure and tell them.'

'I will. And, under pain of death, you ring me again in a couple of days, right? We have to have a serious chat about this.'

'OK. And tell Jimmy I'll ring him too.'

'Sure. Now you *mind* yourself, do you hear me? Don't do anything I wouldn't do!' She laughed deep in her throat. 'Don't you go and – oh, dear God! *Sydney!* Use the *tongs*.' Then back to me: 'Gotta go, Bel.'

'Say hello to everyone—' But she had already hung up. I retrieved my card and turned to walk back to Mary Wu's trailer.

The phone kiosk is stationed at one of the little crossroads on the site; it has a bench seat alongside, presumably to accommodate anyone waiting to use it. All of a sudden I didn't want to go back to Mary's, not yet anyhow. I sat.

Ten minutes after I hung up that phone, I'm still here, roasting, boiling, smiling inanely at passers-by and others who've been using the phone, most of whom, I have to say, smile back although I'm sure they think I'm soft in the head, sitting here with no shade and trying to look as if I'm waiting for the phone to ring for me.

They're right: I *am* soft in the head. I'll probably get sunburn as bad as Rowan's, because although I've used a factor twelve sunscreen the air has become strangely humid and factors one to eleven have probably evaporated by now.

I'm not just postponing going back to Mary's trailer. I'm reviewing things once and for all. I have to make some decisions because, up to now, I've been like a loose branch swinging in the wind, and if I'm not careful I'll come off the tree altogether.

For someone whose life is regulated by a tin alarm clock and the rigid processes and hygiene of a hotel kitchen it has been an extraordinary twenty-four hours. Not even twenty-four hours – it's been an extraordinary few days. Mentally, I count off what's happened recently and since I got here: meeting my mother for the first time in nearly four decades; Rowan turning into a human being, falling off his perch, then, by disarming that Eddie creep, flying on to it again so spectacularly; my surprise party, the emotional flood at the chapel, the pressure of Dale's mouth and his body against mine . . .

I force myself not to indulge in that last one. I have to keep thinking straight.

For instance, what had happened there with Greta? Ten minutes ago, I'd picked up that phone with the full intention of asking her to tell the management of the Leicester Hotel I'd be going back to work within a day or two. I'd hung up having asked her no such thing.

I decide that at present there are only two things I can control. I can stop shilly-shallying about Jimmy Porter and put the poor man out of his misery; and I can examine the fantasy of staying on here. The seed sown when I was watching the horses has continued to sprout – or why had I told Greta I'd be staying on?

Bel Moraghan, who are you fooling? No one's listening so you can come clean. It's Dale, isn't it?

To give a simple 'yes' or 'no' answer to that one is too dodgy (suppose I base any decision to stay here on a possible relationship with him and he rejects me?) so I try to cut him out of the equation and look objectively at both issues.

No matter how I look at them these are the results:

(a) Jimmy and I are going nowhere and (b) on balance, having seen the lifestyle – even if it is only in a trailer park and only for a few days – I'd love to give America a go, with or without Dale. For instance, my mother and I are only beginning to get to know one another.

You can't live in your mother's pocket. That's sick.

Yes. But I'm sure Eve's gang wouldn't turn their backs on me, so I'd have a ready-made group of friends to start with before branching out on my own. From my handbag, I extract the Polaroid photo taken of me at my birthday party. I look dreadful in it, but in the background I can see Eve, part of Mario's grinning face, Dale's right arm and someone else's back probably Gina's, to judge by the combat gear. They're nice people, all of them. They'd be happy to have me here.

What about Greta?

This is the twenty-first century. She could come and visit.

Is this just a silly fantasy? Like that time in Tenerife when you got carried away?

321

I'd had a few drinks that night in Tenerife. I was half attracted to the manager of the bar we were in. I'm stone cold sober now and the idea keeps coming back.

I could try it, couldn't I? And if it didn't work out, I could go back to Ireland, and I'd do so in the knowledge that at least, like that eagle up there at the chapel, I had spread my wings and wouldn't go to my grave having lived and worked all my life within a few miles of where I was born. That's the bottom line. I've led a most constricted existence.

And nothing is irrevocable. Giving up the Leicester isn't the end of the world. I'm a hard worker, a trained old-school waitress, and in Ireland these days they're crying out for what they're now calling 'workers in the hospitality industry'. You have to laugh at the jargon these days. We have no binmen or dustmen any more: they're all 'operatives' or 'engineers' in the sanitation industry. And while I mightn't be much of a playgoer, I do read my *Irish Independent* and apparently nobody any longer writes plays, acts in or directs them in a theatre, they all 'make theatre' in a 'space'.

This second decision – whether to try to stay – is more complicated than the first, and before I have time to waver, I'm on my feet again, shoving the phone card back into the slot, punching in numbers. Jimmy's probably still asleep. But so what? Feck him. It's half past eight in Ireland. He should be up.

'Hello?'

When he comes on all sleepy and slow, I nearly lose my nerve but shore it up by being brisk and schoolmarmy. 'Jimmy? It's me. Bella.'

'Oh.' He wakes up properly, remembers that he's miffed with me and his tone changes. 'It's only half past eight over here, Arabella. You know I don't get up until after nine. And I'd have thought that after our last conversation I'd have heard from you before now. When are you coming home?'

'I'm sorry, Jimmy. Look—' I clench my toes so hard that they cramp and I have to kick off my sandals to spread them. 'I'm ringing you now, aren't I? I'm staying on for an extra few days.'

'Oh?' He doesn't sound pleased.

'Yes. I am. There have been a few developments over here. Rowan is in hospital. It's not serious but I should stay.'

Now don't weaken. You're not staying for Rowan. Tell him. Tell him.

'As a matter of fact, Jimmy, there's something I have to tell you about coming home. It's very possible I might be coming back just to put my affairs in order. I love it over here. I'm thinking of giving it a go. For one thing, I'd like to get to know my mother. I'm sure you can understand. But it's not only that—'

'Hold on a minute, Arabella.' I can almost hear him jumping out of the bed. 'Are you telling me you're leaving your job? Everything here? What about us?'

This is it. I was right about him standing up because, through the silence on the line, I can hear the groan of the springs on his old bed as he sits down again. I've been at him for years to get rid of it but it was his parents' and he's sentimentally attached to it. 'I want to give it a go, Jimmy.'

'So you're asking me to up sticks and go to America? Not bloody likely. Have you lost your wits, Bella?'

'I'm not asking you to come here, Jimmy. This is something I'm doing by myself.'

'You're not asking me . . .' The truth starts to dawn on him. 'You mean I'm not welcome?'

'I didn't say that. I said this is something I'm doing for myself. And there's nothing definite. There's a lot I have to find out and I mightn't even be allowed to come and live here. Look, we've got into a habit of each other, Jimmy—'

'Let's get this straight here,' he cuts across me. 'Are you breaking off our relationship?'

My toes cramp in the opposite direction.

And so, typically, here's Arabella Moraghan handling one of the crunch moments of her life in full public view in a telephone box, cradling the phone between shoulder and ear while crouching to pull at the toes on both feet. Lovely.

'Arabella? Are you there? Hello? Hello?' In my ear, Jimmy's voice is rising.

The toes straighten out and so do I. I stand as tall as I can and take a very deep breath: 'I'm afraid that, given the circumstances, you're right. I am breaking it off. But you mean a lot to me, Jimmy,' I rush on before he can interrupt me. 'We've meant a lot to each other, haven't we?'

'Thanks a lot, Bella,' he erupts. 'Thanks a bleeding lot. Oh, this is real nice, this is. This is a lovely way to wake up on a sunny morning.' Then, sneering: '"We've meant a lot to each other." Well, you can mean what you like to *yourself* for the rest of your life. You won't be seeing much of James Porter or meaning very much to him. Thank you for nothing, Arabella. Good*bye*.'

As I take my card out of the phone, I feel lightheaded, whether from the heat, or shame that I've done this to another human being, or relief—

I'm not going to question.

I realise that in the couple of minutes I've been on the phone, the sun has gone behind a cloud and the temperature has cooled considerably. I look up at the sky and see that it has turned a glowering shade of greeny-black. Nevertheless, I want a cold drink. A cold shower. Ice on the back of my neck. And I'm hungry.

Slowly, very slowly, with my head low, I make my way back towards Mary Wu's. Luckily, I see no one I know because I must look weird. It's not only the hanging head, it's that, like a heron, I'm stretching each foot hard with each step, attempting to ease the cramps that have gripped again.

Poor Jimmy, I think, but at the same time a sneaky bubble of excitement is forming in my chest. How am I going to communicate to Dale Genscher that I'm no longer another man's woman? And what's going to happen then?'

CHAPTER FIFTY

Remember I was talking about an action-packed twenty-four hours when it wasn't even twenty-four and there were a couple of hours to go?

Well, the roller-coaster continues. I'll tell you how in a minute. It's just after eleven o'clock in the evening and I'm staying in Mary Wu's trailer for tonight; she couldn't be on her own and I volunteered. I'm on a pullout bed in her cramped living area – hers is the smallest trailer I've been in so far and I have the feeling it's been furnished largely from charity shops. It has that bleachy, heavily cleaned smell.

Mary has taken a sleeping pill and is snoring away in her bed. She's a very heavy sleeper and trailer walls are thin (in Dale's you don't hear much because the two bedrooms are at opposite ends; I'm becoming a connoisseur!) and I'm as awake right now as a six-month-old kitten. This, however, is not due to the noise: it's because my brain won't switch off. The only way I'll get to sleep tonight is if someone clocks me on the head. It's just as well the weather has cooled because Mary has no air-conditioning.

You might think it's odd that I was the one to volunteer for Mary-duty, given that I've fallen in love with Dale.

Yes, I'm admitting it. I've fallen in love with that man, pony-tail, tattoos and all. And before you scoff, my head hasn't been turned by one kiss. It's an accumulation of little things, big things, his quietness, his generosity, his intelligence, his chest, his mouth . . .

Oh, God. Who am I now? Barbara Cartland? But not having experienced this kind of thing since I was about seventeen and 'in love' with a sixteen-year-old kitchen porter, the first boy who tried it on with me, I had almost forgotten how mushy this stuff can be. If I ever gave it a recent thought, I'd have said I was long past being moony. I know differently

now. I'm far from past it. I'm revelling in it. It's wonderful. It's a fizz fountain in my blood.

Speaking of Barbara Cartland, I wouldn't be all that big of a fan, but
in my present mood I can see that books like hers certainly get one thing
right. The first days of 'falling in love' have to be the most thrilling experience of a human being's life: fluttery emotions, silly smiles, planning,
plotting, dreaming, not to speak of the what-ifs, and the terror – a thrill
in itself – of rejection. So I'm seventeen again, poised at the top of the
slope above the ski jump, assessing what's ahead but not ready to kick off
down that steep, scary hill, close my eyes and take off.

*Will Arabella Moraghan crash into the rocks buried under the snow or will she
land safely on both feet?*

Danger is part of the whole delicious deal.

I know I'm sounding like a twit here, but you'll just have to bear with
me. Think of this as an antidote to all the hand-wringing I've been going
on with. I couldn't wring a hand now if you threatened to slice me up
like a ripe tomato. I'm more likely to swing on Mary's light fitting if I
was sure I wouldn't topple the trailer.

I think Dale was surprised to hear me offering to stay with Mary. I
did so in the first place to help her, of course, but also for selfish reasons.
Having finally accepted I was in love, I knew I had to calm down if I
was going to handle it properly. Like, I am not a teenager. I have to find
some appropriate behaviour.

Interestingly, he didn't put up a fight for me this time, like he did with
Eve. I think that's a good sign. He's as shook as I am.

Shut up! Eejit!

There's another reason I'm here rather than with him tonight: it's out
of respect for Jimmy. Does that make sense? Like, it was all right to accept
Dale's hospitality when we were just host and guest but now that this has
happened, even if nothing comes of it in the long run, I didn't want to
jump straight in, even if it was only to sleep under the same roof and at
opposite ends of the trailer. I would have been super-conscious all night
of Dale's presence only a few yards away. And after dumping Jimmy, it
would have felt, I don't know, cheap maybe.

Arabella! Enough of this twittering! Get back to the story.

I reached Mary's again at around half past three to find a police car
parked outside and two cops waiting to escort her. She was in the bath-

room while Dale was on his mobile to Gina, instructing her to drive Rowan straight from the hospital to the courthouse instead of coming back to the site. Eddie was being brought to court in less than an hour.

Eve, who had initially said she'd come along to support Mary, cried off at the last minute, announcing that she was tired. She didn't look tired. In fact, she was bubbling but trying not to show it – out of consideration for Mary, I presume. There was little if any trace of the sick woman I had met when my sister and I first arrived. She indicated she wanted to talk privately to me outside.

'I'm not really tired,' she said, when we were safely on Mary's steps. 'I've never been so happy, ever, in my whole life and I don't think I'd be able to keep it bottled up. That wouldn't be fair on poor Mary. It'd be like rubbing her nose in it. Anyway, if I'm honest, I want to enjoy this. It's Christmas every minute. You're here and Rowan's a hero and now we've found Maura, thanks to Willow.' She beamed widely.

From inside, I could hear the bathroom door opening and Mary saying something to Dale. I patted Eve's arm. 'Of course you don't need to come, Eve. You weren't there, you didn't see anything and there are plenty of us. Don't worry about it.'

'Sure I will. Big day tomorrow, this damned cast being replaced at last and . . .' her eyes narrowed to gauge my reaction '. . . I'll be calling Willow to get Maura's phone number. I'll be damned if I'm going to wait for an oul' letter. And while I'm talking to her, I'll be able to see what's what with Willow too.'

Lots of luck there, sunshine, I thought, then had to hope that her mind-reading radar wasn't operating.

It turned out that Robinia Meadows, where both offences had taken place, is in a different county with a different administration from that of Sedona so we weren't going there. To tell you the truth, I can't remember the name of the town we went to, or the details of the short trip. We'd dashed straight back to the site from Sedona, so Dale still hadn't collected his pickup and the three of us were again in Robert's car. Given our mission, the atmosphere was surprisingly relaxed. This could have been because, while we were concerned for Mary, none of us is related to her or her son. Also, since I was in the back seat, with Dale's ponytail dangling invitingly in front of me, I can't tell you much about the scenery.

327

Oh, yes. There was one thing. We had left the rocks behind and, with our destination in sight, were crossing a flat desert plain when Dale pointed at something moving in the distance. It was a goods train, yellow and black locomotive, dull brown wagons, picked out against a sky getting darker by the minute. 'You seen one of these before, Arabella?' He turned to smile at me. I looked for twinkles. Glimmers. Conspiracy. Anything that would refer back to that moment on the plaza in front of the chapel.

Nothing. *Nada*. 'No, I haven't actually.'

If he noticed I was a little miffed, he didn't show it. Instead he turned back to our obliging, patient driver. 'We're only five minutes away, Robert, we got time. Why don't we pull over and see if we can't hear the horn? She can't come to the States for the first time and not hear one of our anthems.'

So we stopped, Robert cut the engine and we lowered all the windows. I felt a little ridiculous, as if I were a child at the zoo waiting for the gorilla to wake up or the hippo to *do* something.

There was no traffic on our stretch of road and while we waited the silence seemed to buzz, to grow in weight, piggybacking on the humidity seeping into the car. I could smell the weather changing, but also Essence of Genscher. Slowly, agonisingly so, the train moved along the distant tracks. I was about to say we should get a move on when Dale chuckled, 'There you go!' and I heard it, a long, mournful, lonely honking that proved to be worth the wait.

Up to the time I saw those Stetsons and cowboy boots at Phoenix airport, I think that, like many Europeans, as you know, I'd half believed America wasn't real, that the place was an illusion created for movies. I suppose the two men who had stopped for me to hear that sound were the equivalent of us directing our tourists to Jameson's Distillery, Guinness's Brewery, or the Abbey Theatre. 'Marvellous!' I said, as the horn sounded for the second time. 'I wouldn't have missed it. Thanks, Robert.'

'You're welcome. All done?' He started the engine.

'You know, Robert,' I went on cheerily, 'when I go back to Ireland I'll have to send you the biggest, fattest thank-you card I can find.'

I waited. But, dammit, there was no stir from Dale at the mention of me going home.

Just like I forget the name of the little town we went to, I forget what they called the hearing at the courthouse. It wasn't a full trial, it was an appearance before the judge with the lawyers present, and witnesses if they were needed, to see if there was enough evidence to send Eddie Montgomery for a real trial later.

On the steps outside the white painted courthouse, we talked beforehand to the prosecuting solicitor, all wasp-waist and impeccably blonde. 'It's just a formality, ma'am,' she couldn't have missed my sudden nervousness, 'and you probably won't be called today. Hi, kid!' She waved at someone driving by who'd greeted her through the open window of his car, then turned back to me. 'If you are, simply tell the judge what you saw.'

Rowan, looking like something from a horror film with the burned side of his face plastered in some kind of greenish-white gunge, arrived with Gina about five minutes after we went into the courtroom (stifling, modern, blond wood, Arizona seal and a US flag). There was no room left on our bench so they had to stand near the back. I mouthed, 'Hello,' then turned back to watch Eddie's court-appointed lawyer. Feeble-looking, probably still in his twenties, with acne and a brave moustache, he was having difficulty juggling an enormous number of files. Was he really as incompetent as he looked, or was his appearance a clever ploy to lull people into a false sense of security? (*My Cousin Vinny* has always been one of my favourite movies)

Yet the whole thing wasn't as dramatic as what you'd see on TV. For a start, everyone mumbled, court clerk, lawyers, the misfortunates brought up on driving offences or abuse of one substance or another; even the judge, middle-aged, stern-looking, with chocolate-coloured skin and eyes as big as cricket balls behind Coke-bottle glasses, spoke in a tone that didn't carry beyond the front row.

Even if they had been speaking clearly they would have been difficult to understand above the weather outside. Shortly after Rowan and Gina arrived, the clouds cracked open with forked lightning, spread after jagged, dazzling spread in such rapid succession that the entire sky seemed cut up like a jigsaw and about to fall through the cloudburst. This rain was not rain as I know it but a solid, bouncing sheet so that within two or three minutes the vehicles in the car park outside were swamped up to the hubcaps in a foaming, muddy lake.

The weather show stopped as Eddie was brought in, although the lightning, warning of more to come, continued to flash and flicker as the first policeman took the Bible oath.

Our hearing lasted five or six minutes, with only the two policemen from today's episode called to the stand. I strained to hear, but they were mumbling as fast and low as everybody else. The defence lawyer entered a plea of 'not guilty' on his client's behalf, then made a quiet attempt to get bail for him – at least, I think that was what he was asking – but the judge dismissed this and set a trial date for six weeks' time. Eddie, who seemed uninterested in what was going on, was herded off again to the cells and I felt so sorry for Mary, who had sobbed quietly throughout his appearance; she'd been told that if his case were to go to trial, she'd be called to give evidence whether she wanted to or not. Talk about *Sophie's Choice*.

What must have been really upsetting for her was that her son hadn't cast her a glance.

I was sitting between Dale and Robert so I couldn't put my arm round her until we all stood up and went outside into the air, now fresh and cool. I hugged her then, being careful because of her injuries, but what could I say to her? You can't call a woman's son a gouger to her face, can you? You can't say you hope justice will be done. So I muttered something crappy about us all getting through this and that things would work out. That was when I offered to stay with her.

She's stopped snoring. I hope she's not waking up. It's mean, I know, but I don't want to have to console her again. I want to be selfish.

Wey-hey, and let's have a hoedown. I'm hugging. I'm kissing. I'm Millsing and Booning . . . And I don't care if you think I'm over the top – for once I just don't care.

Dear God, between Eve and me there's enough fairy dust floating around Robinia Meadows tonight to light up the Christmas pantomime at the Gaiety Theatre.

CHAPTER FIFTY-ONE

I'm not going to be able to tell you well what's just happened. I don't have the proper words to describe the emotions. Not the suitable words in anyway.

First, there's good and bad news. I couldn't wait until tomorrow to make my phone calls to Ireland and the bad news is that I didn't get very far with Willow. Well, maybe a little ways.

It started badly. 'Why are you ringing me, Mother?' she goes. 'I told Bella to tell you that your friend will be writing,' and then, when I insisted, she gave me Maura's number as quick as she could so I couldn't prolong things. And when I did, she would talk to me only in little short sentences, 'I'm fine. Everyone's fine,' when I asked her how she was getting on, that kind of thing – I had to work hard to get her to say more than three words together.

At least I got her to talk about being on TV. That was great, a real surprise. She's obviously real intelligent and resourceful. 'Just tell me how you found Maura. Please, Willow. I'm very grateful, of course, but I won't be able to rest until I know.'

'For God's sake, Mother, what does it matter?'

'It matters.'

She didn't say anything for a few seconds. I held my breath. I didn't really need to know the whys and wherefores, I just wanted to get a little deeper into what makes Willow tick. Instinct is all very well but I'm new at this mothering stuff and I'm learning that you have to be a bit tricksy. 'All right,' she said reluctantly. 'I contacted a newspaper and I went on TV to make an appeal.'

'You went on TV?' Tricksiness on the floor. Our repressed Willow volunteering to go on TV? I was blown away.

'Yes. That's what I said, isn't it? I did an interview on a television programme. Your friend responded. Now, can we leave it at that, Mother?'

I didn't push: I wanted to leave some space for another day because, you see, I'm hoping that there'll be time for things to get better. Actually, I know there will. It'll take a while, and after all my years of experience in dealing with people, some of them fairly difficult, I feel this'll come good. I really do.

And if it doesn't, Eve?

We won't talk about that. We won't jinx it.

Because the good news, the brilliant news, is that next thing, immediately after Willow, I talked to Maura. She was in the middle of writing to me, she said, when she came on the phone. She burst out crying. I burst out crying too. The two of us were running like faucets and I was afraid my telephone card would run out but I couldn't stop.

Maybe, while it's still fresh in my mind, I should tell you the way the conversation went. It'll be good to tell someone because then I can check and I won't be pinching myself and asking myself if it's real, what's happened.

I'll tell you everything from the first ring.

Ring ring! Ring ring! Ring ring! Ring ring! Four times. Until I called Willow I'd forgotten that in Ireland it's a double.

When it was answered, it was a man's voice: 'Hello?'

'May I speak to Maura, please?'

'Who's this?'

'It's – it's—' I was afraid to say it. 'It's an old friend of hers. I'm ringing from America.'

The phone was put down and I could hear him shouting at her to come quickly, that there was a call from America. I remember thinking: What kind of a hall does she have? I was trying to picture it. Did it have wallpaper and maybe plants and a stand for holding umbrellas? She didn't have carpet on her floor in anyway because I could hear the man's footsteps going away from the phone.

Who was the man?

Next thing I heard her voice. 'Hello? Who's this?' Kind of trembly.

'Maura?'

'Is that you, Eve?'

That's when we burst out crying.

Then everything was a jumble. Her saying, 'Oh, God, Eve, I was writing to you, I have the paper here in my hand,' and me saying, 'I'm so sorry,

Maura, I'm sorry about the money, I'm going to pay you back every penny and with interest,' then her saying, 'Shut up about the money, I don't want to hear about the money, I've plenty of money now, tell me about yourself . . .'

We calmed down a bit then. I told her a summary of what's been happening and where I'm living and all about Rowan and Arabella and Willow coming to see me and so on. 'You know what, Maura? I'm going to come home for a visit. After all these years. Can we meet?'

'Can we meet? Oh, Eve, what do you mean, "can we meet"? Of course we can meet. It's been so long. You could have been dead, for all I knew!' She started to cry again and of course that made me cry again. It was bedlam.

Then after we calmed down it was her turn to tell me what was going on. After we'd sorted out why she hadn't received any of my letters, she told me that her son, the little boy I'd known, is now some kind of banker in Finland and that after a few years of raising him on her own, she went to Blackpool for a bit of a holiday one weekend and she met a lovely man, an artist. They're not married but they have two boys, grown up now and left home to do their own thing; one's a teacher and the other one is travelling around the world. So she now has three sons! Maura and her man now live in County Laois in the middle of the country. 'He's good to me, Eve. He's very successful. If you lived here you'd know his name – bloody hell, Eve, this is no good on the telephone. I want you to meet him and come and stay with us. We have donkeys and geese and a little river and long grass and in a month we'll have the may blossom. When are you coming?' Everything so far from the concrete and noise of the tenement house where we were friends.

I told her I'd be coming when I'd had the second cast off and was fit to walk properly. I said I'd call her as soon as I'd made the arrangements. We cried again and then it was time to say goodbye.

I'm so happy this evening. I wish Arabella was here so I could tell her but she's staying with poor Mary and it's best not to disturb them. I have bubbles in my blood and I want to tell the world.

Willow'll come good. I know she will. I feel it in my bones. Otherwise why would she have gone to all this trouble to find my friend for me?

CHAPTER FIFTY-TWO

It has been an hour or so since our mother telephoned me from Arizona. I am still disturbed.

I know what she is doing: she is love-bombing, using any and every excuse to communicate with me. She could have waited until she got the letter from her friend, but seized on the opportunity to speak to me, to draw me in, make me part of her life, however tenuously. Does she think I am stupid? That I have not figured out that she is trying to get in by the back door, and wear me down. Arabella and Rowan are not enough for her. My guess is that she thinks more about me now than she does about them, and that she will not leave me alone until she gets what she considers 'a result'.

'Willow, it's lovely to talk to you again,' when I lifted the phone. Immediately. Without even 'hello'.

My heart thumped. I *hate* that sensation of feelings running away with me. 'Who is it?' Although I knew full well.

'This is your mother. Eve.'

'I can't talk now, Mother. I'm very busy. I'm helping Maeve with a project for her homework.' In fact this had been finished an hour previously. 'Why are you ringing?'

'How are you? How's everyone?'

'I'm fine. Everyone's fine.'

She wasn't put off, apparently, because she carried on blithely: 'That's good. Now, I know you're busy but this won't take long. I would love it if you'd give me Maura's telephone number.'

'I told Arabella to tell you she will be writing to you.'

'Do you not have it right there? Should I call back later?'

'No. I have it. Hold on.' The last thing I need, I thought, is to get jumpy every time the telephone rings. As I rummaged through my

334

handbag for the piece of paper I got from TV3 – yes, the response was that quick, I was having my makeup removed when the researcher came in with a note that my mother's friend had called in – I could hear her humming a tune. *Humming!*

When I gave her the number, she started burbling on about her appreciation. How she could never thank me enough for going to 'all that trouble'.

'You're welcome.' I cut her off as brusquely as I could without being overtly rude. I am not normally a rude person.

'Thank you anyway.'

She left a silence. That is another thing I hate, when people go quiet in the middle of a tense conversation, forcing you to say something. 'Actually, the children loved coming with me to the TV station. They got autographs from some famous pop star who was being interviewed after me.'

'You went on TV to find Maura?'

She is quick. I'll grant her that. 'Yes. It seemed like the quickest way. I contacted a newspaper and I did an interview on a television programme. Your friend responded. They showed the photograph and interviewed me. Now, could we leave it at that, Mother?'

But she did not want to. 'My! You're wonderful, Willow. Thank you so much.'

'Maeve's waiting. I'm afraid I really have to go.'

'Of course. Just one last thing. Tell me, how are my grandchildren? Has Dermot recovered from his chest infection?'

Was this deliberate? She knew full well that the chest infection had been an invention. The woman was impossible. 'They're both fine. I'm fine too. Now if you don't mind . . .'

'I can't wait to see them,' she went on, as if I had not spoken. 'Please give them a big hug for me. All right? Tell them I'll see them real soon. That's if you will allow me to, Willow. They're my grandchildren, after all.'

'Of course I'll let you see them. Why wouldn't I?'

'Great! Thank you. And I'll bring them a real, genuine Stetson each. Will you tell them that?'

'I will. Goodbye now.'

After I had hung up, I stood looking at the telephone as if it was something I had killed. It is difficult to describe what I felt. 'Uneasy' is probably most apt.

I tell you, she is getting under my skin. Since I got back from the US, I have heard her voice all the time. I've been haunted, that is the only word, by the expression in those eyes while I was shouting at her in the heat and dust of the roadway in that damned trailer park. She has obviously decided to behave as if that never happened.

I am dreaming about her too.

And now she is coming to Ireland.

CHAPTER FIFTY-THREE

Everything You Will Ever Need to Know When Visiting Sedona – I'm flipping through booklets, leaflets, brochures and maps over a cup of coffee. Some time during the night the storm has travelled on, leaving the air refreshed and pleasantly cool. Still in a great mood, I'm thoroughly enjoying myself.

I chose to start my 'big day out' in this café, located in the same mall as Robert and Mario's gallery, because I know the town by reference to it. The décor in the café is similar to that of the Saddle Horn, but not as brash and – presumably for the day trade – the tables have been covered with cheerful gingham napery. Robert's in his gallery: I saw him through the glass and waved at him as I passed but didn't go in. I want to be on my own for a while and for the first time since I got here, I'm behaving like a real tourist. It's difficult to believe that I've been here for only a week because I already think of all these people as 'my gang'. I even catch myself wondering when Mario's coming home.

My cunning plan this morning had been to re-establish contact with Dale by asking him for a lift to town, but when I checked, the pickup wasn't parked beside his trailer and he wasn't at home. I was disappointed beyond logic, then angry – how dare he not be available when I'd screwed up my courage to tell him how I felt about him? I marched straight to the phone box and rang one of the taxi companies advertised there. Hang the expense. Eve was delighted to see me while I waited for it. Well, I thought grimly, at least there was one place on this earth where I was sure of a welcome.

Then I realised how ridiculous it was to be behaving like this, calmed down and helped her feed her cat. With Ginger it's not just a question of opening a tin. This cat has chicken minced and mixed in with his pro-prietary dry food. 'How old is he now?'

'Nobody knows. The vet thinks maybe eight or nine. He turned up on this deck five years ago, liked what he saw apparently, and just stayed. Funny thing about cats,' Eve had been sprinkling fragments of bacon rind on Ginger's mix and straightened up. 'You're very flattered when they choose to live with you. Especially when you're alone.'

I searched for self-pity, but found not a trace. 'I suppose any pet would be good company. They don't allow them in my house, though. Listen, Eve, would you look in on Mary this morning? I don't want her to think I've abandoned her but she was still asleep when I left and I thought it'd be a shame to wake her. Will you explain that I went into town?'

'Sure thing, honey. My hospital appointment isn't until twelve thirty. And rather than leave her here on her own, sure can't I take her with me if you're not here? So enjoy yourself and don't you be hurrying back now – but listen up! Wait till you hear this.' Eyes dancing, she told me she'd made contact the previous night with her old pal. 'Can you believe it? And we're going to meet. She lives in the midlands now and she's plenty of money and I'm going to Ireland . . .' She became cautious. 'But only if that's OK with you and the others.'

'Of course it is, Eve! Wasn't that what we'd planned? It's wonderful news. Congratulations.'

'And there's more.' Triumphantly, she punched the air. 'I found Janice too.'

'Janice?' Stupidly.

'Dale's daughter. I found her in California.'

'Of course, I'd just temporarily forgotten her name. That's fantastic! Well done on both counts, Eve.' But now I was not at all sure I'd done the right thing in mentioning this in the first place. Some surprise parties go horribly wrong. Clearly this had not occurred to Eve – but it would be a shame to dampen her enthusiasm. 'You're amazing, the Miss Marple of Robinia Meadows.'

'Who?' She was puzzled.

'Miss Marple? Agatha Christie? Forget it. So, is she coming? What's the next step?'

'She's thinking about it. She'll let me know. I've to call her back.'

'Eve, we should tell Dale in advance.'

'Mmm. We'll see.'

I decided to move off the subject. 'And how'd it go with Willow?'

She made a so-so gesture with her hand. 'I think we've made a bit of progress but I don't know what Willow might say. At least she knows now to expect me to visit my grandchildren – oh, good boy! You ate all your breakfast.' She picked up the cat. 'But I refuse to let anything dampen all these good things that are happening.' As Ginger nuzzled into her she stroked the thick fur on his head. 'Willow and I will be fine. Eventually. I'll bet you a hundred bucks.'

I saw the taxi coming. 'Done.' I smiled at her. 'But if I lose it'll probably be an IOU!'

My coffee's going cold while I page through all this bumpf I've collected from the visitor centre near the Y. I have a whole free day to myself, so what should I do? A vortex tour 'with experienced Native American guides'? An 'aerial nature walk' in a hot air balloon? Myofacial Release to return me to a pain-free active lifestyle? Or should I go on a Trail Horse Adventure to include Rare Horseback Creek Crossings?

I could even ride to the Grand Canyon on a Historic Train that will take me 'right up to the South Rim'. If I had the time. And the money.

I decide to browse the shops.

With apologies to Robert and his mall, the most interesting-looking place is an arts-and-crafts complex with an unpronounceable name: Tlaquepaque. It's just a short stroll away so, having stuffed all the literature into my shoulder-bag, off I go, happy as a sandgirl. It's downhill and I'm taking my life in my hands because space for pedestrians is minimal. This is a country where few people walk. They hike, trek, jog and power-walk, but to get from A to B you have to have wheels.

The low-level open-air mall is shaded with trees and is quiet at this time of day; many of the little galleries and shops are empty and only a handful of people, mostly trippers like me, I suspect, are sunning themselves on the benches in the central plaza around a tinkling fountain. No music to distract me from the birds calling in the leaf canopy: I'd almost come to expect it – maybe the mall's tape deck is broken.

I avoid the obviously ritzy places and go in search of small souvenir gifts for Greta and her husband, also for Dermot and Maeve – I didn't think it wise or even appropriate to buy something for Willow. There are plenty of decorated pottery canoes, silver and turquoise jewellery, replica cacti and dreamcatchers in every size imaginable. I put off buying anything for the time being: it isn't often I get this kind of free time and I want to make the most of it. The best thing about shopping is the anticipation – when every purchase is still just a possibility.

And every time I see a leather belt or a pair of cowboy boots, even toy ones, I allow myself a sort of giddy personal hug. Only a few hours and Dale and I will see each other again.

In one shop, I'm so relaxed I'm not thinking. Out of habit, I pick up a leather string tie – bolas, or bolos or something, I think they call it. With a movable clasp in the shape of a cow's head or a horse? *Jimmy Porter would get a kick out of this!*

Hastily, I put it back on its stand. Relaxation dented.

I won't allow it. Not when I'm having such a good time. No matter what happens next, I did the right thing in splitting up with Jimmy. I go into the shop next door. It offers posters and old black-and-white photographs of cowpokes with their horses at rodeos or riding the range. They're very expensive: the prints I like come in at between $100 and $250, but it's fun to look through them and the proprietor seems content to daydream behind his counter, so I don't feel hassled, or guilty that I don't buy.

I decide to treat myself to some ice-cream from a booth. When I'm standing at the counter watching the vendor scoop and swirl it into a double cone, my attention is caught by a laugh. Not just any old laugh, it's familiar. It's Dale.

Everything leaps, heart, tongue, tonsils . . . I look around but can't see him.

I pay for the ice-cream and hurry into the main avenue, scanning right and left. I can't help it: of its own volition, my face has broken into a grin of anticipation that would rival Daffy Duck's.

The grin freezes.

It's Dale, all right. Oh, yes, it's unmistakably Dale, strolling along the pathway in front of me, one arm draped casually round the slim waist of an immaculate blonde.

She is as tall as he is, dressed in a pale grey trouser suit; to judge by its softness and the way it flows with her casual yet elegant gait, I would guess it's cut from silk. She is carrying an embroidered clutch-bag. Her shoes match it. Dale says something and she throws her head back. Her laugh is what they describe in novels as 'silvery'.

He laughs now too. They're having a great time. What had Eve written in her diary? *It's funny the things you remember.* Then she had gone on to describe what her husband's floozy was wearing as he and she perambulated down Gardiner Street. History is repeating itself and I, too, am noticing details as though committing them to memory: the unusual smell from the red flowers on a nearby shrub, a waiter clattering plates as he sets tables on the terrace of a restaurant, the faint hum of an aircraft high overhead. As I stand there, unable to move, the woman drops her bag and Dale stoops to retrieve it. While he is handing it to her, something catches his eyes and he glances over his shoulder. He sees me.

His turn to freeze.

He recovers, whispers urgently to the woman and she, too, looks at me. Now he leaves her and hurries towards me.

Quickly, I try to rearrange my shocked face so its expression resembles something pleasant and welcoming. Under no circumstances must I let on that I'm upset. 'Good morning, Dale. It's gorgeous here, isn't it?'

'Arabella!' Under his all-weather skin, he's grey: no sign now of Mr Cool. 'How are you? Didn't expect to see you here.'

'Oh, it was an impulse.' My smile feels now as if, like crazy paving, it's cracking all over my face. 'I thought I'd explore a little, do some shopping.'

Then I couldn't stop myself: 'Won't you introduce me?'

'Sure. Of course!'

He walks beside me towards this woman, who, meanwhile, has moved on a few paces and is examining the leaves on a large green bush. 'Don't tell me.' I cackle. 'She's your horticultural adviser!' I could kick myself because the wisecrack helps him regain some of his composure.

'No,' he smiles, 'she's not.' We're beside her now. 'Hannah, this is Arabella, a friend of mine from Ireland. She's the daughter of Eve – you remember, the woman on the site I told you about.'

'Indeed I do. Welcome to Arizona, Arabella. This your first time in the States?'

Her voice is low and mellow; it's impossible to guess her age. Body and face mid-fifties, could be older or younger, impossible to tell, poise and grace of someone born to money. Jewellery discreet: small diamond in each ear, an expensive watch. You can tell aristocrats a mile off in the Leicester; no one will ever tell me that money isn't important where looks are concerned. 'It is my first time, Hannah, yes. I've had a wonderful time, but this is my last day and I thought I'd do a little sightseeing.'

I'm loud and boring. I'm package holiday. She's a sleek yacht cruising the Greek Islands.

'This is your last day?' Dale is knocked for six. 'You didn't tell me.'

'Alas, yes!' I bathe both of them in the brilliance of my personality. 'I telephoned work last night and – as I think I told you, Dale – the place is very short-staffed. It's a madhouse back there at the moment. They won't extend my leave, I'm afraid. At least I got to do a bit of shopping. You see, Hannah, I'm a waitress,' I explain earnestly, concentrating on her, 'and there's a shortage of us back there. We're like gold dust. Gold dust, I tell you.'

'Oh, that's a shame you have to go.'

She seems to be a very nice person. I'd like her if I didn't hate her with such passion I think I'll burst. 'It is a shame, but I have to tell you, Hannah, having been here for a whole week, I'm hooked. I'll certainly come back to America again. Maybe I'll try another state – California, perhaps.'

Dale is listening to this babble, wearing a look of what I can only describe as disbelief. But now it's his turn to be dazzled by my scintillating small-talk. 'Would that be a good idea, Dale? Would I like California, do you think? No, don't answer that!'

I turn back to her. 'The hospitality here is fantastic, Hannah. Dale couldn't have been more wonderful!' The more I gush, the higher the fires of rage and jealousy burn. This is the secret life he's been leading. And don't let him try it on that this is his sister or his long-lost cousin. 'By the way, has he told you what a hero he is? Has he shown you his war wounds?'

Her affectionate laugh – *silver bells and cockle shells* – is directed solely at him. 'He did mention something, yes.'

I can't stand it. 'Oh, and by the way, Dale, is there a travel agent in this mall? I have to book my flight and get my ticket fixed up.'

'Yeah. Sure thing.' He galvanises, pointing. 'Right over there. Will I go with you?'

'Oh, dearie me, no! No thanks. I'll be fine.'

'But we will see each other before you go?'

'I'm not sure.' I pretend to think hard. 'If I remember correctly, when Willow left, one of the flight options was at around six o'clock. What time are you planning to get home?'

'Oh, I'll be there in plenty of time to give you a ride to the airport.'

My turn to laugh. *Tinkle-tinkle-tinkle* like cheap glass. 'That won't be necessary, Dale, you've been too good to me already. But I will need to take some of my stuff out of your trailer.' I don't look at yer woman. Let her draw her own conclusions. 'Have you guys known each other long?'

They exchange a glance – I think it's involuntary – of such comfortable intimacy that I know now I'm thoroughly beaten. 'Oh, we're old friends, Dale and I,' says she.

'Are you sure you don't want a ride to the airport, Arabella?' he cuts across her.

Pretty quick change of subject, wouldn't you say? 'Thank you so much, Dale, but I'll be absolutely grand. You've done far too much for me already.' I'm repeating myself now. 'Anyhow, I'm sure Eve would like to come with me. We can take a taxi. She'll be much more mobile now with the new cast rather than carting around that old heavy thing. Thanks for the offer, but she and I still have a lot to say to each other. You know how it is. Well,' I hold out my hand to the woman, who takes it in hers, 'I won't detain you. It was very nice to meet you, Hannah.'

Then, to him: 'See you back at the ranch, Dale! Oh, by the way, how do I get into your trailer?' To her: 'To collect my stuff, you see.'

'It's not locked.' He lowers his head, eyebrows beetling.

'Fine. Well, enjoy your day, both of you!' With jaunty steps, I head in the direction of the travel agent.

I don't look back. I'm afraid that if I do I'll turn into a pillar of salt.

On the other hand, a pillar would be nice. It might put supports around the emptiness.

CHAPTER FIFTY-FOUR

E mpty, hollow, plunge, pain, fury, anguish, *humiliation* . . .
We're sitting, the three of us, Rowan, Eve and I, on Eve's deck. I've
packed. My suitcase is at the foot of her steps, tucked out of the way so
no one will trip over it. My taxi is due in twenty minutes. Eve is delighted
with her new cast. She says it's made a new woman of her. She's upset
that I'm going so unexpectedly, but buoyed up that we'll meet again so
soon in Ireland.

Shrieking, crying, weeping, scrabbling, mortification . . .

She has bought, I think, the story that I have to get back to work but,
even so, has asked me ten times now if anything is wrong; that I don't
seem to be myself. I've told her I hate flying and am nervous. I don't
think she believes that, but without a bright light and electrodes, what
can she do?

She has asked me why the taxi. Why not Robert or – looking closely
– Dale?

I have told her that I don't want to take Robert from his work and
that Dale isn't around.

'But he'll be back. Does he know you're going?'

'I'll write to him to apologise for not saying goodbye.' I avoid the question. 'I'll have to write anyway, to thank him.'

'But—'

'Eve!'

She got the message and clammed up.

We've all been silent since.

Grief, heartache, screaming, wretched, fury, shame, rage . . .

Now Eve waves at someone in a passing car. 'Mario is due back tonight.
He'll be sorry he missed you.'

'I'll write to him too. I'll be writing to everyone. Be sure to say goodbye

344

to Mary for me.' Having gone to the fracture clinic with Eve, Mary Wu had decided that, rather than come back immediately to the scene of the crime, or crimes, she would visit a friend. She's not expected back on the site until tonight.

'She's very grateful to you, Arabella. Poor thing. I don't know how she's going to cope with all of this.'

'Human beings are resilient. It'll be tough, but she'll settle down. She has all of you. You'll look after her.' I'd had the savvy to detour to the police station on my way back to inform them I was leaving. There wasn't any problem: I was peripheral to the charges against Eddie but they took my address and phone number just in case.

Rowan is uneasy, constantly fidgeting. Maybe his ruined face is hurting him, although he says it's not. The suit he's been wearing since he got here has cashed in its chips, obviously, because he's wearing a brand-new T-shirt and a pair of khaki shorts, proving that Irish skin in its natural state comes in a shade of violet-grey. He's still wearing the shoes. Still with no socks. We're both smoking like chimneys. 'That's nice gear, Rowan.' I force myself to sound casual. 'Is it new?'

'Yeah. Gina bought it for me. I'm going to pay her back.'

'Of course.' I decide not to bring up the issue of money. I don't give a fiddler's about the money now, to tell you the truth. 'You'll need sandals too, Rowan. Go the whole hog. Where is she, by the way?'

'She had to go in to a meeting at work. She said she wouldn't be long.'

Fourteen minutes to go to the taxi's arrival, if it's punctual. No reason to think it won't be.

Sting, hurt, pain, appalled, embarrassment, null, void, damn shit fuck!

'Will the weather stay nice like this for a while, Eve?'

'No telling, honey. But I guess we'll get a few days. I'm used to the summers here now but they're . . .' She raises her eyes to heaven.

Rowan shifts in his chair. 'Look,' he shifts again, 'since you're going, I might as well tell – I've something to tell youse, the two of youse.'

Eve and I both turn to him.

'I know you'll think this is crap . . .' He glares at me in particular.

Eve reacts as though she's surprised but says nothing. I have no time now for psychology. 'Get on with it. The taxi'll be here any minute.'

He sees that the lace on one of his shoes is untied and proceeds to tie it. 'Gina and me think we might try and make a go of things.' Muttering.

'That's nice, Rowan.'

He looks up. Wary. He must have been expecting a lash. Irony of ironies, I think, having to stifle a most ungenerous thought: why does *he* end up with a relationship? 'What else is there to say? I wish you all the luck in the world. Genuinely. I'm very happy for you.'

'I am too, honey. That's the best news I've had for, oh, half an hour!' Still on her personal cloud nine, Eve gets up and hugs him.

He smiles delightedly at her when she releases him. 'So you don't think we're mad?'

'Of course not, honey. You'll be dead long enough, the pair of you.' Eve chuckles and goes back to her seat. 'I'm presuming when you say "make a go of it" you're not referring to the state of holy matrimony?'

'Give us a break.' Rowan is still smiling broadly, probably from relief as much as anything else. He seems much younger.

I look at my watch, willing it to tick faster. Twelve minutes or thereabouts.

Arabella dumps Jimmy for Dale.

Dale dumps Arabella.

Rowan – *Rowan!* – triumphs in love.

Eve has no such unworthy thoughts. 'Does this mean you're going to stick around?'

'That's all to be worked out. I've been offered a job.'

'What?' He's stealing my thunder here too?

'In one of the places Gina works. It's nice. The manager offered me. He says I'll have no difficulty learning the ropes. And he says I'll get away with working illegally.' His eyes flare. 'It's fucking deadly, isn't it, the whole thing? Can you fucking believe it?'

'*Language!*' But Eve takes both his hands in hers and kisses them, big smackeroos. She's so happy she can't speak.

I can't speak either, but for a different reason. I'm so jealous I could spit. I can't even summon up enough charity to acknowledge that this is exactly what I would have prayed for if I'd been in the habit of prayer. *Be careful what you wish for. Why can't it be me?* 'When did you make this happy decision?'

He looks steadily at me. 'We talked about it at the hospital and then again in the car coming home from the court. What's the matter, Bel? Why aren't you happy for me? I thought this would be a dream come true for you. No more worrying about the black sheep of the family. I'm out of your hair.'

'Don't be ridiculous. I *am* happy for you. Of course I am.'

'You don't sound it.'

'Well, take it as read. I am *happy* for you. OK?' I hear myself and now the truth hits me as if it's a falling tree: this mean-mindedness is more than simple jealousy of his finding love while I lose it. Could I be upset that my problem brother might be a problem no longer?

Devoutly to be wished. Of course it is. Of course I wanted – want – him to be happy and fulfilled and independent.

But—

Where do I fit in now? Whom do I worry about? With Rowan detaching himself from me, what's left?

For the first time I see the plain truth. I've been losing sleep over Rowan for so long it has become a way of life, a steel core to my own self. I could gloss over all my own inadequacies because I had to look after Rowan. I had to worry about him. I had to rescue him. I had a mission in life. I had to be the Good One.

He's still looking at me from his damaged face with Eve's eyes.

Eve is looking at me with his eyes.

'What are you both staring at?'

'Are you sure you're OK, Arabella?' Eve, who has dropped Rowan's hands, lays one of hers on my knee. 'You've gone very pale.'

'I'm fine. Really. I'm just nervous about flying. I told you.' I turn to Rowan. 'It was a bit of a surprise, that's all. I'm thrilled, actually.'

'But you think I'm going to blow it, don't you? That's what's wrong.'

'No, I don't. It's the best thing that could ever happen.' I don't even have to work on meaning this now: I'm sincere.

Greta talks about cutting cords, visualising it. She's a great one for the visualising: you imagine this cord attached to yourself and someone you know and want to set free; when the time is right, you 'see' yourself freeing each other by cutting this cord with an implement like a rose or golden scissors. I always thought it was bizarre but now I think that, with Rowan and me, it's worth a go. I'll try it in the privacy of my own thoughts. Maybe even in the taxi on the way to the airport.

I'll be so sad to see Rowan float away, but happy for him too. My baby brother is all grown up. He probably won't need me any more. That's hard.

347

Nearly as hard as finding Dale Genscher and losing him in the next breath.

I stand up and scan the gravelled roadway for the first sign of the taxi. Eve is not coming. She offered, but I refused to let her. I told her that I'd prefer to leave her here 'and next time we meet, imagine! I'll be the hostess!' 'Listen to me, Rowan. I'm really proud of you. Ten days ago, you're right, I would have thought you'd be in danger of messing up as I'm programmed to believe you will. I've to change that programme now because I've seen a miracle here – well, the beginnings of one. Because there's no point being dishonest, it's very early days. Things were a bit dodgy as lately as yesterday, I think you'll admit.'

Now I can manage to look him in the eye. 'But something really big has happened, and I do wish you all the best in the world. You and Gina both, of course, but really you.' Before he can react, I'm hugging him tightly. After a couple of seconds, he gets to his feet and hugs me back.

'You're right,' he whispers in my ear. 'I'm not out of the woods. But thank you, Bel. For everything.'

As far as I know, it's the first time in our lives that my brother and I have had our arms round one another. I don't remember any other time, even when he was a baby.

When we disengage, Eve is crying. 'God, don't start, Eve. You'll have us all in bits.' I manage to laugh, a little shakily.

She blows her nose but then, over the tissue, looks across me. 'Oh, good! Here's Dale. Talk about the nick of time. Thank God. I'd hate you to leave without seeing him.'

Damn! Blast! Shit!

I turn to look. Sure enough, there he is. I morph into my Pollyanna impersonation. 'Hi, Dale!'

He doesn't acknowledge me. 'Eve, Rowan,' he stands at the bottom of the steps, 'will you excuse us for a moment, please? I need to talk with Arabella.'

'Sure.' Eve heaves herself to her feet. 'Inside, Rowan. Anyway, I could do with a cuppa.'

'No need. She has to come with me to my place.'

Eh? What is this *has to?* I look to Eve for support but she's smiling idiotically at him. Right. If that's the way they want it, I can handle it. 'No can do, I'm afraid, Dale. My taxi is about due. I don't want to miss my check-in.'

'You'll make your check-in. This won't take long. Come with me, Arabella, please.' It's not a request. He comes up the steps and stands beside me, one hand hovering a couple of inches from my back. Who the hell does this man think he is? 'Sorry. I can't. No time. Say what you have to say to me here.'

'Will you stop being such a ninny? We're wasting time.'

By this time, Eve and Rowan have both gone into the trailer and we're alone. I'm seriously angry. 'Who's being a ninny? How dare you—'

'Arabella,' he looms over me, dangerously close, 'I don't want to do the Quiet Man on you, but for the last time, will you come with me?'

I can see he's serious. I'm still mad but I decide to be prudent. 'Five minutes. OK? I'll give you five minutes.' I call inside to Eve and Rowan that if the taxi comes before I get back they're to hold it for me.

'Sure thing, dear.' Eve calls back as, deliberately slowly, I walk in front of Dale and down the steps. We're silent as we trudge the short distance to his trailer. I make sure to stay a little in front. I'm livid, I'm furious, I'm heartbroken.

At the same time I'm curious. Who wouldn't be? His pickup is there. 'How'd you get here without us seeing you pass?'

'This site is set out on a grid system. I can approach my trailer from any direction. I drove up from behind.'

'I see.'

There's another car, unfamiliar, parked outside the trailer opposite – a Jaguar, I think: it has that silvery cat on the bonnet. Instinctively I know who this belongs to and whirl to face him. 'Is she in there? Is this what this is about? A showdown? You're sick, Dale Genscher. And if you think—'

'Go inside.'

'No.' I stop dead, knowing how ridiculously childish this must seem. But I can't face her. Frantically, I search for some dignified way to run.

'I can't force you, of course,' he says quietly, 'but I would have thought you might be a little more grown-up, and have a little more courage.'

That did it. Nobody calls Arabella Moraghan a coward. If he wants a showdown, I think coldly, he's got himself a showdown. I march up to his door and, without waiting for an invitation, step through.

Still impossibly elegant, poised as a ballerina, she's sitting on the couch, a glass of ice water in her hand. 'Hello there.'

349

'Hello, Hannah.' I turn immediately to Dale, who has followed me in. 'So. I'm here, and I now have about four minutes to spare. Let's get on with it.' I look from one to the other and, in doing so, intercept another exchange of those meaningful, intimate looks. I can't stand it. 'For Christ's sake! I'm off. This is pointless.' I go to pass him but he blocks the doorway with his good arm. And without ducking under it, which would be totally degrading, especially in front of *her*, I have to give way.

He takes me by the shoulder and turns me to face her. I resist, but even with only one good arm he's stronger. 'Arabella, meet my mother.'

CHAPTER FIFTY-FIVE

Stupefied, I look from Dale to this woman, Hannah, and back again. Now I hear the sound of footsteps on the deck outside. 'Bella?' It's Rowan. 'Your taxi's here.' He sticks his head through the open doorway – 'Oh, howayiz!' taking in the other two. Then, back to me: 'He wants to know how long you'll be.'

I look at my watch. I can't read it, the face is blurred. 'I'll be up in five minutes. Less, probably. No. I don't know. Look, just ask him to wait.'

'Let him go.' Dale takes a twenty-dollar bill from his breast pocket, gets up and gives it to Rowan. 'We'll call another one when we're through here.'

'Whatever.' Rowan shrugs. 'See yiz.' He goes off.

Dale sits down and indicates that I should too. He's watching me the way you'd watch a dangerous animal that's just discovered the door of its cage has been left open. I don't sit. I'm afraid to. For all kinds of reasons. Also, I'm sure this woman already thinks I'm a crazy person and it would make her uncomfortable for me sit beside her. I'm afraid she might be right: I am a crazy person.

But he did have his arm round her. I certainly didn't imagine that. And she certainly doesn't look old or harassed enough to be his mother. On the other hand she didn't object when he said she was his mother.

I'm not a crazy person, dammit: Dale Genscher distinctly told me that both his parents were dead.

I feel queasy and I do sit, but on a kitchen stool, as far from them as I can manage. 'Could someone please explain to me what's going on?'

The explanation is simple and sad. Dale and his mother have been communicating with each other all along, unknown to the rest of the family and their colleagues in the Jehovah's Witnesses. They talk on their mobile phones and she gives him news of his children, with whom she

351

is in touch. Occasionally she visits him or he sees her at some neutral venue where no one knows them – and only when his father is safely away on business. 'Yes.' Dale's watching me. 'My father is alive too. But he's a very senior person in the fellowship, it's the most important part of his life and he's a bit – well . . .' He glances at his mother.

'Rigid,' she supplies. 'I don't mind if you say it, darling. And he's not just a bit rigid, "rigid" is his middle name. He is also very certain about the teachings of our religion. That doesn't mean he's a bad man. He has other qualities, good ones.' She smiles.

'I couldn't tell you, Arabella.' Dale takes up the story. 'Please try to understand. I couldn't tell you any of it.'

Light bulb: I remember what I thought was uncharacteristic shiftiness when he was telling me first about this JW stuff and his family.

'We're trusting you with this information, Arabella.' The mother, Hannah, is now watching me. 'Dale wants it so. I've tried to change my husband's mind but I've given up. Joey married into the fellowship, so he, too, is in a difficult situation. But now . . .' She falters, looking at Dale for guidance.

'Mother has told me about Eve contacting Janny. I suppose you know?'

'Yes. I'm sorry if you think we were interfering.'

'Don't be. She's an adult. I'm an adult. If she doesn't come, what's changed? The rejection is already comprehensive.'

'How did she take it?'

Again Dale looks at his mother for guidance. 'She was shocked, naturally.' She responds to me and not to him. 'Dale and I discussed it this morning and I think he should leave the first move to her. She has some of her father's qualities and will not be railroaded. I believe she will come round, though, in the end. For instance, she's dating a very nice guy at the moment and if they decide to get married that should provide a crunch point. Yes?'

'Maybe.' Dale shrugs, but he has looked away and I can't read what he feels.

I can take all this on board only in chunks. There have to be ramifications for me, but I'm too confused to know yet what they might be. Easier to concentrate on the two of them. 'But, Hannah, why do you stay in that religion when they insist on splitting up families like this?'

'It's the custom. It's not insisted on everywhere, there are no hard and fast rules, but it's widespread, and among the people who practise it, it's immovable. I do live in hope that at some stage the family can be united again. I love my husband and I've decided to deal with this in my own way.' She sips her water. 'I don't care to think what he'd do if he found out I'd been seeing Dale. I don't know of any members living in this place but we are everywhere. JWs take their mission and their religion very seriously. As Dale says, the fellowship is probably the most important part of my husband's life. Even more so than me.' Her smile is bleak. 'As of now, only you know the truth about Dale and me being in communication. Even your mother doesn't know about that.' She looks to Dale for confirmation and he nods. 'I hope you can honour that confidence, Arabella, for I'm taking quite a risk. It was even risky in the mall. It's the first time I've been to this part of Arizona but I did want to see where my son hung out and couldn't resist it when he—' She looks from Dale to me and clams up.

'What she hasn't told you, Arabella,' Dale's turn again apparently, 'is that it was my idea for her to come to Sedona. I didn't tell her why because I didn't want to scare her, but I was going to wangle it somehow for you two to meet. I'm afraid you jumped the gun on me.' He sits back and crosses one knee over the other.

She takes another sip of her water. The joint recital is clearly over and they're waiting. She has his gift of silence – or I suppose it would be more correct to say he inherited it from her – but as it drags on, and as neither of them shows an inclination to break it, I feel it's up to me.

'I don't know what to say.' I gaze from one to the other. 'I'm sorry, but I just don't.'

'You know, darling,' Dale's mother stands up and puts her glass on the table, 'you two have a lot to talk about so I think it's time for me to go. It's a long drive, and where the housekeeper is concerned, I'm supposed to be having a lazy day at the beauty parlour. I'll have to arrive home looking wonderful.'

'You do look wonderful, Hannah.' I stand up too and so does Dale. 'So wonderful I thought – oh, I don't know what I thought.' I blush so hard my face could be used as an aviation light.

'It doesn't matter now, does it? It's been a pleasure.' Tactfully, she opens her clutch-bag and pretends to search for her keys. 'Short, but a pleasure. I hope we can get to know each other better, however limited the opportunities.' She turns to Dale. 'You were right about her, darling. And whatever you do, it'll be the right thing. You know I'll support you as much as I can.' She turns to me. 'He's marvellous with figures, you know. His father doesn't know, and never will, I hope, but Dale is my guardian angel where my accounts are concerned.'

'I see.'

Accounts? What accounts?

'But I wish he'd cut his hair and do something about those dreadful tattoos,' she continues. 'He's a bit late for Woodstock, don't you think, Arabella? Maybe you can get him to see sense.' She pats his cheek.

'Thanks, Mother. I'll walk you to your car.' He makes a move towards the door but she stops him. 'Better not. Keep in touch now, you hear? Call me on my cell.'

'Sure. Tomorrow. Drive safely.'

'I will. 'Bye, Arabella. Take care of him.'

And she's gone. Leaving behind a light scent of flowers. Freesia. Leaving Dale and me looking at each other. Leaving me in a lather. 'How old is she?'

'Sixty-eight. Shall I call you a taxi now?' He's leaning against the door jamb. He looks *very* tall.

'So why did you want me to meet her?'

'Do I have to spell it out? I'm laying out my hand because you might be leaving and we might never see each other again. But my original statement stands, I'm afraid. I don't trespass.'

'What's that your mother said about accounts? What accounts?'

'Are you being deliberately dense, Arabella? Did you hear what I said? It had nothing to do with my mother's business.'

'I'm very serious. I don't think you've laid out your hand at all. I don't know what I'm dealing with here. Where I come from, we like to know what kind of people we're dealing with . . .' I trail off because he's glaring.

'We don't have time for this pussyfootin' if you're going to catch a plane. I'm taking a risk here. How do you feel about me, Arabella?'

'Are you always this bossy?'

'I leave that to you to decide. Was it just my imagination or did what happened up there at the chapel mean somethin'?'

I don't say anything. I can't. And sometimes, as now, silence acts as a lever. 'All right,' he says gruffly. 'Since you insist. My mother runs a business.

Completely separate from my dad's and far more successful. He has a factory manufacturing light machinery. She started a flower boutique and it's now franchised in thirty-one states. I help her with her accounts. OK? It gives us a chance to meet. Dad thinks my name is Marvin O'Brien.'

'I see. What are you mad at?'

'I'm not mad.'

'You're giving a good imitation of being mad.' I'm the one who's mad now. 'It's important. Things like this are important. I thought I knew you and now I see I didn't know the first thing about you. Not the first *real* thing. And she's clearly a very classy lady. A *rich* classy lady, if I know anything about clothes. And you do her accounts. So what's with the tattoos? What's with living in a trailer park, if it comes to that?'

'I don't care about money. I don't care about status or clothes – you have to have figured that, Arabella. As for the tattoos,' he shrugs, 'after I left the fellowship I fell into a bad life. Drink, drugs, it's all a bit hazy. Don't even remember gettin' most of these done. Probably seemed like a good idea at the time.' He comes off the jamb and walks towards me. 'Quit stalling, Arabella. It's decision time.'

I pace the floor of the trailer, away from him as far as I can go, and then confining myself to a little circle in the kitchen area. I pace so hard that the trailer rocks on its foundation of concrete blocks. I make as much noise as I can.

The more agitated I get, the calmer he seems.

'You know, this isn't fair.' I come right up to his face. 'I was as high as a kite about you last night and then I saw you today in that place—'

'And you jumped to the wrong conclusion. That's hardly my fault.'

'All right. But—'

'But what? And what about this boyfriend of yours?'

I get the waft of lemons from him again, dammit. 'What do you bloody use for aftershave, Dale? Washing-up liquid?'

At this, he laughs uproariously. Then: 'For God's sake, Arabella. Will you answer one question straight. This boyfriend—'

'I've broken it off.'

The sentence detonates the air between us.

He backs off a little. 'Well, thank you for telling me that at least.'

Someone outside blows a car horn. Calls Dale's name. 'It's Mario.' He doesn't move. 'He's back early.'

The horn sounds again. Twice this time. More impatiently.

Muttering something I don't catch, Dale takes two strides to the door, yells at Mario that he'll see him later, then slams it. 'I've probably insulted him. I'll probably have to take him a potted plant. This place! It's like living in a fishbowl.'

'I asked you about that yonks ago and you said—'

'Do you ever stop talking, Arabella?' He puts his hand across my mouth and then, before I know it, replaces it with his lips. The kiss is long and searching, more intense, if that's possible, than the first one up by the chapel. It has an equally marshmallowing effect on me.

He pulls back. 'We have to get a few things straight. I'm not an easy man to live with, Arabella. I carry family issues with me, as you've discovered. I've developed the habit of secrecy because I've had to, and I wouldn't be surprised if people think I'm moody. You? You think I got moods?'

'It has occurred to me.' My head is whirling. I'm hardly daring to think what all this means. He walks away from me, looks through the window with his back turned. 'Well, now you know why. I've had to keep an awful lot to myself. As a result, I'm very independent.' He turns to face me. 'And, as you also know, I'm a non-drinking alcoholic. That presents its own problems.'

'Aren't we being a little presumptuous?' I had to say this. I don't know why, but I had to hold back this overwhelming tide.

He ignores me. 'I'm forty-nine years old as I've told you and, while I'll do my best to accommodate your wishes, it'll be a learning curve. I've been living alone so long I'm used to doing things my way without anybody asking questions, and you don't seem to me to be the type that won't ask questions.'

'You got it!'

We stare at one another, he from the window. From behind, the light is catching a few snowy strands in his iron-grey hair. The only sound is the low murmur of the air-conditioner, turned way down because of the cooler weather. I straighten my shoulders, the way I always do when I have something difficult to do or say. What feels like a steel rod, ceiling to floor, seems to have pinned me to this spot. 'Are you backing in or backing out, Dale?'

His mouth curves briefly, then settles again to its tight, firm line. 'Not a very romantic lady, are you?'

'You're avoiding the question. Are you in or out?'

He lowers his head but continues to gaze at me and I flash on the picture we present: him the bull about to charge, me the immovable object in his way. 'I'm simply layin' out all the bad stuff,' he says quietly, 'so you can never turn around to me later and say you didn't know.'

'I have bad stuff too.' I remain very still. 'I have family issues and I've been living alone for most of my life and I'm probably as settled in my ways as you are. I'm untidy, I read a lot and neglect the housework. I wouldn't be the greatest cook in the world so I eat fast food because I can't be bothered. I love slushy movies and I'm qualified for nothing except to be a waitress.'

'I can live with all of that.' He has moved away from the window and slowly towards me.

'But I'm a really *good* waitress.' I don't want to sell me and Greta short here. I don't want to be disloyal to us or our profession.

'I think I get the picture.' He moves nearer, if that's possible. He's looming over me so I'm overwhelmed by the smell of those dratted lemons. 'We can learn the good stuff about each other together. I'm willin' if you are. So, do you want to be my woman or not?'

'Now who's unromantic?' For myself, I'm dying, dissolving, *dying* in his presence. 'Let's get this straight,' I manage. 'Are you talking about us living together?'

'Let's practise . . .' And I find myself in bed with Dale Genscher. We don't take off our clothes. We don't have time. I'm careful with his shoulder. He's not at all careful with any part of me.

CHAPTER FIFTY-SIX

I called in sick to the department this morning. As it happens, I am not sick but I slept not a wink last night – although they do say that this is an illusion, that when you think you have spent an entirely wakeful night, you will have cat-napped at least some of the time. Whether I did or not, when I attempted to stand this morning to go into the shower, I felt so tired, almost hallucinatory, that my legs shook.

I do not feel guilty about taking this sick day. Apart from maternity leave, which is a statutory entitlement, I have taken exactly eight days' uncertified sick leave since I joined the service more than twenty years ago. In addition, Maeve and Dermot both have a day off, something to do with a teachers' union meeting. So, after leaving a message on my immediate boss's voicemail from the bedside phone, I also cancelled the arrangements whereby the children were to go to a friend's house where the mother doesn't work outside the home. I decided I was going to have a day with my son and daughter. It would stabilise me, perhaps. It would also be good for them.

And we had a lovely morning: we had an unhurried breakfast – they were delighted to have me with them and told me all their little news. They even helped with the washing-up. Then we walked together down to the shops, where I bought a newspaper along with the bread and milk. I consulted them about what we would have for lunch and didn't raise any objections when they chose frozen chicken wings and quarter-pounders along with oven chips. Then, without their asking, I bought them chocolate and comics. They were thrilled – I caught them pucking one another as if to ask themselves if this was for real. I have to admit that my conscience twinged.

Back home, we read our newspaper and comics, had lunch and then I came up here to my bedroom where, intending to have a short snooze,

I passed out it seems, because, to my surprise, it is now after six o'clock. I have been asleep for almost three hours.

Paddy will be home shortly. I must get up to start the tea. He eats his main meal in the department's canteen, we both do, so we don't have elaborate meals in the evening: eggs, or a salad, or mushrooms on toast.

I can hear the TV downstairs. Maeve and Dermot are no doubt glued to some programme, eating cereal and toast, scattering crumbs and sugar all over the living-room carpet. I will not hassle them about it. I will not get angry with anyone today.

For here it comes again, going round and round in my head as it has done since last night. Psalm thirty-seven.

Leave off from wrath, and let go displeasure; fret not thyself, else shalt thou be moved to do evil.

Maeve had to write an essay on this psalm in light of the war on Iraq, and after tea last night, she asked me to help her. Pretty advanced stuff, I thought, for a twelve year old, but she is in a very progressive school. Where education is concerned, Paddy and I do not scrimp.

So I helped her, without actually writing it for her, of course. But then, a while later, that disturbing telephone call came from my mother and after I came to bed, exhausted, or so I thought, the psalm parked itself in my consciousness and would not move.

At one point, I got out of bed, went downstairs, heated some milk and sat in the living room in front of the blank television screen, forcing myself to dwell on calm, pleasant things: our forthcoming trip to the Aran Islands with the children; the medal (runner-up in the under-tens) that Dermot won at his school's chess tournament, the praise I had had from my immediate boss for a project I had completed for the department. But, like two dark underground streams running in parallel, *that* phone call and *that* psalm ran under everything and would not be ignored.

Yes, I am very angry, boiling with wrath and displeasure. But at four o'clock in the morning, entirely unexpectedly, I found myself regretting the tone I had used with my mother on the telephone. Also the hate-filled words I had unleashed on her during that awful scene at Robinia Meadows.

Here, fourteen hours later, in my soft, warm bed, with rain pattering quietly on the gutter over the window, I realise that unless I do something to dam the stream of self-condemnation and censure, I will go seething to my grave.

Perhaps I should try counselling.

It would be a bitter pill, an admission of failure, since I have always prided myself on my independence and rationality.

Anyway, what can a counsellor tell me that I don't already know intellectually? That my mother's sudden appearance in my tidy life has made splinters of the cast-iron cover I had placed over my emotions? That feelings, once released from captivity, cannot be contained as before? That I have to face them and deal with them before I can heal? That I must embrace change? That this is going to take time?

I am a reserved person by nature, as I am sure you have noticed. And I do not think I would enjoy talking to a counsellor.

For instance, I did not enjoy the solicitousness of my colleagues yesterday – two people had seen my appearance on the TV programme and, of course, the newspaper article (over five pages!) was widely circulated and was the talk of the department. I have to say, though, that while I found the attention intrusive, I was touched. On the whole, people seemed not voyeuristic but amazed and sympathetic. I even received several animated assurances that 'There's a book in it!'

I am sure they will put my absence today down to some sort of emotional reaction. With reality TV, confessional radio programmes and 'agony aunt' newspaper columns, everyone in Ireland is now an amateur psychologist.

Where counselling is concerned, there is also the matter of cost. I wonder how Paddy would react to the notion. He is of the view that since Ireland lurched into *à la carte* Catholicism, as he calls it, psychiatrists and counsellors have had a field day; he believes that all anyone really needs is a good confessor.

With everything, is it any wonder I could not sleep last night?

One thing is clear. I cannot let the situation lie as it is.

Leave off from wrath, and let go displeasure; fret not thyself, else shalt thou be moved to do evil.

Perhaps not evil, exactly, but damage to myself.

I can hear Paddy's key in the front door. I get up, grab my dressing-gown and head downstairs.

'Were you in bed all day?' He looks up from stowing his briefcase in the cupboard under the stairs.

'No. I've had a nap.'

'Well, I hope you'll be able to sleep tonight.'

'Paddy, I've something to ask you.' I am not normally a blurter but this was a blurt.

'Fire ahead.' He closes the cupboard door.

'Would it be OK with you if I organised to talk to someone?'

'Am I not enough for you?' He chuckles, but it's forced. His expression is cagey.

'Of course you're great – you've been great about this whole thing – but I feel I need to talk to someone outside. Someone who's not involved.'

'You mean a shrink?'

'Maybe. A counsellor anyhow – I know they're very expensive and I know you think that all I probably need to do is to talk to a priest but I really think . . .' I stop because I've been expecting him to blow a fuse and there is no sign of this.

Instead, he is looking over his shoulder at the closed sitting-room door. 'Are the kids in there?'

'They can't hear us. The television's on.'

'Right. Come into the kitchen. Let's discuss it.'

I follow him in. He sits immediately so I sit too, in Maeve's chair, which is at right angles to his and quite close. 'Right,' he says flatly. 'I've been expecting this. Do you have anyone in mind?'

'No.' Then it dawns on me what he has just said. 'You've been expecting it?'

'Do you think I'm an eejit, Willow? That I haven't seen what you've been going through? What has happened to you is a cataclysmic event in anyone's life. And for someone like you it's nuclear.'

'But—' Then I get annoyed. 'What do you mean, "someone like me"?'

'You know quite well what I mean. I mightn't be the brightest hammer in the toolbox and I may not be the most free-spirited man in the world either, but you're so uptight most of the time I'm actually glad this has happened.' He leaned across the table and, for a moment, I thought he was going to take my hand. He did not, however, and I was glad. I was so confused by his unexpected reaction that I could not have coped with physical contact too. He watches my face. 'I was going to suggest it, as a matter of fact,' he says quietly.

'You were?'

'Yes, I was. I'm getting older too, you know, and like you, I have only one life. We have great kids. We have good jobs. The world has been kind to us and I'd like to see if we can actually enjoy it. We can't if we're afraid of it, you know.'

In all the years we had been married, I had never had a conversation like this with my husband. It felt truthful, naked, but it was new territory and, despite the changes I had felt stirring in myself, it was unsettling.

Too unsettling. My instinct was to pull right back into turtle – or mole – mode. 'You don't understand, Paddy,' I said, as brightly as I could. 'I'm not afraid of the world. This is just a shock I've had and I need to have one conversation – *one* conversation – with someone who might be able to give me a little advice. Steer me in the right direction as to how best to deal with it.'

'I predict you'll need more than one conversation, Willow.'

'We'll see.' I avoid his eyes because now they hold an expression I have not seen often. Understanding.

As I said, too unsettling.

'But let's not get carried away,' he continues, as though I have not said a word. 'There are some great counsellors in the public-health area. I know a few guys. I'll get you bumped up the queue. No point in mortgaging the house just to pay for someone's fancy address in Fitzwilliam Square.' Fitzwilliam Square is the Harley Street of Dublin. None of us had darkened any of its Georgian doors.

'I suppose not.' I glance back at him.

This time he does take my hand. 'I know I'll regret saying this, but forget what I just said there about Fitzwilliam Square. Whatever it takes, Willow. If we have to sell the house—'

'We won't. I promise.'

'That's good news anyway.' We smile at one another. Tentatively. Then Dermot bursts through the door as only a nine-year-old boy can. 'What's for tea?' He sees us holding hands and looks startled. 'Hey! What's going on?'

'Nothing much.' Paddy releases my hand. 'Your mother and I are talking, that's all. So, missus,' he says, sitting back into his chair, 'the boy's right. What's for tea? Any chance that normal service could be resumed around here?'

'Set the table, Dermot, will you?' I get up and go to the fridge to select eggs and a few rashers. I feel quite light-hearted, actually. What happened at that table was unusual. Communication. We both know that Paddy is not going to become Mother Teresa, nor will I become Madonna, but the first few tendrils of change are out and feeling the air. I can sense them and I can tell he can too.

It is very frightening. But exhilarating, in a way.

CHAPTER FIFTY-SEVEN

The second time we make love is slower, kissier, getting to know each other . . . Dale Genscher is very fit. I'm not so fit but he says that's OK: he'll walk the fat off me in no time. I give him a pretend clout. He pretend-clouts me back. We grab each other's clouting arms and melt.

I wake many minutes or hours later and, among the tumbled bedclothes, feel as light as a leaf. I turn my head. Dale is up on his good elbow, his head supported on his hand, eyes and mouth smiling. 'Have you been watching me sleep? That's not fair. For feck's sake, nobody looks good when they're asleep.'

'There are exceptions to every rule, sweetheart.' He kisses the tip of my nose. 'Your mother sent you a note.'

'What?'

'This came under the door about ten minutes ago. I know it's from her. She has very distinctive handwriting.'

I tear it open.

My dearest Arabella,
Thank God. Were all delighted about you and Dale. We were all very upset
when you were going home erly. When your redy, come on over here and
well have a selebration. Mario's done his special chicken.
Your loving mother,
Eve

Yeah. Fishbowl. I don't care. Nothing bothers me right at this minute. 'Well, her spelling hasn't improved.' I'm filled with affection for her. I'm filled with affection for the whole world.

I hand the note to Dale, but instead of reading it he kisses my forehead. 'Do you think you and I . . .'

364

'I thought we just did.'

'You know what I mean. What next?'

Dreamily, I gaze at the ceiling. The recessed light fixture is glowing golden yellow from the reflected sunset outside. 'You can't expect me to answer that, Dale Genscher. Not yet. Not for years and years and years. And certainly not until you've answered a question for me that you wouldn't answer before. Why did you want to skedaddle to Mexico that first day you saw me at the airport?'

He laughs. 'I thought you looked terrifyingly efficient. You looked as if you were searching the airport for problems to fix. I was afraid you'd identify me as one of your projects.'

I put that aside for later analysis. 'And the second day?'

'Ah. The second day. I saw your mouth and your wonderful eyes and your hair – the hair you had all bundled up like a bird's nest on that first day. You let it down on the second. I fell in love with you. With your ridiculous clothes and your skin and your hands and all that talk, talk, talk. You do talk a lot, you know, but I sure do love you for it. I love you for your shame when you have a hangover, and the way you get so angry when you don't understand things, the way you wear your heart on your sleeve, the allowances and excuses you make for people who behave badly. You have a huge heart, Arabella.'

'Enough enough! I'm a walking Coke advert!' But I'm so happy I could fuel a rainbow.

'Here's the big question.' He traces my eyebrows with his finger. 'Are you ready to face the massed gossip-armies of Robinia Meadows?'

The army, including a subdued Mary Wu, is on Eve's deck when we get there. To my embarrassment, we get a round of applause as we climb the steps, but it's so well meant and everyone is so delighted for us that, although I'm a bit pink-faced (Dale, of course, is his usual, impassive self), it's impossible not to go with the flow.

His mobile phone rings as we are settling in to eat Mario's chicken. 'Maybe I'll let this one go.' He looks at its face, then, seriously, 'It's from Ireland.'

What now? Jimmy Porter calling to harangue? To beg? My conscience is bothering me about Jimmy, but I suppose happiness always comes with some sort of price tag. 'We'd better take it, Dale.'

It's not Jimmy, though, it's Willow. And this time she's asking, not for me, but for Eve.

CHAPTER FIFTY-EIGHT

With the lighter cast on my leg, I am able to hop to it. Coming so soon after my call to her last night when she was so bolshy, instinct tells me this is an important callback. Willow is either going to tell me to take a hike, or she has decided to soften. Perhaps for the children's sake. Whichever it is, I decide not to talk to her with others listening. 'Hold on a minute, Willow, I'm going inside,' I say to her when Dale hands me the cellphone.

My heart is shivering as I go into the trailer. Isn't it odd that we can be afraid of our children? To anyone listening, I might have sounded cheery and upbeat while I was on to her last night but I was really nervous.

I settle myself in my chair. 'Hello?'

'Mother?' She sounds composed. And brisk.

'You bet. This is me.'

'I've been thinking, Mother. Although I haven't had any reaction to the note left with you when you were found, it was broadcast so something may come of it in due course. I was wondering if you would like me to initiate enquiries about your own parentage before you come to Ireland. After all, you may have relatives still alive here.'

My heart's shiver is an all-out banging now. This was only the opener. There is something else she wants to say. I can hear her fright but it sounds as if it might be good. *Dear God, let it be good.* I should help her. I can't think how. 'That would be great, Willow.'

'I would need some assistance, of course, but that should be no problem. And I might get lucky. After all, I did with your friend.'

'You certainly did. And so quickly. I'm very grateful, Willow, and if there's anything I can do at this end . . .' I'm not thinking of possible relatives. The penny hasn't dropped there. I'm thinking instead that this is the most delicate conversation I've ever had.

366

'No, I don't think there is. Better leave it to me.'

'OK.'

'OK.'

Silence.

I close my eyes and go for broke. 'I got the impression last night that you're still very upset, Willow.'

Silence. Then, quietly: 'Of course I am. But another reason I'm ringing is to say I'm sorry for my outbursts.'

'Willow—'

She interrupts me and continues all in a rush: 'I can't say I'm sorry I feel the way I do. In my opinion I'm perfectly justified – but I should have had more self-control. And I'm going to try to put things in perspective. For all our sakes.'

'That would be wonderful.'

'No overnight sensations, Mother. I have to warn you that it might take me some time.'

'If there was any way I could turn back the clock—'

'But there isn't.'

'I know.'

Silence.

'Willow . . .'

'Yes?'

I can hear the warning tone loud and clear. I had been about to dig in to find another slice of the real Willow but I hold back. Time for another bit of trickiness. 'Dammit – I don't know what I was going to ask you. Something flashed into my mind there but it was gone as quickly as it came in.' I make myself giggle. 'This kind of thing is what's ahead of me from now on. I found myself standing in the middle of the trailer this morning with a spoon in my hand and not having an idea why. Would you believe that? So enjoy those memory cells while you got 'em, honey.'

'OK.' I could hear she had relaxed a little. 'I meant it, Mother,' she says. 'I've – I've been thinking a lot and I will try to get some perspective on this whole thing. I promise. And when you come over,' she hesitates a little, then again the rush, 'Maeve and Dermot have asked that you stay with us. They're already planning the sleeping arrangements.'

'That would be lovely.' I think my heart is going to explode with delight. 'Thank you,' I say calmly.

Another silence. Shorter this time.

'So that's it, Mother.' She's brisk again. 'We'll stay in touch. I'll let you know if there are any developments on the other thing.'

'Willow?'

'Yes?'

'Thank you. I mean it. Thank you.'

'You're welcome, Mother. Goodbye for the present.'

I sit for a while in my chair, listening to the voices chatting outside. It's dim and cool, even without my air-conditioner. The storm has cleared away the mugginess and humidity and the forecast is for better, more typical weather for late April and early May. I find my eyes are spilling tears of gratitude for undeserved happiness.

My stomach turns over. *Now* I'm thinking of what she has offered. *Now* I'm thinking that I might have real flesh-and-blood relatives . . . *Now* I'm thinking I might learn where I came from.

CHAPTER FIFTY-NINE

'Everything OK, Eve?' I look anxiously at her: she seems a bit flushed and teary-eyed. The longer she had stayed inside taking that call, the more I had worried. She might have been getting quite an ear-bashing. When Willow gets going . . .

'I'm grand, Arabella. Grand.' She beams. 'In fact I couldn't be grander.' She tells us then about Willow's offer to initiate a trace from the note. 'I don't think anything will come of it, to tell you the truth, although you never know, but that's not the real deal. The real deal is Willow. Remember I told you, Arabella, that I thought things would work out. Well, they *will*! I think they *have*!'

I'm longing to ask her for details, of course, but this has to be a private thing for her. She'll tell me eventually, if she wants to. But before I can say anything, Mario rushes across to her, grabs her and kisses her on both cheeks with so much enthusiasm he nearly knocks her over. 'Oh, Eve! It's a fairy-tale! No one deserves the breaks more than you do.'

'It's far from a fairy-tale,' but she laughs. 'We're just at the beginning, Willow and me. All of us, actually.' She looks around at us all. 'I doubt if everything will turn out nice and neat and tied up with ribbon. This is real life and it's hard to see us all living happily ever after. But compared to just a month ago, before that SUV hit me, look at what's happened. I should contact that driver. *I* should pay *him*!'

'Don't you dare.' Robert fetches Eve's plate from where she had discarded it. 'You'll take all the money owing to you and you'll enjoy spending it. Now, sit down, dear, and eat.'

The evening turns into a virtual rerun of my birthday celebration, without the fairy-lights, music and cake – or Chris 'n' Mandy – but there is enough warmth, happiness and friendship sparking around on this deck to illuminate a small city. Even Mary Wu, with the help of a couple of mai-tais, has put aside her misery for the time being.

Eve is right, of course. I'm not living in a novel and nothing in real life is ever tied up nice and neat for ever after. And in the case of our group, composed of such a diverse and eclectic collection of individuals from such messy and strange backgrounds, chances are that there will be unravelling, roughness and falls. But as of this evening, we are all looking forward. With the possible exception of poor Mary (and with Eddie off the scene things might settle down even for her, given time) I get the impression there is a communal feeling of hope and expectation. Especially among my family.

I have a real family. And maybe – who knows? – more to be discovered! The realisation comes and goes like bursts of sunshine . . .

I will go back to Ireland in a few days' time and Dale will come to Ireland with Eve, who's already announced that she's going to wait until she's fully mobile.

He and I discussed his visit while we were lying in each other's arms after making love. I did broach the subject of whether I might stay on right now, confessing my fantasy of finding work in the American 'hospitality industry', but he talked me out of it. 'Better to wait a little. See how you feel about things in a coupla months' time. See how you feel about me, Arabella. This could be only a passing romance, you know, and when you see me in the cold light of your own country, you might change your mind.'

'Who's got a good opinion of himself? It's not just because of you, you know.' I tried to make myself sound indignant.

'I've nothing to do with this plan?'

'Nothing at all! It's a *lifestyle* thing, Dale.'

'Yeah. Lifestyle.'

'It *is*!'

'C'mere to me, you—'

'But *you* might change your mind about *me* when you see me under those grey skies over there. I'm probably different at home.' I got such a fright at the thought I sat bolt upright in the bed so the covers fell off my shoulders. 'A passing romance. Is that what you feel this is?'

'Come back here, babe! That's an order.' He pulled me down again on the pillow beside him and stroked my face. 'Listen,' his eyes were so close to mine I couldn't focus properly but the glare in them was so fierce it was almost frightening, 'I don't do passing romances. I'm ornery, I can be pernickety, I'm getting on for my middle age, you'll have a lot to put up with, but I know when I'm in love.'

My heart nearly stopped with the rush of feeling.

No one had ever before said that to me. Neither had I ever said it to anyone. Not in that way. 'I'm in love too.' I swallowed the words. Despite what we had just done together, I felt shy.

'Well, ain't that dandy!' Gently, he kissed one breast and then, not so gently, took the nipple of the other into his mouth. 'A matched pair!' he mumbled, looking up at me with wicked eyes, and we might have made love again right then – as we did later – but he let me go. I think we were both a little overwhelmed by the declaration we'd made. Certainly I was. So we snuggled in and fell asleep in each other's arms. When we woke up we became practical. I became practical. I decided that he was dead right, and that if I was to move here in any permanent way, it had to be done in an orderly fashion, considering his own family situation. 'There's your daughter. Do you think she'll come round?'

'I think my mom's advice is the best. I'll leave it to Janny herself. But I'm hopeful. And if things go my way with her, maybe Joey will come round too. She's always had an influence on him. Nothing's gonna happen tomorrow.'

'We have the rest of our lives to decide these things, Dale.'

'We have indeed.' Rather than kissing me in response to this, which I thought he might, he just touched my shoulder and, in many ways, this was the best moment of all. It was a commitment. Does that sound weird? It *felt* like a commitment . . .

Rowan and Gina are holding hands, I see. I'm ashamed of my nit-picking envy earlier. Thank God I didn't let either of them see it, and although I fear it's not going to be smooth sailing for them – but, then, who gets that? – I mustn't be cynical about them either.

I notice she never lets him out of her sight. Love, for sure, but Rowan's drinking binge must have been scary for her to witness. At the same time, she's bursting with pride that he disarmed Mary's son, and the change in him is startling: he has softened and the frequency of his effing and blinding has radically decreased – for the moment anyhow.

All of that being said, I always felt Rowan's hard, macho core was something he had acquired out of necessity. I had no proof: it just seemed to me that his reaction to the mildest, most well-meant criticism – or even effort to help him – was always too quick and too fierce.

This job offer he has seems for real, four shifts a week, no questions asked about work permits. Gina seems quite confident that it will go fine, particularly as he's a local hero now. The more I see of her, the more she reminds me of myself – stubborn but a born optimist.

Ah, they'll work things out between them.

As I sit and watch my mother and her open-hearted friends celebrating on my behalf and Rowan's, I wonder what Willow is thinking right now. I miss her. I wish she could be here, celebrating too. Whatever has transpired between herself and Eve has obviously been good.

And Greta? Can't wait to telephone her tomorrow. Wait till I tell her what's after happening now . . .

Arizona has been kind to my family. It gave us a mother. It worked magic on my brother. As for my own future, who knows? This euphoria cannot last, I know that, but happiness can and I'm planning to take it day by day. I've learned an important lesson here. Happiness isn't earned, it's grabbed.

Dale and I are eating our chicken sitting back-to-back on the floor of Eve's deck. I twist my head to smile at him and he smiles back: we're remembering . . .

Eve catches the exchange: her grin is wide and benevolent. I blush. You don't like your mother to know what you're up to.

I concentrate on eating. For now I can feel Dale's spine, his ribs, the warmth of his skin through his shirt. I can feel him settled against me. That's plenty to be going on with.